THE
ISLAND

THE

ISLAND

Katrine Engberg

Translated by Tara Chace

HODDER

First published in Great Britain in 2023 by Hodder & Stoughton
An Hachette UK company

Published in the United States in 2023 by Scout Press as *The Sanctuary*

This paperback edition published in 2023

2

A CIP catalogue record for this title is available from the British Library

Paperback ISBN 978 1 529 37966 2
ebook ISBN 978 1 529 37964 8

Typeset in Adobe Caslon Pro by Manipal Technologies Limited

Printed and bound in Great Britain by Clays Ltd, Elcograf S.p.A.

Hodder & Stoughton policy is to use papers that are natural, renewable and
recyclable products and made from wood grown in sustainable forests.
The logging and manufacturing processes are expected to conform
to the environmental regulations of the country of origin.

Hodder & Stoughton Ltd
Carmelite House
50 Victoria Embankment
London EC4Y 0DZ

www.hodder.co.uk

To Laura Höger,
beloved sister and ally

It was the noise that woke him, a throbbing rhythm like a locomotive moving at high speed. He tried to drift back to sleep, but the rumbling in his eardrums forced him to consciousness. He shifted restlessly and felt a sharp pain on the back of his head, struggled to open his eyes, but they were stuck shut. When he attempted to raise his hand to rub them, it wouldn't obey.

I'm having a nightmare, he thought, *one of those where I dream I'm awake. I'll wake up fully in a minute, get up, and the day will begin.* He repeated this sentence like a mantra, but even as he tried to regain control, he knew this wasn't right.

He clenched his fists cautiously and noted, to his relief, that his fingers responded. But the relief was short-lived. A zip tie cut into his wrist. He was tied up.

He blinked and forced his eyes open. His field of vision was blurred, as if he were looking through a greasy camera lens; he was lying on his side and could only make out dim light and trees in the distance. Something that looked like a figure. Where was he?

The last thing he remembered was parking on a strip of dirt

somewhere he hadn't been before, walking through tall grass under a blue-black sky past the outlines of buildings and getting his trouser legs wet. He remembered that he had come here to find something. He had gone in the door of a big building, he remembered that much. And then?

Pain shot upward from the back of his head, making it hard to think. The noise sapped the last of his concentration. Had he been punched?

He mobilized all his strength and raised his head so he could look toward his feet. Not far from the soles of his shoes a light flickered in time with the noise, and in a lucid moment he realized what it was. An industrial saw. He was moving toward it.

A scream drowned out the noise. It took several seconds before he realized it was his own. He tugged at the zip ties, in vain. They wouldn't break. He was hopelessly trapped, at the mercy of the blade, which was closing in on his feet. He threw himself from side to side, his shoulders bashing into whatever was underneath him, blood dripping from a wound on his head. There must be some way for him to twist one arm free.

If only he could see properly, maybe he could loosen the zip ties around his wrists and stop the saw. But he couldn't do anything. This was the end of the line.

He screamed for help, a wild animal's roar, but there was no response.

MONDAY, NOVEMBER 18

CHAPTER 1

At first glance the suitcase looked like something out of an old movie, a big, square travel bag with reinforced corners and a wide handle, attached with rusty metal clasps. It lay in some scraggly snowberry bushes, and the damp soil had discolored the leather and loosened the stickers, mementos from hotels in Trondheim and Hanover.

Violent Crimes Department detective Anette Werner gazed down at the playground in Østre Anlæg Park. On the top of the hill there was a plateau with a bench facing one lone tree, which drew a silhouette against the sky's low-hanging clouds. The kids at the playground didn't go up there much. The people who used the space often left hypodermic needles and condoms on the ground, and it was best not to go near those.

The on-duty investigations officer stood in the clearing, calling the crime scene technicians and the medical examiner. His shoulders were pulled well up around his ears so the woolen trench coat formed an arch over his back. On either side of the clearing, sets of stone steps led down the slope, both cordoned off with striped crime scene tape, which was fluttering in the wind. One of the two young officers who had called for backup stood by the farther staircase, keeping watch.

Anette turned back around to the suitcase, pushed aside a dripping branch, and squatted down in the bushes beside the other young officer. The muddy soil between the bushes revealed roots from the surrounding trees, and the branches' yellow leaves hung limp.

"Who found it?" She nearly lost her balance and grabbed the officer's shoulder.

"A first grader from Krebs' School. They use the playground at recess and strayed up here even though they're not allowed to. The suitcase was still covered with dirt, but one corner was sticking out." The young officer pointed to the top right corner of the suitcase.

"A fox, maybe?"

"Probably. The kids got their teacher, and she was alarmed by the odor and called the police."

The odor. Anette smelled wet soil and autumnal decay. The fallen leaves were already well on their way to becoming dirt, and mushrooms were starting to grow. There was a sweet, underlying note of spoiled meat behind the November scents.

"When we arrived, we carefully removed the dirt from around the suitcase, intending to open it, but . . ." The young officer cleared his throat awkwardly. "Well, it hasn't been that long since I finished the academy here in Copenhagen, and you don't forget the smell of a cadaver that fast."

Anette glanced at him and said, "So it hasn't been opened yet?"

"We just lifted the lid a little and then called you."

"Right."

They heard a child's yell from the playground.

"We haven't had time to cordon things off properly yet." The officer squirmed uncomfortably. "There were only two of us here, you know, until you arrived."

"I can hear the damn *swish-swish* sounds from the kids' snow-suits; they're that close."

Anette pulled out a pair of latex gloves from her pocket. Her own daughter, Gudrun, had just gotten a new snowsuit for the winter, size 2T, sky blue with white clouds. Her golden curls got stuck in the zipper every time she insisted she could zip it up herself. At the moment, Gudrun, her snowsuit, and Svend were all off on a week-long vacation with Svend's sister in Kerteminde. Anette had started missing them as soon as the car drove down their residential street the previous day.

"I'm going to open the suitcase so we're absolutely sure, just so we don't set everything in motion for no reason."

"Oh, I don't have any doubts at all," the officer protested, wiping his dripping nose with the back of his hand.

Anette slid her hands under the edge of the lid and felt the cold pinch her fingertips. They hadn't had their first frost yet, not even at night, but the air was heavy with that typical Danish winter damp, the kind that penetrated deep into her bones and numbed her hands and feet.

The hinges creaked, and she heard the officer next to her gasp. In the open suitcase lay a body. Its skin was brownish purple with white moldy stains, and it took Anette a second to even recognize the shape as human. The body had only one arm and one leg; its head was squashed into one corner and had been sliced clean through.

Instinctively she lifted her eyes away from the body. The sky above her was gray and the air dense with fine little beads of water. The stench was overwhelming. A guttural sound escaped the young officer. Anette quickly closed the lid before he threw up.

"EARTH TO EARTH." The pastor stuck his shovel into a pile of dirt and carefully threw it down onto the white coffin while pushing a pair of glasses farther up his nose with the index finger of his other hand. "Ashes to ashes, dust to dust."

The small group clustered around the grave stood motionless in the drizzle, following the rites. Jeppe Kørner put his arm around Esther de Laurenti and felt her skinny body shaking under the fabric of her coat. His hand on her shoulder was still sore from carrying the casket. Jeppe surveyed the other burial guests, surprised at the absence of Gregers's own relatives. Other than Esther and himself, only a few former colleagues and elderly acquaintances had shown up. The three adult children and who knows how many grandchildren and great-grandchildren hadn't come, pushed away in an ugly divorce many years ago and never reconciled, not even for the final farewell.

Gregers had not left behind much of a mark on the world.

The pastor said the Lord's Prayer and gave the benediction, and Jeppe felt a little choked up. His sadness was for both Gregers's insignificance and his own, the fleeting presence of all beings here on this earth. The doctors had discovered the lung cancer in the spring and given up treatment at the peak of summer. Now they stood on the threshold of winter, burying Gregers Hermansen, retired typographer, Esther's roommate, and father of three children he no longer knew.

Esther had tended him until the end and managed to keep him at home, so he didn't have to go into hospice. Jeppe lacked the imagination to conceive of how hard that must have been, but he sensed that her previously slender figure had shrunk even more and saw more gray in her henna-dyed hair.

Fearless, when our path below,
Pleases God our Father . . .

The group's voices sounded fragile among the headstones. Jeppe's toes were numb inside his dress shoes as he shook hands and parted ways with the other mourners. Esther only made it a few yards before she turned to him. He folded his arms around her and let her cry against his chest until she was calm.

They continued together to the nearest cemetery exit, side by side on the paved paths along cypresses and stone angels.

"No wake?"

She shook her head and said, "I called Jakob, his eldest son, but *the family doesn't wish to participate*. And I don't know any of Gregers's former colleagues, so I didn't have anyone to arrange it for."

"Isn't there a café right out here on Tagensvej? Could I buy you lunch?" He smiled at her.

She had dressed colorfully, as she usually did, in a blue wool coat and orange silk blouse, but her face was set to black.

"Or we could just have coffee, whatever we'd like."

"What I'd like is a glass of wine, even if it's early."

"Then that's what we'll do."

The café was high-ceilinged and bright with big windows facing the street and bentwood chairs around crowded marble tables. Apart from a sleepy waitperson, the place was empty. They sat down by the window. The server stretched and started rooting around for menus.

"I haven't been out since Gregers got sick, you know. And now ..."

Jeppe was about to say something about how life goes on but stopped himself. The last thing a grieving person needs is to be reminded that the world keeps going unaffected, indifferent to their misfortune.

The server placed menus on their table and began describing the day's specials. Jeppe interrupted him.

"We're going to start with a bottle of the house red and some water, thanks. Then maybe we'll take a look at lunch afterward." Jeppe let the server disappear behind the bar before he took Esther's hand. "It must have been hard on you, taking care of him all on your own."

"A home health aide came every day," she said with a smile, "so I had breaks. It was much harder for Gregers than it was for me, having to depend on someone else for help."

"But still . . ."

"Do you know what was hard?" Her gaze wandered out to the street and back again. "When there wasn't any hope left. After that scan they did at Herlev Hospital, where they saw that the cancer had metastasized to his brain, and it was only a matter of weeks. I think I was really good at fighting and keeping Gregers's spirits up until then, even when he couldn't eat or sleep. But that scan broke us both. How do you keep your spirits up when there's no hope of improvement?"

The server unscrewed a metal cap and poured wine into their glasses, set the bottle on the table with a clunk, and hurried off before they could remind him of the water he had forgotten.

Jeppe pulled out a blister pack of ibuprofen and washed down two with a sip of lukewarm, mediocre red wine. Esther did not seem to have any objections to it.

"In reality, we're all dying," he attempted.

"Yes, but we *think* we're immortal. That's what gets us through all the meaningless things: we somehow think that we're impervious to death. As soon as there's an end date, life becomes completely absurd. Especially when you're in pain."

Her voice faltered on those last words.

"Was he in a lot of pain?"

Esther drank and set her glass down carefully, as if she was afraid she might knock it over.

"Let's talk about something else, Jeppe. The beard suits you."

"You think?" He touched his unaccustomed facial hair self-consciously. "It's mostly laziness, actually. I've never let it grow out before."

"So, tell me," she said, cocking her head to the side and studying him. "Are you enjoying your leave of absence?"

"Yes, I think so . . . I haven't missed the police or Copenhagen so far."

Jeppe contemplated whether that was actually true. He was getting so used to giving that same answer without really thinking about it. He had been on an unpaid leave from his job as a detective in the Violent Crimes Department since June, and in August he had sublet his apartment to a sweet, elderly couple who routinely sent him messages about how much they were enjoying city life and the view of Nyhavn.

"But a lumberjack? Isn't that . . . That just seems like such a drastic step for a talented detective, to sort of run off to an island and go chop down trees because of a broken heart. Almost a little . . ."

"Cliché? Maybe, yeah. It was my mother's suggestion. She knows the neighbor of the guy who runs the logging company, otherwise it would never have occurred to me. But when you're sick of things, nothing helps more than hard physical labor. It gets you out of your own head. Plus it pays well, so I'll be able to afford to travel afterward. And it's only temporary after all."

Esther drank a sip of her wine and looked sadly at the bottom of her glass, which was approaching.

"Are you and Sara in touch at all?"

"No . . ." Jeppe was about to explain but realized that her name still hurt in his mouth. "I've shut down contact with my coworkers in general. I don't need to know what's going on in their new super-police-headquarters."

"Surely you have to admit that Sara's more than a coworker?"

"Hmm." Jeppe refilled Esther's glass. His own was still full. "Are you still coming out to the island this afternoon? I'm catching the four-thirty ferry."

Esther nodded.

"Remind me again why you're going?" Jeppe screwed the lid back onto the wine bottle and set it down.

"Do you remember that biography I was working on in the spring? Margrethe Dybris, award-winning anthropologist and somewhat of an icon. She actually got in touch with me a few years ago through a mutual connection at the university, and I was very honored that she took an interest. Unfortunately nothing really came of our contact; I'm not really sure why. And then she died before I ever really got the chance to know her. But I tell myself she wanted me to write her biography."

Esther smiled, looking calmer now, her forehead smoother, and the corners of her eyes less tense.

"Margrethe researched death rituals all over the world and was a pioneering feminist. She lived alone but had several *friends* and adopted two children on her own. She moved to Bornholm back in the 1970s, then died two years ago. I've been corresponding with her adult daughter about coming over to see the house in Bølshavn."

"Are you sure it's a good idea to do it right now?"

Esther raised one shoulder up toward her ear and then let it fall again in an indecisive gesture.

"Gregers's kids are coming to empty out his rooms tomorrow. I don't particularly want to be home for that."

"Ah, okay." Jeppe looked at his watch. "Listen, I have an errand in the city, but I can swing by and pick you up at your place around two o'clock?"

"Great, thank you. That will be perfect. I'll go pack a bag and bring Dóxa upstairs to the neighbor. They've promised to dog-sit her while I'm away, probably just until the end of the week."

The server appeared at their table with a plate of vanilla butter cookies. They smelled freshly baked.

"On the house. The chef is practicing his Christmas baking. You look like someone who could use a little pampering."

He set down the plate and disappeared again. The scent of cookies fresh from the oven wafted up and spread through the room. Jeppe took a cookie and smiled across the table. Esther looked down, avoiding his eyes.

CHAPTER 2

"Tell me again—what are we waiting for?"

Anette tugged irritably at the elastic holding the surgical scrub hat in place over her hair. On the stainless steel table in front of her sat the leather suitcase containing half a body waiting to be autopsied. Bright lights seemed to make the corpse's darkly mottled skin smolder like coals in a campfire.

On the other side of the table stood crime scene investigator J. H. Clausen holding a single-lens reflex camera, with which he had already taken at least a hundred pictures, next to forensic pathologist and professor Nyboe, who had just finished collecting samples of the skin and now flashed her an annoyed look over his mask.

"As I said, we need to fingerprint the deceased before we can lift the body out and proceed with the examination," he said. "The dactylographer's on his way. That's how it is when we rush autopsies, the whole process ends up being a little harried. We wouldn't normally do the exam before tomorrow."

"So, to what do owe the honor?" Anette glanced indiscreetly at her watch.

"Tomorrow wasn't convenient for me," Nyboe replied, and then pulled his face mask down below his chin. "My wife and I are celebrating our silver wedding anniversary and are expecting sixty-five guests for brunch."

"Congratulations!"

"Thanks."

Anette peered down into the suitcase, impatient to get started. In her ten years as a detective, she had encountered body parts and dismemberment several times, but she'd never seen half a person before. In an investigation she was leading, no less.

"What's the white stuff?"

"The swollen section?" Nyboe pointed to the corpse's thigh. "The skin has become pasty from putrefaction, moisture, and temperature fluctuations. The deceased must have been in the suitcase for quite a while, not long enough for the flesh to disappear but for several weeks, maybe even months."

A younger man in a green lab coat and scrub hat joined them at the table. He wrinkled up his nose before pulling up his face mask to cover his stubble.

"Whoa, what the fuck? That reeks! Can I get right to it?"

"Language!" Nyboe eyed the newly arrived dactylographer sternly. "And yes, we were only waiting for you. But be careful, the skin is loose!"

The dactylographer lifted the body's left hand and started rolling the fingers one by one first on the ink plate, then on paper.

"Is there just one hand?"

"Yes, you got off easy today. Done?" Nyboe took a step toward the table.

The dactylographer nodded and left the room. Nyboe tied his plastic apron and put on a fresh pair of gloves.

"Come on, let's lift!"

The forensic pathologist stepped up, and they carefully lifted the half corpse out of the suitcase and onto the metal table, positioning it so it lay on its back. Crime scene investigator Clausen sealed the suitcase in white plastic and then started photographing again while Nyboe measured the body with a measuring tape while dictating the results into his Dictaphone. At regular intervals the technician turned the deceased so Clausen could take pictures from all sides. Nyboe walked back and forth, muttering observations about possible stab wounds, skull fractures, or bullet holes.

Anette stayed back a couple of paces so as not to get in the way and had to crane her neck to catch everything. Even though the body was far along in the putrefaction process, and its muscles and organs had long since turned soft and gray, it still looked like an anatomy drawing. The face was split down the nasal bone, the rib cage open, and the pelvis halved. The remnants of a scrotum revealed the victim's sex as male, but beyond that it was hard to get an impression of the person from his earthly remains. The eye sockets were empty, and in the mouth, behind the teeth, there was only a stump of what had once been a tongue.

"He's been there for a minimum of six weeks and a maximum of twelve. I'll be able to narrow that down more once we've looked at the organs. But we're in the ballpark." Nyboe nodded to the crime scene technician. "Let's prepare for the internal exams."

The pathologist loosened the skin on the face with a snip behind the ear and opened the skullcap so the half brain could be lifted and transferred into a stainless steel bowl without being damaged any further. Or to be more precise: poured. To Anette's untrained eye, it looked liquid. The pathologist proceeded to remove the heart, spleen, and other organs out of the body and weigh them in stainless steel bowls.

"How will we identify him if his fingerprint isn't in the registry?" Anette asked. "His teeth? Is half a mouth enough?"

"I'm not sure." Nyboe spoke without raising his face from the body's nose, on which he was pointing a small and very bright flashlight. "We'll need to hear from the forensic dentists how far they can get with an X-ray and CT scan. We're also taking a DNA sample from the femur for our forensic geneticists. It'll take them a few days. But no matter what, their results will have to be compared to something before they can be of use."

"We'll check up on missing people, men, from the last three months. That will give us something to work with. Can you say anything about his age?"

Nyboe straightened up and snorted.

"Right now I can barely establish the fundamentals such as skin and hair color, because the putrefaction is so advanced. But based on his general physique, I would think we're talking about a full-grown man, who does not yet show serious signs of wear and tear. You know: arthritis, prolapses, hip surgery . . . My conservative estimate would be somewhere between thirty and fifty."

"Oh, come on, that's no help."

"Sorry." Nyboe bent back down over the body and poked the half nose with a small metal pin. "On the other hand, he has a nice hole here in the bridge of his nose, which could well indicate excessive cocaine use. If that's the case, we'll be able to confirm it from the organs once we get them under the microscope."

Nyboe went to stand next to the technician, who was still weighing organs, and started writing on a whiteboard in black and red dry-erase markers.

Anette approached the body. Normal-size head, strong jaw, average build, as far as she could assess. Just halved.

"What did he die of?" she asked.

Nyboe stopped with the pen in midair and gave her a look.

"He was sawed in half."

"Come on, Nyboe! Are you telling me that's what he died of?"

He sighed.

"At least so far, there is no indication of other trauma, although it's too early to say anything definitive."

"Wait a minute!" Anette pointed to the body. "Are you telling me that he was alive when he was sawed over?"

"Yes, Werner, I'm afraid I am."

ESTHER CLOSED THE door of her apartment on Peblinge Dossering, ignoring the nameplate like she had for the past six months. It had been too painful to read, because she had known it would soon be out of date.

Esther de Laurenti & Gregers Hermansen

Now diminished by a dizzying 50 percent. A whole home with only half its population of residents. How would that ever work?

Dóxa came clicking across the parquet flooring and greeted her with a lazy growl, before retiring to her bed in the kitchen. The days when the pug had barked and jumped around every time Esther came home were long gone.

"It's only you and me now, sweetie."

Esther tried to let those words sink in. Death was as hard to fathom as the end of the universe. From now on Gregers would no longer pick up rolls for their Saturday breakfast or steal her crossword puzzle from the weekend paper; he would never again complain that the frying pan smelled of garlic or that the volume of her Puccini was too high.

She packed toiletries and clothes for a few days into a bag and set it in the front hall, ready to go, then opened the fridge but was forced to admit that she didn't have any appetite. There was still an hour to kill before Jeppe came to pick her up, she might as well have another glass of wine.

It had been a long time since she had last cut loose. When you're taking care of a helpless patient, you don't get drunk. But she didn't have anyone to stay sober for anymore. The cork let go of the bottle neck with a sympathetic sigh.

Gregers would have made fun of her and accused her of being a part-time alcoholic if he had been home.

"Ah, but you're not here, my friend. So I'll drink what I want." Esther tilted her head back and gulped down big mouthfuls of Ripasso. It was *also* a relief that he was dead. Was it okay to admit that?

A relief to be done with the bedpan and the blood pressure cuff, the oxygen machine, keeping track of pills, and the hospital bed, which the health aide had set up in Gregers's room. She also wouldn't miss the fits of pain, the swollen legs, the constipation that compelled him to move around the apartment because he couldn't bear being in his own body, and she definitely wouldn't miss his nightly panic attacks, when he thought his death was imminent and fear kept them both awake. She could still see his unfocused eyes in the dark and hear his gasping breaths, as far from being ready to meet his end as anyone could be.

No, Esther wouldn't miss the sickness and death. But Gregers . . . was it Bukowski who had said something like solitude can be one of the most beautiful things on earth?

Maybe if you were young and agile and could be alone on a mountaintop or in a Scottish fishing village, but not when you were a seventy-one-year-old woman, who had lost all the people you were closest to.

"Who do I have left?" she asked Dóxa in her dog bed. "Who'll take care of me if I get sick?"

That question hovered like an echo between the white walls. Once upon a time she had had colleagues, lovers, dinner guests, a social circle of people she saw regularly and could depend on. But so much had imperceptibly slipped away, evaporated into the layers that make up the busy routines of everyday life. But busy with what? What could be more important than the people you love?

She finished her glass and saw the kitchen counter tilting. When had she last seen Frank and Lisbeth, for example? Or good old Bertil?

Esther put her hand over the medallion that hung around her neck, resting against her breastbone as a constant reminder of the greatest loss of them all. A gold pendant with a date engraved on it, March 18, 1966, in remembrance of the baby she had carried, given birth to, and then given up when she was seventeen. Heavily pressured by her parents, forced, even, to give the illegitimate child up for adoption. Should she have defied her parents? Could she have done anything?

She had asked herself that question countless times in an attempt to keep regrets at bay. The answer wasn't clear. What remained was the consequence, the painful truth:

Esther had no one.

She had never had more children and never married. Her closest friends were either dead or forgotten.

"I have you," she said to the dog bed and realized her speech sounded a little slurred, "plus I have Jeppe and my book."

She walked over to the petroleum-colored desk and looked at the stacks of papers, printed articles, and pictures from Margrethe Dybris's anthropological field studies in Indonesia and Central Africa. A fine layer of dust had settled over it all since Gregers got sick last spring, and she was forced to stop working on the book. The thought of getting back to research and writing seemed pointless right now. Why write a book no one is waiting for when your best friend is dead?

Because work was the only thing keeping her going.

CHAPTER 3

The fluorescent tubes in the ceiling came on with a peevish flicker, conjuring up a world of glass and beech veneer. Anette left the door to her and Jeppe's office open behind her, so the hum of her colleagues' voices could fill the room with some life. She tossed her purse on the double desk and hung her coat over Jeppe's unused desk chair, fetched a cup of coffee with extra sugar, and set it next to the two old cups she hadn't cleared away yet. That would never happen if Jeppe were here, she reminded herself as she turned on her computer. Her partner's anal uptightness was one of the traits she most definitely did not miss about him. The empty office, on the other hand, still took some getting used to.

She found the case report that the on-duty investigations officer had already created in POLSAS and added her own notes and pictures from the autopsy.

Manner of death: murder, she wrote, and hesitated as she tried to formulate the wording for the next section . . . *Cause of death: laceration caused by motorized saw, with subsequent arterial hemorrhage. The deceased was found in a halved state (left).*

That would have to do. The crew would understand what it was about. She didn't need to elaborate all the gory details.

"Are you ready?" The commissioner's throaty voice interrupted Anette's thoughts. PC, as everyone called her, stood in the doorway watching Anette with serious eyes under heavy lids.

"It's four o'clock. They're waiting for you in the meeting room. I rolled the flat screen in so you can show pictures on it. Just leave it there. I might need it myself for the press conference tomorrow morning."

"Thanks, PC." Anette saved the report and put her computer to sleep. "One second, I just have to . . ." She reached for her purse and nearly knocked the coffee cup onto the floor.

"Nervous?" A pair of small earrings shone from PC's earlobes, turquoise maybe, something colorful but understated.

"Nah, let's do this!" Anette stood up and nonchalantly sipped some coffee before leaving. PC followed with a slight nod.

The flooring in the new police station was a gray linoleum-like product that made funny noises under the detectives' rubber soles. PC and Anette walked in silence, trying to pretend their shoes weren't squeaking. They opened the door to the meeting room and faced nine pairs of eyes and a general murmur that died away quickly.

PC began.

"I assume that you're all up-to-date on the discovery of a half body in Østre Anlæg Park this morning? Detective Werner will be leading this investigation. She'll brief you now on the autopsy and assign tasks."

As she spoke, Anette looked around at her colleagues. There sat Sara Saidani with a grim look on her face and her black curls in a tight ponytail. Pale and chronically somber, what had Jeppe ever seen in her?

Torben Falck, who was nearing retirement age, was in the seat beside Saidani's, leaning on his elbows and pressing his prodigious potbelly against the table, the shoulders of his old blazer up, kissing his earlobes. Beside him sat the two young officers she had met in the park, flanked by five more uniformed colleagues she hadn't seen before.

The unfamiliar sensation in her diaphragm increased, her mouth felt dry, and her lips stuck to her teeth.

"Detective Werner?"

Anette realized that PC had said her name and not for the first time. She took a step closer to her boss.

"Thank you, PC, and welcome everyone. Have you all read the report?"

The room filled with nods.

"Good. So you already know we're dealing with a really grim case. The murder was exceptionally brutal, and since the body wasn't discovered for a long time, a lot of evidence has been destroyed and identification is going to be difficult. Forensics determined that the deceased has been dead for ten to twelve weeks and has been lying in the suitcase in the dirt for most of that time. That means that our perpetrator placed the suitcase in Østre Anlæg Park in late August or early September." Anette cleared the lump in her throat and looked at the officers. "You went door-to-door. Did anything useful come up?"

"I have put together the statements that we've managed to collect so far," one of the uniformed officers responded. "To begin with, we're focusing on the people who use the park daily—park employees, gardeners, employees of the two museums located in the park—but so far no one has seen anything unusual."

"Isn't it odd," Saidani commented, "that a large suitcase could sit around partially buried in a downtown Copenhagen park for weeks without anyone noticing it?"

"The bushes it was hidden in are dense and grow on a slope," Anette answered, "so it's not a location that people really walk by. What I don't understand is how the perpetrator transported the suitcase into the park unnoticed and had the peace and quiet to bury it. It must have happened at night, right?"

This was met by nods from the rows of chairs.

"We are ringing doorbells on Stockholmsgade," the uniformed officer explained. "The residents have a view of the park. They're slowly coming home from work now, but we're a little struck by how long ago this was. People generally can't remember several months ago. One of the residents, however, claims he saw a suspicious delivery van sometime last fall."

"Suspicious in what way?"

"It was parked late at night with its lights on, as if it was waiting or watching someone. The resident called the police the night of September tenth, because he was afraid it might be a burglar, staking out a location."

"And?" Anette eyed him expectantly. "What did we do?"

"Nothing, I'm afraid," the officer said, and tilted his head apologetically to one side. "No report was written."

Anette sighed. It would have been too good to be true anyway.

"Okay," she said. "Pursue that. Ask around and find out if anyone else saw that van."

"Roger!"

"Falck, check with Clausen when he and the other crime scene investigators will have news on the suitcase."

Falck winked and tucked his thumbs under his polka-dot suspender straps.

"Saidani, you track down all the cases of missing men between the ages of thirty and fifty. Focus on the Copenhagen area but include the whole country."

"He could just as easily be from Sweden, Germany, or anywhere in Europe. It's just a car ride away," Sara protested.

"As long as we don't have any specific descriptions or witness statements, we'll have to cross our fingers that he's Danish."

Saidani looked down, as if she was either checking something on the screen in front of her or was dissatisfied with the order. Anette chose to believe it was the former.

"Also check with our colleagues in Organized Crime, Falck, and see if sawing as a murder method rings any bells with them. It's possible that this could be related to gangs or organized crime, rivalries between hash dealers, how would I know?"

Anette received a little nod from PC and felt the knot in her stomach gradually relaxing. Of course she could lead a murder case, the crew wouldn't even notice that Jeppe wasn't here.

"That's it for now, folks. Remember: everything gets noted in the report as we go. Any developments are communicated directly to me. PC will handle the press, so refer any journalists to her. And then the obvious!" Anette held both index fingers up in the air and then brought them together in front of her face. "We found half a body. That means that there's another half out there somewhere."

JEPPE FOLLOWED A set of red taillights over the deck of the ferry, down the ramp, and out onto the wharf in Rønne. Though it was only just past six in the evening, darkness had long since settled over the island of Bornholm and the surrounding Baltic Sea like a heavy winter blanket. The first Christmas decorations hung from select lampposts. A few lights were on; the streets wet and deserted.

"Do you know the way?" Esther suppressed a yawn in the passenger's seat. The car smelled of body heat and red wine.

"Bølshavn, right? That's almost on the way to Allinge. It should only take half an hour."

They drove north in silence, past Knudsker in the middle of the island and along the forested area of Almindingen, where Jeppe spent his days. He followed the road's familiar turns and hills until they reached the north shore.

"The address is Bølshavn Twenty-One," Esther mumbled, and pointed. "It must be up ahead a little on this side of the street, because the house here is number twenty-nine."

"Could that be it?"

They stopped in front of a white, half-timbered building with lights on in the windows and got out of the car. A woman who was about fifty opened the moss-green front door and came out to greet them. She was small and nimble with wavy, gray-and-brown-streaked hair surrounding her smiling face.

"Esther de Laurenti? I'm Ida Dybris. Welcome!"

They greeted each other, and Jeppe took Esther's bag out of the trunk and carried it over to the front door.

"I'll leave you to it, then. Esther, I'll talk to you tomorrow, okay? And remember, I'm only a half hour away if you need me."

He gave her a hug, got back behind the wheel, and continued to Bornholm's northernmost town, Allinge-Sandvig. He had spent every summer here, at the Strand Hotel, until he turned sixteen and told his mother that he didn't want to go anymore. In hindsight now, those summers loomed for him as the last uncomplicated era of his life, like bubbles of harmony in an otherwise average childhood. *But,* he thought, as he drove past the miniature golf place, down the hill, and parked by the little red wooden cabins by the marina, *that's what we do, hold memories out at arm's length so they can sparkle in an uncritical light and allow us to resent the present.*

He grabbed a small paper bag from the back seat, locked the car, and walked back up the hill until he reached Orla's red fisherman's cottage, number 6. Light poured out the mullioned windows; someone was home. But, of course, where would he go, Jeppe thought, and knocked on the blue door.

He heard the radio being turned down and shuffling footsteps approaching before the door opened and Orla's wrinkled face came into view at around the height of the doorknob. The usual scent of canned fish and wet animal bedding billowed out to meet Jeppe along with Orla's smile.

"Is that you, Jeppe?" Orla asked, gray-white curls topping his head like a disheveled halo. He scrunched up his eyes. "Good thing you made the ferry. The girls are loose. Quick, come in, before they get out!"

Jeppe shut the door behind him and took off his coat, ducking his head in the low-ceilinged entryway. He felt something dart across his foot.

"Watch your step! I think Jane came to say hello. Or maybe that's Harriet. Does she have white ears?"

Jeppe looked down at the rat, which had come to a stop by his toes and seemed to be contemplating its next move.

"Yes."

"Then that's Harriet. She's still just a baby. I'll put them back in the cage now."

Orla bent down unsteadily. The rat shook its ears, ran over to Orla's hand, and allowed itself to be picked up. He walked over to one of the two cages in the living room—the cage dedicated to the six females out of his total of fifteen tame rats—and gently deposited Harriet onto a climbing tree. The rat immediately started darting up and down, and within a few seconds the sound had attracted the other female rats, and they climbed back up and into the cage.

"Are all six of them in there? Can you tell, Jeppe?" Orla put his forehead against the bars of the cage.

"They're there. You can close it."

Orla closed the cage door, straightened up, and smiled again.

"Well," he said, "how was the funeral?"

Before Jeppe had a chance to respond, Orla waved toward the sofa.

"Wait, come sit down. You must be tired. I'll just fetch us a little something to fortify ourselves with." He walked over to the mahogany secretary and reached up for a bottle of Four Roses, which sat on top next to a black-and-white photo of Orla and his late wife. He poured two glasses half full of bourbon and carried them with shaky hands to the coffee table, then sat down in his burnished recliner.

"There, now we can relax. How did it go in Copenhagen?"

"As well as that sort of thing can, I suppose. To be honest, it was a sad affair. Gregers's own children didn't even come to say goodbye." Jeppe drank a sip of the sweet liquor and felt exhaustion catching up with him, from his day, from his trip, from his life.

"That's too bad. No one deserves that. But *you* were there. And your friend. So he didn't leave without a send-off." Orla slithered his feet out of the slippers and flexed his toes in a motion that looked like it was meant to get his circulation going. "Did you hear about that half body they found in a park over there? It's been on the news all afternoon."

"Half body?"

"Yes, cut in half down the middle and thrown in a suitcase." Orla sounded equal parts outraged and entertained.

Jeppe's instincts kicked in. You don't work as a detective for twelve years without it leaving marks in your soul's annual rings. A policeman's acuity sharpens over time. But this was no longer his job to deal with. He curbed his follow-up question with a sip of bourbon and reached for the paper bag.

"I got ahold of that book you asked for. Here you go!"

Orla's face lit up.

"Ah, you found it. That was sweet of you. Thank you." He took the bag and unpacked the book. "*Selkirk's Island* by Diana Souhami. Oh, I'm looking forward to this. Do you want to read?" He held the book out to Jeppe.

When Jeppe had moved into the house next door in August, Orla was the first person to welcome him with coffee and cake, and Jeppe had made it a habit to check in on the retired widower when he came home from work. Usually just for a quick chat, but every now and then he stayed to read aloud from one of the books Orla himself had a hard time making out the print in. And though at first he might have mostly done it for Orla's sake, the arrangement had turned out to suit them both well. There wasn't much to do at night in Sandvig if one didn't care to watch TV or hang out at the local pub.

"Can we dive into it tomorrow? It's been a long day." Jeppe finished his drink. "In fact, I think I'm about ready to head home and turn in."

"Of course, my friend. You can show yourself out, can't you?" Orla winked at him and raised the book right up under his nose.

Jeppe let himself out onto the street, turned his face into the salty sea wind, and walked the few steps to number 4. He found his house key in his pocket but stood at the front door for a second. Over the ocean a black sky looked massive, yet full of shadows, which alternately attracted and frightened him. Sometimes when he was alone, he felt overwhelmed by the urge to go out into the darkness and let it engulf him.

CHAPTER 4

Esther set down her bag on the floral bedspread with an exhausted sigh. The guest bedroom in the old house was on the first floor, and you wouldn't have to be much taller than Esther's five-foot-four frame before you hit your head on the low ceiling. A lamp with a loose shade on the peeling nightstand was the only source of light in the room and didn't stand much chance against the November darkness. It was a nice house, although a bit worse for wear, and the furnishings were of the cost-effective kind, with more focus on intellect than aesthetics, in the most literal sense.

Most walls were covered with letters, postcards, drawings, envelopes, sticky notes, and greetings, all stapled up and faded by the ravages of time. Esther had the thought that she could read the whole family's history just by walking through the rooms.

"So you see why I thought you should come see the house, right?" Ida stood in the doorway. "This says more about my mother than any book or article she's ever written."

Esther leaned closer to a colorful theater pamphlet so she could read the text.

"Has it always looked like this, the house?"

"Always," Ida laughed. "My mother was the type who wrote letters by hand and sent them by snail mail, even long after she had started doing her work on a computer. She liked the textural effect of the physical letters, even if my younger brother and I were embarrassed when we had friends over. All those pieces of paper on the walls—it was such a hippie thing compared to how nice everyone else's homes were. Come on, I'll show you the rest."

They went down the creaky stairs to the ground floor. The ceilings were just as low, with small windows to keep the sea fog out and walls either covered with bookshelves or thickly layered with letters. There was a musty smell, and the furniture was worn beyond cozy to a stage where most people would have gotten rid of it a long time ago. The dining table wobbled, and the cane chairs were full of holes.

They sat down carefully. Ida opened a bottle of merlot and poured some into wineglasses. Esther's head was already heavy from the wine she had consumed earlier, but it would be impolite to say no.

"It's been more than two years since your mother died. How is it that you haven't sold the house yet?"

"We did actually try to sell it as is, but after a few months without any takers, we took it off the market and Nikolaj decided to move in instead. He might as well live here until we get rid of it."

Ida gathered her hair into a bun at the nape of her neck as she spoke. She was slender with delicate features but had the strong shoulders and arms of a lifelong athlete. Her eyes were blue and surrounded by the beginnings of a network of smile wrinkles. She looked nice, Esther thought, kind and intelligent.

"Has he changed anything in the house?"

"Not in the least. It's just like it was when Mother was alive." Ida's facial expression changed, but only for a second, and then she smiled again.

"My little brother is . . . how should I put it . . . not the domestic sort. Having a place where he can live cheaply is enough for him. And I live with my husband, Adam, and our two kids in Copenhagen, so it doesn't matter to me if he's here or not. If only he would maintain the house a little."

She glanced around at spiderwebs and wall cracks from the house settling.

"That's actually why Nikolaj and I agreed that I would come over: We're going to repair some of the minor damage and get the house ready for winter. So it's perfect that you wanted to come keep us company."

"If I can be of any help . . ."

Ida laughed out loud. She looked like someone who laughed often.

"I didn't mean it like that," Ida said. "You should just absorb it all and write the best possible book about our mother. That's what she would have wanted." She stood and held the wine bottle up questioningly to Esther.

"No, thank you," Esther said, getting up as well. "I'm sure I've reached my limit for today. Where's your brother?"

"I don't know, actually." Ida led the way to a small kitchen with blue-floral tiles and a matte copper hood and started unloading groceries from two shopping bags and putting them away. "We arranged for me to come out this week a long time ago, but I haven't talked to him lately. My brother likes to take a walk sometimes."

"A walk?" Esther asked.

"He's got a crew up in Allinge that he hangs out with. He could easily be at some kind of party." Ida closed a kitchen cupboard and smiled at Esther. "You absolutely shouldn't worry about it at all. Come on, I'll show you my mom's study."

Ida led the way through the house groping for light switches along the way. The kitchen was hidden to the left of the front door, behind the stairs that led up to the second floor. To the right there were three adjoining rooms: the dining room, the living room, and a study. An overhead light fixture glowed dimly above the dining table, but none of the lamps in the living room worked. The room looked run-down and half-empty, with dust on the lone armchair and full black garbage bags in the corner.

At the far end of the house they found the study, where Esther could make out the outlines of a bay window facing out toward the water. Ida managed to find a functional light, and a large desk came into view in the bay window, positioned so that whoever sat at it had an unimpeded view of the Baltic Sea. Stacks of books and papers were all over the desk, the floor, and most of the horizontal surfaces in the room. Here, too, the walls were covered with letters, drawings, and postcards—to the right of the bay window a red-and-green Bornholm sawmill poster beamed among sheets of white paper.

Ida walked over to a radiator in the corner and turned it up.

"Make yourself at home! Like I said, the house is full of memories and correspondence, and you hereby have my blessing to look at any of it. She wouldn't have had anything against that."

"None of it is . . . too private?" Esther ran her fingers cautiously over a stack of handwritten papers on the desk.

"My mom wasn't the type to keep secrets. I think she held on to every letter she ever received and many of them are hanging on the walls. When she wrote letters herself, she usually put a sheet of carbon paper underneath so she could keep a copy. Read anything you want, and if you come across something that seems sensitive, then just run it by me or Nikolaj before you write about it. Can we agree to something like that?"

"That sounds fine." Esther skimmed the first few lines of the piece of paper on the top of the stack on the desk. "This looks like a letter, to *Dear E.*"

Ida leaned closer to look.

"Elias, my mother's colleague and *friend*." She made air quotes around the word *friend*. "They married briefly when she wanted to have kids. It was hard to adopt back then as a single parent, but they never lived together and also got divorced shortly after Nikolaj was adopted. I always suspected that they got married purely for show, but my mother flatly refused to comment on it. Maybe you'll be able to shed some light on that for us."

"So perhaps Margrethe kept a few secrets from you two after all ..." Ida began laughing again.

"Maybe you're onto something. It's a shame you never got to really meet her. You would have liked each other. Did she ask you if you would write her biography?"

"No, she didn't get that far. She got in touch with me through a colleague, but for some reason, when I wrote back to her she didn't answer."

"Was it by email? My mother wasn't so good with digital stuff, especially not during the last few years of her life. Ah well, now it will be a posthumous biography, and I'm sure my mother is looking down contentedly from her cloud or wherever she's sitting." Ida smiled warmly. "I'll go find some sheets and make the beds for us. You stay in here and look around as long as you'd like." She left the study and went back to the staircase and then up.

Esther stood at the desk, inhaling the scent of old books, dust, and dampness. The waves broke rhythmically on the rocky shoreline outside, and she suddenly had the sense that the darkness had eyes, that someone or something out there was watching her in the lit-up bay window, that they could see everything, and she could see nothing.

Nonsense! She dismissed the thought and sat down in the old desk chair. Margrethe Dybris had lived and worked in this house for the last forty-five years of her life. If there was anywhere Esther could get a better understanding of the woman she felt so drawn to but had never gotten to know, this was it.

She ran her hands over the desk chair's wooden armrests, worn smooth in some places, rough in others, and pulled closer the stack of rough-draft letters.

Bølshavn, Wednesday, January 11, 2017
Dear E,

I've been planning to write you for a long time. At the risk of sounding sentimental, I'm writing to say goodbye. And to explain. I feel that I'm losing my strength. This is the end of the line, but that's fine.

Winter is upon us. The cold and dark have settled in to stay, and everything is frozen outside. It seems like a fitting time of year to say goodbye. The home-care nurse has a hard time getting through the snowdrifts, and I only heat the kitchen and the bedroom. It will be a relief to let go. I'm ready to die, whatever that entails, but first—as they say—I need to confess my sins.

I hope I manage to get it all down on paper before it's too late and that you'll read it with an open mind.
If I regret anything in this life, it's moving to Bornholm—or not moving away again in time. I firmly believed it was the right thing to do. I knew that bringing the kids over here would make it possible for me to give them a nice, safe childhood. If I had known then what I know now, we would never have come. But no matter how much I might like to, I can't change the past or do things over. It's possible that I've failed as a human being and as a mother, but maybe you can find some understanding for my choices, yes, even forgiveness?

Esther turned the page over, but the back was blank. There must be a missing page. She flipped through the top of the stack but found only copies of letters to other friends and colleagues, some cheerfully addressed to *Professor so-and-so*, others more familiarly to *Dearest Argy*, or simply *Beloved*, followed by a term of endearment. *Elias*, *Pallemand*, *Mim*, *E*, and *A*, Margrethe clearly did not let herself be constrained by rigid naming conventions.

Based on a quick estimate, there were probably around two hundred carbon-copy letters in front of Esther, all mixed together without any sort of system or order. The vast majority of them were addressed to Elias or Argy, the remaining letters were generally short and of a more professional nature. Confirmation that she would attend a conference or notes saying that she would not be attending a student reunion, those weren't immediately of any interest.

Esther sorted them and arranged the personal letters in chronological order with the oldest one on top. It was hard to read the cramped writing, and the carbon turned her fingers black, but after an hour she was looking at the first letter Margrethe had written after arriving on Bornholm.

Esther sighed in satisfaction. Now she was getting going. She got her notebook ready and started reading.

Bølshavn, Friday, August 3, 1973
Dear Argy,

We're finally here! Our trip from Havnegade in Copenhagen to Bornholm on the MS Kongedybet *could not have gone any better. After you and Jørgen helped us haul our suitcases down to the ship's dormitory room and we waved goodbye to you, we stayed on deck to wave goodbye to the city as well. The kids were tired but still understood the solemnity of the moment. Ida stood at the railing with her small back in the wool coat and said goodbye to the city's towers. Nikolaj clung to me, but the fireworks over Tivoli revived him, and in the end he was yelling so excitedly that people were pointing and laughing. Our city said a beautiful farewell. It was touching. Now a new era awaits.*

The ferry docked in Rønne Harbor early the next morning, and we drove up to the north coast in the 2CV, which was loaded so full that it barely made it up the hills. Of course I managed to make a wrong turn, but we got there and were met by our new neighbor, Finn, with the key.

Finn looks like a movie star with his mustache, white teeth, and man-of-the-world manners. He gestured with his arms like a car salesman, or perhaps rather the leader of a religious sect. "Welcome!" he exclaimed, and swung Ida around in a circle. She was infatuated with him right away, took his hand, and walked with him into the house. Nikolaj was more cautious and stuck with me.

The house is beautiful! White walls, thatched roof, half timbering with the most beautiful green yard and a view of the shore and the Baltic. My very own fig tree! Where else in the country could an academic and a single mother be able to afford that?

There is a lot to do, but one thing at a time. Right now we mostly need to land, unpack, and get Ida set up at school, which starts on Monday. She's looking forward to it, the poor dear, and I refuse to tell her how bored I was in school. Being cleverer than your average bear is both a blessing and a burden.

I start my new position as history and religion teacher at Rønne State School in two weeks. The high school didn't have any other applicants and hired me even though I don't have the requisite teacher training.

As you know, it's a big step down on the career ladder from my position in the anthropology department, but honestly I'm so tired of the factions of Marxist men who would rather theorize everything to death with each other than listen to a competent female associate professor. The students weren't really up to

*delving into ethnography studies, and I just can't fight that battle
anymore. Instead, I'm still wagering on being able to apply for
funding with Elias, who is still working in the department, so I
can conduct my field studies and continue my research. I don't give
a damn about the prestige, and my teacher's salary over here is
enough to pay for a good life for our little family. Fresh air, forests,
fields, and gobs of space. The childhood I never got.*

*The nature here is so different from the rest of Denmark, less
friendly and groomed. Here it's raw, windblown, and harsh,
and I love it.*

*Even the rocky shoreline right in front of the house is an
adventure. Nikolaj wants to spend all his time climbing there,
wild and fearless. He gets angry every time I come to get him
and flings himself to the ground in a tantrum. That boy is going
to get in trouble someday!*

*Finn stopped by this morning with herring he had
caught and smoked himself for lunch and an ice-cold bottle
of schnapps, brewed from berries he picked himself along
the coast—I've forgotten their name. In Copenhagen I
would never have tolerated unexpected visitors, but here it's
delightful. Finn feels at home over here. He's knowledgeable
and fun, and it's not hard for me to relax in his company. After
lunch he sat at the table with his shirt buttoned halfway up
and Ida in his lap and told us how Bølshavn got its name. It
came from "Bødlens Havn," meaning "Hangman's Harbor,"
and was named after hangman and executioner Haagen
Nielsen, who executed criminals at the end of the 1600s by
hanging them or beheading them with an ax. Perhaps that
doesn't sound pleasant, but there you have it.*

And now I need to go make dinner!

Your Margy

ANETTE HELD HER phone squeezed between her shoulder and cheek as she buttered two pieces of rye bread with liverwurst, trying to keep the dogs away with her feet. It was a good thing Svend couldn't see what she was planning to eat. To him, anything other than a hot, homemade dinner was throwing your life away.

"I'm sorry, honey, but PC asked me to lead the investigation into the half corpse in the suitcase, so I won't be able to join you after all."

Svend moaned on the other end of the phone call, but she knew that his irritation didn't run too deep. He knew the routine.

"Well, you're going to miss Egeskov Castle, the bouncy houses, and the antique cars, so . . . just so you know."

"But then, I get to examine a bloody, old suitcase along with Clausen and the other forensic guys tomorrow." Anette carried her plate to the dining table, hotly pursued by the couple's three border collies.

"At the end of the day, that sounds more like you." Svend was smiling now, she could hear it in his voice. "Do you have any idea who the body is?"

"No. We have one lone tip, about a delivery van by Østre Anlæg Park. We've got two officers making the rounds in the neighborhood tonight to see if anyone knows more."

"Exciting," Svend remarked sarcastically. "Do you want to say good night to Gudrun? I was just about to put her down when you called."

Anette's daughter came on the phone.

"Mamma?"

Her little voice was so high-pitched and lovely, Anette's heart contracted.

"Hi, sweetie! How are you?"

Gudrun didn't respond.

"I miss you so much! Are you having a good time with Auntie?"

"Mamma?"

"I'm here, sweetie. Are you looking forward to the bouncy houses?"

"You can lower your voice by an octave again," Svend laughed. "She's back to watching *Peppa Pig*."

"Did she catch a cold? She sounds a little stuffed up, doesn't she?"

"Maybe a little."

"Have you taken her temperature? Remember to give her the children's Tylenol if she has a ... She doesn't like the strawberry-flavored medicine. So you have to ..."

"I've got it under control." Svend gently interrupted her.

Of course he had things under control, he might even be coping better than she would. He spent more time with their daughter than she did, at least at times. Anette bit her lip and resisted the impulse to elaborate.

"Give her a kiss from me and say hello to everyone else. Good night!"

"Good night, honey. And remember: you're the best thing in the world."

She smiled and hung up. He had said that same goodbye for more than twenty years. It still filled her chest with a hum, best described as happiness. She was someone's "best thing"; it didn't get any better than that.

Anette turned on her computer and devoured her sandwiches while she skimmed the report in POLSAS and read the most recently added notes.

11/18 7:12 p.m.:
Peter Ingerslev, resident of Stockholmsgade 43, fourth floor, on the right, says that he saw a light blue delivery van with a company name on the side several times from about September 1 through-out the month. He also observed it at night. He doesn't remember

the name but is sure that it was a construction company. Thinks
there was a slogan on it that included the word "drywall." He
doesn't remember any more than that.
Statement taken by PA Jensen.

Drywall?

Anette typed the word into her browser and was rewarded with countless DIY videos where friendly men in plaid shirts explained how they made partition walls out of metal strips and drywall. It didn't look particularly sinister.

She hesitated and typed in the words *saw* and *murder*, all the while feeling a strong need to explain to the algorithms that she wasn't some drama-craving crime fetishist. As expected, the search brought up a series of murder cases in which the dead body had been dismembered with a saw. Anette skimmed the articles about bloody gloves, hand-saws, and amateurish killers, who left behind evidence as clear as the Milky Way, before she closed the tabs with a sigh of impatience.

The man in the suitcase hadn't been killed and then subsequently cut up with a handsaw. He had been sawed down the middle while still alive.

While Anette chewed her bread, she contemplated what that could potentially mean. Some gang-related act of brutal revenge or a tough lesson that got way out of hand?

Nyboe hadn't wanted to say anything specific about the murder weapon yet, other than that it involved a large, high-powered chain saw or band saw.

Murder by chain saw. It sounded like one of those horror movies that always came out over Christmas break to counterbalance all the coziness. It sounded absurd.

A notification on the computer screen lit up with an email from Saidani. Anette pushed her plate of rye bread crumbs aside and opened it.

Hi, Werner. Here's a list of the missing people.

The number of people missing nationally from August 15 until now: 322. Of those, 316 of the cases have been closed again because the missing people turned up. Four of the remaining six cases involved women, which leaves two who might be relevant to us:

Jan Søgård, age 52, single, no children, address Solbærvej 11 in Næstved, works as a teacher at Ellebæk School, but was on a medical leave of absence due to stress before the school year began and hasn't responded to inquiries since. Last seen in early July. Reported missing on November 3 by school admin. No immediate family, no activity on his phone number or credit card since August 3.

Bo Winther Tjørnelund, age 29, single, no children, address Viktoriagade 17, ground floor on the left, Copenhagen V, works as a bookkeeper for a construction company, the Drywall Experts. Last seen September 5. Reported missing by his parents. No contact with immediate family members, no activity on his phone or credit card since September 5.

S

Anette wrote back and asked Saidani to follow up on both missing men and also start the canine units searching all green areas near where the suitcase was found for the second half of the body. She skimmed through Saidani's email again.

The Drywall Experts? The company name on the delivery van that was seen at Østre Anlæg Park supposedly contained the word *drywall*. Anette did a search and found their home page right away. A construction company that specialized in new construction, including partition walls, for both private and business clients, headquartered in the suburb of Vanløse. She sent an email asking them to get back to her as soon as possible, then she clicked through a gallery of construction sites and renovation work. One of the pictures showed a light blue commercial vehicle with the company name on the side parked in front of a building covered in scaffolding.

Anette took a screenshot and moved on to the next photo. It showed a half wall made of drywall in an office, which looked to be undergoing a major renovation, wooden planks stacked on the floor, metal supports all over the place, and a large workbench along one wall.

Anette enlarged the photo. The skin between her shoulder blades pricked up in tiny goose bumps. A heavy-duty plastic handle and gray metal teeth peeked up over the edge at the end of the workbench. The blade of a large band saw.

TUESDAY,
NOVEMBER 19

CHAPTER 5

"Walked when I shoulda run / Ran when I shoulda walked / And don't I know it / And don't I know it . . ."

Jamie Woon's verses ran in a stubborn loop through Jeppe's brain, competing with the roar of the chain saw. He hummed along, had long given up trying to turn off the internal soundtrack that sometimes accompanied his thoughts. Maybe some small part of him had hoped that the tranquility of the woods would merit tranquility in his head as well, but unfortunately it was the other way around: the peacefulness around him made room for even more noise in his mind. Fortunately, it felt childishly good to smash the jumbled thoughts with a sledgehammer.

He pulled a metal wedge out of a bucket, pounded it into place with the marking hammer, and saw it disappear into the saw cut in the Douglas fir. With each blow, the tree released a cloud of forest scent, as if it at the brink of death wanted to remind its murderer that it had lived longer than he had and made more of a difference.

Jeppe picked the saw back up and depressed the safety. Even through his ear protectors and the jukebox in his frontal lobe, he

could hear his coworkers sawing away nearby. Today they were felling around Segen in the western section of the Almindingen forest,
and even though they had started at dawn, they needed to hurry to
get through the trees the forester had marked with his marking knife
before they ran out of light at three in the afternoon.

Sara had been with him the previous night. She had yelled at
him and eyed him with disdain. The aftereffects lingered in his body
even now, reminding him that he missed her.

What am I doing here? he thought, and drowned out his answer
with the drone of the saw. When life is limping, there's nothing to
do but hit Pause, and chop down trees one at a time. Right now that
was the only thing he needed to think about.

"Coffee?"

"Damn it, Andrzej! You can't sneak up on me like that when the
saw is going! How many times do I have to tell you?"

Jeppe released the button and turned to his coworker, who
stood holding an insulated cup, with a broad grin. Andrzej spoke
Polish, and the communication between them consisted primar-
ily of gestures and facial expressions. Their boss, Louis Kofoed,
explained that Andrzej had gotten tired of farming pigs back
home in Rosnówko and had come to Bornholm to seek his fortune. He claimed that Andrzej was more than happy felling trees
for Louis's little forestry enterprise, which supplied wood to the
island's sawmills.

Jeppe wondered if Andrzej had family back in Poland and
planned to return to them someday. He accepted the coffee, raised
the face shield on his helmet, and blew on the surface.

"Thanks. How many have you done?" Jeppe said, and used his
fingers to ask the question as well.

"Small," Andrzej replied, patting a tape measure he had hanging
from his belt. He pointed to the top of the tree Jeppe was cutting
down. "Tree, okay?"

Jeppe looked up, following his finger, but did not understand what his coworker meant. He might feel lonely at times on this island, but it couldn't compare to being a foreigner in a place where he didn't even speak the language.

A branch snapped, and Louis Kofoed came into view in the clearing behind them. He was in charge of their three-man crew and was the only one of them born and raised on the island, a fact that he never tired of reminding them of. He was also the only one who refused to wear a face shield on his helmet because it was "girly," and instead cultivated a long pinky fingernail that he used to fish bits of wood out of his eye.

"What the hell is going on here? You guys taking a coffee break without me?"

Jeppe received a hard punch on the shoulder, sloshing coffee onto his safety boots. Louis was neither especially tall nor muscular, but he had this certain look in his eyes that Jeppe recognized, the kind of guy he didn't want to get into a bar fight with. Louis wasn't afraid of anyone or anything and certainly not a policeman from Copenhagen.

"You guys over here necking? Is that why you don't want me to join in?" Louis's face broke into a laugh, revealing a gray-black front tooth, whose nerve had long ago given up and died. "A guy can't turn his back on you two for five minutes before you start French kissing."

"Andrzej's trying to ask me something," Jeppe said, not taking Louis's bait, "but I don't understand what he means. Something about measuring."

"He's asking if you're sure about the height," Louis replied without hesitating. "It looks a bit short. There, where there's a bunch of branches coming off, there'll be a bunch of knots. And where there's a bunch of knots, the quality is for shit."

"But the tree was marked!"

"The forester marks all the trees he wants thinned. Your job is to pick the ones we can get the most money for. Got it?" Louis blew his nose onto the forest floor and then wiped it on his sleeve. "A-trees are worth five times as much as C-trees. This isn't rocket science, Kørner."

Jeppe drank the rest of his coffee and handed the cup back to Andrzej with a nod.

"This tree is plenty tall, the quality is good, and it's coming down now. So unless you're planning to catch it, you guys better skedaddle."

Louis thumped Andrzej conspiratorially on the shoulder.

"Guess we pissed the Copenhagen boy off, huh?" Louis teased. "Didn't take much, did it?! As long as you get some proper trees cut down in the end, I won't interfere."

He pulled a worn pocketknife out of his back pocket and opened it.

"Look here, Kørner, a tip: if you want to speed things up a little, just block the chain break with your knife so the saw doesn't stop. Then you can cut with one hand and scratch your ass with the other."

His laughter reverberated up into the treetops, Andrzej laughing awkwardly along with him. Jeppe put his face shield down and raised the saw.

"THE SAW BLADE went right through his spine from the tailbone right up to his head, cutting the body in half. As I said, the cut is jagged, not clean, which indicates a saw, an extremely powerful chain saw." Nyboe cleared his throat into the phone. "The victim was dead before the blade reached the heart, but until then . . . He was probably conscious when the saw cut through his genitals and abdomen. I can't remember ever seeing anything like this before."

"Me either," Anette replied. "I did a search on the internet yesterday but couldn't find a single case involving a person being cut up while they were alive."

"It's a gruesome way to kill someone. And there's something even more ghastly, by the way. The crime scene must have been covered in blood, bone marrow, and bits of brain tissue about the size of a pinhead."

"Oh, gross!" Anette gasped, and made a face at Falck, who was sitting in the passenger's seat next to her. They were parked on the street in front of Viktoriagade 17 in Vesterbro waiting for missing person Bo Tjørnelund's parents, who had agreed to let them into his apartment.

"Remember, this is a human being we're talking about, Werner!" Nyboe swallowed, probably a sip of the bitter hot plate coffee he was always drinking. "Clausen and his crime scene investigators are making castings of the bone fragments and doing the corresponding microscopy studies to get a better sense of the saw blade itself, thickness, material, size of the teeth, and so on. We also need to figure out if the blade was clean or if there were traces of any other material on it. All those things together can help us figure out where the murder took place."

"Good, Nyboe. What are we looking at in terms of timing for these tests?"

"We've expedited them, so I'm hoping forty-eight hours. I'll call when there's news." He hung up.

Anette looked at her phone's screen. Svend had texted that Gudrun had a fever, not a bad one, but he gave her Tylenol and was going to wait and see. She put the phone back in her pocket with a knot in her stomach. Just what she needed in the middle of a murder case: to worry about her daughter's health.

Falck chuckled to himself, and she turned just in time to see his plaid-covered belly jiggling cheerfully.

"What are you laughing at, Falck?"

"Oh, I was just thinking about something funny. Villads, my eldest grandchild, he's five, and he's just started telling jokes." Falck wiggled his gray eyebrows. "How did Captain Hook die?"

Anette groaned, dreading what was about to follow, but Falck didn't hear her.

"He picked his nose with the wrong hand! I mean, that's pretty cute, isn't it?"

"Dad joke!"

"Ah, yeah, I suppose so." Falck straightened up in his seat and rolled his eyes, mildly offended.

Anette reined in her annoyance. Jeppe, she reminded herself, always kept his cool when he led an investigation.

"What did Organized Crime have to say about the murder?"

"It doesn't match anything," Falck replied. "The dominant gangs in Copenhagen right now shoot each other at close range or through car windows. They don't saw each other up and stuff the bodies into old suitcases."

"Hmm." She looked at the clock. "It's ten past nine. They're late. You would think they would be here right on the dot. Aren't they worried about their son?"

Falck looked out the window as if to make sure that the sidewalk really was empty and grunted neutrally.

"Nyboe says it must have made a hell of a mess," Anette continued. "Where can you use a loud saw *and* clean up the crime scene before anyone sees it?"

"The Pathology Department?" Falck chuckled but quickly wiped the smile off his face when he saw her expression. "No, in all honesty, um, what about a slaughterhouse? Or maybe a building supply store, you know, where they saw off planks and boards to people's specifications."

"Are you suggesting our victim was murdered at the local home improvement store?"

"Or an auto chop shop with piles of scrap metal and wrecked cars parked out front." Falck was adjusting one of his polka-dot suspender straps. First it was too short, then too long, eventually he gave up.

"You watch too many movies, Falck. People don't use chain saws on cars." Anette spotted a couple hurrying down the street toward number 17.

"Here they come."

Anette and Detective Falck got out of the car and walked over to meet the couple. They introduced themselves and followed them into the ground-floor apartment on the left without further conversation.

The couple looked young, too young to be the parents of a man who was twenty-nine, and sunburned, as if they had just come home from a Mediterranean vacation.

"Yes, well, this is the apartment. I'll just turn on the light." Bo's mother, Beate Tjørnelund, took the lead. She was wearing a trench coat with a plaid lining and pair of big sunglasses pushed up on top of her head. "But there's nothing to find. Like I said, we've been here several times."

"When was the last contact with your son?"

"He came over for coffee and cake on September second, for my birthday." Beate pulled the sunglasses forward onto her forehead and back again like a headband. "We haven't heard from him since. We've called a thousand times, but his phone is turned off."

And all digital platforms inactive, credit cards unused, and social media accounts silent. According to the report, Bo had vanished into thin air.

"There isn't anyone who's heard from him? Maybe someone he was dating or one of his friends?"

Beate frowned and instantly looked older.

"Bo's not in a relationship right now. His friends don't know anything. We've called them all."

"Is it all right with you if we look around a little?"

Beate nodded and sat down on the sofa an arm's length from her husband; both were still wearing their coats. The room they were in looked like a no-nonsense combination living room/dining room. A table with four chairs, a sofa, and a big flat-screen television. No shelves, nothing on the walls, no knickknacks. Anette waved for Falck to follow her and walked into the apartment's only other room, where there was a bed, a dresser made of pine, and a large wardrobe.

"You take the dresser. I'll look in the wardrobe." She opened the white laminate doors. Jeans, long-sleeved T-shirts, regular everyday clothes, but not that much of it. Anette counted and found only three pairs of socks.

"It looks like some clothes might be missing. Unless he's quite a minimalist. Are you finding anything? A computer, for example?"

"Nothing. No airplane ticket to French Guyana, no collection of false mustaches." Falck squatted down in front of the dresser and groaned in discomfort. "There are some papers here, nothing of immediate interest to us, but I'll run through them again just to be on the safe side."

Anette went back out to the parents, who sat at either end of the sofa, not speaking to each other.

"What about his passport, have you found that?"

"No."

She stayed where she was, watching them. They were looking off in a different direction, neither of them at her. The father had propped his elbows on his thighs, his face turned down toward the floor, as if he had given up. The mother shifted around uneasily. Both were conspicuously silent. If Anette's own daughter were missing, she would yell, scream, ask questions, and make demands until she got her back again.

"Where do *you* think he is?" Anette asked. "Do you have any idea?"

Beate blinked nervously. Anette reminded herself that people always react differently in a crisis.

"In the beginning we thought he must have had an accident. I mean, you hear about young guys walking home from a night out and falling in the harbor on their way home. But now we don't know anymore."

Maybe we do, Anette thought.

"I need to ask you something a little unpleasant. Probably not something that you were asked in any of the previous interviews, but still not pleasant." She lowered her chin and looked directly at the mother. "Could Bo have gotten involved in anything stupid? Did he have friends with any criminal ties, gambling debts, maybe?"

That got the father to look up. His cheeks were flushed, maybe from looking down for so long.

"Bo had his first paper route when he was thirteen, he was saving up. Not for a PlayStation or anything silly like that, but for an online investment class. At thirteen! He visited his grandmother every Friday on his way home from school until she died. My son was the student council president and a scout leader. He was a good kid, through and through. He's not a criminal. He's just gone!"

"Honey!" Beate put a hand on her husband's arm.

"I'm tired of the same song and dance the whole time, everyone insinuating things instead of doing your jobs and finding our son." He looked back down at the floor.

Beate moved her hand around to his back and stroked him soothingly.

"The uncertainty is starting to wear us down. We just want to know."

"Completely understandable. I very much hope we can make some progress."

Falck walked into the room and made a face telling Anette that the papers in the dresser hadn't yielded anything. He came over to stand next to her, clasping his hands in front of his body so his belly rested on his forearms, breathing heavily. Anette didn't normally care about that kind of thing, but as team leader, Falck's obvious poor shape cast her in an unfortunate light. His huffing and puffing grated on her nerves, and she had to hold back an irritated sigh.

"I'd like to ask your permission to bring a team of crime scene investigators into the apartment to collect some samples. We'll also need to get in touch with Bo's dentist."

Anette saw the parents exchange a look, as if that was something they had discussed before. Then they nodded. Anette shook their hands goodbye.

"We'll contact you again when we know the specifics. Until then, thank you for your time."

On the way to the car, Anette asked Falck to drive so she could send an email to Saidani and ask her to arrange the crime scene investigators. Even though they were on their way to the National Criminal Technology Center, NCTC, themselves, these types of arrangements had to follow a certain procedure. Besides, she could tell from looking at the clock that they had time for a detour before meeting crime scene investigator Clausen. She typed and hit Send, while Falck felt around for his seat belt.

"Falck, listen to this. Bo worked as a bookkeeper for a construction company called the Drywall Experts. Interestingly, their company van is light blue with the name painted on the side, which matches the van that was seen in the neighborhood around Østre Anlæg Park. Uh, what are you doing?"

"I can't find the damn doohickey."

Anette reached over and fastened his seat belt for him with a click. Falck mumbled grumpily and started the engine.

"We have a little time before we need to be at NCTC, so I'll just call the Drywall Experts and see if the boss can talk to us now. Their headquarters are in Vanløse, but they're currently doing a job in Kødbyen. Tell me, are you listening?"

"Yeah, yeah!" Falck pointed his fleshy index finger at the GPS. "You said Hillerød, right?"

CHAPTER 6

Sleep did not release its hold on Esther until the pale winter sun rose above the horizon at nine thirty. She had passed a fitful night in the unfamiliar guest room, tossing and turning. Even though she knew her hostess was sleeping just down the hall, she felt alone and had to fight an urge to get up and check if Ida was actually in her room. The creaky woodwork had woken her up, or maybe it was the seagulls crying over the water. They made such a plaintive sound, like newborn babies crying, and it left Esther's heart pounding in the dark.

She got up, gathered her toiletries and a change of clothes, and went down the hall to the green seventies bathroom. From the ground floor she heard sounds of dishes and the coffee machine and felt a twinge in her heart remembering how she now lived alone back in Copenhagen. The shower washed away the pang and also the last of her grogginess, and when she came down to the kitchen ten minutes later she was surprisingly ready for breakfast. She actually felt hungry.

"Good morning! Did you sleep well?" Ida looked up from her plate and smiled. Her long hair was gathered into a bun, and she wasn't wearing any makeup. Despite the fine network of wrinkles, she looked rested, almost young, Esther thought as she took a seat.

"Yes, thank you, more or less. It smells wonderful in here."

"I felt like baking. Help yourself! And if there's anything you need, just help yourself to the fridge."

Esther poured coffee into a thick, ceramic mug and took a warm bun from the bread basket.

"Is your brother okay with my moving in like this for a couple of days? I wouldn't want to . . ."

"Nikolaj is pretty relaxed about that kind of thing. Besides, it's as much my house as it is his." Ida unscrewed the lid off a jar of berry jam and spread some on her bread. "You have to try this! My mother's old friend, Finn Sonne, who lived in the house across the street when I was a kid, always makes strawberry jam in July, so we can enjoy the taste of summer when it's cold and dark out." She took a bite and chewed pensively. "Have you gotten started on the letters?"

"Yes, thank you. She mostly writes to Elias and then someone named Argy. Who is that?"

"My mom's sister, Arendse. She and my mom called each other Argy and Margy. Argy lives in Copenhagen with her husband, Jør-gen. I see them often."

Esther nodded, her mouth full of strawberry jam.

"It is good, isn't it?" Ida smiled. "I think I'm going to go for a drive after we've eaten. Nikolaj isn't home yet and doesn't respond to my texts or answer his phone, so I'm going to visit his job. It would be just like him to have changed his number without telling me."

"Where does he work?" Esther got a little thrill from the straw-berries. It was true, they tasted like midsummer and bright nights.

"My brother doesn't have a steady job, but last time I talked to him, he was helping out at Hedegaarden. It's a decent-size farm. They raise organic livestock and have their own slaughterhouse.

There's some meat from the farm in the freezer that we can have for dinner. I think it's chuck rib."

"Sounds wonderful. We could make boeuf bourguignon."

"Yes!" Ida said with a smile. "A good simmering dish is just what we need in this weather. I'll go grocery shopping on the way home. Will you be okay here on your own while I'm out?"

"Absolutely. I'm going to sit in the study and read. Maybe I'll take a stroll through town." Esther washed down a mouthful of bread with some coffee and cleared her throat. "Have you read your mother's letters?"

"Nah. I tried right after she died, but it was too soon." Ida got up, washed her plate, and set it in the rack to dry. "My mother was a person with big feelings who took up a lot of space. I think she worried about me and my brother a lot, but even so, she would still go off for months at a time, from when we were little, without a thought as to what that would do to us. I don't really know how to explain it, but she was both unbelievably loving and at the same time very self-absorbed. So if she sounds dramatic in her letters, you can assume it's fair to dial the volume down a notch."

"Okay, noted."

"I hope that doesn't sound like I'm speaking ill of my mother. That's not how I mean it."

"No, I think I understand," Esther said.

"Good." Ida dried her hands on a hand towel and grabbed her purse from the back of the chair. "I'll see you in a few hours. Enjoy your work!"

Esther finished eating and cleaned up, poured herself another cup of coffee, and brought it to the desk. The room seemed friendlier in the daylight, although the disrepair and dirt were more evident. A film of dust covered the furniture, and the house had clearly been wired for electricity after it was built, the cords running along the surface of the walls, hanging loose with bits of copper wire exposed.

The rancid smell was stronger than the day before, almost sweet, and she felt an urgent need to throw stuff out, give the place a good scrub, and let the house breathe again.

She hesitated in front of the window but reminded herself that it wasn't her job to clean the place.

The view of the sea from the bay window truly was glorious. It was only 150 feet down to the waves, crashing against the pinkish-gray rocks, painting them black where water and stone met.

She set down her mug and inspected the shelves. Academic anthropology literature and scholarly articles, but a good collection of fiction, too, both older and more recent, from Homer and Joyce to Hustvedt and Sayers, apparently not arranged in any particular order.

But what interested her were the letters Margrethe Dybris had written; the dialogue with her colleagues, friends, and children. Esther looked at the stacks and thought of Gregers's few possessions, which his estranged children were carrying out of the apartment back in Copenhagen at this very moment. Would they appreciate what he'd left them and remember him by it, or would they just throw it away?

———————

Bølshavn, Tuesday, May 7, 1974
Dear Elias,

In the month of May there is no place more beautiful
anywhere in the world than Denmark and no place more
beautiful in Denmark than the island of Bornholm. I know
you don't agree—that you would always choose the Serengeti or
Sulawesi—but I am adamant!

The lilacs in my yard are blooming in every shade of purple,
sending their amazingly vulgar perfume all over the whole
neighborhood, the chestnuts' flowers look like white candles, and
the moonflowers are baby blue. We found orpine stonecrop in
the woods and planted it in the cracks in the stone fence, and the

She's sweet enough, though, Dorthe is, just not my type. A
nice girl, stay-at-home mom, who looks askance at a single
working mother like myself. Finn has been trying to bring us
together, if for nothing else than for the sake of our little boys.
So far without any luck. She came over for coffee last week with
her dress buttoned all the way up to the chin and something she
had baked for the occasion. Told me in a muted voice about her
congregation, which awaits me with open arms, and nervously
inquired after my children's father.

We will never be friends.

Ida, on the other hand, dragged a new friend home from
school with her the other day, a fisherman's daughter from
Årsdale, whose hair was so tangled on the back of her head
that it stuck out in the air like an M16 helmet from the war.
She spoke in such a thick dialect that I could barely understand
her, and when I offered her a cookie from the pantry, she took
two without saying thank you. But she was sweet to include
little Nikolaj in their game, even though Ida didn't want him
to play. Of course he ended up adoring the girl and treated her
to one of his rare hugs when it was time for her to go home.
His big sister can't even get a hug out of him. Not to mention
his mother.

Now, work calls!

Yours sincerely,
Margrethe

THE SILVER-GRAY PASSAT was just pulling onto Vesterbrogade
when Anette lost her patience with Falck's leaned-back driving.

"Stop! Pull over!"

"Right now? Well, all right, then . . ." Falck turned on his blinker
and moved right across the lanes so the other drivers had to make

heavy use of their brakes and horns. As soon as the car came to a stop in the bike lane, Anette leaped out of the passenger's seat and darted around the car to pull the driver's side door open.

"We're switching. I'll drive! If we spend the rest of the day moving at this pace, I'll be dead before lunch."

Falck muttered something and struggled out of the driver's seat.

"Øksnehallen, right?" she said. "Wasn't that where the master drywaller is working?"

"You're the one who talked to them," Falck reminded her.

Anette stepped on the gas, heading toward the meatpacking district.

"The Drywall Experts," she snapped, "is owned by a man named Flemming Lykke. I talked to his wife, Nille or Mille was her name. She answers their phone. It's a small family business with three full-time drywallers, one of whom is their adult son, plus two apprentices."

"And a bookkeeper, who's missing."

"Exactly. The missing Bo Winther Tjørnelund was their part-time bookkeeper, three days a week. Nille says that he just stopped coming to work all of a sudden. She has no idea what happened to him."

After a five-minute drive, Anette parked the car in front of Øksnehallen's light-brown brick facade. The meatpacking district's hundred-year-old cattle market now served as a convention center and exhibition space. It hosted a succession of high-end flea markets, beer festivals, and corporate parties, but at the moment the large space was obviously empty. *Under construction* announced a hand-painted sign that had been taped to the door's glass panels. The door was locked, but a smaller door on the side of the building opened without difficulty.

Inside, scant daylight shone through the skylights in the vaulted wooden roof down onto the tile floor and white support columns. At the far end of the football-field-size space was a large area sealed off with plastic sheeting draped in long sheets from the roof. Idle chatter from an ad-financed radio station could be heard from behind the plastic. Anette walked toward the sound, with Falck following her.

On the other side of the plastic curtain stood an unfinished wall with its metal skeleton exposed, and behind that another one, as if someone were building a labyrinth. A thick layer of dust covered the floor, and there were rulers and power tools sitting around with disarrays of power cords tangled in knots. Anette proceeded toward the radio, which had begun to play an up-tempo pop hit about eating cake by the ocean. Someone was whistling along with the melody.

She rounded yet another unfinished wall and reached an open space where sheets of drywall sat in tall stacks and four bright lights shone on the plastic curtain that hung on all sides. In the middle of the room was the workbench she had seen on the internet and around it three men in white overalls.

"Can I help you with something?" the eldest of the three tradesmen asked. He had close-cropped chalk-white hair and his facial coloring suggested a fondness for red meat.

"Flemming Lykke? Anette Werner with the Copenhagen Police." She held out her hand. "My colleague, Torben Falck, will be with us momentarily. We wonder if we could ask you a few questions about your bookkeeper, Bo Tjørnelund?"

"Yes, of course." He moved his box cutter over to his left hand and then squeezed her fingers in the kind of handshake you only get from people with physically heavy jobs. "Hey, Patrick, turn off the radio! We can't really offer you a seat unless you want to sit on the drywall?"

She shook her head.

Falck finally appeared from around one of the half-finished

walls, looking like someone who had run a sprint. He nodded to those present and came over to stand next to Anette.

"That's my son, Patrick, and this's Kenny, one of our new apprentices. Right, Kenny?" Flemming Lykke pointed his thumb at the apprentice. "Have you found him? Bo, I mean?"

"Unfortunately not. You haven't heard from him, either?"

"Not since the beginning of September. He's not answering his phone, either, which is really weird." Flemming Lykke pursed his lips thoughtfully.

"How long has he been working for the company?"

"Two years, but only three days a week. He has other clients as well."

Anette jotted that down.

"Is he a good bookkeeper?" she asked.

There was no response. She looked up from her notepad and saw Flemming raise his shoulders vaguely.

"He was all right."

Was. Past tense.

"And you have no idea where he might be?" Anette asked, glancing over at the son.

"He's probably in fucking Miami, the asshole!" Patrick hissed the words out in a one breath, so quietly that it was almost inaudible.

"Patrick!" Flemming turned to face his son.

"In Miami? What do you mean?" Anette took two steps toward the young man, who stood with his arms crossed, looking grumpy. "Do you know something?"

"Patrick! We don't want trouble." Flemming retracted the blade back into the shaft of the box cutter and tossed it angrily onto the workbench. Patrick looked down at the floor.

Anette turned to Falck.

"Maybe it would be better if we continued this conversation down at the station. What do you say, Falck?"

"Sure!"

"No, there's no reason for that." Flemming exchanged a long glance with Patrick. "Kids, go take a smoke break. We'll continue in ten minutes."

Patrick went on his way without looking right or left, and Kenny, who had obviously picked up on the vibe, hurried after him.

Once they were gone, Flemming smiled disarmingly at Anette.

"Forgive my son. He's young, and he has the temper to fit." He sighed. "A couple of weeks after Bo disappeared, we realized that he had taken some money with him, a tidy sum."

"How much?"

"One hundred and fifty thousand kroner. We're a small firm, so that hurt. Patrick is furious about it. Bo is one of his old pals, so of course we thought we could trust him."

"Embezzlement?" Anette eyed him skeptically. "Why didn't you report him to the police?"

Flemming didn't bat an eyelid.

"Ah, okay!" Anette smiled. Under-the-table money was easy to steal because the tradesman couldn't go to the police. Whether he wanted it or not, Flemming had just given himself a gold-framed motive for murder.

"One of your company vans was seen on Stockholmsgade in Østerbro this fall, at night and over the weekend, too. Did you do a job there that required around-the-clock work or what?"

Flemming returned her wry smile.

"That must be a mistake. We've been working here in Øksnehallen since summer vacation, and we only have the one van."

"A mistake? A witness saw the van multiple times!"

"I don't know anything about that."

"Who has access to it?" Anette held his gaze; his smile was gone.

"Myself and my son. We only use it for work, so if someone claims to have seen it late at night, then it wasn't our van."

"Aha."

She walked over to the workbench and squatted down in front of the saw. A layer of fine dust had settled like a membrane over all the surfaces on the tool. She ran a finger through the dust.

"How often do you clean up the construction site?"

"Uh, we sweep every day. Is that what you mean?"

"Do you wash off the saw?"

His eyebrows wrinkled over the bridge of his nose.

"No, we don't wash the band saw. Why would we do that?"

"It could get greasy or something." Anette stood back up and brushed off her hands. "I'll just give you my card in case you or anyone in your family should happen to think of something else that you want to share."

CHAPTER 7

The dogs' barking echoed between the trees and made the windows of Jeppe's rented Japanese pickup vibrate. He swallowed the last bite of his sandwich, got out of the pickup, and coolly greeted the two black Labs that accompanied sawmill owner Finn Sonne wherever he went. They eagerly jumped up on Jeppe, leaving muddy stripes on his clothes.

"Down, girls. Come here!" The dogs obeyed right away, running back to their owner. Finn appeared in his usual blue coveralls, which did not in any way reveal his extreme affluence. His tall form, slim stature, and clear blue eyes made him seem younger than nearly eighty, which Jeppe knew to be his actual age. His hair was still thick and a confident mustache gave his face a cosmopolitan flair. The only visible sign of age was the beginning of a curve to his torso, which made his neck shorter and pushed his shoulders forward.

"Hello, sorry to bother you in the middle of lunch. It's Jeppe, right?"

"Jeppe Kørner, hi. And that's fine. I was done eating."

"Good, good." Finn patted his thigh, and the dogs immediately sat down by his feet. "Everything going well? What's wrong with your helmet?"

"My face shield came loose on the left side. It's a little annoying. But Louis doesn't have any spares. It'll be fine."

"I have an extra helmet at the sawmill you can borrow. Just swing by and pick it up when you have a chance." Finn looked over his shoulder. "Can I coax you into honking your horn? I need to have a chat with Louis."

Jeppe opened the door of the pickup, turned the key in the ignition, and pressed the horn multiple times, the signal the crew used in the woods to gather everyone. He heard the saws turn off somewhere and closed the car door again. The dogs started whining and acting frantic, and Jeppe saw Finn's daughter come into view between the trees. Camille Sonne helped run the sawmill and had developed a line of oak plate that had brought both the company and the island international acclaim in design circles.

She had her father's height and authoritarian bearing, but that's where the similarities ended. Where he was blond, she was dark; where he was sharp, she was soft.

As she approached, the dogs could no longer control themselves and ran to meet her. Camille didn't pet them.

Jeppe, on the other hand, received an intense look, lasting several seconds. Her lips parted into a smile.

"Hi, Jeppe."

She came over, so close that he for a second thought she was planning to kiss him. Instead she studied him without any shyness, as if she knew something about him that he himself did not. Her scent mixed with the forest's, jasmine and wet wood. Jeppe's palms started to tingle.

"Hi, Camille."

"How's it going, policeman? Are you settling in here in the woods, or are you bored?" She winked jauntily and called the dogs to her without waiting for his response, then proceeded into the woods with the dogs leaping around her legs.

Finn turned to a group of larch trees, from which Andrzej and Louis emerged, each with a chain saw in hand and a helmet under an arm.

Finn smiled at Jeppe.

"Maybe you and Andrzej can have a cup of coffee and warm up in the truck while I talk to Louis ...?" It was worded as a question, but it seemed more like an order.

Jeppe waved Andrzej over to the car and got into the driver's seat, turned up the heat, and got out his thermos.

"Coffee break." He handed Andrzej a cup, and he took it with both hands. Andrzej's hair was wet from sweating under the helmet. Jeppe poured himself a cup and drank as he watched the others through the windshield. They stood ahead of the car, talking together, Louis with his face turned toward Jeppe's pickup. He looked stressed.

Jeppe discreetly opened his window a bit.

"That *is* your problem!"

Finn's voice had taken on a sharp edge. The next thing he said vanished amid the soughing of the trees. He put his hand on Louis's shoulder and leaned in close. Louis nodded, his eyes glued to the ground.

Then Finn patted him on the shoulder and walked back past Jeppe's pickup.

"Have a good shift, folks! They say snow's on the way."

Finn continued into the woods, the same way Camille had gone with the dogs. Andrzej finished his coffee and held the helmet up with a questioning look.

"Yes, I suppose we'd better get started again!" Jeppe got out and walked over to Louis, who was still in the same spot, staring at the forest floor.

"What was that about?"

Louise raised his head with a jerk and looked as if he had forgotten he wasn't alone. Then his face broke into a cheeky smile.

"What do you think? We're behind. You're too slow, and now the sawmill's starting to complain. If only you guys could match my pace. I'm so fast, I ought to get a medal, a gold coin with my name on it hanging from a fucking silk ribbon around my neck." Louis halfheartedly grabbed his crotch and then picked up his chain saw from the forest floor.

"Well, let's get going!"

Jeppe watched his thin silhouette disappear into the woods and grabbed his own equipment from the bed of the pickup, his saw, helmet, and bucket of wedges. The conversation hadn't been about the team's output. Even though Louis was trying to seem like he had the upper hand, Jeppe had picked up on his true reaction to the conversation. He was nervous.

"WE'RE GOING INTO the blood room," crime scene investigator Clausen said, unlocking a door and holding it open for Anette Werner and Torben Falck. The light came on automatically and reflected off the stainless steel table and shiny vinyl floors.

"The blood room?" Falck looked around skeptically.

The Forensics Department at NCTC had recently been merged with Cybercrime and moved into a modern headquarters building in Glostrup, not unlike the detectives' own new offices at Teglholmen. The investigators were now housed in a square of light gray brick built around an interior courtyard, like a Minecraft version of Kampmann's old police headquarters in downtown Copenhagen. A flat roof and tall windows made the building seem dismissive, as if it were saying, *Beat it* instead of *welcome*.

"The blood room is the examination room where we study blood evidence, Falck. Since we've combined the investigations of physical and digital evidence under one roof, we've been able to optimize our cooperation with IT and make it tremendously efficient, and we've achieved a significantly improved workflow between the departments." Clausen straightened and looked almost youthful in his black T-shirt with POLICE Crime Scene Investigator printed on the back. "We've even started developing a new analysis method in collaboration with the Forensic Chemistry Department, so we can determine the age of biological specimens. TraceAge, you've probably heard of it."

"Of course," Anette replied with no idea what he was talking about. "It's great to hear that you're pleased with your new digs. I wish I could say the same."

Clausen's smile pulled wrinkles all the way to his hairline.

"TraceAge is one of the most exciting things that's happened in years. Soon, hopefully, we will be able to determine the age of blood traces and fingerprints. You see, the biological decomposition of blood resembles the decomposition of foodstuffs . . ."

"Clausen!" Anette looked at her watch. "The suitcase!"

"Yeah, yeah, it's over here. We've collected the samples we need, but let's just put on a face mask and gloves for good measure." He rolled a metal table on wheels over from the corner and removed a layer of protective plastic.

On the table lay the light brown suitcase, now without its gruesome contents. Clausen undid the lock and opened the lid so they could see for themselves that it was currently empty. The beige paper liner with a pattern of leaves was covered with rust brown stains. A deeply autumnal smell rose and spread across the table.

"To begin with the essentials, we have found traces of only one blood type in the suitcase and it matches the body's. There are no fingerprints or other biological evidence left after being in the ground so long." Clausen pointed. "Those stains you see on the inside are blood and bodily fluids. The actual killing must have caused a tremendous amount of bleeding, and some of that blood has wound up in the suitcase. As you know, once the heart stops, a body will stop bleeding, but with a wound with such a large surface area, the inside of the suitcase will get bloody anyway. Yeah, and then the suitcase had been buried relatively soon after the killing, my estimate is a maximum of two to three days."

"Okay, that supports what Nyboe has said so far." Anette tugged irritably at her face mask, which was tickling under her nose. "Why would the perpetrator put the body in a leather suitcase at all?"

"Practical considerations, I imagine. A body is big and unwieldy, but if you divide it up and put it into suitcases, it's easier. I wonder if we won't find that the other half has been treated the same way?" Clausen suggested.

"Leaving it in a park in the middle of the city is a big risk to take." Falck tucked his thumbs under his suspender straps. "Why not drive it out to some nature preserve or other deserted place?"

"Yeah, that's been bugging me, too." Anette leaned over the suitcase. When she got close she detected a faint whiff of basement on top of the woodsy smell.

"What are those stripes on the bottom?"

"Good eye, Werner!" Clausen sounded almost proud of her. "The suitcase was sitting on something grooved, maybe when it was being transported to Østre Anlæg Park. The bodily fluids that seeped through the leather made those wide stripes that you see."

"Can you tell anything about where it might have come from?" Anette asked, standing back up again.

"I can tell you more than that. I can tell you exactly where it was purchased!" Clausen beamed. He closed the lid and pointed to the stickers that decorated the outside of the suitcase. "It's an old case, I would estimate somewhere between sixty and eighty years old, and it looks like it might originally have been used as a touring case for a theater or something like that. There's no manufacturer's name in it, so I don't know who made it back then."

Clausen carefully lifted the suitcase and turned it upside down, revealing a small orange tag on the bottom.

"But, it was sold in this store at any rate."

Anette squinted and read out loud, "Olsker Antiques. Twenty-five kroner. Wow, that must have been a few years ago if that was the price!"

"Yes, nowadays you could probably put a zero after that, maybe even two."

"Do you know where that store is?"

"I do, indeed!" Clausen turned the suitcase back over and set it on the metal table. "Olsker Antiques is a well-known old antiques store in the village of Olsker. It's on the island of Bornholm."

"On Bornholm?" Anette exclaimed.

Falck cleared his throat and said, "We ought to call the Investigations Unit over there."

"Yes." Anette pulled her phone out of her pocket and started searching through her call log. "Or . . ."

"Or what?"

She put the phone to her ear and smiled at Falck.

"I know just the person who could swing by Olsker and ask."

CHAPTER 8

"You want me to do what?"

Anette laughed, and the microphone made a scratchy sound.

"Relax, Jepsen, you just need to swing by the store, show them a picture of the suitcase, and find out if they can remember it!"

Jeppe found a pack of cigarettes in one of the pockets of the lined nylon jacket, which kept the cold out and the sweat in, and lit one. He tried to limit himself to five a day, and the one at the end of his work day was the best. When he inhaled and the smoke burned his throat, he hit that perfect balance between healthy forestry worker and run-down policeman that made him feel most like his true self. On his way up and on his way down, but mostly on his way out. Away from conformity and midlife crises, away from life as a family man, away from the thought of Sara.

He exhaled the smoke in a thick jet.

"You get that I'm on leave, don't you? I'm sure you've got some excellent colleagues in Rønne, eagerly waiting for you to call and delegate such an exciting task to them. You want me to google their number for you?"

"Oh, come on! You know just as well as I do that I need to go through official channels if I want to involve the Investigations Unit on Bornholm, and that kind of thing takes time. If there turns out to be anything to it, I will obviously do just that, but right now we only need to know if they remember the suitcase at the secondhand shop. It'll take you five minutes."

Jeppe leaned against the pickup and gazed up at the treetops; they would soon become invisible in the afternoon twilight. It was not like he had better things to do.

"Fine, I'll swing by and ask."

"I knew I could count on you." She laughed again, and Jeppe had to hold the phone away from his ear. "Tell me, when are you going to be done playing lumberjack? We miss you at headquarters."

He put the cigarette out on his heel, opened the door of the pickup truck, and put the butt in the ashtray. His neck ached, and his calves burned from the day's work.

"Just send me the pictures and the address, and I'll drive over right away. Ciao!"

Jeppe started the car and hung up the call. Right when he put down the phone, a text arrived from Esther inviting him to dinner in Bølshavn that night. He replied, *Yes please!* and set his phone on the seat next to him. Olsker, he could be there in twenty minutes. He coasted off the forestry road and then hit the gas when he reached the pavement. His phone buzzed as Anette's pictures arrived and the sound became a rhythm that suggested the first few lines of an old song.

"*Whoa, Black Betty (Bam-ba-lam) / Whoa, Black Betty (Bam-ba-lam) / Black Betty had a child (Bam-ba-lam) / The damn thing gone wild (Bam-ba-lam).*"

The woods turned to fields and the fields to villages with lights on in every third or fourth house. Very rarely he would pass another car and have to pull over to the side, but beyond that he didn't see any other life. Even though the island was green and not covered in snow, it reminded him of the time he had spent two lonely winter weeks in Ilulissat in Greenland.

Olsker Antiques turned out to be easy to find. The store was right on the main road in a white building, the front of which was covered with plaques and old signs. The sidewalk in front of the building was packed full of shelves, chairs, and baskets of old shoes, toys, and magazines. Jeppe parked in front of the store and carefully walked through the densely displayed wares to the entrance, which was hidden under a dartboard and strings of blinking lights.

The store was empty but so stuffed full of things that it triggered his claustrophobia. It looked like everything that had been thrown out or left behind on the island for the last forty to fifty years had been allocated a place somewhere in this two-story building. Dolls with pale faces and missing limbs, glasses for every conceivable type of beverage, oil lamps with colored glass chimneys, and clothes racks filled with moth-eaten furs. It looked like a place where one could destroy things worth thousands of kroner with one slightly too vigorous arm movement, and it reminded Jeppe of the flea markets his ex-wife used to drag him to on the weekends when they were together. He had loathed every single minute of that.

"Can I help you?"

The voice came from somewhere behind a shelf of porcelain and plastic baskets full of tarnished silverware. Jeppe walked around the end of the shelf and discovered an elderly woman dressed in layers of gray wool standing behind a counter.

"Are you looking for anything in particular or just browsing?"

"Hi," Jeppe said, taking out his phone. "I'm looking for a suitcase. Apparently it came from your store. Do you recognize it?"

The woman moved the pair of eyeglasses that hung in front of her chest on a gold chain up onto her nose and leaned forward.

"An old-fashioned suitcase like that? You'll need to go up the stairs and to the right. That's where we have our luggage department."

"Um, I'm here to ask about the specific suitcase in the picture. It has a price tag on it from your store, so it pretty much has to come from here."

She leaned forward to the phone again and scrunched up her eyes. Then she straightened up and yelled:

"Aage! Aage, come here a minute!"

An elderly gentleman with a big gray beard came hobbling in from the back room. He nodded to Jeppe and sat down on a chair by the wall.

"It's the knee," he said. "It always locks up when it's water-cold."

"A cold fog and windy at the same time," his wife explained. "It's often like this before the first snow. Even if something tells me that we have had our last real winter in this country. Now it's just rainy weather from November until March. May I?" She reached out her hand, and Jeppe handed her his phone so she could show the picture to her husband.

His face curled in toward the screen and then spread into a smile.

"Yes, that's one of the touring suitcases we bought when the Royal Theater held a sale in Copenhagen. I think there were a total of four of them. Don't you remember, dear?"

"Oh my Lord, that must be thirty years ago." She turned to Jeppe. "Why are you interested in them?"

"So it's from Copenhagen? Can you remember exactly when you bought them?" Jeppe found it wisest to answer her question with another.

The couple looked at each other; Aage scratched his beard.

"Well, we've been running the store since 1988, and it must have been right around then."

"And there were four of them? Can you remember who bought them?"

Aage nodded.

"I believe they were sold in pairs, but now to whom . . ."

"Didn't Jacob Wulff buy two of them?" his wife interjected.

"No, those were the upholstered ones from the Rønne Theater." Aage eyed Jeppe with a wrinkle in the middle of his forehead. "Is it important?"

"It is, actually. Very important, even."

"Hmm, back in the eighties and the early nineties we didn't have a cash register yet. We didn't buy one of those until the taxman insisted. Before that we kept handwritten sales ledgers, and we've still got those someplace."

He looked questioningly at his wife, who folded her arms over her chest and scowled at him over the tops of her glasses.

"Oh, come on," he said. "Don't be like that, sweetie. After all, we have nothing but time here in the winter. I might as well take a look around since the young man is asking so nicely. It's more fun than doing crossword puzzles."

"Thank you so much. It would really be tremendously helpful if you could look into it. You can reach me at this number." Jeppe wrote down his number on a notepad that was sitting on the counter. "Otherwise I'm living in the house next door to Orla Klostermann up in Allinge-Sandvig. Pretty much everyone knows him."

"Orla Klostermann, yes, sure. He's originally from Pedersker. And you know what they say . . ." Aage ran his hand over his beard and stifled a chuckle. "There are three types of people on Bornholm: the good, the bad, and the ones from Pedersker, ha!"

Jeppe could hear him chuckling all the way out to his car.

ESTHER WALKED ALONG the rocky shoreline without considering where she put her feet. Like a child following her gut instinct and letting her body take over. Soft pillows of moss in delicate greens and brilliant yellow welcomed her feet as she stepped over tidepools and piles of animal dung.

The granite rocks along the water's edge were shiny emeralds and, farther ashore, highland cattle in their winter coats watched her lazily from the heather and grass. When she looked down the coast, twisted deciduous trees grew all the way out to the steep cliffs, and she felt as if she had been transported to a deserted island in the tropics. Wild, rugged, and lonely, it frightened her a little.

Late migratory birds flew low over the sea. Esther stopped and felt for a moment just as liberatingly insignificant as she did under the stars on a cloudless night. But then the birds were gone, the moment passed, and her grief subsumed her again. Gregers.

She found a path that led through a fenced area with grazing sheep and let her thoughts wander to the book she was there to write. She hadn't planned on reading Margrethe Dybris's letters, but then on the other hand, what was she there for if not to get to know the anthropologist better?

As Esther deliberated to herself, darkness fell over Bølshavn, slowly and apologetically, as if November were well aware that days this short were unreasonable. The outlines of the yellow tufts of grass, the rocks, and the isolated trees were erased, and Esther realized that there weren't any artificial lights there. It was only quarter past three in the afternoon, but soon the path beneath her feet would be transformed into an ankle-breaking tripping hazard. Probably best to be heading home.

She found her way up to the main road and let out a sigh of relief once she felt the asphalt under her feet again. The last mile back to the center of town she walked quickly, so that her heart was pounding behind her ribs and beads of sweat formed on her upper lip. She didn't encounter anyone on the road and wasn't passed by a single car, either. Bornholm in the winter was truly the antithesis of the grass-hopper swarm of tourists it experienced in the summer.

When she was a few hundred feet from the house she noticed the car, which was parked out front. At first she thought it was Ida, who had finally come home, but as she got closer, she realized it was a totally different car. This one was older and, as far as she could tell, gray and not blue like Ida's.

Someone had come to visit. And yet the house was dark.

Esther slowed down, but her heart raced along steadily in her chest.

"Hello? Is anyone here?" Her voice sounded feeble and tentative. She coughed audibly and then opened the garden gate.

No response.

She took two steps and then stopped abruptly. A shadow was moving in the backyard and she heard footsteps.

"Who's there?!"

A figure burst out of the darkness and came toward her. Esther stood nailed to the spot.

"Hi." A man's voice, high and hoarse, not one she recognized. "I didn't realize there was anyone home."

A short man, about forty and dressed in work gear, stepped out into the light.

"I just stopped by to pick up something that Nikolaj borrowed from me."

"Who are you?" Esther tried to calm her breathing.

"Who are *you*?" He smiled suddenly, revealing a deficiency of oral hygiene. "I'm Louis. I'm a friend of Nikolaj's, who lives here, but I've never seen you before."

"I'm Esther de Laurenti, and I'm here because I'm writing a book about Nikolaj's mother. His older sister, Ida, invited me."

"A book, well, well . . ." He nodded approvingly. "I don't suppose you could let me into the house? I just need to pick up some tools Nikolaj borrowed that I need."

Esther hesitated. Alone in a strange house with a strange man on an island in the middle of nowhere.

"I think you'd better come back another day when Ida's here. It's not my house, and . . ."

He cocked his head to the side. "I just need to run in and grab something. It'll only take two minutes . . ."

Esther took a deep breath and dug in her heels. "That's unfortunate! But I can give you Ida's number, so you can call her and work something out."

Louis looked at her without responding. The silence between them grew and turned into unspoken threats in Esther's head. Just as she was about to repeat herself, mostly to fill the void, he stuck his hands in his pockets, turned around, and walked over to his car. A half minute later he was out of sight.

Esther stood on the garden path, suddenly hesitant about letting herself into the house. The wind crawled up her ankles, into her pants legs, and sent shivers up her spine to the short hair at the nape of her neck. She pulled her coat around her and tried to see inside, but the twilight had turned into a nighttime blackness and the house was dark. It seemed abandoned, a place that offered no protection.

A set of headlights swept over her from the top of the hill. She recognized Ida's blue Volkswagen and allowed the relief to wash through her.

Ida parked, turned off the car, and got out.

"Esther, why are you standing out here?"

"I just came back from a walk. You've been gone for a long time . . ."

Ida took two grocery bags from the passenger's seat. She looked like someone who had had a long day.

"I went grocery shopping, so we have supplies for a few days." She found a key and opened the front door. "But I still haven't been able to get ahold of my brother. His work doesn't know where he is. I ended up driving to the police station in Rønne to report him missing."

She turned on the light and went in. Esther followed.

Ida set the grocery bags in the kitchen and flopped down in a chair. She had a horizontal wrinkle across her forehead.

"I need a glass of wine."

"Allow me." Esther found glasses, got out a bottle, and poured some for both of them. "What did the police have to say?"

"That's just it! They said . . ." Ida paused to drink a sip of wine and then sighed. "They wouldn't accept the report. They said that they knew my brother and that I should just chill out and wait. He was bound to turn up."

"Are you okay with that?"

"They said to call if there was any indication that he was in trouble." Ida set down her glass and rubbed her face till her cheeks glowed. "They thought he would most likely come home again soon."

"Do you think they're right?" Esther asked cautiously.

"I don't know. I so rarely come to Bornholm, and Nikolaj and I haven't been close for years, so I don't know what he gets up to. My visit was all arranged back before the summer holidays, but I reminded him about it several times by text. And I'm sure he would prioritize getting together with me even if something else came up." Ida shook her head to herself.

"One of his friends came by just now, just before you got back. Louis?"

Ida narrowed her eyes.

"Louis Kofoed—I've met him, he's the one who cuts down trees on the island. He's a little younger than my brother, but I suppose they work on projects together sometimes. I don't have much confidence in him, I have to confess."

"He wanted to get into the house. He said Nikolaj had borrowed some tools that he wanted back and asked me to let him in. Of course I didn't. I should have asked if he knew where Nikolaj was, but I forgot."

"What if my brother's in trouble? What the heck am I supposed to do?"

Esther put her hand on Ida's.

"I know someone who might be able to help."

Bølshavn, Friday, April 18, 1975
My dearest Argy!

Would you believe that I've been offered a professorship at Berkeley! A thirty-six-year-old woman on an indefinite leave of absence being offered a position most anthropologists would give their right arm for. Elias says that the department is abuzz with excitement, and I'm bursting with pride. And schadenfreude!

It was the award, of course, that led to the offer. Very few Europeans receive the sort of accolades I got for my book from the renowned American Anthropological Association. Despite my exile to Bornholm, I've managed to make my mark internationally. Not that that would impress the locals here, but at least I can hold my head up in the teachers' lounge.

Elias is proud of me and asks when I'm leaving. I need to suck it up and tell him that I won't be accepting the offer.

I've thought about it a lot. No, that's an understatement. You know me. I've been lying awake at night ever since the letter arrived in March. What a birthday present! My life's ambition, and one which I hadn't expected to accomplish so soon. I thought it would take years, and that's exactly the problem.

The timing doesn't work. The kids are too small. I hope you don't think I'm being overprotective, but I don't have the heart to uproot their lives again so soon after we moved here. And to a totally different country with foreign customs and a different language.

Ida is in the second grade and has made friends she likes and gets along well with. Nikolaj is only four and still wakes up at night because he's scared of the dark.

I simply can't bring myself to do it. I'll have to hope that they'll make the offer again when the kids are bigger. Alternatively I'll be begging the department in Copenhagen in a few years that maybe I can teach two or three days a week so I can divide my time between the island and the city, the children and my career.

So I'm turning down Berkeley, but, oh, how it fills my thoughts!

Something else that fills them—and you'll have to be even more patient with me now—is my neighbor Finn Sonne. It's not love, don't worry, he's too one-dimensional for me, a businessman with broad shoulders and a narrow mind. He goes to church on Sundays and alphabetizes his books. Even so, the attraction is as powerful as it is mutual. And impractical. He's married and lives with his wife and kids right across the street, and we all know the saying: don't shit where you eat! It's a little messy. But the pickings on a small island aren't the same as in Copenhagen, and people have needs, you know. Finn is handsome and strong, and I, who've always fallen for poetry and intellect, am finding a man's man to be surprisingly refreshing. It's just for fun.

I just need to make sure it doesn't affect the kids.

Did you and Jørgen have a good New Year's? And how are things going with my naughty nephews? Give them a hug from me and tell them I owe them a Christmas present.

Love,
Margy

ANETTE BIT A mouthful of hot pepperoni off her La Mafia pizza and saw strands of melted cheese dangling like suspension bridges from her mouth out to the triangle of crust in her hand. As she chewed, she realized that she hadn't eaten a proper dinner since Svend and Gudrun had left for Kerteminde three days earlier. He always did the cooking, and she often teased him that his way of showing love was with tomato sauce and stew. That thought planted an acute pang of longing. She wasn't used to being without her family for days on end, and the feeling chafed at her like a new pair of shoes. Not entirely uncomfortable, just unaccustomed.

She dropped the crust onto her plate and pushed both it and the thoughts of her family aside. Since she was leading a murder investigation on her own, she had to just decide that being home alone was a relief.

She looked up at Saidani and Falck. It hadn't been hard to convince them to hold the day's debriefing at the local pizzeria.

"While you finish eating, I'll update you on the suitcase," she began, and then paused to wipe tomato sauce off her lips with a thin paper napkin. "Kørner asked at the secondhand shop on Bornholm and the suitcase *was* bought there, about thirty years ago."

It was not strictly by the book to involve a colleague who was on a leave of absence, but Anette didn't plan on justifying her methods.

"They had four touring suitcases of that style, and the owner is trying to find out exactly when they were sold and to whom. But there is a connection to Bornholm."

"That doesn't necessarily mean anything," Falck protested. "My wife and I go to Bornholm every summer, and you wouldn't believe how much junk we drag home with us from all the island's antiques shops and flea markets. The suitcase could have been bought and sold ten times since it was on Bornholm."

"Which is why we're still interested in checking whether Bo Tjørnelund or anyone he knows tends to go over there. His employer, for example. If Bo actually did embezzle a large amount from the company, you could easily imagine . . ."

"Them sawing him to death? No!" Saidani raised her voice. "It simply doesn't fit that murder method. Would a master carpenter saw his bookkeeper in two because he helped himself to the till?"

"Relax, Saidani."

Anette looked over her shoulder. Saidani had a fiery temper in general, but Anette couldn't help wondering whether the reason she was getting worked up was that Anette had involved Jeppe in the investigation.

Saidani drank from her water bottle and meticulously screwed the lid back on. It grew quiet around the pizzeria's little plastic table, apart from Falck's chewing his way through a calzone.

"Do you think he was conscious when . . ." Saidani tentatively broke the silence. She sounded as if she had calmed down again.

"Let's hope he was far gone and had no idea what was happening," Anette said, but didn't feel convinced.

"What would make someone saw a person in half?" Saidani cocked her head to the side to indicate that the question was rhetorical. "Maybe we should ask Mosbæk to weigh in on the murder method. It might help us come up with a profile of our killer."

"You're right. I'll give him a call." Anette wrote a note in her calendar to call the police psychologist. "Falck, was it just me, or were Bo Tjørnelund's parents trying really hard to convince us that he had never been involved in anything shady?"

"Hmm, maybe?" Falck took another bite while considering her question.

"Weren't they worried about him?" Saidani pushed ever so slightly at Falck's plate as if she wanted to distance herself from his chomping sounds.

"Yeah, maybe. But they were acting weird."

"Maybe because they know he's sitting on a beach in Mexico, drinking mojitos with the company's money?" Saidani's lips curled into a quick smile. "But not necessarily the company you're thinking of. I did a little digging today into the backgrounds of both missing men. Bo didn't just work for the Drywall Experts. Two days a week he kept the books for a company called Food King, which runs a number of fast-food restaurants and stores that sell bulk pick-and-mix candy in the Copenhagen metropolitan area."

"Pick-and-mix candy?" Anette's eyes widened. "Isn't that . . . ?"

"Exactly. According to Organized Crime, that's a classic front for laundering drug money. Which is not to say that this company does that, but it is a possibility. But then we're back to the gangs," Saidani said with an exasperated shrug.

"And none of us are buying that angle." Anette poured some more soda into her glass, drank it, and burped discreetly. "Were the crime scene investigators able to collect any DNA from Bo Tjørn-elund's apartment?"

"Yes, and the parents provided contact info for his dentist. Clausen will let us know once he's compared it to the body." Saidani scooted her chair farther away from Falck, who just then dropped a glob of cheese in his lap without noticing. "I found pictures, both of him and the other missing person, Jan Søgård, on Facebook and added them to the report."

Anette's phone rang from inside her coat over the back of her chair, and she bent over to get it. The number on the screen was from police headquarters.

"Werner speaking."

"Good afternoon, this is the main dispatch desk. I hope you haven't sent your team home yet. We need you over at the Citadel. They found another suitcase."

CHAPTER 9

Jeppe gathered the silverware on the right side of his plate and tried to decode the subtle tension that hung over the table. In principle, everything was cozy and pleasant in the white half-timbered home in Bølshavn. Ida Dybris was an attentive hostess, the table lit with candles, the food delicious, and Esther obviously happy to see him. And yet through the whole meal, he had a sense of dissonance in the musical score.

It wasn't until Ida started carrying things back out to the kitchen that the tension broke. Esther leaned over and whispered, "Ida's brother is missing, and the police won't help. She doesn't want me to say anything, because she doesn't want to burden you, but ... what should she do to find him?"

"Uh ..."

Ida returned to the dining room with dessert plates, but stopped just inside the door, brought to a halt by the silence at the table.

"Have you told him?"

"Something could have happened to him. Jeppe doesn't mind our asking him for advice." Esther eyed him pleadingly. "Well, Jeppe?"

You can remove the policeman from the community, but you can never get the community to look at the man as anything other than a policeman, he thought, and drank a sip of water.

"Maybe you should have a seat, Ida, and tell me what's wrong. And then we'll see if I can help. When did you last speak to him?"

Ida set the dessert plates on the table and sat down.

"August tenth. I wrote to him a few times after that, but he hasn't answered."

Jeppe did the math in his head and furrowed his brow.

"Three months. Why won't the police help?"

"Nikolaj has apparently *gone underground* before. Yeah, that's what they called it at the police station. Four years ago, before our mom died. I haven't heard about it before now, she never told me anything, but he was gone for almost three months. The police say that we should wait and see if he doesn't turn up again on his own this time as well."

"But what happened the last time?" Jeppe asked. "Did he not tell anyone he was going away?"

Ida slowly ran both hands over her hair, as if she could smooth away her wrinkles and worries.

"Like I said, I haven't talked to him about it myself, but the general theory is that he stole the Christmas Joy from the Hut and then went somewhere warm with the money."

"The Christmas Joy?"

"Yes, sorry." Ida grinned, embarrassed. "Are you familiar with Hut Li Hut in Allinge, the bar?"

Jeppe nodded. Hut Li Hut—or "the Hut" as the locals called it—was one of the island's few bars that was open year-round, a place where hard-core drinkers hung out. He had gone down there himself one night, but he had quickly realized he wasn't going to find his new social circle there unless he planned to spend the winter drinking himself half to death.

"The Hut keeps a sort of piggy bank," Ida continued, "for forty of their regulars. Every week all year long they each put at least a hundred crowns into the pig, and one night in early December they kill the pig and throw a big party with all the money. They call this whole arrangement the Christmas Joy. But four years ago, someone stole it, at the same time my brother disappeared. It contained almost three hundred thousand kroner."

"Three hundred thousand?!" Esther's mouth hung open.

"Wow, that's quite a sum," Jeppe agreed. "But Nikolaj came home again, right? How ..."

"According to the police, his version was that he had taken a job on a container ship and been on long-haul trip to Asia. The Hut dropped the case, and the police never brought charges. I don't know if he talked to the Hut and the regulars, but they resolved it on their own somehow." Ida collected crumbs off the table with her index finger and fell silent.

Jeppe looked down. It didn't take much imagination to picture how that matter had been settled. With an ass whooping.

She sighed.

"I don't think Nikolaj had anything to do with it, but now he's gone again."

"And you don't know if he's all right or if he disappeared voluntarily?" Jeppe was far too familiar with this sort of family story. The black sheep, veering in and out of criminality, and the puzzled family, trying to help from the sidelines. It never turned out well.

"Have you considered that your brother might not *want* to be found?" Jeppe said. "Not even by you?"

Ida sat for a long while, looking down at the tabletop. Esther placed a hand over hers and gave it a squeeze.

"I'm afraid something serious has happened to him. My brother is maybe ... what do you call it ... a bit of a con man, but he has a big heart."

Jeppe nodded. Ida had just described the prototypical sort of criminal the police usually fished out of Copenhagen Harbor with something heavy around his feet.

"What can I do?" He regretted the words the instant they were out. But Esther looked at him gratefully, and Jeppe knew it was too late to withdraw his assistance. "Does your brother have a job?"

Ida wiped her cheeks with the backs of her hands and nodded.

"He helped out at the farm Hedegaarden. I drove there today, but the boss wasn't in, and the other employees hadn't heard of Nikolaj."

"Friends? Acquaintances? Is he seeing anyone?"

"I only know that he's still seeing Marco Sonne and Louis Kofoed. That's all."

That got Jeppe's attention.

"I know Louis. I can easily ask him. And Marco Sonne, you say? Is he related to Finn Sonne?"

"He's Finn's son."

"Okay. Listen, I can't promise anything, and there's also a limit to what I'm even *allowed* to do as a private person, but I'll ask around some for Nikolaj the next few days. That said, the local police are probably right that your brother disappeared of his free will and will turn up again when he's ready."

Jeppe got up, suddenly heavy in both body and soul. Whatever you flee from, you carry it with you. Just when you think you can be at peace, the chaos finds its way and pushes you out into the deep again.

"I'd best say thank you for a lovely meal and head north. It's late, and I promised my neighbor I'd stop by. I'll call you tomorrow if I find out anything about your brother."

THE OLD FORTIFICATIONS from the Middle Ages still run around downtown Copenhagen like a star-shaped wreath of water.

Looking at a map of the inner city, one can see clearly how the lakes in Ørsted Park and Østre Anlæg Park, and yes, even the lake in Tivoli are vestiges of the old city moat. The Citadel remains as one of the most distinctive remnants of the old fortifications: a perfect, five-pointed star-shaped citadel, extending between the bastions and ravelins and still in use as barracks by the Danish military. Only 1,500 feet as the crow flies from where the first suitcase was found in Østre Anlæg Park.

The second suitcase lay at the water's edge under a fallen tree near the Ved Kongeporten bridge. The fall's wet weather had left the ground in the ramparts waterlogged and soft, which resulted in landslides and areas collapsing. The hidden suitcase had been washed down into the lake Copenhagen children skated on in winter and referred to as the Vanilla Ice, and was found by one of the police's canine patrols just as it was getting dark.

Anette made her way awkwardly down the slippery slope. The old wooden windmill stood still atop the rampart, its sails up like condemning fingers pointing at the evening sky. She looked up at it and gave a thought to the three border collies waiting for her back home in Greve. At least they had one another.

A team of crime scene technicians stood by the water's edge with bright work lights and their joint attention focused on a large leather suitcase, just like the one Anette had seen near the playground. Forensic pathologist Nyboe squatted beside the open suitcase, his tall form bent over its contents.

"Hi, Nyboe. Is this what I think it is?"

"Yes," he replied without looking up. "I can pretty safely say that already. The other half of the dead man from Østre Anlæg Park, the right side of the same body in an equivalent state of decay."

"Falck," Anette said, turning around to face Torben Falck, who stood behind her on the slope, "check where the perpetrator could have parked and get a team of officers started going door-to-door along the perimeter of the Citadel! Have them ask people specifically about activity at night, people with suitcases, and any parked blue workmen's vans. And gather all the surveillance footage you can find. This is an embassy neighborhood. There must be cameras all over the place!"

"Surveillance?" Falck took a cautious step and slipped in the mud so that he had to flail his arms around to keep from falling. "Isn't it a waste of time to sit around staring at video from all the streets around the Citadel and Østre Anlæg Park as long as we can't narrow down the time frame any further than August or September?"

Anette raised her eyebrows.

Falck stood for a second, then slowly scrabbled back up to the path and out to the street that ran along the Citadel. Anette waited until he was out of sight before letting out a heavy sigh. Danish hierarchies were as flat as the country's topography. Being the boss was draining when everyone thought they had just as much right to make decisions.

She walked back to Nyboe and squatted down by the water's edge. He was collecting samples from the body with little white sticks that he rubbed against the brownish-purple skin and placed into labeled evidence bags. His fingers worked quickly and easily, the way they do in people who have been practicing a skill for so long that it no longer requires thought.

"Are you familiar with Caligula?" Nyboe asked without breaking the rhythm of his hands' work.

"Is that some new method you guys are using?"

He shot her a look.

"Caligula was a Roman emperor. His preferred method of torture was sawing. He would have the victim hung upside down so it would take them longer to faint and then saw them lengthwise, from top to bottom."

Anette pictured it and felt her shoulders shake in a shudder.

"They say sawing was also a common method of execution in Europe in the Middle Ages," Nyboe continued, "but honestly I have a hard time believing that. No society is that barbaric."

"But ..." Anette pointed to the half corpse in the suitcase, "apparently someone is that barbaric. Are we dealing with some kind of medieval cult, Nyboe? Is that what you're trying to say?"

Nyboe sealed yet another paper bag and shook his head.

"I lack the imagination to picture what's behind such a killing. That missing person you've been looking for ..."

"Bo Tjørnelund."

"Would a ritual killing fit his profile?"

Anette moaned and said, "I'm having a hard time seeing that. Did you see the pictures of him that Saidani uploaded, by the way?"

"Let me just check."

Nyboe stood up and took out his phone. He typed slowly and with concentration, like someone who didn't feel at home with modern technology.

"Yes, here he is. Bo Winther Tjørnelund."

"Can I see?" Anette came over next to Nyboe and watched his screen. Photos of a young man at a family birthday party with a paper flag in his hand, in tight-fitting Lycra on a racing bicycle, and in swim trunks at a beach, a portrait in a soldier's beret worn at an angle.

"Hey, what do we have here?" Nyboe went back to the beach photo. "He has a tattoo on his right shoulder. See!"

Anette leaned closer to the screen and just caught a glimpse of a yin-yang symbol in black ink before Nyboe stuck his phone back in his pocket and squatted down again. He pointed a light at the body's shoulder and studied the area closely, his nose dangerously close to the swollen skin.

"Do you see anything, Nyboe?"

"Give me just a sec!" Nyboe kept studying the body's shoulder, occasionally grumbling to himself. After a minute he turned off the light.

"No tattoo. I can't say who our poor Caligula victim is, but he definitely is not Bo Tjørnelund."

ESTHER CLOSED THE guest bedroom door and, after a moment's deliberation, turned the key in the lock. Whether it was because of Ida's worrying about her missing brother or Louis Kofoed's odd visit wasn't clear to her, but she felt apprehensive.

After dessert, she had insisted on clearing the table and washing up, and Ida had gratefully put an arm around her and then gone to bed. Normally Esther enjoyed doing the dishes after a good dinner, but when she stood at the sink in front of the kitchen window, a choking sensation crept in on her. As if the lack of light prevented her from breathing deeply.

She ditched her plan of working in the study and brewed a cup of tea instead and took the letters up to her room.

The wind whistled into the cracks in the old house, and the stairs complained ominously every time she stepped on them. She had to feel her way along and regretted that she hadn't left the light on in the front hall. It was blowing harder, and the trees in the yard whooshed and made loud snapping sounds every now and then.

A figure came toward her.

Esther heard her own breath speeding up.

"Ida?"

No answer.

Esther saw the silhouette of a person right in front of her and realized it was Louis, who had returned. To steal, maybe even to kill? Now that she'd seen him, she surely wouldn't survive.

She raised an arm in a gesture of self-defense and saw the shadow do the same.

In that moment she remembered the mirror on the wall at the end of the hallway. It hung just outside her room. She had done her hair in front of it that very morning.

Esther exhaled in relief and took two steps toward her own terrified reflection.

"You old fool!"

She hurried into her room and closed the door. It wasn't until she was sitting on the bed with the curtains drawn and all the lights turned on that she felt safe. She let her tea steep on the nightstand, placed a letter in her lap, and read.

Bølshavn, Sunday, December 3, 1977
Dear friend, my own E,

It's funny how the youth revolution has hit Bornholm, only after years of delay and a surreal lack of any connection to its political origin. The students here aren't so much revolting against an ossified educational system as they are enjoying the new music and the concept of free sex. Principal Bjørn Henriksen leads the school's 150 students with loving attention and a firm hand, and there's not that much to be dissatisfied with. We only had one student strike last year, when the students left the school for two hours—they spent one of the hours marching around Store Torv in downtown Rønne in protest and the other drinking beer at Hintzegård—and then they basically returned to class with sheepish grins. It's cute and not very dramatic.

We had our fill of drama here this weekend, though! On Friday Ida found a dove when she got off the school bus. It was flapping around on the street, disoriented, but couldn't fly and was obviously injured. She carried it home wrapped in her coat, so it wouldn't get hurt any worse. For an eleven-year-old, she's remarkably empathetic.

We set it up in the laundry room in the basement with water and food. Ida dug branches and dry leaves free from the snow and carried them inside so the bird could feel at home. I think it had been hit by a car and had broken something vital. The most merciful thing would probably have been to wring its neck. But Ida would never have forgiven me, she was determined to cure the creature so it could go back out and fly again.

The next morning, she ran over to Finn and brought him back so he could see the dove. My neighbor is a pillar of Christian charity during the day and a frequent guest in my double bed at night. I've already regaled you with stories about him, and there's not that much else to add, besides the fact that we all enjoy his company. It's great to have a man around the house, especially since he goes back to his own place again.

Now, please don't ask me if I am not missing something! Of course I am, I have longings and feel lonely just like everyone else. I just don't believe the solution to that problem can be found in the (so-called) monogamous marriage. And I don't see many examples that convince me otherwise.

Finn thought one of the dove's wings was broken and tied two sticks around it to stabilize the bone so it could have a chance to mend. That would also relieve the pain, he said, and it seems that he was right, because after a few hours the dove perked up and started eating.

Ida was delighted. Nikolaj tried to pick the bird up in his arms to cuddle it, but he was far too rough (he's only seven). I finally had to ban them both from the basement for the rest of the day so the poor animal could rest.

At night, after the kids were in bed, I checked on it myself before Finn came over with a bottle of red wine. It's become somewhat of a weekly tradition, depending on our busy schedules. We both need to laugh and talk about adult topics without the children every now and then. Dorthe rarely joins him, and honestly that's a relief. But I don't know how he defends coming over to my place to drink wine with me several times a month! He doesn't say, and I don't ask.

This morning Ida got up before dawn and ran down to the patient. Her screams woke me up, and I hurried down to her. The dove lay on the basement floor with its head on crooked, bloody, as if its neck had been broken. It must have been a cat or a fox. The poor creature.

We buried it in the yard. It was hell digging a grave in the frozen soil. Ida nailed together a little cross and cried as if she'd been beaten. After several hours, I forbade her to talk about it anymore. She was so obsessed with that damn bird. Not my finest parenting moment, but you know how my temper has a way of getting the best of me. And she needs to learn. Life goes on.

That's a little glimpse into our everyday lives here in the country. When will we hear back about the application, do you know?

Yours,
Margrethe

———————

"YOU'RE IN COPENHAGEN with a body in two suitcases from Bornholm, and I'm on Bornholm missing a man." Jeppe took a final puff of the cigarette he had declared to be the day's last and tossed the butt into the water. The wind was blowing in off the Baltic, and the waves were crashing against the stone breakwater at Sandvig Marina. He had to hold his hand up to shield the phone's microphone so that Anette could hear him. "Could it be the same guy?"

"Hmm, what do the local police say?" She yelled to drown out the wind.

"They won't even report him missing yet. Nikolaj Dybris apparently gets a little too into alcohol sometimes, and he once disappeared for an extended period when the ground under his feet got too hot."

Jeppe could hear a door open and dogs barking like crazy.

"Sorry, I only just got home. The dogs have been alone all day, and they're bonkers." Anette shushed them. "I'm taking them out for a walk; we can talk on the way."

There was rattling and clanking, then the door closing again.

"What do you think? Is Nikolaj sitting on a beach on Grand Canary, or could he be the one in my suitcases?"

"It's worth investigating. Are you looking at anybody else?"

"We thought it could be a bookkeeper at a construction company whose van was seen in the evenings by the park. But it's not him, so I wonder if the van wasn't there for some kind of job they were doing under the table."

"You should probably contact the Bornholm Police and have them check Nikolaj's house."

Pause. The sound of her breathing was the only thing connecting them.

"Yes, I suppose I should, but . . . Jepsen?"

Here it came. He should have known to say no when she had first asked. "Yes?"

"Would you mind asking around a little first? Just the obvious places. I can't bear starting up the whole song and dance if Nikolaj's drinking buddies talked to him on the phone the day before yesterday and his sister just hasn't heard about it."

Jeppe couldn't help but laugh dryly. This was the second time in one evening that he'd been asked to look for Nikolaj. Maybe there was a simple explanation for his disappearance, but underneath it could also be a massive root network of secrets that extended far wider and deeper than any of them could imagine. And Jeppe knew from experience what could happen if they started pulling on the branch that was sticking up out of the ground. The thought alone was exhausting. But the scorpion will always sting the turtle that's carrying it across the river, even if doing so kills them both. Because that's its nature.

"Okay. I guess I can take the day off tomorrow to look for him. But only one day; then you're on your own!"

"Thank you. You're a rock!

"Yeah, right. Bye!"

Jeppe hung up and walked across the windswept hill to red cottage number 6 and knocked. Orla opened and lit up into a radiant smile.

"Ah, you made it, Jeppe! Wonderful. Hurry up and close the door behind you. The boys are out tonight."

Jeppe stepped into the brown interior, took off his shoes, and enjoyed the shaggy feel of the worn wall-to-wall carpets under his feet. The warmth embraced him like a comforter and even the smell of animal husbandry and the home nursing service's ground beef and potatoes felt familiar and safe. He flopped down on the sofa, feeling like he had come home. Orla set a glass of cheap bourbon in front of him before he assumed his place in the recliner and let a gray rat settle on his shoulder.

"This is Wickham, my party animal. If something's going on, he always wants to be in the thick of it." Orla pet the rat with his index finger. "How was your day?"

"Fine, I guess. Long."

"Is he driving you hard, your boss, to keep the good Finn supplied with wood?"

"I suppose you could say that. I'm pretty beat at any rate." Jeppe laughed and rolled his neck and shoulders sorely.

But Orla looked at him gravely.

"The Sonne family has always had a reputation for being tough. Righteous and moral with the one hand and greedy and power-hungry with the other. The closest you get to a family of rural nobility in this millennium."

"Okay," Jeppe said hesitantly. "I don't have that much to do with them. My team works in the woods. We don't go to the sawmills."

"But you've met them, haven't you? What do you think of the daughter?" Orla's eyes widened. "A looker, eh?"

"Could be."

"Camille Sonne turns men's heads, even the ones who are married. She's not shy." Orla waited for a moment, sensing Jeppe's obvious hesitation. He picked up the rat and set him in his lap, rubbing it behind the ears.

"Any news on the body in the suitcase?"

"Not that I know of." Jeppe didn't see any reason to discuss a case he wasn't even involved in with his curious neighbor. He sipped his bourbon and noted that he was getting used to the taste. "Hey, do you know Nikolaj Dybris?"

"Margrethe's son? Yeah, I know him." Orla cocked his head. "Why do you ask?"

"His sister can't get ahold of him. No one's seen him, and she's starting to get a little concerned."

"Little Ida," Orla sighed. "She used to work the cash register at the grocery store, always so smiley and sweet. Her brother, on the other hand, has always given the family cause for concern, a bit of a scammer. But I don't know where he is. I don't really get out much anymore."

Jeppe took another sip. The sofa beneath him was far too soft and offered no support for his back, which was stiffening up after his long day in the forest. The ibuprofen was calling him, maybe along with an oxycodone for a change. But he knew that Orla had been sitting here alone all day and that his visit was pretty much the only human contact he had.

"Shall I read to you?"

"That would be wonderful! I started the new book, but I'm making slow progress." Orla gathered up the book from the coffee table.

"It's about a sailor named Alexander Selkirk, who sails off as a privateer on a British ship to plunder French and Spanish galleons along the South American coast. We're in 1703, and piracy is apparently completely normal. But conditions on board the ship are terrible, and the crew is dying left and right from scurvy and dysentery. Selkirk has a falling out with the captain, who then maroons him on a deserted island off the coast of Chile. And now he has to manage there all by himself."

Orla handed him the book over the coffee table.

Jeppe opened it to the brass bookmark shaped like a feather pen. The words on the page swam in front of his tired eyes. He blinked a few times and started reading.

The island was never quiet, never still. There was the chatter and whirr of hummingbirds, the barking of seals, the squealing of rats, the susurrus of waves, the wind in the trees. There were sounds of contentment, of killing and of casual disaster. A nocturnal seabird, the fardela, screaming in the night like a frightened child . . .

As the days passed, day after day after day after day, he got inured to solitude. Company was not essential. His relationship was to The Island. He was a rough man but it seduced him. He had so much time to observe the sunlight on the sea, the mist in the valley, the shapes of the mountains, the shadows of evening. He came to know The Island's edible plants, its thorny shrubs, scented laurels and palms, its useful animals and freshwater springs, its natural shelters, birds and fishes, its lizards that basked in the sun, its rocks covered in barnacles . . .

Here was a paradox of freedom: he was free from responsibility, debt, relationship, the expectations of others, yet he yearned for the constraints of the past, for the squalor and confinement of shipboard life.

Jeppe snuck a peek at Orla, who sat with his eyes closed, chin resting on his chest. The rat in his lap had begun to wash itself with small, meticulous motions. A snoring sound escaped the elderly man.

Jeppe set down the book, covered Orla's knees with a blanket, and tiptoed to the front door. In the foyer, he stopped and listened but heard only the soft snoring from the recliner in the living room. Carefully, so as not to risk the rats escaping, he opened the door and let himself out and into number 4.

His cottage was chilly and quiet. Nothing had changed since he left home early that morning. He went upstairs without turning on the light, brushed his teeth, and crawled into a bed that was too short for him and yet still too big.

Freedom's paradox.

WEDNESDAY, NOVEMBER 20

CHAPTER 10

"You can put your shoes on the mat!"

Anette looked down at her sneakers. Strictly speaking, she would prefer to spend her morning reviewing witness statements and tracking suitcase clues back to Bornholm—concrete tasks—rather than speculating about perpetrator profiles in Mosbæk's home office. She had mixed feelings about the use of police psychologists in investigative work in general, and she always had. Not out of some calcified prejudice over the profession, even though Jeppe often wrongly accused her of that. The problem was that their observations extremely rarely brought the investigation closer to resolution. As a rule, the criminal psychologists' expertise was more relevant once the culprit had been found and people were trying to understand his thinking and motive so that preventative actions could be taken in the future.

But, she reminded herself, all tasks had been delegated, and the team was working in full swing. When you were investigative lead, you needed to turn over every stone even if you had to do it in your stocking feet.

She untied her shoes, set them on the mat on the floor, and walked into Mosbæk's home office.

It was warm and had a faint scent of garden shop or a nursery.

"You don't mind dogs, do you? I let Maslow come to work with me today." Mosbæk smiled fondly at the dog whose leash he was holding. The psychologist's checked shirt and knit vest matched the dog's brown and orangey-gold colors, his feet screamed loudly in green-and-purple-striped woolen socks. Tufts of shed dog fur floated over the room's worn Persian rugs and revealed that Maslow was no doubt allowed to come to work with his owner on most days.

"He's an Australian shepherd, isn't he?" Anette squatted down and pet the enthusiastic Maslow. The discomfort in her chest dissolved in time with the dog's affectionate wagging. "I have three border collies myself. Older than this guy, I can see, but still healthy and with beautiful coats."

"I had no idea you were a dog person," Mosbæk said, sounding as if she had just risen significantly in his esteem. "Your partner isn't so keen."

"Oh, Jeppe's just afraid of germs. And he's nuts. Is this where we sit?" Anette pointed to the room's sofa arrangement by the glass wall facing an overgrown yard. A climbing plant on the fence outside had fallen over and drooped in an arc toward the ground. Winter moss covered the crooked stone patio pavers, and the garden furniture was still out, getting wet.

"You sit on the sofa, then you can use the little table for your computer. There's a cup of tea for you on the side table. It's sage leaves from the garden."

"Aha, okay." Anette sat down and got the iPad out of her bag. She appreciated home-grown herbal tea about as much as an itchy rash. "I assume you've read the report?"

"Yes, it's deeply disturbing reading. What's the status? Any suspects yet?" Mosbæk sat down in a bottle-green armchair facing the sofa, teacup in hand. The steam fogged up his glasses. He took them off and wiped them on his sleeve with an apologetic smile.

"I'm afraid we don't even know the victim's identity yet. And the witness statements we've gathered so far haven't led to anything concrete. That's why I'm hoping the two of us can gain some insight from analyzing the murder method itself. It's so . . . unusual." Anette was about to pull her own reading glasses out of their case in her purse, but one glimpse of Mosbæk's greasy lenses stopped her. No matter how vain it was, she couldn't sit here looking middle-aged and visually impaired with him. "Nyboe mentioned a Roman emperor who sawed his victims in half."

"Caligula, yes," Mosbæk replied, drinking a slurpy sip of his herbal tea. "The comparison is obvious. Here, too, we're talking about an unusually brutal murderer, who let his or her victim understand just how painful the death awaiting him was. Regardless of whether the person in question was working alone or as part of a group, that suggests a perpetrator with either a serious mental illness or pent-up rage of a caliber you and I would have trouble comprehending."

Mosbæk ran a hand over his reddish-brown beard and glanced out at the yard.

"Incidentally, Caligula isn't the only one associated with sawing victims to death. Have you heard of Simon the Zealot?"

She shook her head.

"He was one of Jesus's twelve disciples, probably not one of the better-known ones. He is normally depicted with a saw, because the legend says that he was executed by sawing, hoisted up into a tree by his feet and sawed down the middle from his crotch to his head." Mosbæk nodded to himself. "This murder method could just as well be a reference to the Zealot. Though he didn't commit any crime against Jesus as far as I can remember from Sunday school, and this murder looks like an act of vengeance."

"You're saying you don't think the perpetrator sawed his victim in half for the fun of it?" Anette raised one eyebrow.

"No." Mosbæk didn't catch the sarcasm in her voice. "Even if sadism exists in many forms, I don't believe this murder is about that. If the perpetrator was driven by a desire to torment and kill, he would probably already have done it again. That sort of need has to be fed more than once."

"Could it be a religious sect? Punishing a dissenter, for example?"

"Yes, or for some other crime the sect considers unforgiveable. Infidelity, theft, blasphemy . . ." Mosbæk took off his glasses and wiped them absentmindedly on his shirt. It didn't seem to help. "What about the suitcases? Where exactly did you find them?"

"One was buried in the bushes behind the playground in Østre Anlæg Park. It must have been heavy to carry it from the car all the way through park and up the hill, not to mention how hard it must have been to bury it. We found the other suitcase under a tree trunk by the moat at the Citadel."

"So a slightly easier undertaking, then. Could it have been carried out by a lone perpetrator?"

Anette thought it over. "Maybe he buried the first one and was totally exhausted when he returned to his van by Østre Anlæg Park. So he skipped burying suitcase number two in the same spot and instead drove to the Citadel, where he could get by with just carrying it a few hundred yards and hiding it in the muck under a tree by the edge of the water."

Mosbæk reached down and scratched Maslow behind the ears. "But why hide them in the middle of the city? Why not drive them to a secluded beach and throw them in the water?"

"Because bodies that get thrown in the water have a habit of washing back up on shore very quickly."

"But," Mosbæk protested again, "he must have known that two suitcases in the middle of Copenhagen were sure to be found as well."

"Yes. But apparently not until a good chunk of time had passed and the body was so decayed that it was hard to identify."

"Okay. An identity that needed to be obscured could fit with a motive of punishing someone. A religious sect that wants to eliminate a former member might decide to . . ."

Anette's phone lit up with Sara Saidani's number on the screen. She signaled to Mosbæk that she needed to take it, got up, and walked to the window overlooking the yard.

"Hi, Saidani. Any news?"

"Do you remember Jan Søgård from Næstved?"

"The schoolteacher, who was on sick leave due to stress and then disappeared?"

Maslow came over and rubbed against her leg. Anette leaned down and petted him.

"What about him?"

"I was gathering background info on him, dental records and so on, but—and I don't want to point any fingers at our coworkers here—the investigation into him has to be described as halfhearted. The police have only talked to a few of his colleagues and rung his neighbors' doorbells. That's it. There's a clue that no one has followed up on, and I don't know why."

"Which clue are we talking about?"

"According to one of Jan Søgård's neighbors, he has a second house where he spends his vacations. And as far as I can see in the report, no one has been by there to look for him."

Anette had one of those premonitions that sometimes felt as tangible as hearing a coin drop into a slot.

"Wait a minute. You're not saying that—"

"Yes, I am," Saidani cut her off. "His vacation house is on Bornholm."

JEPPE WOKE FROM a dream before the alarm clock rang, and he lay in bed, groggy, under the sloped ceiling of the fisherman's cottage. Even with the window closed, he could hear the sea. You would think that would have a calming effect, but for him it was the opposite. In the gap between sleep and consciously awake, he felt he could hear the waves in multiple layers, ever deeper, stacked on top of one another. The current carried him in and out against the rocky shore, growling like a wild animal in the depths, crackling softly on the surface. Jeppe listened with a sensation that he was sinking to the bottom and being subsumed.

At eight he got up, his brain wrapped in cotton, and checked his phone. Louis had reluctantly given him permission to take the day off, all the while impressing on him how busy they were if they were to make their quota before the snow arrived. Jeppe replied with an okay and put away his phone.

He managed to make coffee without putting grounds in the filter and burn his oatmeal before he pulled himself together. Two of the round pills and two of the oval pills helped. They relieved his back pain and spread a welcome calm through his nervous system. Maybe it was just as well that he wouldn't be handling a chain saw today.

He brought the coffee cup out to the cold pickup truck and found Hedegaarden's address on his phone. Nikolaj Dybris's workplace was located in a section of the center of the island that Jeppe wasn't familiar with, where the wilds were flat and the woods dense with conifers. He drove past fallow fields with flocks of black birds and through plots that gleamed emerald green with winter-sown crops. The clouds had fallen to the ground forming a dense fog with no horizon.

Hedegaarden lay whitewashed and square at the end of a pot-holed dirt road. A large modern building had been built as an extension of the farm; Jeppe guessed it was the slaughterhouse. Fat sheep stood around in the folds next to the buildings, looking like contented animal welfare models in the shadow of the slaughterhouse. Jeppe parked in front of a metal door, got out, and looked around. Not a soul in sight.

He knocked on the slaughterhouse door, waited, cautiously grasped the handle, and opened it. The space he stepped into had a high ceiling and was brightly lit and just as cold as outdoors. The walls and ceiling were white and crisscrossed with metal structures with hooks and a hoist system, the no-slip surface of the floor full of puddles. Bloody stains around floor drains suggested that something had been slaughtered recently and that the subsequent wash-down had not been able to remove all the traces. A sweet smell of fresh meat lingered in the air.

"Hello? Is anyone here?"

Jeppe's call echoed back from the bare walls, but there was no answer. He walked farther into the slaughter hall. A series of skinned heads stared at him from a rack with entrails hanging out of their neck openings. Their eyeballs were milky but intact and looked like marbles surrounded by the exposed flesh on the skulls. There were heaps of entrails on the floor in one corner—it looked like stomachs and intestines—and next to that a shovel leaning against the wall.

"It's waiting to be inspected by the vet before Daka picks it up for disposal," an older man said, entering with full buckets in his hands and knee-high rubber boots. His shoulder-length hair was streaked with gray, clipped straight across the forehead, and smelled freshly washed. A bloodstained plastic apron hung from his broad shoulders. He set down the buckets and kept talking as if he and Jeppe were in the middle of a conversation.

"The scraps need to go all the way to Randers. That costs sixty kroner per bucket plus transport and weight. We'd rather take it to Aakirkeby to be used for biogas, but that's not up to us." He pulled a rag out of his pocket and wiped his hands, eyeing Jeppe expectantly.

Jeppe wasn't sure how to respond. Ultimately he held out his hand.

"Jeppe Kørner. I'm looking for Nikolaj Dybris."

"Anton Hedegaard." The man carefully folded up his rag, put it back in his pocket, and returned the handshake. If he was surprised by Jeppe's visit, there was no sign of it.

"Are you the owner of the slaughterhouse?"

"I own the whole farm. I inherited it from my parents and have been running it for forty-two years. The slaughterhouse was added on five years ago. I got sick of having to transport the poor animals to Køge." The man brushed hair off his forehead and looked around proudly at the hall. "As you can see, we were just slaughtering this morning. You want me to show you around?"

"Thanks, but like I said, I'm just looking for Nikolaj . . ."

"Nikolaj, you say? I have no idea where he is. Haven't seen him since sometime last summer."

"Can you remember when?" Jeppe looked down at his sneakers. The toe of one was pink from bloody water.

"Hmm, it was at the end of the season, so maybe late August. He drove goods for us a few times a week, until we couldn't get ahold of him. Then we found someone else."

"Did he quit?"

Anton Hedegaard looked at Jeppe and ran the tongue around in his mouth. Maybe he was hard of hearing, maybe just the contemplative type.

"No," he finally said.

"Didn't it surprise you that he just disappeared?"

"Oh, yes," Anton replied, not seeming surprised at all. "But it was seasonal work. Maybe he just didn't want it anymore."

Jeppe's fingers were cold, and he stuck his hands in his coat pockets. There was something awry with the casual way the farm owner downplayed the problem. On a small island, where most people know each other, people don't just disappear like that without anyone raising an eyebrow.

"Did he come claim his paycheck before he vanished or leave any of his stuff behind? Or was everything resolved at the end?"

"We didn't have any outstanding business with each other; I would remember that. I'm really sorry I can't be of any more help." Anton shifted and seemed like he was about to wrap up the conversation.

"Where do you think he is? If you had to guess . . ."

Again that calm look and a long pause.

"Tell me, how do you know Nikolaj?" Anton asked. "Why are you looking for him?"

"I'm a friend of his sister, Ida's. She's worried about him." Jeppe tried to soften the questioning with a smile, but his cheeks were stiff from the cold. "Anything you might remember or think of concerning Nikolaj's disappearance would be helpful."

"There was a rumor . . ." Anton shook his head angrily. "I don't know if there's anything to it, and I'm sure it's best not to pass it along to Ida. But there was someone who mentioned that he probably headed out to the Sanctuary Rocks and jumped into the sea."

"Why would he do that?"

"That's what I said, too! Why in the world would he do that?" Anton rubbed his hands together and looked up at a digital clock on the wall. "I have to get going. I have two animals I need to break down before lunch. Was there anything else?"

"No, thank you for your time."

Jeppe watched the farm owner walk over to a panel and push a button, which turned on a winch. Slowly the winch hoisted a dehaired and headless animal carcass up by its hind legs.

"I'll just leave you my number. Call me if you hear anything that could help us find him," Jeppe yelled over the noise of the motor and the chain's clinking. He pulled his notebook out of his jacket pocket and ripped out a page.

While he searched for a pen, Anton stepped onto an open lift and let it raise him into the air. When he reached the animal's hind legs, he stopped the lift and tilted a roof-mounted chain saw over the cadaver.

Jeppe scrawled his number onto the slip of paper and left it on a stainless steel table just inside the door, with a clear sense that the butcher would leave it there. His goodbye was drowned out by the noise of the blade hitting the animal's femur.

———————

Bølshavn, Thursday, February 22, 1979
Dear Argy,

Bornholm summers may be paradise, but the winters, on the other hand, are hell. I've gotten used to it now, but I still feel like a figure in a Hieronymus Bosch painting sometimes, a freak among freaks. We become odd when it gets dark, weird and crotchety island dwellers who let our secrets crawl up from the basement and take over our living room.

I heard about someone from Svaneke they call Peder Panty, who snips the undergarments off of people's clotheslines and hides them in his dresser. They say he's a pedophile. He's dating Drunk-Bente, but really it's her daughter he wants. On New Year's he beat and raped the poor girl, but instead of reporting him to the police, the fishermen beat Peder Panty until he bled out of his eyes. And so he learned his lesson, people here say, as they repeat the story over coffee and cake.

More and more details are added every time. Nothing tastes as good as other people's misfortune served on a slice of almond cake.

I've buried myself in work. Elias and I were finally granted a portion of the research funding we need for our fieldwork in southeast Asia so now we need to plan and apply for additional funding.

It has hung over me, like a guilty conscience, for the longest time. After my daily teaching at the high school, grading papers, grocery shopping, and helping my own kids with their homework, there's just nothing left. But now is the time! I promised Elias, so I'll just have to burn the candle at both ends if necessary.

It's a blessing that Ida has gotten big and conscientious— twice a week she goes horseback riding and brings Nikolaj with her so I don't have to worry about them until dinnertime. They go there by themselves, those two little people, and then he helps muck out and pets the barn cats while Ida rides. I enjoy the extra work time and endure the usual mixture of pride and guilt when I see them get off the bus.

By the way, Finn and Dorthe have had another baby! A real straggler, a little girl, who will be named Camille. Not Camilla with an a, but with an e at the end. I was scolded when I said it wrong. Dorthe still doesn't like me, and I can't blame her. I'm sure she knows what's going on. Even so, I wish (at the risk of sounding like I have double standards) we could be friends. She honestly seems a little lonely. I think that's why she's so dismissive, and not just to me.

In her defense, Finn says, she's had two difficult pregnancies, both with Marco and now Camille. And she doesn't look well. She's troubled by pelvic instability and breast pains that makes it hard to nurse. I think—but don't say it out loud, I can't afford to—that all pregnancies and births are a trial, and that in the long run you can't use that as an excuse for being unhappy. If that's what she is?

To be completely honest, the pregnancy caught me off guard to begin with. Why bring more children into a lifeless marriage?

The other night, when we were alone, I asked Finn outright. He mumbled something about it being God's will.

and how a man can't deny his wife a baby. Can you believe that?!

He and Dorthe attend a free church where the minister calls himself Father Samuel and behaves as if he's responsible for the pastoral care of the entire island. I've only met him once, and he kindly offered to find me a good husband who could support me and the children. That Christian male chauvinism, which occasionally rears its ugly head here, makes me feel as much of a stranger on Bornholm as I do in Mali. It makes me want to move home to the city. Maybe someday?

Give the beasts a hug.

M

ESTHER LOOKED UP from the paper and observed Ida. They were both sitting in the study, Esther at the desk with Margrethe's letters in front of her, and Ida on the floor by a shelf she was removing the books from one by one.

"What are you doing?"

Ida stopped with a book in her lap and smiled, embarrassed.

"When we were little, our mother often made treasure hunts and hid clues and notes for us around the house. I thought . . ." She opened the book and started flipping through it. "Maybe it's silly, but I was just thinking that it's possible Nikolaj hid a note for me somewhere."

"About where he went, you mean?"

Ida shrugged.

"It's just the sort of thing my brother might come up with. He's always been a little bit of a conspiracy theorist, you know, a deep-seated distrust of the government and telecommunications and that sort of thing. Our mother should never have let him read Orwell." She laughed and put the book back on the shelf.

"Are you worried about him?"

"I don't know. I'm limited by not really being up-to-date on his life and what he does on a daily basis. Even if Nikolaj and I feel connected, there are long periods of time when we don't talk to each other, especially since Mom died. I don't really have any friends left on the island, and I can't remember the last time he came to Copenhagen to see his nieces. Who are his friends? What does he like to do? Is he seeing anyone? I've asked Finn, I've been to the farm, and I've checked with Marco. No one has seen him since August." Ida took another book and started flipping through it with a small sigh.

"Marco, that's Finn's son, right? Does he still live on Bornholm?"

"He moved to London years ago. He works in finance." Ida turned her head and looked out the bay window's sea-sprayed panes. "He and my brother couldn't be more different today, but as kids they were inseparable. We grew up together, after all, and they've managed to hold on to their friendship despite their differences. But Marco hasn't seen or heard from Nikolaj since he was home over summer vacation."

Esther followed Ida's gaze out to the Baltic's gray waves. Bornholm seemed to be a place where it would be easy to disappear forever if that was what you wanted to do. Just one small step off the rocky coastline, and you would be sucked out and down and away. Was Ida searching for a suicide note?

"Let's hope my friend Jeppe finds him. Or at least clears up where he is. Jeppe is thorough. I bet he'll find something."

Ida nodded but did not look very reassured.

"Do you have any brothers or sisters?" she asked.

"I'm an only child." Esther smiled, pained, used to having to almost apologize for not having any siblings.

"What about kids?" Ida instantly seemed to regret the question. "I'm sorry. I don't know if it's okay for me to ask that . . ."

Esther put her hand protectively over the medallion she wore around her neck. Do you have a child if you've given it away?

It was too hard to explain and still too painful for her to really comprehend.

"I'm alone. My roommate died last week—Gregers. We just buried him. Now it's just me and my little dog, Doxá."

"I'm so sorry to hear it." Ida looked down. "Were you close to your roommate, Gregers?"

"What's funny is that we lived in the same building for many years without really getting to know each other. Gregers could come off as a bit grumpy, and I kept my distance. But over time we became friends. Actually really good . . ." Esther's voice began to tremble, and she stopped talking.

She closed her eyes. After sitting like that for a moment, she felt Ida's arm around her back and let herself be drawn into a hug. The human closeness made it possible to breathe again and helped ease her grief.

She hadn't realized that she needed it.

CHAPTER 11

"One toasted with the works, thanks. And a Cocio."

Anette put her elbow on the counter of the gas station café and tried to block out the morning traffic on the highway behind her. All the noise was really getting on her nerves. She wasn't usually sensitive to noise, or to anything at all for that matter, but some sort of protective layer seemed to have been removed, leaving her like an orange without its peel. Sensitive like her grandmother who used to shush her grandchildren the instant they stepped in the door.

She dipped her sausage in ketchup and spicy mustard and took a bite. It wasn't anywhere near lunchtime, but a sausage didn't really count as a proper meal, and besides, she had the feeling it would help soothe the uneasiness in her stomach.

As she ate, she checked her phone. The Bornholm Police had sent a car with two officers over to Jan Søgård's summer beach home by Balka to ring the doorbell, and she was waiting to hear back from them. She had also left a long message on Svend's voice mail, mostly just to say good morning, but she may have happened to remind him how much children's Tylenol Gudrun could have and how important it was to check whether the fever came back.

He hadn't returned her call. When he did, she would do her best to keep the tone casual and loving.

She washed down the last bite with a swig of chocolate milk, got back in her car, and pulled out onto the E47 toward Næstved. The principal of Ellebæk School had canceled a meeting to talk to her and seemed relieved that she was coming right away. The search report for the missing Jan Søgård did not mention any immediate family, so his employer was the best place to start.

As she passed Haslev, Nyboe called.

"Hi, Nyboe."

"We're still waiting on test results with regard to the saw-blade details." As always, the forensic pathologist got right down to business. He sounded distracted, as if he were reading off a piece of paper. "But we're talking about a large-blade saw with teeth up to half an inch long."

"Bigger than a standard chain saw?"

"It's possible that there are handheld saws with this type of cutting edge, but I doubt it. I believe we're looking at some form of band saw."

Nyboe drank and swallowed without moving the phone. "The deceased had no external characteristics of note such as tattoos, piercings, or pronounced scars. All organs and extremities were intact, and there was no sign of any surgical procedures. You know: he had all his toes, no evidence of healed broken bones . . ."

"And he hadn't donated a kidney to anyone, I get it."

"When we compare the length of the femur to our tables, we estimate the deceased's height to be right around five foot eleven. And our forensic anthropologist took a look at the cranial sutures, in other words the tissues connecting the cranial bones, and set the age somewhat higher than we first assumed. The deceased was around fifty, give or take five years."

"Fifty?" Anette swerved in her lane and earned herself an angry honk. Jan Søgård was fifty-two.

"I was surprised, too. The deceased was in very good shape, slim with a strong musculature, so I thought he was a fair bit younger. But this is supported by the forensic odontologist's examinations of his teeth. Based on the degree of calcification in the roots of the teeth, their determination of the age is the same. That having been said . . ."

"Yes?" Anette turned up the volume.

"Do you remember that I found a hole in the bridge of the body's nose that suggested cocaine abuse? Well, the examinations of the liver and kidneys confirmed that the deceased had a prolonged abuse of both alcohol and drugs. So his being in good shape is not synonymous with a healthy lifestyle."

Anette weighed whether she could picture a middle-aged schoolteacher from Næstved using coke during recess and landed on yes. The most dangerous thing she could do as a detective was to think conservatively. In the "far out" category, reality always trumped imagination.

"Okay, well, I guess that's it." Nyboe hung up without saying goodbye. The social niceties of starting and concluding conversations had never been his strong suit.

Anette turned up the car radio and drove the rest of the way to the tunes of pop music from her youth, which apparently would not die. She hummed along to "Sailor of the World" by Dodo and the Dodos and put the trip to Næstved behind her in about twenty-five minutes.

Ellebæk School's principal received her in his office with a view of the playground and weak coffee on the warmer plate.

Anette didn't manage to say, "No, thank you" in time and was seated by the desk with a mug of sludge in her hand and the principal across from her.

"I hope you don't take milk. We ran out . . ."

Anette hurriedly waved her hand no. The principal poured himself a cup, glanced discreetly at the time, and folded his hands. He was a short, stocky man in his thirties with the beginning of laugh lines at the corners of his eyes and a bald spot in his thinning, black hair. His shirtsleeves were rolled up to the elbows and revealed surprisingly hairy forearms.

"I must admit that I'm positively surprised to see that you're taking this seriously," he began. "Jan's medical leave of absence was valid until November first, and then the plan was for him to call. But we haven't heard anything and haven't been able to get in touch with him, so we're starting to get worried that something happened to him."

His last few words were drowned out by squeals and joyful shouts from kids playing on the playground. Anette smiled at the sound. In a few years it would be Gudrun's turn to go to school and make friends. The thought was bittersweet.

"When were you last in contact with him?"

"Jan called me in the middle of July and went on sick leave due to stress. He was terribly sorry to do it so late, so close to the beginning of the school year, but right up until then he had been hoping things would turn around. I told him of course, that he should just take all the time he needed and report back when he could. He also sent a note from his doctor. Jan's always very by the book." The principal squinted at a piece of paper in front of him and set it aside, as if the text on it distracted him.

"What was his stress due to, do you know?"

"That's basically not something I get involved in . . ."

"But if you had to guess? Given that Jan is missing now," Anette insisted.

He looked out the window for a long moment.

"Jan has worked here at the school for twenty-two years, and I've been here for only four, so there's a limit to how well I know him. But he is highly regarded by both coworkers and students and, as far as I'm aware, he hasn't been out sick for more than a handful of days the whole time he's worked here."

"Until now."

He gave her a look. "The school had a hectic spring due to some reorganization and illnesses, so Jan—and all the other teachers— were under a lot of pressure. He's a science teacher, but he was asked to sub in English and shepherd a ninth-grade class through their exams in German on top of his own classes. That's hard work. And then he lost his wife last year. That kind of thing also taxes your reserves, you know?"

"Of course." Anette drank a sip of the coffee and couldn't help but make a face. "Is he in good shape physically?"

"Huh?" The principal looked really surprised. "Well, I suppose he is. He's in good shape for a man in his fifties. Not overweight, if that's what you mean."

"Does he have a muscular build? The type of person who works out?"

That made him laugh.

"I'm sorry," he said. "I don't mean to . . . No, I don't think Jan's the type who works out. I don't think he really spends much time lifting weights, but he does go for long walks, and he's an avid birder. He has a route along the coast on Bornholm. He has a cottage there and walks it every day."

"Is that where he spends his summer vacation?"

"Jan goes to his cottage every time he's off work. He loves it there. We made the police aware of that when we reported him missing."

"We've asked the Bornholm Police to go check if he's there." Anette cursed her colleagues for not immediately following up on such an obvious clue in their investigation. "One more thing, and I apologize if this falls a little outside the normal scope of a professional relationship . . . Do you happen to know if Jan used any illegal drugs?"

The belly laugh was spontaneous and so hearty that the window-panes practically shook. The principal had to wipe his eyes before he could answer her.

"I'm sorry, but in my wildest imagination I just can't picture that. I mean, of course you never know what people do in their own time, but . . . no, not Jan."

Anette wasn't laughing. There were two missing men who fit the body in the suitcase. They had already ruled one out, so now it really had to be the other one.

"Are you one hundred percent sure?"

"Uh . . ." The principal opened his mouth and closed it again. "Well, no, there's no way I could be." He regarded her with a growing skepticism.

"Okay." Anette stood up and held out her hand to shake his goodbye, trying to ignore his disappointed look. It drew her attention to the least favorite part of her job: the unsolved cases. "Thank you for your time. I'll be in touch as soon as we have news about Jan."

THE SMELL HIT Jeppe like a brick wall when he stepped into Hut Li Hut, Allinge's only year-round bar. Decades of unrelenting cigarette smoking had seeped into the furniture, curtains, and carpets, and had turned the place's customers into caste-marked underlings, recognizable to the rest of the world with a single sniff. The smoke was acrid and so thick it was almost viscous, like the tar it left behind in its victims' lungs. Jeppe's eyes started watering instantly.

He walked up to the bar and nodded to the short-haired woman behind the counter who stood cross-armed and looked to be the owner of the place. She wore an extra-large T-shirt with THE HUT printed over her free-hanging breasts and round belly. A lit cigarette hung from the corner of her mouth.

"Mona, we've got guests. The police stopped by."

Jeppe sat down on the barstool next to the patron who had very unnecessarily announced his arrival.

"Could I have a cola, please?"

Mona pulled out a refrigerated drawer, grabbed a bottle, and opened it in one graceful motion, the cigarette still balanced on her bottom lip.

"Glass?" she asked.

"I'll just drink it out of the bottle." Jeppe tilted his head back, allowing the sugary liquid to tingle in his throat.

"Don't you want some rum in that soda?" the patron next to him asked, with a wry chuckle made through his cigarette. The chuckle turned into a cough that lasted several seconds before he smothered the last rattle of it with beer. He set the empty bottle on the counter and received a new one without asking.

Jeppe noticed that he had a little round box in the middle of his throat and guessed that was there to make breathing easier after some procedure on his throat.

"It's a little too early for alcohol for me," Jeppe replied, and nodded to the clock behind the bar, which showed it was only 11:20 a.m.

"I always start the day with an Underberg," the other patron said. "It does wonders. Hit us both, Mona!"

Mona set two shot glasses on the counter and filled them with Gammel Dansk. She managed to carry out the procedure without lifting her feet off the floor or taking the cigarette out of her mouth.

"You live up next to Orla in Sandvig, don't you? I'm Gråpæren." He raised his shot glass up in a greeting and smiled. Worn teeth came into view behind his narrow lips.

There was no way out. Jeppe raised his glass and clinked.

"Jeppe. And I don't work for the police anymore."

"Then we'll be great friends." Gråpæren winked and downed his bitter in one go. "My real name is Anders, but I had a fruit orchard down south for many years, so everyone calls me Gråpæren, you know, after the pear."

"Down south?"

"In Aakirkeby, down in southern Bornholm. But I don't own it anymore. I took a tree to the head several years ago, and after that it was hard for me to tend the fruit trees. Everything grew and grew—cherries, apples, pears, plums—all hung on the branches, rotting." Gråpæren stubbed out his cigarette and lit a new one.

"Now it's someone else's headache. And you know what I'm going to do with the money I got for the farm?"

Jeppe drank his Gammel Dansk and reached for the cola to wash it down.

"I'm going to Madeira! Have you been? Madeira is the most beautiful place in the world. You won't find a prettier island than that. So that's where I'm going, damn it!" He slapped the counter gently, and Mona refilled his Gammel Dansk.

"Madeira, you say?" Jeppe took out his own pack of cigarettes and lit his first of the day. Better to howl like the wolf he was among. Mona eyed Jeppe expectantly and poured him another shot as well.

"Yup, I'm getting away from this crap climate the minute I get the chance. And I'm not going to miss a single one of these assholes!"

"Before you move abroad," Jeppe said with a smile, "do you mind if I ask you about something? I'm looking for Nikolaj Dybris, or to be more accurate, his sister is and I'm helping her. She says he usually comes here . . ."

The silence that followed was deafening. Jeppe might as well have knocked all the glasses onto the floor, it was that quiet. Hadn't the jukebox just played Johnny Cash?

"Could be the Holy Spirit finally got his revenge." Gråpæren chuckled to himself and raised his glass to an imaginary Lord.

Before Jeppe had a chance to ask what he meant by that, Mona tossed a dishcloth on the counter and started cleaning it off in big circles. Jeppe had to pick up his soda bottle so it didn't get knocked over.

"Nikolaj isn't welcome here and hasn't been for years." She tossed the cloth into the sink and folded her arms in front of her chest. "When you find him, you tell him that that still goes. The soda's on the house."

Jeppe sat for a moment to see if she really meant it, but when she stood unmovingly he finally got up and put out his cigarette in the overflowing ashtray.

"Well, then, thanks for the drink."

Mona turned around and loaded dirty glasses into a dishwasher tray. As Jeppe began to leave, Gråpæren grabbed him and whispered: "He hangs out behind the grocery store Netto. Just ask for the Can, you'll find him!"

———————

Bølshavn, Sunday, September 20, 1981
Dear sister,

Yesterday we went to Market Day at Hedegaarden. Finn invited us; he knows the farm's owner. Dorthe stayed home with the little one, but Marco was allowed to come.

The weather was on our side. It was one of those blessedly warm late summer days that we have so few of. The courtyard was decorated, and in the farm's biggest barn were strings of lights and hay bales and trays of fruit. I felt like I was in a Morten Korch movie. My inner big-city snob acted up, I must admit, but live music was playing (a dubious pairing of harmonica and guitar), and there was roast lamb and a lovely atmosphere, so I ended up giving in to it.

Ida was impractically dressed in jeans that looked like they had been painted onto her legs and a low-cut top she had borrowed from a friend. She was cold the minute we got out of the car. But even in that somewhat provocative outfit, she was radiantly beautiful. There is something completely delightful about the sheer beauty that teenagers wear so unconsciously. Something downright touching.

I watched her all day with a lump in my throat. My own femininity is gradually preparing for retirement, and my big girl will be leaving me soon. I mourn all the things I never had a chance to give her while there was time. The attention that lacked, not enough, never enough, the security, the honesty. And now it's too late.

Finn and I sat with some of the people from Bølshavn, the grocer was there and Aggers and several others. Father Samuel came, too, but I made sure not to end up next to him. Everyone speaks so warmly of him and everything he and the church do for the island, but I don't like him.

Ida doesn't like to be seen in her mother's proximity these days, so she walked around visiting the booths with a classmate. Nikolaj and Marco started crawling around underneath the long tables, teasing people by putting apples in their purses and tying their shoelaces together. Nikolaj is only two years older than Marco but was clearly masterminding the game. Marco may be a little introverted and quiet, but he looks up to Nikolaj and worships him the way only children can. It's pretty cute.

Unfortunately one of the attendees did not quite share that opinion. I don't know what made him so angry, but a young man suddenly shouted and picked up Nikolaj by the collar, until he hung wriggling in the air. Because he's tall, people often think he's older than his eleven years.

Finn and the farm's owner quickly intervened and got the man calmed down, while I comforted the boys, who were both

scared and crying. Luckily there was an ice cream stand, and
two big waffle cones quickly got them thinking about something
else. Ten minutes later they were playing again, although this
time outside of the barn.

The farm's owner, his name is Anton, walked the angry man
out and waited until he had driven away. I hope he wasn't
drunk! Oh, but it was a relief that he wasn't allowed to stay.
Finn bought us coffee and explained that the angry man was a
fisherman who runs three cutters out of Nexø Harbor. He's not
even thirty, but he's already made his first million kroner trawling
cod from the Baltic and selling it to the Americans. It has gone to
his head, Finn explained, and not just him. Apparently people are
talking about a "fishing bubble." The island's youngsters only want
to be fishermen or work in the filleting factories. A kind of gold
fever, but with salmon and herring instead of precious metals.
To someone like me who's never heard of anything but quotas,
endangered stocks, and boats being scrapped, these types of stories
give the island a gleam of the Klondike.

It's as if Bornholm is its own universe—liberated from the
mainland but also a little forgotten, relegated to its own rules
and ways. Maybe Bornholm is the wardrobe that leads to
Narnia, where the kids can disappear into a fairy tale and hide
from reality?

Your letter arrived a few days ago, dear Argy. What you
wrote about taking long walks along the Lakes and searching for
the year's first scrawny chestnuts gave me a pang of homesickness
for the city and life as it once was. Life before the island, life
before children.

With love,
Margy

JEPPE HAD TO go into the Netto by the harbor and ask the cashier for directions before he found the Can that Gråpæren had mentioned. A battered construction trailer and a picnic table with a panoramic view of the water sat on an empty lot behind the grocery store. The trailer had been put there by the harbor, the cashier explained, for residents of Allinge who liked to get together and drink beer but couldn't afford the Hut. The trailer provided shelter from the frost and wind, and its door was always open. She couldn't tell him why the place was called the Can, but she thought it was good that the "boozers" had a place to meet so they didn't "bother the grocery store customers" as she put it.

Even before Jeppe had opened the trailer door, he recognized the hoarse laughter from inside: Louis. Jeppe pulled the door open and was met by the same thick smoke as at the bar. There were no lights on in the trailer, and in the scant daylight, the interior faded away in the smoke. Jeppe could make out a wooden coffee table and some dated armchairs, a bulletin board on the wall with pictures on it, and two figures each with a lit cigarette at the back of the room.

"Well, we've got ourselves a fancy visitor here, Lassie. If it isn't my Chøpenhagen coworker." Louis pronounced Copenhagen with a heavily exaggerated Bornholm accent. It sounded like a provocation. "What are you doing here, Jeppe?"

Jeppe moved closer.

Louis stood with an unusually tall, clean-shaven man, who had the vacant gaze of a drug addict and a thin red windbreaker zipped all the way up to his chin. They were leaning against the wall by a small refrigerator, where they had set their strong beers and a coffee cup of cigarette butts.

"Cozy place. Celebrating getting off work already?" Jeppe squinted at his watch as he asked. It was only twelve fifteen. "I thought we were busy."

"This, from someone I gave the whole day off?! Should I have presented you with a note from my mom? It's my company. I manage my own work hours. You're not the only one who has a life outside the woods." Louis finished his bottle of beer and belched. "You don't usually hang out here in the Can. To what do we owe this honor?"

"I'm looking for Nikolaj Dybris. I was led to believe that he hangs out here?"

"Nikolaj? Didn't he get a sailing job?" the guy in the windbreaker asked.

"I don't know. But maybe you do?" Jeppe nodded over at Louis. "I understand you two are friends . . ."

Louis leaned down to the mini fridge and took out three bottles of Guldøl. He pulled a key out of his pocket that he used to open the beers and then handed Jeppe one.

"Friends? Who the hell told you that? I hardly know the guy." He smiled, showing his gray front tooth. "Cheers."

Jeppe drank hesitantly. "Didn't you loan him some tools that you wanted to get back? His sister told me you stopped by the house yesterday."

"You know Ida?" The question spilled out of Louis, and Jeppe could tell that he regretted it right away.

"Yes" was all Jeppe said. No reason to elaborate.

"Well, I've met Nikolaj many times. He knows the Sonne family, you know? But we're not friends. I wouldn't call it that."

"But you loaned him some tools anyway?"

Louis shrugged. "I actually really want them back, but he's not answering his phone." He pointed to his buddy with the bottle. "So maybe you're right and he's out sailing, Lassie."

"Aww, come on," Lasse objected. "You're the one who told me. That he had taken a job as an engineer on a container ship and was sailing to Asia for six months."

Louis stopped with the bottle suspended in the air in front of his mouth.

"That is a fucking lie. I never said that." He laughed. "Did you forget to take your Risperidone or whatever the hell it's called, your antipsychotic thing?"

Lasse laughed along with him.

Jeppe let their laughter fade before he asked his next question.

"Ida hasn't heard from him since August. Wouldn't he have let his sister know before going away for so long? Let alone his boss or maybe his neighbor?"

Louis studied the label on the back of his beer.

His buddy nodded and said, "You'd almost think he's dead."

Jeppe looked at him and drank again. It had been a long time since he had drunk strong beer. His temples were tingling.

"Who else might know where he is? You say he knows the Sonne family. Is Finn the one I should ask?"

Louis rolled his eyes and sighed as if he was starting to get bored with all of Jeppe's questions. "Well, I don't know. I only met him at the sawmill at some point."

"Lots of times, didn't you say?" Jeppe surveyed the trailer's moth-eaten armchairs and the bulletin board with its photos and nodded appreciatively. "Nice place you've got here."

"Zealot's Children set this up," Louis's buddy replied readily. "One of the island's free churches. They do a lot for the local community, for people who are vulnerable or lonely. I've never subscribed to him, Jesus, but it's not just shit that comes out of his religion."

"Zealot's Children? I've never heard of them."

"Yeah, don't ask me what they are." The buddy laughed. "But rumor has it that they've got their hands deep in the sawmill's till."

"That's enough, Lassie!" Louis set down his beer so hard it foamed over.

"Hey, you're the one who fucking told me! That the sawmill lady was a believer and spent a fortune on her church before she suddenly up and died."

"You're being a jerk! You've had one too many, you fool." Louis grabbed his friend's arm and pulled him away. "Come on, I'll walk you home. Jeppe, I'll see you first thing tomorrow!" They squeezed inelegantly past Jeppe and left, the friend protesting loudly and Louis tensely silent.

Jeppe let the trailer's thin door smack shut behind them before he found a pack of Kleenex in his jacket pocket, pulled out one paper tissue, and fished Louis Kofoed's still warm cigarette butt carefully out of the coffee cup on top of the mini fridge. Once he had made sure the butt was thoroughly extinguished, he wrapped it up and stuck it in his pocket. Although he wouldn't be able to avoid leaving his own traces on it, they would still be able to extract Louis's DNA from the butt, if they needed to. He then photographed the unknown faces on the bulletin board with his phone camera before stepping back out into the fresh air.

The ground swayed slightly under his feet, and he knew the sensation wasn't from the alcohol. It was the policeman in him, coming back to life. Before he started the car to head to the sawmill, he looked at himself in the rearview mirror. The spark was back in his eyes.

CHAPTER 12

Anette greeted Torben Falck by the coffee machine and stepped into her office just as the Bornholm Police called her back. The voice on the line sounded so young that at first Anette was confused.

"Tell me, who am I speaking to?"

"Ditte Vollmer, sergeant, I work as a detective with the Bornholm Police Investigations Unit." The young woman spoke slowly and clearly as if to an elderly, somewhat dim-witted person. "I'm calling in regards to Jan Søgård."

"Yes, thank you. I understand that. I was just expecting it to be a grown-up who called." The silence on the line told Anette that she had gone too far. "Sorry, that was supposed to be a joke."

"Ha ha."

Anette pulled off her coat and tossed it over the back of a chair. She cast a long glance at the rum ball she had bought at the bakery to go with her coffee, which was now sweating in its paper sack. It would have to wait a little longer.

"Let's get to the point, Jan Søgård's summer house. What did you find?"

"It turned out to be no easy task. The two officers we sent to Balka Strand arrived at a dark house with the curtains drawn and a mailbox full of local newspapers. There was no doorbell, so they knocked and waited. After a few minutes, they walked around the perimeter of the house."

"Mm-hmm." Anette resisted the urge to hurry the young detective along. She obviously liked delving into a level of detail that went beyond what was necessary, but Anette had probably already pissed her off enough for one day.

"At first glance it looked nice and well maintained and, well, like all the other summer homes out here, which get closed up for the winter and then reopened in the spring. There didn't seem to be anything out of place . . ."

Anette waited. Was there going to be a *but*?

"Luckily the officers took a walk through the neighborhood and rang the doorbells of some of the permanent residents. When they got around to the next street and the house whose property is adjacent to Jan Søgård's, they got a bite. A ceramics artist lives there, and she knows Jan and often chats with him on the beach. She was able to say that as far as she could tell he had spent the whole summer on Bornholm, because she'd seen him swimming almost every morning up until the beginning of August."

"And then?"

"Well, then she figured he'd gone home, the way the seasonal residents do. But she had actually been trying to get ahold of him for days, to no avail, and was getting desperate."

"Why?" Anette felt yet another warning chill graze the back of her neck.

"Because she was having trouble with flies and was more and more convinced that the insects came from Jan's summer house."

Anette sighed. She knew what was next. The recurring tragedy of people who die alone and forgotten. Jan Søgård wasn't the man who had ended up in two old suitcases in Copenhagen.

"Have you been inside?"

"The officers broke the door down and found him on the floor of the living room. It looks like a stroke, but it's hard to say. He has decomposed so much that he has fused to the carpet."

IN THE GRAY afternoon light, the sawmill in Østerlars looked like a place drug lords would hang out in an eighties movie. Big, modern industrial buildings with electric lights shining from the few and far between windows, outdoor stacks of posts and beams stacked crosswise and an older half-timbered building hidden behind a high fence. Jeppe had been here before and knew that the office was behind that fence.

He opened the gate, stopped, and listened for the dogs. There was still a little buzz from the alcohol, a state that was amplified by the painkillers he had taken. He shouldn't be driving or questioning people in this condition. Normally, he would never have. But different rules applied on the island, and besides, he was just a regular guy, helping an acquaintance.

He knocked on the front door.

Camille Sonne opened and smiled at him in surprise.

"The policeman?! What's wrong?" She stayed with her hand on the doorknob. Her dark hair hung loose and looked like it would be as soft as silk to touch. She had on a soft-looking sweater and tight jeans.

Jeppe hurriedly raised his eyes to her face.

"Is Finn in the office? I was supposed to come pick up a helmet."

"My father left early today. But he set out the helmet. Would you like to come in, or do you prefer to stand in the cold?"

"Thanks." He stepped into the foyer. She moved away only

slightly from the door, and he couldn't avoid brushing her breast with his arm. The air inside was warm and smelled sweetly of cheap scented candles. He unzipped his jacket and pointed to the door to the office. "That way?"

"The helmet's in the kitchen. I was just getting ready to knock off for the night. Would you like a glass of wine? Or are you a beer man?"

Jeppe let her lead the way and followed, glancing fleetingly at her denim-clad butt. If he drank any more, he was going to do something stupid.

"Wine sounds great. Thank you." He didn't have to have more than a sip or two, after all.

The kitchen turned out to be small and old-fashioned with linoleum countertops and low-hanging overhead lights. The helmet sat on the counter. Jeppe gave it a pat.

"I was actually hoping I could ask your dad if he knows where Nikolaj Dybris is, but you probably know him, too, yes?"

"Mm-hmm." She opened a screw-top bottle of wine and rummaged around in the cupboards for glasses. "I'm afraid it's going to be coffee cups. At least they're not chipped. Watch out, I filled it a little too full."

Camille handed him a ceramic coffee cup full of wine, leaned against the counter, and drank from her own.

"Ah, white wine o'clock is the best time of day! Nikolaj? What do you need him for?" Her tone was carefree, her voice light as a spring day.

"Ida's worried about him. Do you know where he is?"

"He's my older brother's friend, not mine," she said, shaking her head. "I've always thought he was a bit of a fuckup."

"A fuckup?"

"Yeah, you know . . . the type who drops the birthday cake on the floor right before it's supposed to be served. Always excited about big plans that never amount to anything. Drinking, drugs, getting fired from jobs. Nikolaj is nice enough, just a little pathetic. I never understood what my smart, successful big brother saw in him." Camille cocked her head to the side to show how confounding it was.

Jeppe drank a little and instantly regretted it. His head started slowly spinning.

"Do you think Marco knows where he is? Ida's asked him, but maybe he knows more than he's telling her?"

"He hasn't said anything, but I'll ask him. How's that?" She raised one eyebrow. It seemed like an invitation for more.

"Yes, that would be great." Jeppe looked down into his coffee cup. "There's a rumor going around that Nikolaj went sailing . . ."

"Ha! What did he steal this time?"

Her teeth were pointy like a child's, her eyelashes long and thick, making her eyes seem enormous. They were studying him in a way that made him feel naked.

"Do you believe he stole the Christmas Joy?"

"Oh, stop. Everyone knows that!" Camille calmly raised her coffee cup as if in a toast. Her sweater slid up to reveal a section of exposed skin on her belly.

Jeppe returned the toast and set his cup down on the kitchen counter.

"There's another rumor that he jumped off the Sanctuary Rocks."

"Nikolaj would never do that. He doesn't have the balls to commit suicide."

"But could he have the . . . desire?" Jeppe sighed. "That's the wrong word, but you know what I mean."

Camille thought that over before answering.

"I don't know if Nikolaj was suicidal. He was pretty consistent about attracting fiascos and pain, but aren't men generally like that?"

"Are we?"

"Yes. Men seek out pain. We women already carry it within us," she said firmly. "More wine?"

"No, thanks." He ought to be going. "I'll try to catch Finn sometime in the next couple of days. Thank you for the wine."

"Anytime."

She smiled again, revealing her pointy canines. Like a ferret, Jeppe thought.

He grabbed the helmet and started to leave, this time the floor really was swaying. He turned around in the doorway.

"Hey, I came across something called Zealot's Children, a free church. Does that mean anything to you?"

Her facial expression didn't change. She continued to smile.

"You don't need to say free church, as if it's a rotten egg someone forced in your mouth. Zealot's Children is a completely ordinary Christian church, and coincidentally the one my family goes to, when we go, that is. What does that have to do with Nikolaj?"

"Nothing. I was just wondering."

Jeppe's phone started ringing. He raised a hand to wave goodbye, but Camille had already turned her back to him.

———————

Bølshavn, Saturday, January 29, 1983
Dear A,

Dorthe Sonne is dead!

Finn's wife died last Friday. She was only thirty-nine and mother to two children. After a long illness, as they say. Cancer. She was found in her bed, had discreetly drawn her last breath, and left no disturbing bodily fluids behind, if one is to believe the official report.

The tragedy is occupying the local community, as a conversational topic, as gossip, as grief. I, too, find myself unexpectedly sad. Considering that I never really got to know her and that she always kept me at arm's length, I suppose I shouldn't be so affected by it. But I'm grieving—for Finn, for the kids, and for Dorthe, who never got to enjoy life before she died.

A woman is expected to sacrifice herself when she has kids, cheerfully and without reservation. That's what it was like when I got Ida seventeen years ago, and as far as I can tell, nothing has changed much despite a lot of talk about equality and maternity-leave legislation.

I tried to do it differently—by adopting on my own (Elias was only pro forma, after all) and to reclaim control over motherhood, by insisting on preserving my professional ambitions and by continuing to travel. Lord knows my children paid a price for their mother being able to have her freedom (well, some of it), but hopefully they gained something else in exchange, don't you think?

The problems more likely occur if you DON'T make demands and just give in to society's unrealistic expectations of self-sacrifice and absolute motherly love. I think that's what Dorthe Sonne did—because that's what her era and her religion prescribed— and now it's cost her her life. I'm sorry, I don't mean to sound so dramatic. Or yes, I darn well do! It's possible she had cancer, but I think she died of a broken heart. Broken by grief at her life.

The danger signs started when Camille was born just under four years ago. At first it was just small signs that led to a sense that something was wrong. Dorthe wouldn't pick up the baby when she cried and took the baby carriage out for a walk without wearing her shoes—the kind of things you could easily ascribe to general exhaustion during the postpartum period. But eventually it became clear to me that things weren't as they should be.

Finn started taking the baby to work with him, even though Dorthe was home and expected to take care of the children while he managed the sawmill. A traditional marriage. I don't know what went wrong. We didn't talk about that sort of thing at all, but after a few months Finn was the one minding the baby. Maybe he was afraid that she would hurt the baby.

That was about the same time when Dorthe found faith for real. Or to be more precise, she had always been a believer, but after Camille's birth she became more and more active in that silly free church the family belongs to, and she spent several evenings a week at events and doing volunteer work.

It affected the whole family, also Marco. He had always craved his parents' attention but never really received it. The firstborn son of a wealthy Christian family, how could he be neglected, you wonder? But he is! Finn told me the other day while rolling his eyes that Marco has started wetting his bed again. At the age of ten! Good Lord, he just lost his mother! I wish I could do something for the boy, but what? Talk to Finn, who is so shut down with grief that he can hardly look me in the eyes anymore?

I comfort myself with the fact that Nikolaj at least still likes to spend time with Marco, even though he's actually outgrown toys and would rather listen to music or play ball. My heart swells for my big boy, when I see them running around on the rocks playing a game of tag or whatever they come up with. His being so caring is the only mitigating circumstance in this tragic period.

Oh, the winter this year is a doozy! Even my bones are freezing, and I would give anything to sit in your cozy kitchen with the woodstove lit and a pot of tea.

Not a particularly uplifting letter, sorry! I'll do better next time, I promise.

Yours,
Margy

"DO YOU HAVE a minute? I need to bounce this case off someone sensible." Anette pulled her hood up against the beginning drizzle. It was freezing cold and felt like needles pricking her face. She had gone out on the pier to make the call in peace and quiet, but the weather was not cooperating. The parking lot in front of police headquarters was deserted, and if it weren't for Jeppe's voice over the phone, she could easily be the last person alive on a virus-afflicted planet.

She turned her back to the wind and walked along the water.

"The teacher was lying in his summer house decomposing after what was most likely a stroke, so we still don't have any ID for the body in the suitcase."

"Damn!" There was a clunk, as if Jeppe dropped his phone. Then she heard his voice again, hoarse and distant.

"Sorry, I'm back. Hello?"

"Tell me, Jepsen, are you drunk?

"Just tired." The wind hit his phone's microphone, so she could barely hear him. "And maybe just a tad tipsy. I'm going to have to go for a walk before I dare drive."

Anette stopped on the pier.

"Since when did you start drinking in the afternoons? Tell me, are you okay out there on that island?"

"Chill. I just had Gammel Dansk and a little wine, and I didn't do it for my own sake. The alcohol just doesn't mix well with the ibuprofen."

"None of what you're saying is making me feel any better. You're taking painkillers again?"

He sighed heavily, or maybe that was the wind, too.

"I work hard, Anette. Was there something you wanted?"

She bit her tongue. If Jeppe thought he could fall apart without her intervening, then he had some things to learn. But right now, over this windy phone call, it was probably best to focus on the case.

"What did you find out about Nikolaj?"

"He hasn't been seen since the end of August. There are rumors going around about him running off or committing suicide, but no one knows anything concrete. He seems to be a little bit of a shady character, you know: theft, drinking, broken promises. People say he stole money from the local bar, or more accurately from its patrons, so he's not all that popular."

The rain picked up, and Anette searched for somewhere she could get out of it.

"You think he could be addicted to cocaine?"

"Easily! It sounds like he's lived a hard life."

"Our victim snorted a hole in the bridge of his nose. How old is Nikolaj?"

"I'm not exactly sure, but he's Ida's little brother, so probably just shy of fifty." Jeppe sounded winded, as if he were walking uphill. "Listen, if he matches your body in the suitcase, and the suitcase was bought on Bornholm, then you'd better get your ass out here. I'm going back to the woods tomorrow, so I can't help you anymore."

"I don't need your help! Or your advice," Anette snapped, and regretted it right away. "Okay, I didn't mean that. Not like that."

"It's fine, Anette. I know what it's like to be in charge. It rubs you raw, leaves you exposed."

She reached a shelter and stood under it among parked bicycles. The rain melted sky and earth together into a wet mass of misery. "Exposed" was no exaggeration.

"Is it raining where you are, too?"

"Not right now."

Anette wiped her face with her free hand.

"I'd better take a ferry over tonight and get the local police started. The detective I talked to about the missing teacher sounded like she was fourteen. Not all that reassuring."

He chuckled.

"Do you want me to inform Nikolaj's sister of our suspicions? You'll need to get into the house and collect samples, so maybe it's best if she has a little forewarning . . ."

"Can't you just tell her the absolutely necessary for now and then I'll handle it myself in the morning?" Anette shifted her weight to get the circulation going in her cold feet and bumped into a bicycle that threatened to tip over and take the rest of the bikes with it.

"Fuck! Just a sec. Oh, plus I'll have to get my in-laws to watch the dogs. They hate that."

"The dogs or the in-laws?"

"Both."

Jeppe laughed again.

"Once you get over here . . . Well, if I can do anything, just let me know, will you? If you want to chat or need some advice. I don't usually have much going on after work."

"Thanks, Jepsen." Anette smiled down at her phone. "I always want to hear what your instincts are. Turns out I might be missing them. Is your intuition telling you anything right now?"

There was a moment of quiet, and then he responded somberly, "I've come across a free church a few times."

"Really? There's bound to be a bunch of those on Bornholm. What about it?"

"I don't know. As far as I know, Nikolaj doesn't have anything to do with it. It's just . . . it's intuition, nothing more."

"Okay, thanks." Anette ventured back out into the rain and headed for her car with Jeppe still on the line. She did not miss his illogical instincts that much after all. "Mysterious free church, I'll make a mental note of that."

"The family that owns one of the sawmills we deliver wood to is involved in it. And they know Nikolaj. Their son, Marco, is a friend of his. The church donated a trailer to the local alcoholics, so they're engaged with the local community, but . . . Well, like I said, it's just a thought. Look into it if it makes any sense. It's called Zealot's Children."

Anette stopped. The rain hit the her forehead like ice-cold fingertips. "What did you say?"

"Zealot's Children."

Anette blinked up at the dark gray sky. Then she started running to the car.

CHAPTER 13

Esther got up from the desk in the bay window and looked outside. She heard the wind buffeting the trees in the yard but could hardly see anything. Once again, she had the feeling that someone was watching her from out there in the shadows. *You're letting your imagination run away with you*, she told herself sternly, but her anxiety raced along unchecked. She had just hung up after talking to Jeppe and wished she had plucked up her courage and asked him to stop by. She was extremely uncomfortable at the prospect of being alone in the house all night.

Ida had a date with an old family friend, and Esther had assured her that she would be fine on her own. *I'm just going to work. It'll be lovely.* And she'd meant it.

But then it had gotten dark, and the house had come to life. It creaked and rustled, and that strange odor seemed more noticeable than before.

She turned her back to the window and walked through the living room to the kitchen without looking right or left. The countless letters on the walls hissed as she passed them, set in motion by the air currents. She imagined the letters were pale hands reaching out to her and shivered. Out of the corner of her eye she glimpsed the black trash bags, an old chair with a shabby back, and then a sudden motion. She gasped out loud before she realized that it was just the lights of a car driving by, reflected in the breakfront.

A bottle of red wine she had promised herself she wouldn't open sat on the kitchen counter. The most important thing was to not drink alone. The first sip already settled a basic calm within her. The next one added a small dose of indifference. And with the third, her breathing moved from her throat down to the stomach.

It would be fine. The house was old, but so was she, so they should go well together. It's just branches on the roof, she reminded herself and refilled her glass. Just wind and weather, nothing else.

Jeppe hadn't managed to find Nikolaj, but the local police were going to start searching for him the next day. It would all work out.

She carried her glass through the dark living room and paused to take a calming breath despite the smell. She refused to let herself be daunted by her body's cowardice. The wine made her brave.

Another set of headlights shone in through window. Esther set down her glass. Her eyes had adjusted to the dark now, and she felt calmer. The house just needed a dust rag and a little cleaning. Her eyes fell on the black trash bags in the corner of the living room. She counted twelve of them and was already opening the first one before she had a chance to think it over. Maybe this was where the unpleasant odor came from?

She turned on the flashlight on her phone and set it on the floor so it created a little circle of light. The first bag she opened contained clothes, not folded, but wadded up like dirty laundry on the floor of a teenager's bedroom. Jeans and blouses that smelled musty, like cellars and times gone by, but not rot.

The next bag contained stacks of magazines and newspapers, mostly anthropology journals and Margrethe's internationally published articles, journals like *Peoples of the Earth*, *Journal of Anthropology*, and *The Journal of the Royal Anthropological Institute of Great Britain*.

Esther picked one up and held the cover to the light: *Annual Review of Anthropology*, from 1986, one of the headlines read "Indigenous States of Southeast Asia." She put it back in the bag and closed it with a sigh. *We collect so many things over the course of our lives—as we age they make up more and more of our identity—but they have no value to anyone else*, she thought sadly. *They die with us and might as well have been thrown away long ago.*

The next bag was full of worn everyday items, bread baskets, bookends, and candlesticks. Esther admired a pretty, old candelabra that was dented at the base but still gleamed like gold under a layer of dirt. A little wooden box at the bottom of the bag turned out to have been artfully painted with flocks of birds under clouds and a big deciduous tree in front of a farmhouse. Esther picked up the box so she could read the artist's signature at the bottom.

To Margrethe with my undying love. AH 1985

"What are you doing?"

Esther jumped out of sheer terror and dropped the box so it slid across the floor. Her heart was hammering against her ribs, and she broke out into a cold sweat all over her body.

Ida stood just outside the phone's circle of light. Esther hadn't heard her come in.

"Oh, how you scared me!" Esther had to bend over forward, bracing herself on her thighs so as not to lose her balance.

"Why did you open the bags?"

Esther hesitated. Strictly speaking they hadn't agreed that she could look at anything other than books and letters. She had just wanted to . . . well, what had she actually wanted?

"It was just an impulse. I thought maybe the smell was coming from the bags."

Ida gathered up the little box and brushed it off abruptly. Then she set it down with a little bang.

"My brother packed the bags, and I'd rather not open them without his permission. How about we make a deal that you stick to the study?"

"Yes, of course. I'm sorry." Esther stood and watched Ida tie a knot in the top of the bag, not sure what else to say. Then she turned around and climbed the stairs, went into the guest room, and closed the door behind her.

"WOULD YOU LIKE crème fraîche dressing, chili, or garlic?"

Jeppe rested his elbows on the counter at Søjlehuzed, looking straight across the owner's bald head.

"Chili, thanks."

He was handed his shawarma with microwaved pieces of meat and paid the woman at the cash register. Two kids ran around kicking an old mayonnaise bucket, while their mother scolded them. That just made them laugh even louder.

Jeppe got his change, walked out into the cold, and started home. It was a ten-minute walk to the fisherman's cabin from Allinge-Sandvig's only fast-food restaurant.

The streetlights turned on as he passed below them. He had a touch of a hangover and maybe that was what provoked his sense of being lost. Sara and the girls would be done with their dinner by now. He could just hear them teasing each other and bickering in the kitchen, Sara, shushing them, the pot of rice burning on the bottom. Life. And here he was with a plastic take-out bag containing his aluminum-foil-wrapped dinner and no one to talk to. The arguments, remember them, he reminded himself. Remember the animosity and all the conflicts. It just wasn't working. Someone new will come along.

Will someone new ever come along?

What if there was a way to know how many times you would find love in your life? Then you could slow down when you got to the last love and hold on tight through all the hardships.

He sat down on a bench, peeled back the aluminum foil, and ate the shawarma with his face turned out toward the black sea and his back to the deserted asphalt of Strandvejen.

In Copenhagen the streets were never deserted, the city's pulse thrummed twenty-four hours a day, year-round. There the noise grated on your nerves, and lack of space made people snap at each other, because the others were blocking their view, taking up their air, draining their energy. Here, a set of blinking Christmas lights on a house lit up the shoreline rocks, but apart from that the waves and his own chewing were the only indications of life.

The cold crept under his skin. He shivered and tossed the last of his food into the trash can before lighting a cigarette and proceeding home. The walk got his heart rate up and put some warmth back in his body.

In front of Orla's house the home nursing service's car was idling. They were probably dropping off his dinner. Jeppe walked by his windows and saw a strong woman leaning over Orla's armchair, her hands braced on the armrests. Orla sat in the chair looking very small, much smaller than her. The front door was ajar. Jeppe quietly let himself in and stood in the front hall. The woman's voice boomed from the living room.

"Do you understand that? It's unhygienic and disgusting. We're going to stop coming! Then you won't get any food, Orla. What are you going to do then?"

It took Jeppe three steps to reach the living room. He had to restrain himself to keep from yelling.

"What's going on here?"

The aide straightened up with a gasp and turned around, clearly shocked.

"Orla, are you okay?" Jeppe made eye contact with him.

Orla nodded.

"Who are you?" The aide looked at him, her eyes mere slits in her face.

"I'm the neighbor and Orla's good friend. Why are you raising your voice at him like that?"

Her eyes flashed.

"Orla has been told a thousand times that we can't help him if he has rats running around loose. Maybe you can explain to him that he has to do something about this problem."

"You don't need to yell at him!"

"I wasn't yelling." She eyed him with something bordering on contempt. "You try working under these conditions, just for one day. You'd raise your voice sometimes, too!"

The aide walked past him and out to her car. Ten seconds later he heard her drive away.

Orla picked nervously at the plastic lid covering his dinner tray. Jeppe sat down on the sofa.

"Is she always like that?"

Orla smiled weakly.

"Karin can certainly come off as a little strict, but she's nice enough. They all are, the people from the municipality, and they work very hard. I wish they understood that I can't just ditch my pets."

"Maybe we could find a solution where they deliver the food to my place or leave it in front of your door. Then you only need to keep the rats in the cage when they come to clean. Should I give that a try?"

"That's sweet of you, Jeppe." Orla smiled like someone who no longer believed it was achievable.

"I can sort this out," Jeppe said, getting up.

"Won't you stay a little while? I'm not that hungry after all. Did you have a nice day in the woods today?"

Jeppe sat back down. "I actually took the day off and did a little looking around, made some new friends at the Hut."

Orla's eyes widened.

Jeppe laughed self-deprecatingly. "I was looking for Nikolaj Dybris. Apparently he hangs at the Hut. Or he used to." He pulled out his phone and opened the Photos app. "Are you familiar with the Can down by Allinge Harbor?"

"Doesn't ring any bells."

"It's a trailer that a free church, Zealot's Children, set up for the local drunks. People say Nikolaj comes there now."

Jeppe showed Orla the pictures he had taken earlier that day. When they reached the close-up shot of the bulletin board in the trailer, Orla leaned forward.

"What's that? Oh, my eyes, it's too small."

Jeppe zoomed in on the bulletin board. Between recent photos of the Can's regulars and friends, hardened men with beers in their hands, were some caricatures drawn on beer labels, newspaper clippings, and a few photos that were yellowed and clearly older. One of them showed three teenagers with sun-bleached hair, arm in arm standing in the grass in front of an old house. Two boys and a girl.

"That's him!"

"Who?" Jeppe zoomed in farther.

"Nikolaj!" Orla exclaimed happily and pointed to the screen.

"Who, the one in the middle?"

"Yes, I'm positive. He's very young there, of course, but that's Nikolaj Dybris."

Jeppe studied the old photo. The boy in the middle was lanky and blue-eyed with a big mouth in a charming, genuine grin directed at the photographer. The type who would be the first to come to mind if one were searching for words like *cheeky devil* and *imp*, and whom one's grandmother might describe as having a "glint in his eye." His right arm rested casually around the shoulders of a slightly shorter, dark-haired boy, whose face was turned toward Nikolaj, his gaze somewhere between him and the camera. To the left of the boys stood a pretty blond girl with her hands in the pockets of her cutoff jeans. She smiled with closed lips and looked straight at the lens.

"Who are the other two?"

"That I don't know." Orla sounded disappointed at himself. "Also, I can't remember where I've seen Nikolaj as a young man before. I feel like I recognize him from somewhere, though. Maybe he was in the local paper?"

"That could be." Jeppe cast one last glance at the youthful faces and then put his phone away. He clapped his thighs. "Well . . ."

"Maybe we should have a little something to fortify us." Orla nodded at the secretary and the whiskey bottle. "And then you could read out loud a little bit?"

Jeppe looked at his watch and stood up.

"Well, just a few pages," he said. He poured Four Roses into two glasses, only the smallest amount in his, and found the book on the coffee table. "I see you read some more on your own."

"Yep. Selkirk has been shipwrecked alone on the island for four years and four months now." Orla sighed happily into his glass.

Jeppe opened the book and began reading aloud:

Selkirk was cooking food by his hut in the late afternoon, when the ship of rescue came. He judged the month to be late January. He scanned the sea and there, on the horizon, was a wooden ship with white sails. He knew that it was his ship . . .

It was so much the ship of his dreams. In the moment of seeing it time stopped. There seemed no interval between the point of abandonment and this promise of rescue. The same wide bay,

the straight line of the horizon, the high cliffs and wheeling birds.
Nothing had happened between then and now. Only the inchoate
process of his mind. Uncommunicated. Lost. He had been nothing
to anyone. A shadow of self . . .

A second ship came into view. It seemed that here again were
the Cinque Ports *and the* St George. *He felt in conflict, fearing*
the ships would pass, wanting them to pass, fearing the fracture
of his solipsism, the sullying of The Island.

"Do you know what *solipsism* means?" Orla asked.

"Something about being alone?" Jeppe looked up from the book page.

"Solipsism is the thesis that one's own self is the only thing one can be sure really exists. Everything else could be the product of one's own imagination, extraterrestrials, or zombies. You only know for sure that you yourself exist."

"Okay . . ."

Jeppe was about to read on when Orla continued:

"But believing that a person is the sun in his own universe and can manage on his own without other people is the ultimate in egocentrism." Orla nodded to himself. "No one can manage without other people, Jeppe. Not in the long run."

ANETTE DROVE OFF the ferry, pulled out of the line of cars, and found the patrol car parked on the wharf as agreed. An unusual headache had settled behind her eyes after the rainy drive through Sweden to the ferry dock in Ystad, and she felt sluggish and out of sorts. She had tried calling Svend several times on the way, but when she finally managed to reach him, the connection was so bad that they couldn't hear each other and had to hang up. Now the longing for her family rumbled in her stomach along with her hunger and tiredness. *Dinner and a good night's sleep*, she reminded herself, *and then you'll be ready again.*

A woman, who was petite like a teenager, stood in front of the parked police car. Her slender figure was well bundled in wool and Gore-Tex, and she appeared to be standing in an at-ease position with her hands clasped behind her back, like a cadet doing drill training.

Anette rolled down her window.

"Ditte Vollmer, I presume?"

The young detective regarded her without smiling.

"Detective Werner? Follow me. We'll swing by the police station for a briefing. Then we can grab a sandwich to bring back to the hostel we've booked you into. Okay?"

A hostel, ugh! Anette cursed to herself and promised that in her next life she would get a job in the private-business sector so she could at least stay in proper hotels when she was away from home.

She closed the car window and followed the patrol car on the short trip through Rønne to the police station on Zahrtmannsvej. In the dark it looked as square and boringly modern as the one in Copenhagen, just smaller.

Ditte Vollmer typed in the code on the locked door of the building, and they went up to an open-plan office on the second floor.

"Welcome to Bornholm's Investigations Unit! The crew is gone for the day, but this is us."

A handful of desks sat separated by low partition walls, flanked by yucca palms and oversize trash cans. Laminate-covered shelves with chipped corners and faded ring binders revealed that the interior had not been updated for several years.

"You can use that desk over there in the corner while you're here. Brandt, one of our crime scene investigators, is out on maternity leave, so it's free."

Anette sat down in Brandt's creaky desk chair and felt her sitting bones hit wood through the chair's worn upholstery.

Ditte remained standing, her back straight and her jacket still on. Her eyes were big and bright, her face young and makeup-free. She looked like someone who carried around something heavy and never smiled with her mouth open. She looked like someone who did abdominal crunches in front of the television at night. She looked like Anette twenty years ago, just in miniature.

Anette unzipped her jacket and took her iPad out of her purse.

"Posh conditions," she remarked. "But let's see how long I'll be forced to stay before I move in."

Ditte lifted her chin and smiled faintly, as if Anette had said something arrogant. For a moment they looked at each other in silence. Then she, too, unzipped her jacket and sat down at the desk facing Anette, her posture proper like an assistant judge. She pulled up a document on her screen but looked like someone who had already memorized the important bits and knew them by heart.

"I checked Nikolaj Dybris's criminal record. It goes back so far that some of it hasn't been digitized yet. All the pre-1990 cases are still in the basement archives, and he was surely running afoul of the law even before then. Here in the digital records, I have him burglarizing a summer home in September 1991, disturbing the public order in March 1993, fencing stolen goods in October 1993, driving under the influence in January 1995, theft again in April 1996, one single count of a violent act in October 1996—a bar brawl—and it basically continues like that from there. Mostly he has gotten off with fines and conditional sentences, but he did serve time for the one count of violence. More recently he seems to have kept on the right side of the law, though, because there haven't been any reports since 2013."

"Have you met him?"

"Uh, no . . ." Ditte looked at her, as if she had suggested that they play a game of Pictionary.

"I mean," Anette explained, "Bornholm is a small island. Don't most of the residents know each other?"

"I'm from Rødovre and have only lived on Bornholm for a year and a half. But with forty thousand residents, I don't think you should expect everyone to know each other."

"Ah, okay." Feeling annoyed, Anette turned around to her own screen. She wasn't used to being put in her place by a detective half her age. Or any age, for that matter.

"Do we know anything else? Who was the last person to see him, for example?"

"Not yet. We need to make a list of people to question after we've visited his sister at the house tomorrow. I've arranged for us to go there with two crime scene investigators and collect DNA samples at nine o'clock."

"Good. I'm sure I'll be done with my spa treatment at the hostel by then."

"I'm sorry, what . . . ?" Ditte looked genuinely confused.

Anette was a little tickled at that.

"Nine o'clock sounds fine. What about his phone?"

"The call log for his cell phone shows that it was last used to make a call on Thursday, August twenty-ninth, at eleven thirty p.m. The call lasted just under four minutes. My colleague, Detective Poulsen, is checking the masts on the island to see if the phone has been in the area since then. But I'm thinking it was either destroyed or it went to the bottom with our missing person."

Anette raised her head and asked, "Who did he call? Can you tell?"

"We can. The last call Nikolaj Dybris made before he disappeared was to a person by the name of Louis Kofoed."

Bølshavn, Wednesday, August 24, 1984
Dear Elias,

Sunday we celebrated Nikolaj's fourteenth birthday. I could have won first prize for my baking—a layer cake, coconut macaroons, and fresh cardamom buns—and I invited his whole class and all the neighbors over. Even so, it ended up being a miserable affair. Or maybe not exactly miserable, but not particularly successful, either.

Nikolaj is still mad at me because I didn't make it home for his actual birthday on the tenth, and it didn't help when I explained our visa problems to him and how we were detained in Ujung Pandang. I tried! It's not like I decided to take a beach vacation instead of making it home in time for his birthday. But he's too immature to understand force majeure, and maybe I'm too busy explaining myself instead of just apologizing. At any rate, we've been arguing since I finally got home a week ago. Almost a month away and it's not easy for me to come back. The kids have visibly grown—both taller and away from me.

On top of that, I came home to a hornet's nest of accusations and hard feelings, which Mrs. Agger hadn't handled very well. She's usually wonderful with the kids and takes such good care of them when I'm away, but this time apparently she was at her wit's end.

Oh, I understand. Anton Hedegaard can be downright scary when he loses his temper. The Jensens next door say that he came over unannounced and stood out in front of the house yelling when she wouldn't let him in. He claims that Nikolaj and Marco shot at his sheep with their bows and arrows and managed to hit one of them, and he was forced to kill it. Nikolaj absolutely denies that it was them.

I drove over to Hedegaard to make peace, but there wasn't much conciliatory spirit to be had from the farm owner. He kept going on and on about animal cruelty and called the boys sadists and little devils. When I asked how he even knew it was them, he claimed that "one of his employees" had seen them, without wanting to reveal who this employee was. I really tried to mediate *and offered to pay for the poor sheep, but he wouldn't budge. When I pointed out that there really wasn't that much difference between an animal being shot with a bow and arrow or a rifle, the way he does it, he nearly threw me out. I'm sure he'll come around. I must go over there with a bottle of wine one of these days.*

Nikolaj maintains that he's innocent, and I hardly know what to believe. I have this nagging sense that Marco's a bad influence, but I don't know how I feel about that thought. The gods know, he has good reason to act out, the poor boy.

I tried to get Finn to talk, but he evaded the topic. We've slipped further and further from each other since Dorthe's death—well, actually it started before that. Even before Camille was born, he had something going with a young woman who was working at the sawmill, and no matter how I tried to show him that we could easily still be friends, he pulled away. Now he avoids me altogether, and it hasn't improved in the six months since the funeral. He never showed up for the birthday party last weekend and also didn't say he wasn't coming.

Of course I understand his frustrations. A widower with two children, the youngest only five, and his own business—that can't be easy. Maybe he feels guilty, too. What do I know?

I'll survive. I left our personal history behind ages ago, and I don't hold grudges. But it breaks my heart to see how he ignores Ida and Nikolaj, who still idolize him. And Marco! He's only eleven and has to get by without his mother. Finn drags Camille around as if she were still a baby but forgets his son.

I miss carrying my son around, but Nikolaj has gotten big. He's his own person now with his own will and a private life that he keeps secret. It's too late to raise him anymore. All I can do is sit back and enjoy the result.

Enough about that. Did you land well and get unpacked? If I know you, you've already typed and systematized all your notes, you diligent person, you. I will forever be jealous of all your hard work (but also small-mindedly think that it's easier to be diligent when you don't have any children).

By the way, I heard from Kenneth M. George last week! Do you remember, we met him in Jakarta? He was doing fieldwork for his project about headhunters in Southern Sulawesi and now he's in the middle of writing a book about them. I read his letter and felt the wanderlust lifting its wings within me again (so soon!). But of course that might be due to the children's cool welcome.

Lovingly,
Margrethe

THURSDAY, NOVEMBER 21

CHAPTER 14

In the early-morning hours, a storm came in from the east. A hard wind pressed the coastal trees to the ground and whipped the waves up over the rocks. Jeppe lay in bed and listened as it howled through the roof insulation. He sat up, pushed aside the slanted window's blinds, and saw waves foaming iron gray and furious just beyond the marina. It looked like one of his dreams.

Before he could think of an excuse, he pulled a towel down from the shelf, pulled his coat on over his pajamas, and walked outside. A strong gust of wind pushed him along, past red-and-white half-timbered buildings, lavender beds, and the neighbor's calico cat, which was pressing itself against the facade, but still stared at him with fearless eyes, down to the old smokehouse that sold expensive ice cream cones in the summer. Here he tossed his pajamas on the rocks and threw himself naked into the agitated sea. He felt the air get knocked out of his lungs as ten thousand synapses sparked in his body. Only a masochist does this to himself, he thought, and crawled ashore like a shipwreck survivor; the waves were trying to pull back out again.

He hurriedly dried himself off, ran back to his cottage, and warmed up under the shower. He made coffee and ate two eggs with his phone in his hand. Once again he opened the picture from the Can of the three smiling teenagers. He sent it to Esther and asked her to ask Ida if that actually was Nikolaj in the middle—and who the other two were—before he cleared the dishes, walked out to his all-wheel-drive pickup, and headed for the woods. As he reached the top of the hill, Anette called. Her chipper voice crackled through the car's speakers.

"Good morning, island dweller! Did I wake you?"

"Sorry to disappoint you. I've already been for a swim, and now I'm on my way to work." Jeppe slowed down as a pheasant ran across the roadway on short, eager legs. "Have you arrived at the eastern front?"

"I spent the damn night in a bunk bed at the youth hostel in Rønne." She laughed her throaty laugh that sounded like it came all the way from her feet. "I'm returning to my roots, just like you, Jepsen. I wonder if I didn't sleep in that very same bunk bed at some summer camp or scouting retreat. You realize how old and comfortable you've gotten when you have to stand in line for the shared bathroom."

"Did you want something, besides telling me how rough your life is?"

"Hey, Jepsen. We can't all run around chopping down trees to show the world we're invincible."

He tried to protest, but she interrupted him.

"Did you learn anything else about Zealot's Children?"

Jeppe couldn't help but laugh.

"That's *your* job," he said, "not mine, not anymore."

"But isn't it your employer's church?"

"Anette, no."

"You could just ask around a little . . . ," she insisted.

"No thank you." Jeppe turned onto Segenvej headed for the Almindingen forest. The treetops way above him creaked in the wind, and dried leaves swirled across the roadway.

"Couldn't you at least ask your coworkers and the people you're hanging out with if they know Nikolaj Dybris and if he went to the church? You know, casually while chain-sawing, the way real lumber-jacks get things off their chests."

"I already spent my whole day yesterday asking about Nikolaj. I even went by the slaughterhouse where he works, and they don't know where he is, either. Now you need to take over." Jeppe approached the edge of the woods and slowed down. "My boss knows him, actually, so maybe you ought to question him. His name is Louis Kofoed. I can send you his number."

"What?!" Anette yelled, as if something heavy had just fallen on her toes. "The last recorded phone call Nikolaj made was to a Louis Kofoed, on August twenty-ninth at eleven thirty at night."

"Okay . . . According to Esther, Louis was actually trying to gain access to Nikolaj's house the day before yesterday. He said he wanted to pick up some tools Nikolaj had borrowed."

Jeppe reached the edge of the woods and spotted the others' cars, pulled up next to Louis's old beater, and parked.

"I can try to see if I can get anything out of him, but I can't promise you anything. He's already not that crazy about me."

"Pshaw, everyone loves your winning personality. Ask him, then we'll question him later. Should you and I meet for coffee this after-noon?"

"I'll text you a time and place!" He hung up before she had a chance to ask him more favors. His car door caught a gust of wind and slammed shut with a bang. Even here, in lee of the trees, the storm was so loud he could barely hear himself think.

Jeppe gathered his equipment from the back of the truck, put on his helmet, and walked through trees with his chain saw pointing back and the bucket of wedges in his hand. The trunks gleamed in varying shades of brown and gray set against the forest floor's deeper orange and it struck him how he had gotten used to the beauty of the woods, the way you get used to anything attractive. In the beginning, the majestic deciduous trees had taken away his breath every time he made his way through the scents of fungi and moss. The way they connected the earth and the sky, the dead and the new, budding life, the very thought of how old they were made him dizzy. He still appreciated the peace and the fresh air, but the trunks' towering magic no longer caught his eye. The forest had become his everyday life.

Fifty yards in he passed Andrzej, who waved and smiled behind his visor, and shortly thereafter Louis, who was busy trimming a tree he had cut down.

Jeppe set down his equipment and watched Louis saw the side branches off the trunk, while he waited to be noticed. Louis's agile figure worked fast and focused. It wasn't until a branch far above them broke off and dropped to the forest floor a little way from them that he looked up and spotted Jeppe. He turned off his saw and wiped the sweat from his brow with oil-blackened fingers.

"You're late!"

Louis was winded and panting, his upper lip only a thin line above the grayish tooth. His hands held on tightly to the saw, and his knuckles shone white.

"The police have launched an official search for Nikolaj. They can tell that you're the last person he called before he disappeared . . ."

"Huh, you're well informed." Louis wiped his brow again and looked up at the treetops.

"Do you remember that phone call?"

Louis rolled his eyes.

"I can't even remember what I had for breakfast an hour ago. Maybe he just butt-dialed me."

"Fair enough," Jeppe said, gathering up his saw and bucket of wedges. "But you probably shouldn't expect the police to buy that explanation."

Louis glared at him. Even though it felt childish, Jeppe stood there for a second, engaging in the mental cockfight, and it wasn't until Louis turned on the saw and went back to work that he continued in among the tree trunks.

"I GUESS IT'S what you'd call a fixer-upper," Anette mumbled to Ditte, ringing the doorbell of the Dybris family's home in Bølshavn and leaning in to hear whether it was working. The doorframe's green paint was cracked and lifted off in flakes, letting moisture into the rotting wood. Wilted hollyhocks drooped along the brickwork, fighting wild-growing vines for space. At some point someone had clearly loved this house, but it was a long time ago.

The door opened slowly, almost reluctantly, to reveal a slim woman of about fifty with her long hair up in a bun and a vertical crease between her eyebrows.

"Good morning."

Anette held out her hand and smiled.

"Hi, Anette Werner from the Copenhagen Police, and this is Ditte Vollmer from the local Investigations Unit. Thank you for letting us come over."

Ida Dybris opened the door and stepped back so Anette and her Bornholmian coworker could come in. Two crime scene investigators followed them, carrying heavily packed work bags. They nodded and said a friendly good morning to Ida, who returned their greetings in a mumble. The crease in her forehead grew deeper as the police took over the house. She closed the front door after them and crossed her arms nervously in front of her slim body.

"How does this work? I've never been part of anything like it before."

"Is there somewhere where we could talk undisturbed? Meanwhile the investigators can gather their specimens if you could just point in the direction of your brother's belongings?"

Ida looked like someone who would prefer to be anywhere but here.

"The kitchen is that way. There's coffee on the table already. Just make yourselves comfortable there, and I'll get the investigators started."

Ida seemed to get lost in a thought, her eyes glazed over.

"Oh, right, I have a woman staying here at the moment, my mother's biographer. We're not really sure what she should do while all this is . . . ?"

"We'll figure it out." Anette smiled again and tried to look confidence-inspiring. Apparently she did not entirely succeed, for Ida stayed put, blinking anxiously until one of the investigators cleared his throat and finally got her moving.

She led them to a wooden staircase with crooked steps, and they disappeared upstairs. Anette rolled her eyes at Ditte, but Ditte didn't bat an eye. Without saying a word, the young detective managed to make Anette's unspoken commentary on the home's befuddled owner feel inappropriate. Which perhaps it was.

Anette plodded off with a little shake of her head. If youngsters only knew how irritating their moralizing was to everyone else, maybe they would learn to relax a little.

The kitchen was right off the front hall. Anette ducked through the low doorway and spotted an elderly redheaded woman sitting at a small table reading a handwritten sheet of paper. When she looked up, Anette recognized her right away.

"Esther, what are you doing here?"

"Anette! What a surprise." The older woman lit up in a smile, stood, and hugged her. "I'm here writing about Margrethe Dybris. Jeppe didn't say anything about you being the one who would come over! Why are the Copenhagen Police investigating something on Bornholm?"

Anette didn't answer, just patted Esther awkwardly on the back and freed herself from the hug.

"I suppose we'd better wait for Ida. Is there coffee?"

"Of course. Have a seat and I'll find you cups." Esther pulled out chairs for them and shook hands with Ditte. She placed two chipped ceramic mugs on the table. "Good that you're helping find Nikolaj. Ida is nervous, of course, that something might have happened to him. Hopefully she'll have some peace of mind soon."

She smiled expectantly at Anette, who looked away.

Ditte poured coffee and was of no help. The sound of sugar being stirred into the coffee filled the kitchen.

Esther's smile shrank as she looked from the one detective to the other.

Ida stepped into the kitchen's awkward silence like someone who knew what was coming, sat down in the last available chair in the room, and propped her elbows on the table. The shadows under her eyes drew crevices in her narrow face.

"You've found him, haven't you? That's why you're coming to collect samples. You've found my brother's body."

"No, Ida," Esther exclaimed, shocked, and took her hand. "The police do this when they're looking for someone. It's standard procedure." She turned her watery blue eyes to Anette and raised her chin, inviting her to say something.

Anette took a breath and said, "Esther, maybe it would be best if we could speak with Ida alone?"

"She's welcome to stay." Ida's voice sounded tense, and she didn't lift her eyes from the table.

"Okay."

Anette tasted the sweet coffee, mostly to give herself time to sort through the words in her head. It was a matter of saying things as they were, as quickly and gently as possible. The more you tried to wrap up bad news, the worse it got.

"Two days ago we found the body of a man in a park in Copenhagen. We haven't been able to identify him, but we believe he's an ethnic Dane around fifty years old, who's been dead for two to three months. So we're gathering information on all missing people who match that description, including your brother. Forensics needs DNA to compare and contact information for Nikolaj's dentist so we can compare his teeth to the deceased's. We don't know anything definitive yet."

Ida sat in silence for ten seconds and then let out her breath. "So there's hope?"

Anette hesitated.

"As I said," Anette said, "we don't know anything yet."

"How did he die? The guy in the park?"

Ditte, who hadn't said a word since they had arrived, cleared her throat and shot Anette a warning look. As if she weren't aware of the importance of being sensitive! Anette turned away from her young colleague and swallowed her annoyance.

"We're still conducting the forensic testing, but I'm afraid there's no doubt that the deceased was killed."

Ida looked up, like a stag on a country road.

"Killed? You mean intentionally? That can't be Nikolaj. Why would anyone kill my brother?"

"That's exactly what we're hoping you can help us figure out. Did he have any enemies? Did he have money problems? Was he maybe hanging out with the wrong people?"

"I don't think so." Ida thought for a moment. "But I wasn't that close to my brother. Sometimes we weren't in contact for long periods of time . . ."

"When did you talk to him last?"

"I called and wished him a happy birthday on August tenth. He was in a good mood then and sounded like his usual self." Ida's voice was faint. "Is there any concrete indication suggesting that it is my brother? I mean . . . he lives on Bornholm, and you found the body in Copenhagen. Couldn't it pretty much be anyone?"

Anette pulled her phone out of her pocket, opened the file with the photos, and found a picture of the leather suitcase, which she held out to Ida.

"We found this suitcase in connection with the body and have traced it back to Bornholm. Does it look familiar?"

Ida looked at the screen in detail but then shook her head.

"I don't know. *In connection with the body*, what does that mean, anyway?"

Esther made a sound and put her hand over her mouth. She had clearly heard about the halved body in the suitcase.

Ida looked from her to Anette in fear.

"What does it mean?" Ida repeated.

Anette cleared her throat and was beginning to explain the situation when one of the investigators appeared in the doorway.

"Could I just borrow you for a second?"

Anette looked at Ditte, who nodded and stood up.

"Excuse us," Anette said.

They followed the investigator into a low-ceilinged living room, where worn furniture competed with dust and old bottles to create the least possible amount of feng shui. A rancid odor lingered in the space, and there was a horde of black trash bags in one corner.

The forensic tech pointed to one of them with his flashlight.

"We haven't dusted for prints, so put your gloves on, and touch as little as possible. As far as I can tell, we're talking about a significant sum."

Anette walked closer to the bag. The beam of light from the flashlight shone in on a grocery store bag containing bundles of light yellow Danish bills. There was a large *200* next to the word

EURO. She scanned the bundles and quickly counted ten, fifteen, twenty.

"I'll be damned!"

––––––––––––

Bølshavn, Wednesday, February 6, 1985
Dear Elias,

I've started seeing someone. Can you believe, after all these years it's still something I have to work up the courage to tell you even though I know you won't mind. Isn't that silly? Some remnant of my patriarchal indoctrination, maybe. It's not serious, not at all, but I enjoy the attention of a man and have fun sleeping with him sometimes (Ida and Nikolaj mustn't know, so he sneaks in and out of the house).

He's big and strong, good with his hands, and idealistic about his farm, cares more about animal welfare than finances, which I find admirable. Not a man I will have long, philosophical conversations with, or fall in love with, but an excellent distraction for a woman in her prime (I'm forty-six!) who is busy with more important things in life than keeping a man fed and satisfied. I promise you that he's not going to cost me my work time! Quite the contrary, the little romance gives me extra energy to get some writing done on the article.

The children are thriving. Ida is taller than me, almost nineteen and a young lady now, not a girl anymore. She finishes high school next year (she isn't in any of my classes, that would be inappropriate) and is already talking about taking a sabbatical afterward and earning some money to travel. She plans her life and takes charge of both her exams and her equestrian competitions, and my heart swells with pride. The dedication she devotes to everything she does might curtail her social life. She rides every day after school, so there's no time to drink beer with her classmates. But it's a conscious choice, and you can't do anything but respect that. Not even if her dreams will take her away from the island and from me.

Her little brother grows with each passing day, more and more in the diametrically opposite direction. Not big on academics, easily distracted, and a little lazy, but on the other hand so socially adept and with a rare gift for compassion. I still hope that I can light an academic spark in him, maybe after he graduates and is ready to be challenged a little. He's interested in mechanics and science; maybe he'll do something related to engineering, we'll see.

For now I'm pleased with his large circle of friends and especially with the relationship he still has with Marco. They're together every day after school, even though Marco is two grades younger than Nikolaj and a weakling compared to my tall, handsome boy. They like to lie up in his room listening to records together, talking and daydreaming. As close as brothers, but then they have known each other since they were little. Every night when Marco has to go home, they say goodbye with a hug at the front door and I tease them, but really I'm touched. How many teenage boys are so loving and mature?

And speaking of maturity, Nikolaj has been pestering mc for a moped (officially he's not allowed to drive it until he turns sixteen, but here on the island people turn a blind eye to that sort of rule). I say he needs to save up for it himself. Am I being too strict? He has to learn to take responsibility. Maybe he should get a part-time job. He is fourteen, and my friend has actually offered to let him help out at his farm a couple of afternoons a week. The pay isn't stupendous, but better than nothing, and then I wouldn't be the only one keeping him on the up-and-up.

Enough about that. I've prepared an old-fashioned, bourgeois roast for dinner so I'm off to put that on while I listen to the Rachmaninoff concert on the radio and dream of brighter days.

Sincerely,
Margrethe

CHAPTER 15

The east wind gradually picked up, and by eleven it was blowing so hard in the woods that one of the older trees came down on its own. Louis Kofoed reluctantly ordered the crew home with a look on his face that indicated he still blamed them for not reaching the day's quota. He tossed the chain saw onto the back seat of his car and tore off onto the forest road without saying goodbye.

Andrzej looked at Jeppe and put an imaginary bottle to his mouth, but Jeppe pretended not to understand the invitation, waved goodbye, and drove away with a pang of guilty conscience for the lonely Pole. One of these days he would have to set aside time to be social. Today he had other plans.

It took him a good chunk of time to find his way to the church. Finding the address online was easy, but even so he managed to drive past the place twice before realizing he had arrived at his destination. Zealot's Children was located in an older, brown-brick building with a flat roof and a windowless facade. The building was in a drab residential neighborhood on the outskirts of small town Østermarie, and only a discreet golden cross on the front door revealed that it wasn't a family home like the neighboring houses.

Jeppe parked his car on the street and walked down the front yard's neatly curved pea gravel to the front door. The woodwork looked worn in several places and up close it was clear that the mortar between the brown bricks was crumbling and at an advanced stage of decay. An understated doorbell set church bells chiming inside, and then the sound of footsteps approached. The door was opened by a clean-shaven man in his seventies with short gray hair and clear blue eyes. He was wearing a navy blue sweater without a single fuzz ball and a thick silver chain with a cross on it gleamed around his neck.

"God bless you, welcome to Zealot's Children." His smile revealed a string of straight white teeth. His handshake was firm and warm, and he used both hands. An extremely hearty welcome for an uninvited guest, Jeppe thought, deciding to explain his visit with something resembling the truth.

"Jeppe Kørner. I'm sorry to come barging in like this. I've heard about the church and was curious, so I thought I'd just stop by and pick up a brochure."

The man's teeth gleamed almost as brightly as his eyes.

"Come in out of the wind. We don't have any brochures, but I'd be happy to show you around and tell you a little about the church."

The wind slammed the door shut behind them and the sound echoed off the tiled floor in the front hall.

"What a storm. Are you new here?"

"I suppose you could say that. I'm working here for the winter, but who knows, I might decide to settle down permanently . . . Are you the pastor?"

"Father Samuel." He put a hand on Jeppe's shoulder and took a step closer so that they were a bit too close. "I used to work in the fishing sector, just like some of Jesus Christ's disciples. Now I have a church in his name. The Lord truly does work in mysterious ways."

He winked and gave Jeppe's shoulder a squeeze. "Let me show you the interior."

Father Samuel opened a set of double doors made of a golden wood finished with a high-gloss varnish and led the way into a large, square room. He flipped a switch, which turned on sconces along the walls. The room's straight lines and worn gray wall-to-wall carpet framed rows of rustic wooden pews that were facing a carved altarpiece of the same golden wood as the door.

"Are you familiar with Simon the Zealot?" Father Samuel sat down nimbly on an upholstered prayer bench in front of the altar and indicated that Jeppe should do the same.

"Wasn't he one of the disciples?"

"Perhaps you're a church man yourself?" the paster asked, nodding appreciatively.

Jeppe smiled with an expression that he hoped could be interpreted as an affirmation. He needed an alibi for his visit, but if the pastor started speaking in Bible passages, his cover would be blown in a second.

"Where did you hear of us, actually?"

"I work in the forest and sometimes deliver wood to the Sonne family. Camille speaks warmly of the church, so I thought . . ." The lie came easily. Jeppe knew he was heading down a dead end, but he couldn't see any other way to approach this. "I'm looking for a place to . . . exercise my faith."

"You've found it." The pastor put his hand on Jeppe's knee and let it stay there. His eyes twinkled in a friendly way, but the touch seemed uncomfortably intimate. "Zealot's Children is a safe haven for all good men and women who want to be closer to Jesus Christ."

Jeppe nodded, his throat feeling a little dry.

"The Apostle Luke uses the nickname Zealot to distinguish between Jesus's two disciples, Simon Peter and Simon the Zealot," Father Samuel said, sounding as if he were speaking to a child.

"Ostensibly because he belonged to the Jewish sect called the Zealots, who rebelled and fought against the Roman Empire."

He raised the index finger on his free hand and closed his eyes halfway.

"Now you probably think that this is contrary to Jesus's teaching about turning the other cheek and of course you would be right about that. It's all about balance. Here at Zealot's Children we believe in Jesus's commandment to love thy neighbor, but at the same time we are ready to fight for our faith and never bow our heads to anyone."

"What do you mean by that, fight for your faith?" Jeppe asked, adjusting his position so his knee slipped free of the pastor's grasp. "Does the church have enemies?"

"Well, you shouldn't take it as literally as that." The pastor laughed. "The word *zealot* comes from the Greek word *zēlōtēs* meaning 'eager.' Think of the English word *zealous*, 'impassioned,' 'lit up by a holy fire.'"

"Aren't all believers that way?"

Father Samuel sat unmoving. When he spoke again, his voice had an edge to it.

"In this church we overcome all adversity and go to the gates of hell and back again without hesitating. There is no room for doubt here at Zealot's Children, and even when we forgive, we don't forget. I lost my own daughter when she was a teenager, and the rage her death ignited in me still burns and gives me fuel to follow my calling with even greater dedication. The difference between clasping your hands together and clenching them into fists is small. Do you understand?"

The pastor grasped Jeppe again, this time on the back of his head, and the touch felt so transgressive that Jeppe automatically brought his hands up to push him away. Before he was able to do so, the pastor let go and leaned back with a warm smile like a friendly neighbor, who was just offering to help prune the hedge.

Jeppe felt a desperate urge to get up and walk out of the church.

Something about Father Samuel's style gave him the creeps. But he was there and might not get this chance again. He gritted his teeth.

"Did you found the church originally, or was it already here?"

The pastor smiled indulgently as if Jeppe were asking irrelevant questions but apparently decided to humor him.

"Zealot's Children arose as a small breakaway group from the local Pentecostal church. Some of us wanted to do more with our faith than it could offer."

"And was the Sonne family part of that group?"

The pastor hesitated before answering.

"Dorthe Sonne was one of our most esteemed founders at Zealot's Children, very generous with her donations. The Sonne family bought this building and founded the church with me. Now over time we have come to need a new, larger space, but that is coming along."

Jeppe turned around and considered the carved altarpiece. Jesus stood in the middle with his arms out wide in the classic embracing gesture and around him swirled an ornately carved border of flowers, branches, birds, and fish. On either side of Jesus the altarpiece was divided into smaller reliefs of cloaked people in New Testament scenes, which seemed familiar even though Jeppe couldn't specifically place them.

Father Samuel pointed to a bearded man in the bottom-right corner.

"Simon the Zealot suffered a martyr's death and gave his life for the Christian faith. He fought against a superior power and was punished here on earth but rewarded for all eternity in heaven." The pastor stood up. "Now, time is ticking. I hope you've had your questions answered? Otherwise you'll have to come back."

Jeppe got to his feet and followed the pastor back to the front door.

"Thank you," Jeppe said. "That was nice of you. I'll have to see if I can make it to the next service."

"It's on Sunday. But we do hold an evening prayer every weekday at six. It's only half an hour."

"Then I'll try to make it to that tonight."

"You will be most welcome." The pastor opened the door, letting a gust of fresh air into the front hall that rattled the coat hangers behind them. "Kørner, you said? What do you do for work when you're not chopping down trees on Bornholm?"

Jeppe knew he would be shooting himself in the foot if he lied, so he said, "I'm a detective with the Homicide Department at the Copenhagen Police."

Father Samuel raised his eyebrows.

"You can call that a bit of a contrast to chopping down trees. Do you ever feel like . . . *I miss my morning coffee and corpse?*"

Jeppe stared at him blankly.

"It's a quote from the 87th Precinct series," the pastor explained. "The crime novels by Ed McBain."

"I'm sorry. I'm not a big crime reader."

"So I see." Father Samuel exhaled through his nose, the sound seeming oddly like a reprimand. He waited until Jeppe was outside and said, "Thanks for coming. Go in God's peace!"

Then he closed the door.

"WHAT DO YOU think the architect calls that color, sausage meat? Are you sure this is where he lives?" Anette leaned toward the dashboard so she could get a better look at the pink apartment building.

They were at the harbor in Allinge, surrounded by pretty, old Danish buildings in ocher yellows and wine reds, and the modern apartment building seemed completely out of place.

"Høiers Gaard, that's the place." Ditte reached across Anette to set the parking disk to twelve o'clock. "There's a big café and condos with water views around the front of the building, while the units around back here are smaller rental units. He lives on the second floor."

She opened the door and got out. Anette followed and was hit by a fierce gust of wind off the water and the smell of french fries. The combination reminded her of something pleasant, a vacation memory from her childhood, maybe, and made her stomach rumble. The soggy cornflakes from the hostel's spartan breakfast buffet had not laid the most solid foundation for the day. She looked around for the source of the food smells.

"Maybe we should just grab a sandwich?"

"Later!" Ditte continued toward the apartment complex with purpose and did not slow down for a second. Her small body leaned into the wind and did not seem like it could be swayed by anything, certainly not a little hunger.

Anette caught up to her at the building's door.

"That's what I meant, later," Anette said. "Here he is, Kofoed, second on the left." She pressed the buzzer and waited.

"I wonder if he isn't at work?"

"I called the forester and checked. The team knocked off work an hour ago because of the storm. Louis's not answering his phone."

Anette hit the buzzer again.

"Are you trying to ahold of Louis?"

The question came from a French balcony on the right side of the entrance, one floor up. A man leaned on the metal railing, watching them with a lit corncob pipe in his hand. His long, gray hair was tucked behind his ears and came down to the collar of his paisley, terry-cloth bathrobe, which, from what Anette could see, was the only thing he wore.

"I was the one who called, if it's . . ." He stuck the pipe in his mouth and got the glow going again, exhaled smoke, and then looked at them expectantly. "You're from Kivus, the rental agency, right? I left a message."

Anette looked at Ditte, who answered the man without hesitation.

"We understand there've been problems?"

"Yes, damn it. Well, I mean, we all have to coexist, but ... you know?"

"Absolutely. We need to get it taken care of," Ditte confirmed. "Could we come up?"

"Sure, I'll buzz you in." The man disappeared into his apartment. A moment later the lock hummed.

Ditte held the door for Anette, who smiled at her young colleague.

"From the rental company, huh?"

Ditte shrugged.

"There's a better chance that he'll tell them something than the police showing up unannounced."

Anette regarded her with newfound respect. Maybe Bornholm's Investigations Unit wasn't completely useless after all.

One flight up, the man answered the apartment door, still holding his pipe, but gave no indication that he was going to let them in.

"I mean, I don't want to get Louis in trouble or anything, but I'm just really tired of it at this point." He shook his head making the loose skin on his neck wobble.

"Tired of what?" Ditte stood with her legs slightly apart, her hands in the pockets of her blue bomber jacket. The fact that the man hadn't picked up on her being with the police suggested that there was more than just tobacco in his pipe.

"It's all the noise at night, you know? I don't have anything against a little loud music, some noise now and then, but this?! And for months. No, that's not fair, and I've told him so, too."

"He plays loud music?" Ditte asked, sounding almost sympathetic.

The man looked at her, confused.

"No, what? Who said anything about music? It's all the other stuff. He stomps up and down the stairs at all hours of the day and leaves his car idling in front of the door. Who knows what's going on, but it's a real pain in the ass, I'll tell you that. And he can't keep doing it. There's a lot of elderly people living here, you know?" He stuck the pipe back in his mouth. Then he leaned in a little and lowered his voice.

"I think it's drugs. What if people suddenly show up with guns and that sort of thing?"

"Have you asked him what he's doing? Maybe there's a completely normal explanation."

"Oh yeah, I've asked him! He told me to stick my pipe where the sun don't shine and stay out of it." The man shook his head, offended, and crossed his arms. The belt of his bathrobe was ominously loose. "And to top it all off, that damned butcher stopped by, too, the other night and stood down on the street yelling."

"Which butcher?" Ditte asked, keeping her tone casual.

"You know, the one with the sausages at a thousand kroner apiece or whatever they cost now. If you call anything organic, you can charge an arm and a leg for it. People are idiots."

"Can you remember when it was?"

He curled up his upper lip so it touched his nose, trying to remember.

"Was it a week ago? Somewhere around there, late at night. He was yelling that if that little shit didn't come down, he was going to come up and get him."

"And then Louis went down, or what?" Ditte still sounded vaguely uninterested, but sympathetic.

"Yup, and then they stood yelling at each other until the butcher drove away. And that wasn't until about fifteen minutes later. By then they'd woken up the whole building!" The man flung his arms out so his bathrobe opened, fully revealing that, indeed, he was not wearing any underwear. "Are you going to talk to him? Maybe give him a warning?"

"You bet we are." Ditte turned around and gestured to Anette that it was time to go. If she found the situation amusing, there was no sign of it on her pale, serious face. "We'll deal with it. Thank you."

"Great, thanks."

The man waved with his pipe and yelled bye the whole way down the stairs until the building's front door slammed shut behind them. They made it out and into the car before Ditte allowed herself to smile.

"Is that how you do things here on the island?" Anette asked, smiling back.

Ditte raised her eyebrows, making an ambiguous face, which suggested she had a far better sense of humor than Anette had given her credit for thus far. Then she started the car and followed the signs to Rønne.

As they drove out of Allinge, Anette summed up the situation. Or maybe she was just thinking out loud, which was usually her role when Jeppe was the one in the car beside her.

"So far the forensic team has found forty-four thousand euros hidden in a black trash bag at Nikolaj Dybris's house. Ida doesn't know anything about the money and has no guess as to where it came from. But something tells me that the *tool*"—Anette made air quotes with her fingers—"Louis Kofoed wanted to pick up Tuesday night was really the money. No matter where Nikolaj is, both he and Louis must know about the money. How much is forty-four thousand euros in kroner?"

"About three hundred thirty thousand." The answer came promptly.

"Where the heck did all that money come from?"

"Selling drugs?" Ditte suggested. "Maybe they were selling them together?"

"The victim did snort the bridge of his nose to pieces, but outright selling . . . Wouldn't you have heard about that? If we're talking about amounts that large, wouldn't that have brought them to the attention of the police?"

"You're right. So, blackmail?"

Anette looked out the window at the green hills and oak trees with their thick trunks. She tried to put the pieces together but just grew more and more confused.

"Why the hell is Louis running up and down the stairs at night?" she wondered. "And why was there a butcher out in front of his apartment yelling?"

"We could ask him," Ditte said.

Anette looked at her. That demure smile was back on the detective's face.

"Do you know who he was talking about?"

"It could only be Anton Hedegaard. He has a farm with a slaughterhouse on the middle of the island and a butcher's shop in Rønne. It's about five minutes from the police station, and often he's there himself."

"As long as we can't find Louis, I suppose that it's the next best thing." Anette checked her phone. Jeppe had sent a message with the name of a café, a time of three o'clock, and a *GB, J* at the end. The kind who sticks to the formalities even in his text messages. She sighed.

"I have an hour before I need to meet someone at a place called Stampen Smokehouse. Do you know it?"

"It's just south of Rønne. You'll make it there, no problem." Ditte pulled into a roundabout with gas stations and grocery stores at each exit and took the road into the center of town.

"Once we've stopped by the butcher's, you can just drop me off at the police station and take the car down there."

Anette nodded and put her phone back in her pocket. The idea of talking the case over with Jeppe gave her a flutter in her stomach. Or maybe she was just hungry.

AFTER THE TEAM of investigators left the house in Bølshavn with DNA samples and a stack of seized euro bills, the mood was subdued. Esther cautiously tried to show her concern by offering tea and conversation, alternatively to return to Copenhagen so Ida could be left in peace, but Ida absentmindedly shook her head to both. She was obviously worried about Nikolaj now—which was understandable enough, things really didn't look that good—but it left Esther in the painful position of not being able to neither help nor leave.

"I'm sorry," Ida said. "I need to lie down for a bit. Will you be all right on your own? There's rye bread and sandwich fixings in the fridge, so you can make yourself some lunch." Ida's eyes were burdened with worry.

"Of course!" Esther said. "Just let me know if there's anything I can do."

She watched Ida climb the stairs to her room. *Everyone leaves me*, she thought and then immediately shook off her feelings of victimhood. None of this was about her. Life was simply going on. Gregers had died, and Ida's brother had disappeared and turned up in two parts. Esther found her coat. A brisk walk would be just the thing. She could use a good airing out.

This time she followed the road north, passing thatched houses painted red and white, neatly landscaped yards, and trees as tall as the Round Tower back in Copenhagen. The road undulated up and down through the hilly terrain as the houses became increasingly spaced out, and Esther breathed more easily as she grew winded. *Physical exertion is the best way to fight sadness*, she reminded herself, the wind tugging at her coat.

Even in this autumn storm, the view was as pretty as a model village. On one side the tree-dotted meadows unfolded over the crest of the hills, and on the other they dropped down to the rocky coastline.

"The wild, unique natural splendor of Bornholm," she mumbled to herself, appreciating why Margrethe had loved this place so much that she had never moved back to Copenhagen.

Some way north of town she reached a hilltop where the trees had been cleared and the top layer of soil removed. It looked like the earliest stage of a construction site. Whoever built a house there would have a spectacular view of the water. A short gravel path led up the hill from the main road. Esther put the short distance behind her in about fifty strides. The heat rose inside her coat and beads of sweat covered her upper lip.

The view was truly phenomenal: a panorama of the sea and the rugged, rocky coastline. There were whitecaps on the Baltic, and in the distance she could just make out Christiansø, the little island northeast of Bornholm, or maybe it was just a tanker. If she had believed in God, she would have felt closer to him now.

A gust of wind shoved her sideways and she laughed spontaneously. You'd have to be a stubborn fool not to acknowledge the higher powers on a day like this. She had better get back before she was blown up into the sky.

On her way down the path she spotted a sign that she had initially overlooked, because it was tucked in against the bushes. A painted wooden board had been screwed to a post and pounded well down into the soil. UNDER CONSTRUCTION BY THE GLORIA CONSTRUCTION CO., she read, and below that in slightly smaller letters: ZEALOT'S CHILDREN.

She continued down the path to the main road and back to number 21. She opened the door carefully and listened. It was quiet, so Ida was probably still napping.

Good, then Esther would have some peace and quiet to work.

She hung her coat up in the front hall and made a face. That unpleasant odor on the ground floor came and went, but it was never entirely gone. It didn't make sense that they couldn't locate the source. She walked into the living room sniffing, over to the window, to the armchair, to the black bags in the corner.

Esther moved a bag out into the middle of the floor. It was heavy, and the dust came off it in clouds, but she kept pulling out bags until the corner was empty. There was nothing to see, just worn floorboards and dust bunnies.

She squatted down to get a better look. Running her palm over the floorboards, it turned gray from the dust. Right in against the wall there was a height difference between two boards. It wasn't large, but it was there. As she ran her hand over it again, she discovered a gap between the baseboard and the floorboard. Esther put her fingers down into the hole and lifted out the floorboard. It moved without difficulty but only until it was a few inches above the floor, then she couldn't force it up any farther.

She lay down on her stomach. The stench was unbearable, and she scarcely dared think what the dirt would do to her cashmere slacks.

There was a space under the floorboard, but it was too dark for her to see what was down there. Instead she slipped her free hand down, till her fingers hit something soft and wet. She screamed and pulled her hand up, lay there and regained her composure before she reached down again, grabbed the soft thing and picked it up.

A rat. A half-decomposed rat that had surely eaten poison and laid down to die.

The nausea rose up her esophagus, the smell of death stuck to her hands. Esther ran out the front door, kept going all the way to the trash can, and threw the rat away. Slammed the lid on and inhaled the clear November air deep down into her lungs. Imagine that such a small animal could practically ruin a whole house!

In the kitchen she washed her hands with the hottest water she could stand. It felt good to have solved the little mystery and made a difference. She rinsed the soap off her fingers, which she had scrubbed red, then went back to the living room and opened the window to let out the rat smell.

CHAPTER 16

The butcher's shop was one of several food purveyors in an old warehouse. RØNNE MARKET, Anette read, inhaling deeply the aroma of tacos, cracklings, and churros. The white tiled walls were lined with shelves of microbrew beer and cider, freshly centrifuged honey, and locally produced cheeses behind boards displaying prices written in chalk in three languages. A patio with flowerpots and café tables was surely an attraction in the summer months but was deserted now. Many shops looked closed for the season, but some were still open to serve the last of the lunch visitors.

There was a line for the butcher. Judging from the flat take-out cartons people were carrying away, there was quite a demand for the sandwiches.

Anette and Ditte stopped at a bit of a distance and studied the business. A tall, older gentleman with shoulder-length hair—whom Anette guessed must be Anton Hedegaard—stood behind the counter next to a young salesclerk, both wearing leather aprons and friendly smiles. The display case in front of them contained glazed hams, fried meatballs, liver pâté, and sausages, fat, glistening, and looking delicious.

"We could buy a late lunch here, if you're still hungry?" Ditte suggested casually, as if the thought of food hadn't crossed her mind before.

"It's fine. I can easily wait until I meet my friend at the smokehouse." Anette gritted her teeth. "Let's focus on the questioning for now."

The line quickly emptied out, and they walked up to the counter. Anton Hedegaard clasped his hands together.

"And how may I help you pretty girls?"

Anette turned and looked pointedly over her shoulder. *What girls?!* She pulled out her wallet and showed her ID badge, held toward him at straight arm.

"We're with the police. Do you have a minute?"

The young salesclerk's eyes widened, but Hedegaard smiled.

"Of course, we can go in back. Sonja, my friend, will you mind the shop in the meantime?"

He opened a worn wooden door that led them to a small back room with a desk, a milk crate on its side to sit on, and a stack of cardboard packaging on the floor.

"Can I offer you a sample?" Hedegaard said. "We just smoked some sausages."

Anette's mouth started watering against her will, but Ditte replied dryly, "No, thank you. We understand that Nikolaj Dybris works for your slaughterhouse?"

"That's right. He drives goods for us during the high season, but I haven't seen him since the end of the summer." Anton Hedegaard moved his jaw from side to side a bit so that it clicked, then pressed his lips together and ran the tongue around inside his mouth, as if he were adjusting a set of false teeth. A scent of shampoo rose from his considerable volume of gray hair.

"He only works for us during the busy summer months, when the farm is packed with people around the clock. I have no idea where he is now."

Anette heard her stomach grumble and shuffled her feet to cover up the sound. The ensuing silence suggested that she had not succeeded.

Anton Hedegaard took his hands out of his apron and held them up apologetically.

"I'm sorry," he said, "that I can't help you. Was there anything else?"

"There was one thing . . ." Ditte raised her chin slightly. Even though she stood straight as a tin soldier, she was a head shorter than the aging butcher, who had to bend down to hear her speak. She didn't seem to notice.

"One of the neighbors says that you argued with Louis Kofoed out in front of his apartment in Allinge late one evening last week. Are you having some sort of difference of opinion?"

"That was a private matter."

"In an investigation like this, you can't just say *private* and then think that that gets you out of cooperating with the police," Anette attempted. "As far as we know, Louis Kofoed was the last to have contact with Nikolaj before he disappeared. If you two have a dispute, we need to know what it is."

"I can't remember," Hedegaard said, smiling at her.

"It was one week ago!"

"I can't remember."

Once again silence filled the small room.

"It wouldn't happen to have to do with a large sum of money, would it? About forty-four thousand euros?"

The butcher's jaw muscles tensed. It only lasted for a second, then he turned his hands apologetically toward the door.

"Well, Sonja is new," he said. "I'm afraid I'd best get back out there and help." He opened the door to return to the shop and smiled again. "You're sure you wouldn't like a sausage? You won't find any better than these."

"I JUST NEED to understand. Do you have an appointment to speak with a caseworker, or what?"

The woman behind the bright green counter at the municipal services office in Rønne eyed Jeppe sternly. His number blinked in red on the display above her, but that was the only sign of life besides them and a dying monstera palm by the window.

"No," he replied, feeling dumb. Of course he should have made an appointment. You don't just barge into municipal services unannounced if there's a problem in the home nursing service. "I'm sorry, maybe this wasn't very well thought out. I'm here on behalf of my neighbor Orla Klostermann, who lives in Sandvig. His address is . . ."

"Oh, I know Orla very well. His late wife was my mother's cousin." The woman's chilliness thawed visibly. The horizontal line in her forehead vanished and turned into laugh lines instead. "Is he doing well? He must be at least eighty-five by now."

"He's doing quite well, given the circumstances. I look in on him every day and keep him company a little. But he's having trouble with the aide who brings his meals. She says they'll stop coming if he won't get rid of his pets."

"And of course he doesn't want to do that. Is it a dog or a cat?"

Jeppe spread his fingers out in a conciliatory gesture to cushion what came next.

"Rats."

Her eyes widened.

"I know, I know," Jeppe said, "but they're practically his family. He just forgets to shut them into their cages. Couldn't we make some sort of arrangement, where the aide leaves the meal at his front door?"

The woman typed something on a keyboard hidden behind the counter.

"You don't happen to know his civil registration number, do you?"

"Yes, I did have the presence of mind to ask him for that." Jeppe found the number in the notes app on his phone and read it out loud. "Do you think there's anything to be done?"

"I'm sure I don't need to tell you how difficult it is to make special arrangements with a public agency like ours." She looked up awkwardly from her pose, bent over the computer. "But I'll try writing his caseworker to ask for an exemption. Then we'll have to see."

She finished typing and straightened up with a smile that said goodbye. Jeppe didn't move, one hand still on the apple green counter.

"Is there anything else I can help you with?"

Jeppe drummed gently on the countertop, considering how far he could allow himself to go. Then he shook his head and laughed in a way that most women usually interpreted as charmingly shy.

"Well, I don't want to waste your time, but I do actually have a question that you might be able to clear up for me."

She glanced up at the clock on the wall above her and looked around the empty office. Jeppe leaned forward with a conspiratorial smile.

"I'm doing a little family genealogy research here on the island, well, more specifically in Bølshavn, and I ran into one person in the records that I'd really like to interview. But I can't find her. Her name is Dorthe Sonne . . ." His intonation went up on the last syllable of the last name *Son-neh*, so that it sounded like a question.

"Dorthe with a *th*? Let's see." She typed, shook her head, and clicked around with her mouse. "I'm only finding one Dorthe Sonne here on the island, sure enough a resident of Bølshavn. But she died all the way back in January 1983."

The woman altered her tone of voice, in the event that she was breaking bad news to Jeppe.

"She couldn't have been very old, then, could she?"

The woman squinted at her computer.

"Born in 1944, so she would have been just under forty."

"Was she ill?" Jeppe hoped that by maintaining the pace of the conversation, he could avoid arousing her suspicions.

"It doesn't say anything in here about the cause of death, but maybe?" She scrolled through a few pages on her screen. "She was married to Finn Sonne—oh, those are the people who own the sawmill. I thought I recognized the name." She straightened up with a glint in her eye. "They belong to that nutty free church, where you're not allowed to go to the doctor."

She cautiously cleared her throat as if she realized she had gone too far with that last comment.

Jeppe nodded encouragingly to get her to continue.

"I don't remember what it's called, but they have a pastor who's known for healing and distance healing. He claims he can cure cancer by speaking in tongues and a bunch of nonsense like that." She pursed her lips. The wrinkle in her forehead returned. "Well, I suppose you won't be able to speak to Dorthe Sonne after all. I'm sorry."

"Thank you so much for trying." Jeppe flashed her a big smile. "Oh, and by the way since I'm bothering you anyway, there was one other person I was hoping to talk to, a Louis Kofoed. He's younger, so I wonder if we couldn't find him?"

The woman looked like she felt like she ought to say, *Enough was enough for today*, but she typed the name in anyway and then read out loud.

"Louis Kofoed, born 1981, mother: Connie Kofoed, father: unknown, address in Allinge. Could that be him?"

"That sounds right."

She read farther down the screen for a few seconds and then closed the window with her mouse. She stood up and put both of her hands behind the counter in a gesture that could only be interpreted as a *Thanks for stopping by and goodbye.*

"Now, I don't know what you want him for, but I would steer clear if I were you."

"Why?"

She looked over her shoulder and then lowered her voice.

"I shouldn't be telling you this, but ... he's an ex-con. Louis Kofoed served time in Nyborg, a maximum-security prison, from 2005 to 2008."

Jeppe raised his eyebrows questioningly.

"I can't comment on the specific case." She was practically whispering now. "But typically the prisoners who go to Nyborg are the ones convicted of violent crimes. Or worse."

Bølshavn, Monday, April 14, 1986
Dear Argy,

The sun sets in the west and colors the sky yellow and pink like a radiant flower blossom, even here on Bornholm's northern coast. I'm sitting at my desk and feeling a rare contentment. I feel at peace, accomplished, and grateful.

Ida came home from a riding competition today and was happy and tired and chatty in a way she hasn't been in a long time. Not with me, anyway. Maybe the worst of our conflicts is behind us now that she's not a teenager anymore? I hope so.

Nikolaj is home as well, and the three of us have had a cozy, calm evening of laughter and good cheer. I can't remember the last time that happened. I prepared spring lamb for dinner, and they both helped cut the vegetables without my asking. Nikolaj was in a teasing mood, but in a nice way, and he seemed so happy to see his sister. At one point I walked into the kitchen and saw them with their arms around each other. Now that doesn't happen very often,

*either. They've gone off to bed now in their own rooms and I'm
sitting at my bay window with a brandy, writing to you.*

*Imagine having reached a place in my life where my greatest
joy is a peaceful evening with my big kids. How matronly! Ten
years ago I would have laughed scornfully at that prediction.
I would have added goals like "dissertation" and "research
funding" to my ambitions for a good life. And it does have value
to the extent that my work is my identity. But I must have
changed. Time has smoothed those sharp elbows some. Today
happiness is being with my children.*

*The harmonious evening was contrasted by a less harmonious
morning with Finn and little Camille, who's beginning to show
slightly worrisome personality traits, if one can be permitted
to say such a thing about a seven-year-old (and since you're my
sister, I'll permit myself anything).*

*Finn came over this morning and asked if I wanted to go on
an outing to the Sanctuary Rocks with them. He so rarely asks
these days, so I said yes, even though I had planned on working.
I'm honestly okay with our not seeing each other that often,
although despite the distance between us, he's one of the people I
know I can count on. But I miss him.*

*We drove along the coast in Finn's smoke-belching Land
Rover (he sold the red Mustang when Dorthe died), and
Camille squealed with delight as we swooped down the tall hills
by Gudhjem. Finn turned on the radio and hummed along to
the music; the day seemed promising.*

*It's a good time of year to go walking at Helligdommen,
where the Sanctuary Rocks are—everything is in bloom on the
hillsides, and there aren't any tourists yet. I never tire of that
stretch of the coast and its dramatic cliffs. The pretty wooden
stairs and pathways, draped along the cliffs like a cobweb, make
it possible to get all the way down to the water.*

We found one viewpoint where the drop down to the water was so high that we caught our breath. Camille was out of control, running down the stairs and flinging herself against the flimsy barriers, screaming loudly and scaring the birds away. She's little and doesn't know any better, but Finn doesn't do anything to stop or discipline her. She gets her father's undivided love and permission to do whatever she wants.

At the Moonshine Rocks we found a place out of the wind. Finn had packed sandwiches, and Camille took one bite of hers and then amused herself by throwing the rest to the seagulls. She's a strong-willed young lady, and I can only commend that, but still it was nice when she lay down and fell asleep. I've obviously forgotten how exhausting little children can be.

I must admit that I expected Finn wanted to talk to me about something specific, but even so, his confession caught me off guard. He had to try several times before he was able to find the words, and even that is striking because the Finn I know is never unsure of anything. He also made me promise to keep it quiet (a promise I'm breaking now, but since you don't live on the island, it doesn't count).

It turns out he has had a long-term affair with his young secretary at the sawmill—classic!—and gotten her pregnant. After the two of us were finished with each other, he emphasized several times. I patted him soothingly on the hand while I rolled my eyes to myself. What is it with men who think the sun rises and sets in their laps?!

The child is five years old now, and the mother demands that Finn acknowledge his paternity, which he flatly refuses to do. I have the sense that he's bribing her to keep her mouth shut.

Truth be told, I'm not the least bit surprised that Finn has an illegitimate child. He has always been a ladies' man. What's surprising is how guilty he seems to feel. Not about the poor

*secretary as much as about his late wife and—I'm reluctant to
even write it here—God.*

*Finn called himself a sinner and seemed burdened by
Christian guilt. I tried to remind him that consideration for the
woman and the child needed to weigh more heavily than his
own guilt, but he just went on a rant about Judgment Day and
the importance of living purely for Jesus Christ.*

*I sat there in the sunshine with the most beautiful view and
wished I was anywhere else. I seriously missed my old friends
from the university, with whom I could have high-level,
nonreligious conversations. In the end I had to get up and go for
a walk, otherwise I would have said something I regretted.*

*What happened to that strong, handsome man I knew and
loved? Charming Finn, man of the world, with those broad
shoulders and the most dashing mustache in all of Scandinavia.
Was it Dorthe's death that shrank him like that? Did she
confront him about his infidelity on her deathbed and force him
to promise to save himself and all of us infidels from eternal
damnation, or what is this about?*

*I'm sad about the gulf between us, because I suspect it will
only grow wider in the future. As Mother always said: "Never
trust someone who doesn't doubt!"*

*Love,
Margy*

STAMPEN SMOKEHOUSE WAS located in a low, white building
with big windows, and might just as well have been a nursing home
or a conference center, if it weren't for the hand-carved wooden sign
over the door and the scent of fresh meatballs.

Jeppe had found the place online, since he and Anette were to
meet near Rønne, but at a discreet distance from the police station.

There weren't many places on Bornholm open in November, selection was slim, and they might as well meet at a smokehouse as a café. On seeing the place, however, he regretted it a little.

The wind was still blowing heavily, and the sun umbrellas from the patio had been closed and tossed in a pile under a lunch table, where they lay flapping in the wind.

Jeppe breathed in deeply. Despite his racing thoughts, he had been relatively at peace here on the island the last few months and had allowed the time to move more slowly. But that was about to change now that a false value had crept into the equation.

He gathered his fingers around the box of ibuprofen in his pocket, pulled his shoulders up against the wind, and hurried inside.

His feelings of discomfort evaporated the second he spotted the blond woman in jeans, sneakers, and a parka sitting at one of the smokehouse's small tables. She stood up and smiled, the windblown tip of her nose gleaming over her teeth and her blue eyes twinkling. Anette flung out her arms looking like an ad for whole milk or hiking boots. Jeppe walked right into her hug.

"Hi, Werner, welcome to the burbs."

She held him out at arm's length and studied him, her brow furrowed.

"Yeah, you can say that again. Boy, a person can't turn their back for ten seconds without you growing yourself a depression beard. You've got bags under your eyes, Jepsen. Is everything all right?"

"Everything's all right. It's good to see you."

"Good to see you!" She squeezed his upper arms. "You've built some muscle. About time. Come, have a seat, I'm dying of hunger."

"Nothing's changed, then." Jeppe sat down across from Anette with a warm tingly feeling. He had completely forgotten how good it felt to have friends. "I'm just having coffee."

"As long as you're not drinking Gammel Dansk." She scowled at him cheerfully over the laminated menu and then turned to the young waitperson in a polo shirt with braces on his teeth who appeared at their table. "I'll take a Shooting Star Combo Plate with fries and extra bread and butter, thanks."

"Unfortunately our kitchen is closed from three to six. We're only serving coffee and cake right now. Today's cake is a roulade."

Anette looked at Jeppe, as if the whole thing were his fault.

He turned around to the server and said, "We'll both have coffee and cake, thanks."

The server disappeared into the kitchen and Jeppe glanced around the smokehouse dining room. Apart from them it was empty.

"I'm sorry. I should have found a better spot. I just thought you should experience a Bornholm smokehouse since you're here. Maybe there'll be some smoked herring in the cake? You never know, we could luck out." He laughed at Anette, who rolled her eyes in response. "How's your family?"

"Good. Svend's visiting his sister with Gudrun, and they seem like they're having a good time even though she has a bit of a cold. They don't miss me at all." She made a smoothing gesture with her hand over the moss-green tablecloth. "So things couldn't be better."

"Ah!" Jeppe smiled wryly. "And what about the investigation? Are you planning to bring your team over?"

"Not until we get the DNA test results back. We still don't know for sure that the body is Nikolaj Dybris. And then it will be up to the local Investigations Unit, how much help they think they need." One corner of her mouth twitched a little. "Do you need me to warn you before you risk running into Sara in the grocery store?"

Jeppe shrugged.

"Here's the coffee," he said. "Luckily the cake seems to be raspberry and not fish."

Anette watched him as he prodded the slice of roulade with his fork.

"Okay, I suppose I'd better. Though you are obviously over her and couldn't care less."

"Thanks."

"We found a large sum of money—forty-four thousand euros—hidden in a trash bag at Nikolaj's house," Anette said through a mouthful of cake.

"So that's what Louis wanted to go in and get the day before yesterday?"

"It would seem so."

"He did several years in Nyborg Prison." Jeppe opened a container of creamer and poured it into his coffee. "Might be worth looking into his criminal record."

"He's also had some kind of falling-out with Nikolaj's old boss, a butcher, who sadly won't tell us what their conflict is about. Louis seems to be the type of person who attracts trouble." She scraped her plate and then licked her fork clean.

"You're not going to eat your cake?"

"You can have it." Jeppe pushed his plate over the table. "Have you talked to him?"

"It's like he sank into the ground. He doesn't answer his phone."

"I saw him this morning in the woods, but I don't know where he is now. His mother's name is Connie Kofoed, she lives over in Hasle. Maybe she could help. Oh, by the way . . ." Jeppe pulled a plastic bag out of his pocket and set it on the table. "One of Louis Kofoed's cigarette butts. I thought it might come in handy to have his DNA."

"Thank you, Jepsen. I'm glad to see that there's still a little policeman hidden under that lumberjack beard of yours." Anette winked at him and put the plastic bag in her purse. "Do you think he could be involved?"

Jeppe considered this.

"I don't know Louis very well," he said, "but I can easily picture him and Nikolaj having some kind of scam going. They both seem to know how to operate on the wrong side of the law. And Louis knows Nikolaj better than he wants to admit, I'm sure of it. But murder?"

"He's gone underground."

"Yeah, that doesn't exactly speak in his favor."

Anette furrowed her brow and pointed to Jeppe. "Okay," she said, "what about this scenario: Louis and Nikolaj stole money from the butcher shop, then Louis got greedy and killed Nikolaj?"

"Or the other way around: Nikolaj was trying to con Louis, who found out about it and then killed Nikolaj. That would explain why the money was at Nikolaj's place. But a slaughterhouse doesn't exactly keep a lot of cash around, at least not a law-abiding slaughterhouse. So, where did the money come from?"

"Good point!" Anette nodded resignedly and started eating Jeppe's cake.

"Is it good?" he asked.

"Not really. But it's there." She took another bite and licked jam off her fingers.

Jeppe leaned back and watched her.

"By the way, Zealot's Children appears to be a congregation of influential people, including Finn Sonne, who owns Østerlars Sawmill. I swung by the church to chat with the pastor. His name is Father Samuel. Nice man."

Anette smiled.

"I thought you wouldn't be able to stay away. Do either Nikolaj or Louis have anything to do with Zealot's Children?"

"At first glance, only that they know and work for people who are members of it."

"Does the church have anything to do with the body in the suitcase, Jepsen? What do you think?" She scraped up cake crumbs with her fork and stuck them in her mouth.

"Since when do you want to hear what I think?"

"Touché."

"Ida gave me Marco Sonne's phone number. He's Finn's son and Nikolaj's childhood friend, so maybe he knows something. I'll send it to you in a second. He lives in London."

Jeppe felt the phone vibrate between his fingers but didn't recognize the number on the screen.

"Kørner," he said, answering it.

"Yes, this is Aage. I found it."

Jeppe's brain did a somersault.

"Oh, from Olsker Antiques!" Jeppe exclaimed. "Of course. Hi, Aage. What did you find?"

"It was about those suitcases. Sure enough, we found them in the sales ledger for 1988, right after we opened the store. *Two touring cases, twenty-five kroner apiece*, I'm reading the ledger entry right now, although my wife didn't make it easy with these tiny letters. But then, of course, my eyes were better back—"

Jeppe interrupted gently, asking, "Who bought them?" He met Anette's curious gaze. "Does it say?"

"Yeah. I was just getting to that. Like I said, two suitcases at twenty-five kroner apiece, sold on December tenth to Margrethe Dybris, Bølshavn Twenty-One."

CHAPTER 17

"Connie Kofoed in Hasle, can someone find her number?"

Anette posed the question to the open-office landscape, staffed by three local detectives plus Ditte Vollmer. They clustered around a desk behind a tired yucca palm, discussing the problems of the ferry operation, their voices echoing between the cubicle partition walls. Anette's question triggered a quiet snicker that made her look up from her iPad.

"What? What did I say?"

"Sausage Connie," one of the detectives replied with a lukewarm chuckle. "You'll find her in the yellow pages."

"Connie's one of the island's prostitutes," Ditte explained. "And because she's not that young anymore, my male colleagues feel entitled to denigrate her."

"Ah!" Anette said. "But she's also Louis's mother, so when you're done making fun of her, maybe you could get your finger out and call her? She might know where he is."

Her scolding was met with a sulking silence from the three policemen, who wrapped up their conversation and returned to their respective desks. One of them dialed a number on his phone and began a conversation.

Ditte pulled a chair over next to Anette.

"We found Louis's phone. It was lying in a ditch next to the road south of Klemensker in the middle of the island. Maybe he threw it out the car window."

"On which side?"

Ditte understood right away.

"West side of the road. That fits with him heading south and throwing it out the passenger's side window."

"And what's south of there?" Anette scanned the big map of the island that decorated one wall of the office. "He wasn't on his way to the ferry at any rate."

"No, he drove in the direction of the forest, where he works every day, but maybe he was on his way to the airport on the south shore."

Anette stood up and walked over to the map on the wall.

"Have you started a search for him?"

"It's underway. We have officers stationed by the ferry and at the airport now, but he's had half a day to disappear, so maybe we're too late. I requested the surveillance footage and passenger lists from all departures between ten o'clock and three p.m. today. Let's see if we find him in those."

"The two suitcases the body in Copenhagen was found in belonged to Margrethe Dybris." Anette set her index finger on the little dot that corresponded to Bølshavn. "If we assume that the victim was killed here on Bornholm, where could it have happened?"

"If the killer used a chain saw, it could have happened anywhere."

Ditte got up and came over to join Anette at the map. She ran her index finger up along the coastline.

"In the woods or maybe in an old barn or factory building on the north shore. There are a number of empty places around Tejn and Allinge, old fish auction halls and that sort of thing."

Anette shook her head.

"According to our medical examiner, the cut doesn't seem to have come from a chain saw. It's more likely a band saw of some sort. An industrial-grade saw. That's the kind we're looking for."

"Finn Sonne has a sawmill." Ditte's eyes scanned the map, and then she put a finger on the town of Østerlars. "One of the last ones operating on the island. I wonder if they have a saw of that caliber?"

They looked at each other.

"Have you heard back from Copenhagen on the dental exams they did on the body?"

"Nyboe promised we'd get them tomorrow." Anette felt woozy. She was going to need a proper meal soon; the selection at the gas station was not going to cut it tonight.

"Are you okay?"

"Couldn't be better!" Anette shook her head to clear it. "Why don't we call the Østerlars Sawmill and see if we can stop by?"

"I was just about to suggest it."

Ditte walked back over to her desk, sat down at her computer, and looked up the number.

Anette stayed at the map reading the funky names of villages she'd never heard of. Sorthat-Muleby, Knudsker, Gøngeherred.

"Was your colleague able to check the masts?"

"Detective Poulsen checked all the masts on the island for signs after Nikolaj's last call on August twenty-ninth at eleven thirty p.m., but there's nothing. Since that call to Louis, he's gone."

"His phone is anyway." Anette cleared her throat. "By the way, I don't think I told you that my colleague Jeppe Kørner is on the island. He's on a leave of absence from the police and has helped me search for Nikolaj."

Ditte looked up from her computer.

"On his own time," Anette hurried to explain. "Not as part of the official investigation. He's good friends with Esther, whom we met at Ida Dybris's house."

Ditte didn't bat an eyelid, merely turned back to her screen and continued typing.

Anette decided not to elaborate. You explain and apologize only once, anything beyond that is pathetic. She returned to her desk and sat down.

"So, no sign of life since August twenty-ninth. Wouldn't you agree that Nikolaj was most likely killed that same night?"

Ditte murmured her agreement, picked up her phone, and dialed the sawmill.

Anette ran back through the conversation to make sure she hadn't said too much. Maybe Ditte had X-ray vision and sensed that she came straight from meeting Jeppe and that she was still drawing on his help. But originally she had only sought his advice. He was the one who had decided to talk to his contacts here on the island— Anette couldn't stop him from doing that.

She grabbed her jacket from the back of her chair and put it on with a small sigh. It wasn't easy riding solo when she was used to being a double act.

THE EVENING PRAYER at Zealot's Children was not a big draw. Jeppe glanced around from his seat in the back row and counted only twelve people sitting in the church's hard wooden pews. It did not, however, appear to affect Father Samuel in any way that the turnout wasn't better. Wearing an embroidered purple cassock, a mismatch to both his clean-scrubbed face and the ordinary house they were in, he read Bible passages and preached empathically to his congregation, like an eager bingo host. He moved down the center aisle several times and laid a gentle hand on people's shoulders or foreheads as he spoke.

One of those who received a loving touch turned out to be Camille Sonne, who sat facing the pastor, her eyes closed. Her dark hair was covered with a floral scarf, tied loosely at the back of her neck, and at first glance it looked more fashion-conscious than pious, but since they were in a church, maybe it was after all.

Jeppe caught himself dwelling on the curve of her neck, leading up to her chin and beautiful mouth. Even in profile and half-covered, Camille was an attractive woman.

The service was short and devoid of any form of extravaganza such as speaking in tongues or eye-rolling. Jeppe got up along with the rest of the congregation and received Father Samuel's parting blessing with a bit of disappointment before making his way toward the exit.

"I see that curiosity won over prejudice." Camille caught up with Jeppe at the front door, where he stood fiddling with his coat, trying to look like he wasn't waiting for her. "Well, how was it, then, as weird as expected?"

"I'm no expert when it comes to church rituals, but this one seemed to go completely by the book." He held the door open for them both, stepped out into the night air, and took a deep breath. The wind had subsided and a frosty chill taken its place. He flipped up the collar and stuck his hands into his pockets.

"Father Samuel said you'd come by because you were looking for a place to exercise your Christian faith?"

Her tone was as cool as the air, and yet Jeppe sensed a hint of amusement. She wasn't seriously offended. Maybe she had even come to see him?

They walked a few paces out to the street, the gravel crunching under their feet. Camille waved goodbye and good night to the parish children who got into their cars in pairs and drove away.

Then she smiled at him.

"Do you think you could give me a lift? My ride seems to have left. It's not far to the sawmill . . ."

Her smile was sweet.

Jeppe returned it and felt the blood rolling out to parts of his body he had forgotten. A little voice in the back of his head whispered that her suggestion was hardly as spontaneous as it sounded.

"This is me, right here," he said.

His pickup was freezing cold, and the window instantly fogged up from their breath. Jeppe let the motor run with the heat on high, rubbing his hands together and staring straight ahead at the street. It felt awkwardly intimate, sitting there so close next to Camille.

Once the truck had warmed up, Jeppe pulled his sleeve across the inside of the windshield and pulled out. When they reached the rural road she broke the silence.

"My father was pretty upset to hear that you knocked off logging today. He's been trying to get ahold of Louis all day. If he doesn't get in touch soon, you're going to lose the order."

"Isn't that a little drastic?" Jeppe glanced over at her. "The wind was really blowing."

"We're already behind our production schedule." She sounded irritable, as if it wasn't his place to ask critical questions. "How long are you planning to stay, by the way? Are you going home for Christmas?"

"I don't know."

"Don't you have a real job back there waiting for you, a family? Louis can be demanding. You mustn't let him keep you."

Jeppe hesitated. Was this why she had come to the prayer service? To encourage him to go home?

"For now I enjoy being here. Then, we'll have to see."

She pulled off her floral scarf and set it in her lap.

"I'm supposed to tell you hi from my older brother and say that he still doesn't know where Nikolaj is."

"What is he doing these days?"

"Marco works as an investment banker." Camille's voice softened, sounding proud. "At one point he was headhunted by Sachsman and Porter for their London branch, but for the last two years he's been on his own. And he's busy. He bought himself a nice flat in Belgravia and plays tennis at the same club as one of the princes. My brother is insanely good at what he does."

Jeppe grunted his approval.

"But he must wonder what became of Nikolaj, too. Aren't they friends?"

She sighed.

"There are many ways to be friends. They only see each other when Marco comes home for his summer break, and then Nikolaj seems most interested in driving around in my brother's vintage Porsche, partying at the island's summer restaurants. Marco goes along with it for old time's sake, and because he's a loyal person."

"You don't sound especially enthusiastic about Nikolaj."

She shrugged.

"I've known him forever and grew up with him as one of the big kids my brother hung out with. Marco is nearly seven years older than me, and he and his friends seemed unattainable when we were kids. But . . . there's just some people who add value wherever they go and others who foment chaos. Nikolaj belongs to the latter group. A loser, if you ask me."

They were approaching the sawmill. Jeppe slowed down and glanced over at Camille. She sat with her hands in her lap, looking out the window.

He was itching to ask about her mother and what she died of, but he knew it would shatter their nascent trust and stamp him as a policeman doing his job.

"Father Samuel told me he lost a child . . ." he tried instead.

"Did he? That's not generally something he talks about." Her answer was halting, but there was nothing hostile in her voice, more a childlike curiosity that sounded like something she rarely permitted herself to express. "But yes, his daughter died in an accident. I was only nine or ten when it happened, but I remember it clearly. Everyone was crushed. We knew her from church, of course. She was my older brother's age, very pretty, I remember, and had a reputation for being a bit of a rebel. Her parents apparently had their hands full with her, but they only had the one."

"How did she die?" Jeppe pulled into the courtyard and stopped in front of the sawmill leaving the engine idling. He hoped the conversation would keep her in the car a little longer.

"She fell in the Troll Forest. I don't know exactly what happened. I was too little to be told the details."

Camille groaned, half in indignation, half in amusement.

"Christian child-rearing at its best. What they don't know won't hurt them. No understanding of how frightening it is for a child to sense all that despair without having it explained." She smiled at him sideways and held eye contact. "It's still not something we talk about."

Jeppe returned her smile. He couldn't figure out whether Camille was one of those people who flirts because it's effective or whether she was genuinely interested in him.

"I didn't dare set foot in the woods for years because I was terrified of the wild animals." She pushed the hair out of her face, and her eyes caught the light from the streetlamp on the road, shining in the darkness.

"The wild animals?"

"Well, you know how things can grow in a child's imagination. When I asked the grown-ups what happened to the pastor's daughter, they said she fell in the bear cave and died."

———————————

Bølshavn, Sunday, October 12, 1986
Dear Argy,

Nikolaj is stealing from me. He doesn't think I notice, and I let him stay in that belief. I can't deal with the conflict, not right now. It's just spare change from my purse in the hallway and beer from the fridge, and I take comfort in the fact that it isn't any worse than that. It's just something kids have to go through, right?

I don't think Ida ever did it, and I can't remember you mentioning that your boys stole from you, either, but maybe you were just laid-back about it.

The hard thing about being the mother of a teenage boy is that he shares so little about what's going on. He and Marco empty the change out of the coat pockets in the front hall, and I let it slide, because, well, at least it isn't worse. But maybe it IS worse, what do I know? Maybe they're shoplifting, too, taking drugs, getting in fights, breaking the law, doing things I can't even imagine. When do you step in?

The two stick together like peas in a pod, driving all over the island on their souped-up mopeds. Wear holed jeans and smell of beer and cigarettes when they come home. There's not exactly a ton of cafés and bars on the island, and the teenagers mostly hang out at the beach or party in the woods. Marco is only fourteen, but as far as I can tell Finn seems to have given up on the boy and pretty much gives him free rein.

As long as Nikolaj eats dinner at home every day, and we still talk about our days and about life, then I forgive him that he meets his friends later with whatever he can carry of value in his pockets. It'll resolve on its own.

I remember my own transition from childhood to adulthood as an endless stretch of restlessness in body and soul. Being a teenager is so turbulent and full of energy. The worst thing you can do as a parent is limit their freedom and curtail their need to experience things. I let Nikolaj go all over with Marco as long as his homework is done and he gets to bed at a reasonable hour so that he can get up in the morning.

He worked for Anton over fall break. Anton has forgiven his childish boyhood pranks and praises him for being good with his hands. He's taught him how to build fences, weed, and paint woodwork, and even though naturally I have bigger ambitions for my son than unskilled manual-labor jobs, it certainly doesn't hurt for him to get some practical experience.

Finn has even, surprisingly, gotten him an extra temp job as a bricklayer. The gable wall of Finn's church was crumbling, so Nikolaj and the mason are repointing it at Father Samuel's place on the weekends. The long-term plan is to build a whole new church, and Finn is pulling strings with investors and municipal politicians to raise money and obtain building permits—he's good with that kind of thing. But new construction will take a long time, so they're renovating the old church to begin with.

Nikolaj seems to enjoy the work and says that the pastor's family is nice and serves a hot meal for lunch. I've warned him not to listen to them too much, he's at risk of being brainwashed. I honestly can't cope with any more Christian fundamentalism in my life.

By the way, there's a rumor going around about Father Samuel and Dorthe Sonne! That they supposedly had a thing going behind the backs of Finn and the pastor's wife, whose name is Ingeborg or Agnes or something like that.

I don't believe it. Dorthe was hardly the type. Did I tell you about the time she came over for coffee and I suggested she use a diaphragm if she didn't want more kids? I explained how easy it is to use, but her face went ash gray, and the subject seemed to make her so uncomfortable that I dropped it. She's supposed to have had an affair with the pastor?!

I wonder if the rumor didn't start during the period when she was ill and he was trying to heal her? That sort of thing can kind of take off and grow out of proportion on an island like Bornholm. Things have to fit into the existing boxes in a place like this, otherwise people start feeling insecure.

Elias is a little tired of me. I'm having a hard time getting my part of an article for the Peoples of the Earth journal done, and he chews me out and gets impatient, as he does, you know. Sometimes you would think we were still married.

Hug my nephews for me!

M

CHAPTER 18

"Was that Jeppe's pickup?"

Anette turned to look at the car they had just passed, which was fast disappearing into the darkness behind them. She was probably mistaken. With careful fingers she typed the long English phone number into her phone and heard it ringing.

"He's not answering," she murmured to Ditte. "I'll leave a message." She cleared her throat and waited for the beep.

"Hi, Marco, this is Anette Werner with the Copenhagen Police. I need to ask you to call me back at this number. This is regarding your friend Nikolaj Dybris. Thanks."

Ditte pulled into the gravel area in front of the sawmill and they got out of the metallic blue Mercedes. Anette looked around at the elongated buildings and stacks of tree trunks lying all over. It had rained on their way there and the wood was dripping bleakly. Low clouds had rolled in over the island, and in the dim daylight the deserted Østerlars Sawmill looked abandoned. Like a snapshot of something from the past that life had now turned its back on.

Anette zipped her jacket, satisfied with her own observations. With that sense of poetry, what did she need Jeppe for?

"Who are we meeting?" she asked.

"I spoke to the owner, Finn Sonne." Ditte looked around. "The employees've all gone home for the day, but apparently he had something to finish. If we walk around the place, I'm sure we'll find him."

"Okay."

"He did say that he doesn't know where Louis is, but I insisted on coming out anyway so we could see the place."

The building next to them was large and newer-looking, with lights burning in its small windows. They crossed the gravel parking area and grabbed the handle of a red metal door, which opened easily. Inside they encountered an enormous structure made of steel and wood, extending the whole length of the space and up toward the insulation panels in the ceiling. Tracks and crossties made of wood and steel ran from right to left and back again across the hall, spools, wires, and pipes. Buttons glowed green and red in a control panel behind a pane of glass. It looked like a place designed to rumble with energy, but right now it was quiet.

"What do you think they do in here?" Anette asked.

"Ten to one, it's got something to do with sawing up trees."

They followed a steel rail through the hall, peering in between logs and board until they stood in front of a gray metal box that stretched from floor to ceiling. The box was equipped with a row of castors and displays for measuring unspecified units. A little above head height, a dirty window revealed that the box contained a band saw.

Anette jumped up onto a stack of pallets, wiped the glass with her sleeve, and shone her phone's flashlight in.

"That's a powerful saw, no doubt about it. But it's shielded by this box, and there are only narrow openings with room for planks to go through."

"Are you sure?" Ditte stepped onto the pallets, stretched up onto her tiptoes, shielded her eyes with her hands, and checked for herself before hopping back down onto the floor. "Let's keep going!"

Across from the modern building there was a smaller, older version and the wooden door at one end of it was open. Anette stumbled over something on the slippery ground, two metal rails, which led through the doorway and into the hall. She walked closer and heard a rhythmic throb from inside, like a locomotive. She peered in and saw wood paneling on the walls and the ubiquitous sawdust in a thick layer on the floor and hanging in the air like fine particles. Two Labrador retrievers ran to meet them and curiously sniffed their legs.

Anette followed the metal rails to a tree trunk. It was moving toward an old saw with a horizontal blade, which was eating into the tree trunk. An enormous, gray steel frame hung over the saw, and next to it, spools and belts ran around, keeping the blade going.

A tall, older man in blue coveralls stood stooped over the saw and didn't see them coming. He adjusted a grip and bent in over the saw blade so he could monitor the cutting surface. As he straightened back up, he spotted them.

Anette took out her laminated ID badge and held it up. Then she pointed at the machine and yelled: "Can we turn that thing off?"

Finn Sonne blinked. He pulled a cloth out of his pocket, wiped his oil-stained fingers, and found the off switch at knee height. The engine stopped, and the spools spun slower and slower until they, too, came to a stop. He called the dogs over, and they lay down calmly at his feet.

"I don't know where he is," he said.

No hello, no explanation.

"Who are you talking about?"

"Louis. Isn't he the one you're looking for?" Finn folded the cloth up neatly and put it back in his pocket. "Because you think he killed Margrethe's boy."

Anette glanced at Ditte, who was standing beside her with her hands behind her back. She hadn't said anything about Nikolaj Dybris when she called the sawmill, just asked for Louis and whether they could come by.

"And did he?"

"I don't have the foggiest idea. Nikolaj has a tendency of getting on the bad side of people."

"Is he on your bad side? Or anyone you know?"

One corner of Finn's mouth quivered in a sarcastic smile, as if Anette were underestimating him.

"My deceased wife and I were good friends of Nikolaj's mother. My son played with him when they were kids. Believe me, I know him. He's always been a bad boy. That's why I've kept my distance from him for many years."

"But your son hasn't, as far as we've heard. Marco and Nikolaj are still friends . . ."

"No, they're not." Finn interrupted emphatically. "You can ask him yourself."

"Thanks, we will." Anette considered whether Marco's father was trying to control his son and dictate what he told the police. "When did you last see or hear from Louis?"

"I saw him in the woods yesterday. Today he knocked off work early because of the wind, and I've been trying to reach him all day." Finn clenched his teeth and sighed in irritation. "The sawmill can't wait for the delivery."

Ditte handed him a business card.

"Contact us right away," she said, "if you hear from him."

Finn took the card, skimmed it, and stuck it in the pocket of his coveralls. Then he switched on the saw with a push of the button and started working again with his back to his visitors.

Ditte walked briskly toward the door, but Anette's eyes lingered on the saw, the floor, and the sawdust before she joined her. The dogs followed them back to the car. When Ditte started it, the headlights swept across the gravel parking area reflecting in their eyes.

"Do we agree that Finn Sonne's sawmill can't be our crime scene?" Anette asked, buckling the seat belt with her eyes on the building. "That thick layer of sawdust around the band saw can hardly be new, and those raw boards on the wall would be impossible to clean."

"Agreed," Ditte replied. "Besides, the sawmill is a workplace with a lot of employees who use the saw daily. A crime committed there would have been discovered. It would be like murdering someone in a circus ring in front of the audience!"

Anette laughed tiredly at the comparison.

"I'm going to eat a real dinner tonight. Do you know any good spot that's open? We could eat together. My treat."

"Sure, we can do that," Ditte mumbled, sounding surprised. And happy.

AS THE TICKING wall clock in the kitchen passed nine, Esther gave up on waiting any longer and buttered herself a slice of bread for supper. Ida had driven away midafternoon without saying when she would be back. And of course Esther couldn't expect that, either, certainly not in this situation, she reminded herself. She wasn't there as a family friend but rather in a professional context and could certainly spend the evening alone.

The light was on, and the front door was locked. A small glass of red wine would probably take the edge off the last of her out-of-sorts feelings.

She sat down at the little table in the kitchen with her back to the window overlooking the road. Even though the streetlights normalized the view to some extent, she still preferred not to look at the deserted roadway. Each unexpected movement would scare the dickens out of her. There was no reason to tempt fate. Instead, she focused on the lovely open-faced sandwich on her plate, a slice of rye bread topped with smoked mackerel, and filled her glass up the rest of the way with a contented sigh.

Gregers loves mackerel, she thought before remembering the new reality, and her stomach twisted.

With age, appetite had become a fickle guest, but having something to read helped. She got up and went to the study to fetch a letter.

In the living room Ida had set a dented architect lamp by the window facing the water and plugged it into one of the few electrical outlets that worked. As the room's only light source it lit up nothing but the area directly around it and created long shadows in the rest of the room. On top of that it made a dazzling reflection in the window glass, transforming it into a mirror and making it impossible to look out at the sea when it was dark. A situation for which Esther was grateful at the moment.

Her eyes fell on the little painted box she had found in one of the black bags the day before and dropped on the floor. Ida had set it on the windowsill, and now it sat gleaming in the lamplight.

Esther opened the box. It contained big silver rings with turquoises in them, cheap dangly earrings, and narrow bracelets with imitation gems. It looked like the kind of jewelry people bring home from trips and which has more sentimental than material value.

She heard a loud bang from the yard just on the other side of the windowpane. Esther jumped, gasping in fear. She leaned toward the pane and shaded her eyes with her free hand so she could see out, but there was nothing in the yard besides the impenetrable November darkness.

Her breath fogged up the glass and she moved backward and saw the window becoming a mirror again. Maybe it was a falling branch, ripped loose by the wind earlier in the day. The doors were locked, she reminded herself. I'm safe. There's no reason to let my imagination run away with me.

She picked up a bone bracelet set with red stones and smiled. It could only be Margrethe's, possibly a souvenir she had brought home from Africa. It felt soft and warm between her fingers, like touching skin.

Esther put it back, felt around with her fingers, and found a necklace. It was plain, made of silver with a cross for a pendant, surprisingly puritan compared to the other contents of the jewelry box.

There was another bang from the yard, followed by a crunch, which repeated after a second. The sound of footsteps.

Esther reached a shaky hand up to the button on top of the architect lamp and switched it off with a little click. The room around her went dark, and the yard became visible.

She peered out until the blackness turned into bushes, trees, and hedges, held her breath and clutched the chain tightly between her fingers.

What was she doing here, all by herself in a strange house?

Maybe she should just go home to Copenhagen, retrieve her dog, and continue writing the book in her own safe Copenhagen apartment, where the lights worked and there was no carcass smell. Surely Ida would let her take the letters with her.

Esther had better go to bed. Hopefully Ida wouldn't have any objections to her leaving the light on. She turned away from the window, but before she took the first step, some movement in the yard caught her eyes. A movement that was neither swaying trees or a reflection from a passing car.

She turned back slowly to face the windowpane. Without thinking, she started stepping backward, as if the darkness of the room could protect her. She closed her eyes, breathing in bursts. She was alone and defenseless, unable to either hide or run away.

There wasn't a sound from the yard, just her own frightened whimpering. Esther forced open her eyes and tried to get her breathing under control. Beneath the sounds of her breath she heard the recognizable creak of the front door being opened.

THE ONLY RESTAURANT in Rønne open late on a Thursday night in November was an empty running sushi place just off the main square. The electric conveyor belt carried colorful little plastic plates of sushi around a well-lit dining room, between rickety tables, to nonexistent customers.

Anette eyed a tuna roll skeptically and turned to Ditte. "Do you come here often?"

"No," Ditte admitted. "I don't go out to eat that often. Where should we sit?"

"Here!" Anette pulled out the nearest chair and sat down at a table covered in an Easter-yellow velour tablecloth. "Do we just help ourselves, or what?"

Ditte looked around for help. A young woman behind the counter was busy, packing take-out orders into paper bags, and didn't even deign to look at them. Behind her a window into the kitchen showed two men with tattoos on their necks, each bent over a cutting board, rolling seaweed with rough hands. Every once in a while they barked at each other in a Slavic-sounding language. Though it was 9:00 p.m., and the restaurant was empty, they were doing steady business.

"I'm just going to start." Anette felt another spell of dizziness and reached for an orange plate from the belt. It had a spring roll on it that didn't look particularly Japanese. It tasted like it had been frozen for a long time, then fried, but the sensation of food in her mouth was heavenly. She snagged a white plate with salmon nigiri before it sailed out of reach and swallowed the refrigerator-cold fish in two bites. As she chewed she noticed that Ditte was watching her, wide-eyed.

"Aren't you having anything?" Anette asked, her mouth full.

"Yes, of course." She furrowed her brow skeptically. "Is it good?"

Anette grabbed another plate and sighed. "About as good as a condom with no sex."

Ditte made a sound somewhere between a laugh and a cough and grabbed a pink plate with a seaweed salad from the train. The waiter came over to the table and took their order for two colas with great somberness and accompanying notes on a notepad. She explained the place's pricing system, based on the varying colors of the plates, and walked away with energetic footsteps that left their table wobbling.

"Louis Kofoed's mother doesn't know where he is." Ditte struggled to split apart a pair of disposable chopsticks. "Detective Jakobsen just wrote."

"Should we question her ourselves?"

"Nah." Ditte managed to liberate the chopsticks and position them painstakingly in her right hand. "I met her. She's a bit of an institution here on the island. An alcoholic, a former prostitute, as they said. Louis had been in foster care and hasn't had any kind of close relationship with her."

She tried to scoop up some of the seaweed salad with her chopsticks.

"Connie did confirm, though, that Louis and Nikolaj have been good friends since Louis did a traineeship at Hedegaarden twenty years ago. Nikolaj is ten years older but apparently took Louis under his wing. Connie has met Nikolaj a few times, but not in several years."

"Sausage Connie from Hasle," Anette mumbled, scanning the train for plates that looked like they hadn't been circulating since the morning. She selected an interesting-looking omelet with little pieces of ham next to it and caught Ditte's eye across the table. "How is it, being young and female in the Bornholm Police? Your colleagues seem a little . . . old-school?"

"They're all right. I think we all have things we can teach each other. Hopefully I give them a new view of women on the force, and in return they teach me something about being there for people. People on Bornholm take care of each other. Big-city dwellers could learn from that." Ditte smiled and returned to her seaweed salad.

Anette was about to question her further but dropped it. She was too tired. Instead she stacked up her plates and tried to work out what her meal would cost. She was looking forward to telling Svend about this place.

"What's our next move? Beyond finding Louis Kofoed?"

Ditte finished chewing before she responded.

"He hasn't shown up on any surveillance footage from the ferry or the airport, so that's an indication that he could still be on the island."

"He can't be running away from us, can he? I mean, we just want to find out if he knows where Nikolaj went. He hasn't done anything—not that we know of—so why run off like that?"

"I wonder if it isn't about the money . . ." Ditte finished her cola and pulled out her phone. "Something occurred to me, actually, when we were talking to Anton Hedegaard, but then it slipped my mind again. Just a sec."

She typed and scrolled down her screen.

"All businesses have to publish their financials, and I've heard rumors about Hedegaarden . . . and, yup, sure enough. A deficit of millions of kroner for both the farm and the slaughterhouse over the last three years, debts to vendors and overdraft limits exceeded, tax deferment, and net worth at rock bottom. Our good Anton is almost bankrupt."

The phone rang in her hand. Ditte eyed the display skeptically, then answered.

"Hello? Ah, hello." She sounded surprised. "Where?" Pause. "When? Are you sure? Would it be all right if we came by to hear more?" She glanced at her watch. "Tomorrow morning then? Nine o'clock?"

Ditte said goodbye and hung up.

"That was Father Samuel from Zealot's Children. He heard that we were looking for Louis Kofoed and wanted to let us know he had just seen him."

"Where?"

"Apparently he drove by the church half an hour ago." Ditte shot her a look and then raised her hand to request the bill.

Bølshavn, Monday, July 8, 1987
Dear Argy,

I'm sorry you haven't heard from me in a long time, and forgive me for starting my letter with an apology—I know you hate that—I've been busy first with exams at school and then a deadline for an article on the Mesoamerican custom of honoring the dead by cleaning their bones once a year. I'll send it to you once I can make copies again. Read it if you're up to it.

It's summer vacation now and peace has slowly settled over us. Not over the island, of course, which is hopping with families on bicycle vacations and German tourists who've rented the same summer cottage for ten years running. The locals toil away and grumble, making a fortune off the visitors, and at the same time harboring an illogical aversion to serving them.

I've gotten used to it now (although not so that I view myself as one of the locals, ha!). In the beginning I, too, found it tiresome to stand in line at the grocery store and zigzag between

all the towels on the beach to get in the water, but little by little
I've come to see the hectic summer life as a necessary opposite to
winter. The energy is contagious. I fix up the flower beds in the
garden and paint the fence, swim out to the farthest buoy every
day, and read in the hammock in the yard.

It's so pretty here in high summer, even after almost fifteen
years, I haven't sniffed my fill of the strawberry fields, the Scotch
broom, and the smell of the sea salt drying in the sun along the
coast. And the colors! I wish I were a painter and could capture
all the rapeseed yellow, sky blue, and grass green, not to mention
the sparkling gray rocks, which are the opposite of the winter's
boring asphalt colors. Danish colors normally have so much
white in them, but not on Bornholm. Here the colors are deep
and intense, like in Southern Europe.

And now I finally have plenty of time to enjoy the summer.
School is closed, the kids are basically never home, so I have only
my research to consider. I remember with melancholy the days
when I was constantly trying to shake them off my trouser legs
so I could work. Who could have known how much I would miss
their attention?

Ida turned twenty-one this spring. She's allowed to do
everything and doesn't need permission for anything. At Easter
lunch this year she announced that she was planning to attend
a language school in Boston for a year after summer vacation.
She's a cashier in the big, new grocery store in Gudhjem, and
she's saving up the money herself, doesn't need my help anymore.
I feel so proud but, at the same time, devastated. You have
grown children yourself, you understand.

Nikolaj will be seventeen in a month. He's been taller than
me for ages and seems to have gotten a girlfriend. Not that he
tells me anything, but he's more careful about the way he looks
and spends less time with Marco that he used to. He daydreams

through dinner with a goofy smile and then hugs me out of the
blue. So, you see, it can only be a girl!

   The other day I tried to have a talk with him about sex, but it
was so painful for us both that he practically fled from the house.
If only he's careful, then I suppose he's getting to be old enough
for that sort of thing.

   I, on the other hand, am getting to be too old. No, good
gracious, a woman of forty-eight isn't too old for boyfriends
(yes, plural, boyfriends), but I'm over it. Men are simply too
much trouble. I just can't anymore. Either they're too lazy or the
opposite, too eager and want to move in together. It's a myth
that it is women who want to build nests and have proper
relationships. My experience tells me that it's the men who can't
get the hang of being alone.

   Anton is no exception. We've had a lovely time together without
major complications. But in the long run it wasn't enough for him.
He wanted to meet the kids, move in together, and get married,
if I could be persuaded. I tried to explain to him how that would
ruin the good thing we had and that I have always deliberately
steered clear of the constraints of marriage, but he persisted. I
ended up breaking up with him, and he, of course, took it badly.
In English there's a saying that hell hath no fury like a woman
scorned, but it's no comparison to a man scorned!

   Now I'm going to make myself a sandwich and drink a beer
in the sun. Come visit me soon!

                                                Yours,
                                                M

——————————

THE STARS WERE twinkling over Sandvig Harbor as Jeppe finally
reached home and parked the pickup on the wharf, his body humming with unresolved tension. He had let Camille go, even though

she had invited him to stay and his libido was screaming that there were no good reasons not to. The fact that he didn't trust her motives was probably the only valid argument. But now as he put his weight into long strides up the hill, it occurred to him that the real reason was something else. His heart was still in Copenhagen, and that was holding his body back.

The lights were on at Orla's place.

Jeppe peeked in the window and saw his neighbor sitting in his armchair with the book in his lap and his chin down on his chest. A light gray rat asleep on his shoulder.

Jeppe carefully tapped on the windowpane and saw Orla blink, lift his chin, and look up, confused.

Jeppe knocked again.

"Yes, yes." Orla slowly got up and came over to the window and unhooked the hasps to open it. The rat didn't budge from his shoulder.

"Jeppe, is that you? What time is it?"

"Ten thirty. I'm sorry if I woke you. I just wanted to say good night." The stuffy air from the living room hit Jeppe's nostrils, and he took a step back.

"I stopped by the municipal services office today. They agreed to write to your case manager, so we may be able to get the aide to leave your food outside your door instead."

Orla found Jeppe's hand with his own soft one, gave it a squeeze, and smiled gently.

"You're a good boy." Orla noticed the rat on his shoulder and carefully set it down on the floor. "There you go, Harriet. Then maybe we can be left in peace for a bit. That would be nice." Orla straightened up. He looked tired.

"You look like someone who could use a nap," Jeppe said.

"Well, maybe just a short one." Orla fumbled with the window latch.

"Just one thing, very quickly . . ." Jeppe eyed his neighbor questioningly as Orla stood there with his hand on the window latch. "There's a free church on the island, Zealot's Children, and supposedly the pastor lost his daughter in an accident back in the late eighties. Have you heard that story? You know so much about the island."

"Oh yes, you don't forget that sort of thing. Now how did it go . . . ?" Orla wrinkled his brow so much, his nose crinkled. "It's up there in the porridge somewhere," he said, patting his head. "I just need to remember . . ."

"We could talk about it tomorrow."

"Didn't it happen in the Troll Forest up behind Stammershalle?" Orla lit up at the memory. Then he shook his head, exasperated. "I'm not fully awake."

"There might have been something about a, well, it sounds ludicrous, but there might have been something about a bear cave?"

"Oh yeah! That's it." Orla smiled again. "Very few people know this, even among the locals, but there are some ruins from an old zoo back behind Stammershalle Seaside Resort. In the 1930s, the hotel's owner opened a little zoo with lions and bears so the prominent guests had something to enjoy when they were tired of swimming and eating. It closed again shortly thereafter, during the war, but remnants of the bear cave are still there today." Orla interrupted his own recollections with a prolonged yawn.

Jeppe patted the old man's hand.

"We should really be getting to bed, both of us. I'm beat, too. Maybe we can talk about it tomorrow."

Orla nodded dully.

"That's probably best. Nightie night."

He pulled the window closed, and Jeppe walked the few steps over to his own front door. As he inserted his key, his neighbor opened his window again.

"Jeppe?"

"Yes?"

"Thank you, my friend."

Orla closed his window. Jeppe let himself into his place, set his boots inside the front door, and ducked to climb the low-ceilinged stairs to the second floor. He brushed his teeth, took two of the strong ibuprofens, and lay down in bed with his face under the skylight and the stars while the pills spread a comfortable numbness through his body. Maybe he should drive up to see the bear cave the next day after work. If there was any work tomorrow at all.

He closed his eyes. For some reason or other, he had a hard time imagining Louis showing up. Deep down he felt like it would suit him just fine to have another day off from logging.

An unexpected sound brought him back up to the surface. It was only a faint creaking but enough to catch his attention. She stood at the foot of his bed, her eyes shining, reflecting the starry sky over the cottage.

How had she gotten in?

He sat up in bed and opened his mouth to ask but realized that she was naked and could not speak. The moon shone on her skin.

He allowed his eyes to wander from her lips down past her collarbone, over those round breasts, and the skin of her stomach to her crotch and heard his own breathing grow heavier. He flung the comforter aside and reached out to her with both hands.

"I was starting to think you would never come."

FRIDAY, NOVEMBER 22

Esther gasped for breath. It was dark, and she didn't know where she was. She turned her head and saw daylight dawning around the edge of the blinds. An old mattress bulged underneath her, and a quilt with small flowers covered her chest. Reality slowly returned: she was in the guest room in the Dybris family's house on Bornholm.

She pushed the quilt aside and got up, slowly and with difficulty, pulled open the curtain, made the bed, and spotted the silver chain gleaming on the nightstand. Now she remembered that she had been clutching it in her hand the night before when Ida came home and found her in the darkness of the study. The shadows in the yard had been imagined, the fruit of an overactive mind.

She picked up the chain and looked at it in the morning light. A word was engraved on the back of the shiny silver.

Isola.

The shower invigorated her, and Esther caught herself humming under the jets of water. She dressed with an unexpected surge of energy and a feeling that everything would start looking up soon. Someday joy would find its space alongside the grief. Maybe it was just a momentary glimpse of hope and she had no idea where it came from, but it comforted her.

When she came down to the kitchen, Ida was already sitting at the little table eating her usual bread with strawberry jam. She looked up at Esther and smiled.

"Good morning. Did you sleep well?"

"Yes, thank you, really well." Esther sat down and accepted a cup.

"You looked like you could use a good night's sleep, too. I almost couldn't get through to you when I came home." Ida poured coffee into the cup. "I promised to say hello to you from Adam, my husband, and thank you for keeping me company. He had to stay in the city with the twins. They're in ninth grade and can't just get away. And it would have been tough for me to be here alone."

"Of course." Esther smiled in surprise. She was of some use after all. "I do have the book to write as well. Any news about your brother?"

"I went back to the slaughterhouse yesterday."

"Hedegaarden?"

"Yes, exactly." Ida wove her fingers around her cup. "Anton wasn't there when I stopped by the other day to look for Nikolaj. But he was a close friend of my mother's and has helped my brother out with jobs since he was a boy. So I thought he might be one of the people on the island who actually knew my brother. Not as a drinking buddy, but properly."

Esther nodded and remembered the initials on the box she found in the living room. AH, that must be him, Anton Hedegaard, Margrethe's old friend and lover.

"Anton fixed us some food—very touching—after all, he is getting up there. I asked him point-blank if he knew where the money in our living room came from, if Nikolaj had been involved with drugs or anything like that."

"Did he know?"

Ida took a deep breath, her shoulders rose and fell again.

"Nikolaj helped Anton get a loan. The slaughterhouse apparently has liquidity problems, and the banks won't help. So back in the spring Anton asked my brother if he knew someone . . . and he did." Ida took a sip of her coffee, and her eyes welled up.

"Know someone?" Esther looked at her, bewildered.

"A private loan, as they say, no middleman, with sky-high interest rates and no paperwork. Anton says my brother knows the guy who runs the betting at the racetrack and the pinball arcades in Rønne and Hasle. Some guy who works on the ferry during the day and loans out money on the side."

"That sounds . . ."

"Criminal? I thought so, too." Ida sighed. "Anton says that Nikolaj was supposed to repay the first installment to the ferry guy on September first. A hundred thousand kroner, cash. But he never got the money."

Esther fell quiet. The thought that Nikolaj would steal money in such a vile way from his mother's old friend was almost as bad as his disappearance.

"Do you believe him? Anton could have his own reasons for lying. Maybe you should go to the police with this?"

"I don't know, but unfortunately it matches up really well with the police finding a large sum of money here in the house." Ida rubbed her face. "My brother has always lived a little on the wild side, sort of permanently restless, but he's also a warm and loving person. And now . . . I've read the papers and can't help but think that he must be the body in the suitcases."

"Maybe it will all turn out to be a misunderstanding." Esther couldn't resist the urge to comfort her.

Ida gave her a shadow of a smile to show that she appreciated Esther's intentions but couldn't really use them for anything.

"I want to ask you about something in regard to that." Esther got up, hurried up the stairs, and unplugged her phone from its charger cable. On her way back down she found the message from Jeppe and pressed on the picture. "Jeppe wants to know if the boy in this picture here is Nikolaj as a teenager."

Ida took the phone and enlarged the picture with two fingers.

"Yes, that's him. He's so young and cute here! I've never seen this picture before."

"Who are the other two?"

"That one is Marco Sonne. They were inseparable."

"And the girl?" Esther showed her the screen again.

"I'm not totally sure, but I wonder if that wasn't Nikolaj's girl-friend? He looks like he's about seventeen or eighteen in the picture, and he was dating someone then."

Esther took her phone back and zoomed in on the screen. The girl had sky-blue eyes and a confident smile.

"That was while I was away at college in Boston, so I never met her." Ida stood up.

"Not even when you came home?"

"No. During those years, I was more preoccupied with my own American boyfriend, Brian. He was a baseball player, I kid you not. My first great love. We swore we'd stay together after my time there was up, but of course it didn't last."

Ida took her untouched plate and tossed her toast in the trash.

"Actually I never really came to live on Bornholm again, because once I came back from the US, I was accepted into the biology pro-gram and moved to Copenhagen."

She cleared the table in a few motions, putting the butter away in the fridge and the dishes into the sink. She took the dishcloth and turned around. An unexpected smile lit up her face.

"Nikolaj was the world's biggest tease when we were little, a real little comedian. He was always mocking our mother and her preten-tious friends, both the clever ones from Copenhagen and the reli-gious people from the island."

Ida twisted the cloth as she spoke. The smile crinkled the corners of her eyes.

"My favorite was when he made fun of the Sonne family's church. That would make my mother give in, too, though she tried to be the grown-up. Even Marco couldn't help but laugh. And they *were* unwittingly hilarious. The pastor, Father Samuel, held *healing sessions*, that's what he called them, for the sick and downtrodden, and Mother dragged us along to one this one time, probably mostly out of curiosity. She was an anthropologist, after all. But she should never have done that. Dorthe Sonne lay on the floor in front of the altar and was being stroked like this all over her body"—she demonstrated—"by Father Samuel, while he sang and rolled his eyes. Nikolaj and I were practically crying we were laughing so hard. After that my brother healed everything from the washing machine to the mailman for several months."

"What was wrong with her?"

"Dorthe? Some kind of cancer." Ida tossed the rag aside onto the counter and sat down. "It killed her in the end, so the healing wasn't that effective. It's nothing to laugh about," she said with a sad sigh.

"Maybe not." Esther smiled at her. "But you've got to remember the good things when you miss someone."

Ida nodded gratefully.

"I just don't understand how my cute, funny little brother ended up in two suitcases in Copenhagen. Who did he ever hurt?"

———

Bølshavn, Tuesday, March 1, 1988
Dear Argy,

Thanks for your letter. I'm sorry to hear that you've been fighting at home. But—and now I'm clearly speaking from beyond my own personal experience—isn't that to be expected after twenty years and two kids? Desirable, even? Doesn't it just show that you and Jørgen are actively committed to each other?

Until death do us part, what kind of a thing is that to promise each other anyway? Together no matter what has always meant to me that you fossilized and took root, and I honestly can't imagine anything worse. That promise goes against everything love should be: alive, flexible, curious, changeable, all of that stops with the "yes" in church.

I know you don't agree and that you may even feel a little sorry for me for being alone. And it's not always fun. To be honest, I'd much rather have someone. But not a man who treats me like a piece of furniture and acts like a child. What good would that be? I want someone to talk to, laugh with, discover the world with, and be challenged by. Otherwise what's the point?

Don't take this the wrong way. I'm not trying to rub salt in the wound or question your marriage. But maybe this crisis will lead to a revitalized and improved relationship. Not back to what it was, but onward to something new. I hope so, and I'm rooting for you.

And while we're on the subject of romance, Nikolaj is in love. He is so happy and goofy, it's very sweet. He even brings her over, and I think that means he's serious about her. Otherwise he would never let a girl meet his old hippie mom; he's surely far too embarrassed of me for that.

She's unbelievably sweet and lovely and, more important, so bright! She wants to make something of her life, travel and see the world, get an education, and have a career where she calls the shots, as she puts it. Maybe something for the UN (she apparently saw a movie), it's a little vague, but the ambition is there, and I applaud it!

Here on the island people rarely dream that big, especially not girls, and I'm always so happy when young people stand out in such a positive way.

To be completely honest, I'm pleasantly surprised that my

son has chosen himself a strong, independent girlfriend. I had
secretly feared that he would come home with a pretty airhead,
but no! There's a fire burning in her eyes.

   And Nikolaj is seriously in love with her, so wrapped up in
his emotions that I can't fathom that we don't share any DNA.
He gives himself away passionately and just blossoms in her
presence. It's so lovely to see. My brain reminds me that he's
adopted, but my heart says we're the same breed.

   Marco hangs on like a third wheel. Ack, that love!

   Take care of yourself and let me know if I should come to
Copenhagen and—what do I know?—hold your hand or make
coffee.

Yours,

M

FRIDAY MORNING THERE was a bite to the air in the woods.
Nippy, Jeppe thought, thinking fondly of his late father, who had
always claimed that Danish has as many expressions for a cool wind
as the Inuit have for snow. The cold made his skin buzz, like it had
buzzed the night before, and he smiled beneath the treetops.

   Sara had come to him in his dreams again, but this time they
hadn't wasted any time arguing. Their lovemaking had been so life-
like that Jeppe could still feel it in his body. He knew that the feeling
would evaporate quietly and leave a hollow longing, but he would
enjoy it as long as he could.

   "Louis, no?" Andrzej shot him a quizzical look and gave his helmet on the forest floor a little kick. They stood leaning against Jeppe's
pickup, waiting for their boss. Jeppe still felt pretty sure he wouldn't
show up.

   "I don't think he's coming, Andrzej. And I don't dare start without him. I think we're getting another day off." Jeppe found a pack of

cigarettes and offered his Polish coworker one. "Day off! What will you do?"

Andrzej put his hands together as if in prayer, brought them up to one cheek, and then closed his eyes for a second. Then he pulled a cigarette out of the pack and lit both Jeppe's and his own.

"Sleep? Is that what you do when you're not working? What about your family? Where are they?" Jeppe pointed to his ring finger and then rocked an imaginary baby in his arms. "Wife? Children?"

Andrzej smiled and pulled out a worn wallet. He flipped past pictures of adults and children, naming them with tenderness in his voice.

"Are they in Poland?"

Andrzej nodded and closed the wallet.

"Rosnówko."

"How long has it been since you last saw them?" Jeppe pointed to his watch. "How long ago?"

But Andrzej just nodded amicably and pointed at Jeppe.

"Familie?"

"You want to see my family?" Jeppe asked.

Andrzej nodded.

Jeppe contemplated what to show him—a picture of his mother, maybe, or of his police coworkers?

He flung up his hands apologetically and looked at his watch again. "You haven't heard from Louis, have you?"

"Perhaps . . ." Andrzej clenched his teeth in a concentrated attempt to find the right words. "Perhaps, other job."

"He has another job besides the trees?"

Andrzej mimed nailing and using a drill and pointed to himself.

"Craftsman jobs?" Jeppe asked, smiling at his coworker. "Do you go out on jobs with him after work? No wonder you want to sleep when you're off. Where do you guys work?"

Andrzej swung his cigarette around in a circle to show that they worked all over the place and then gathered his hands together in front of him as if in prayer again. This time he didn't raise them up to his cheek.

"Church."

"Which church?" Jeppe looked at him.

"Church of old boss man." Andrzej squinted his eyes. The cigarette between his fingers had burned down to the filter, but he let it burn. "Father Samuel."

Louis had had Andrzej out working on a job for Zealot's Children. How, he wondered, did God's servants pay their tradesmen? Jeppe put out his cigarette.

"Let's leave, Andrzej. He's not coming."

ANETTE TOOK A last bite of the gas station doughnut she had selected to supplement the youth hostel's modest breakfast buffet and sighed contentedly. The car smelled like fried dough and jam.

"You have a little sugar by the corner of your mouth there." Ditte smiled at her. She seemed cheerful this morning.

Anette wiped her mouth.

"It's still there. Here, let me." Ditte reached over and brushed her cheek with her fingertips. "There."

She sat with her hand hovering an inch or two from Anette's face.

Anette raised her eyebrows, surprised at the sudden touch, but just as she was about to say something funny about this motherly attention, Ditte pulled her hand back with a jerk and opened her car door.

"Well, should we get going?"

They crossed the gravel to the church's brown front door. It read ZEALOT'S CHILDREN above the doorbell. Father Samuel opened the door before they had time to ring it.

"Good morning and God's peace. Come in, come in."

He shook their hands and gave Ditte a friendly pat on the shoulder. "There's fresh-brewed coffee in the residence. It's this way."

He led them through the building, past a set of golden wood doors around to a smallish kitchen with a seventies' brown tile backsplash above the linoleum counters. An insulated carafe and three cups sat on a round wooden table under a low-hanging light fixture. The pastor gestured to the table and started pouring coffee.

Anette tried to look out a double-glazed window in the door to the backyard, but there was condensation between the panes, and it was too fogged up to see through. Somewhere nearby a radio was playing Danish pop music.

Ditte set her notebook on the table and flipped it open to a blank page.

"I was the one you spoke to yesterday when you called," Ditte said. "When did you see Louis Kofoed?"

"It was exactly eight thirty p.m., because I went in right after and watched the late TV news almost right from the beginning."

"He drove by, you said . . . ?"

"Yes, right out there on the road." He pointed. "I was just locking up the church for the night. He slowed down and drove by slowly."

"And you're sure it was him?"

The pastor nodded enthusiastically.

"Absolutely. Even though the car confused me. Louis usually drives an old bucket of bolts."

"What was he driving this time?"

"A sports car. I'm not so good with car makes, and it was dark out. But it looked nice." He raised his eyebrows.

Anette leaned forward and nearly bumped her forehead into the light fixture.

"But you still recognized him," she said. "How do you know Louis?"

The pastor looked from Ditte to Anette and smiled, as if he knew not only Louis but her, inside and out.

"Louis delivers wood to my good friend Finn and helps out in the church every now and then. I wouldn't say that I know him well, but well enough to be sure that it was him driving by last night."

"How did you know that we were looking for him?"

"Finn mentioned it. More coffee?"

The pastor raised the carafe, though neither of them had touched their cups.

Anette watched him. He was friendly and answered their questions willingly. And yet there was something cagey about him that she couldn't put her finger on.

"Did I understand correctly that your church has donated a trailer for the folks over in Allinge?"

"That is part of the Christian gospel after all, caring for your neighbors. We try to do our part for society's weak and needy."

"Nice." She smiled. "How do you finance your charitable acts?"

"Private donations," he replied without any hesitation. "Our congregation is comprised of a circle of well-resourced families with their values in order. Making a difference in the local community on the island has always been one of our main undertakings."

"If only everyone thought like that, I wonder if the world wouldn't be a better place?" Anette could feel Ditte's eyes on her cheek. "Does the church work on other projects besides charity?"

"Yes, we've been blessed with large donations, so we're building a new church. As you can see, this one is getting worn down." Father Samuel made a vague gesture toward the fogged-up window. "There's a way to go still, but we've secured the land and will be pouring the foundation any day now."

"That sounds like a major undertaking. Where will it be?"

"On a hilltop overlooking the sea a little north of Bølshavn. We've found a Dutch architecture firm to design the church. It will be exquisite, but then it's been in the works for many years."

Anette and Ditte looked at each other.

"We won't take up any more of your time. But if you see Louis again, could you please let us know?" Ditte passed a business card across the table.

"Of course."

"Oh, by the way, what did he do for the church?" Anette asked as she stood up. "You said that Louis has been helping out. Doing what exactly?"

"He repaired some of our pews and spackled the walls behind the altar. And we got the patio put in last summer." The pastor stood up as he answered.

"Out here?" Anette walked closer to the fogged-up window and tried to see out into the backyard.

"Yes." Father Samuel opened the door and let them out into a large backyard with a campfire pit, tall grass, and a stone patio with tables and benches for a good-size summer camp.

"When the weather permits, we move our devotions out under God's heavens."

Anette walked out onto the patio. It was neatly done, formed of large, square, concrete pavers, a functional but by no means extravagant solution. She felt relatively confident that the church would be able to present a bill for the work that was done. There was no sign of dirty dealings, and yet something was troubling her. Maybe the pastor's willingness or the fact that he had called them so promptly yesterday after having supposedly seen Louis.

She stopped and stuck her hands in her pockets. The November cold bit at her cheeks. When she turned around to return to the kitchen, she noticed that the concrete paver shifted underneath her. She took a step backward and tried again, moving her weight forward and then again. Sure enough. The paver wobbled.

CHAPTER 20

North of Gudhjem on one of the prettiest stretches of coastline in the world lies the Stammershalle Seaside Resort, which gazes out on the Baltic Sea. With its high gables and bright yellow facade, it looks like a historical landmark from an era of lords and ladies and servants and bathing costumes for both sexes.

Jeppe parked in front of the main entrance and knocked on the white double doors. Glass panels revealed that the lights were off inside, but Jeppe could see a man walking around, cleaning, and knocked again. The man saw him, turned off his vacuum cleaner, and opened the door with a friendly smile that showed he didn't mind the interruption.

"Are you here for the job interview?" he asked, and gestured Jeppe to come in. He was under thirty, blond, and had the kind of rosy cheeks typical of people who sleep eight hours a night and never worry about anything. Behind him a white wooden staircase led upstairs and, along with the striped wallpaper, emphasized the seaside hotel aesthetic.

"No, I . . ." Jeppe stopped. It was easier to barge in when he was on official business. "I'm sorry for showing up unannounced. I didn't realize you were closed. I'm doing some genealogy research here on Bornholm, and I came across a story about the hotel that I'd really like to have confirmed. Do you have five minutes?"

The man looked at his watch.

"I'm expecting an applicant for the job of sous-chef in about five or ten minutes, but if we can wrap it up before then?"

Jeppe nodded.

"Let's go into the lounge." The man shook his hand. "I'm Per. I own the hotel, along with my wife." He led the way into a pretty room with high wood panels, antique wicker furniture, and a panoramic view of the rocky coastline and the water.

"We took over the place five years ago, so we're still new, but I do know a little about the hotel's history. Have a seat!"

Jeppe sat down in a wicker chair, which groaned beneath him, and scooted to the front edge of the seat so he wouldn't break through.

"I've heard rumors that the hotel had a zoo back in the 1930s. Is that true?"

"Yes, it definitely is." Per nodded. "Almost a hundred and ten years ago a German wholesaler named Mecklenburg converted Elverhøj Tavern into Stammershalle, and in 1934, he put in a little zoo so the fancy guests from Berlin wouldn't get bored. It was very impressive and decadent, I can assure you. Six acres of land with monkeys, deer, all sorts of birds, and badgers. People came here in droves to see the wild animals." He pointed up at a shelf below the ceiling, where a small taxidermized lion cub was gathering dust on a stand.

"The wholesaler even bought lions and bears. The lion cub up there is from that era. I don't know how or why it died. That remains a mystery."

Jeppe glanced at the shaggy lion cub and heard the echo of a song lyric run through the back of his mind. *"And I'm a bad boy, 'cause I don't even miss her. I am a bad boy for breaking her heart."* He quelled the music by clearing his throat and turned to face Per.

"When did the zoo close?"

"Didn't take long. The war put an end to tourism, and the feed became too expensive. So by 1940, the fairy tale was over. But you can still see what's left of it, if you go into the woods behind the hotel."

"The Troll Forest?"

Per nodded.

"Just follow the path to the left, and you'll get there."

"Thank you so much for your help. It's a really amazing place you have here." Jeppe rose tentatively from the wicker seat. "I imagine the hotel's more recent history is probably exciting as well. Any interesting guest or . . . events?"

"For sure!" Per laughed in agreement. "But then you'll have to ask someone other than me. Like I said, we haven't been here that long and I've only memorized the hotel's origins. And the part about the zoo, well, because it's a good story. I trust you can find your own way out?"

Jeppe followed a path along the facade into the edge of the forest and suddenly found himself in another world. Where the seaside hotel lay bright and windblown at the water's edge, the forest behind it was dense, the treetops crowding out the sky, and perfectly silent.

The path branched into several smaller ones that curved around the hills and disappeared into the foliage. Vines climbed up the trees and fallen trunks lay, slowly disintegrating on the forest floor. It looked almost like a temperate rain forest, it was so lush, even in the middle of November. It was clearly called the Troll Forest for a reason.

Jeppe tripped on overgrown rock formations twice and thought he had found the ruins of the zoo both times. But after walking for five minutes he encountered a shape that was too symmetrical not to be man-made, a poured-concrete wall about three feet tall running between the tree trunks and forming an oval enclosure that was about thirty by fifty feet. The ninety-year-old concrete was covered with moss and ivy, and cracks shot across it like bolts of lightning through the gray surface.

Jeppe approached it. The area inside the wall had been excavated, and it was about ten to twelve feet down to the bottom. A rock formation towered up in the middle of the oval and you could easily imagine a bear climbing around on it. Plants that had likely started as cuttings had now grown out of control throughout the bear exhibit. The woods were working at their own pace to reclaim the German wholesaler's monument to human frivolity.

This was where the pastor's daughter had died thirty-one years ago. According to Camille, she fell into the bear cave and was eaten by the wild animals.

He looked at his watch. It was almost ten thirty in the morning already. Orla was bound to be up and somewhat refreshed now. Maybe he remembered more about the pastor's daughter's tragic death.

Jeppe turned around and walked back to his truck. In time with his footsteps, a line from a song grew in the back of his head and became a chorus that reverberated against the treetops and his temples.

"And I'm free, free falling."

"ARE YOU FAMILIAR with the Karl Skomager case?" Anette propped her elbows on the roof of the car so she and Ditte were eye to eye.

"Not off the top of my head. Why?"

Anette turned to look over the fallow fields. They had pulled the car over just past the little village of Årsballe, a ten-minute drive from the church.

Her excuse was that she needed to clear her head. In reality, she couldn't quell the anxiety boxing around her body. Sitting buckled in behind a steering wheel felt like wearing a straitjacket. Her chest was quivering again in an uncomfortable way, and she was having trouble calming down. The feeling wasn't unfamiliar. It cropped up sometimes when she was in the middle of an investigation. Usually, she would take the dogs running on the beach, and that took care of it.

But her unease had gotten worse after she had had Gudrun. Not that she experienced it more often, but the way it felt had changed. Before she would have described it as tension, but now she was forced to admit it was anxiety. Anxiety about messing up, anxiety about not being enough.

"Karl Skomager went to his summer house to repair a few things and vanished without a trace. Twelve years later they found him buried under his own patio. Do you know what tipped them off to the idea that he was there?"

Ditte shook her head.

"The pavers, they wobbled. As the body decayed, it created empty space that made the patio unstable."

"Are you trying to tell me that there's a body under the church patio?" Ditte raised her eyebrows skeptically. "We've already got an unidentified body, and now you're saying we might have another one? Who would it be?"

"No idea."

"I wonder if it might not just be shoddy craftsmanship. Maybe the dirt just settled or something like that. You get what you pay for."

Anette looked down at the car's metallic blue roof and tried to gather her thoughts, but they were racing in so many directions it made her feel dizzy.

"What I'd really like to know," Ditte continued, "is why Louis Kofoed was driving a sports car."

Anette rubbed her temples with her fingertips.

"Okay," she said. "For now we're working on the theory that Nikolaj was murdered and his body put into his mother's old suitcases. And we know that he and Louis Kofoed were friends."

Ditte nodded.

"The money ties them together. Forty-four thousand euros in a black bag. Where did they get it from?"

"Maybe that's where the donations to Zealot's Children come into the picture? Who actually manages their money; is that something you see somewhere?"

"Well, I can certainly click through to the Ministry for Ecclesiastical Affairs' home page. I'll try if we have cell coverage here." Ditte pulled out her phone and started typing on the screen, mumbling to herself. "It seems to be an investment group in London."

She furrowed her young forehead in the pale winter light.

"Were they stealing the free church's money but then Louis got greedy and liquidated Nikolaj?"

"I don't know. This case feels like climbing Mount Everest and then discovering another mountain behind it." Anette shivered. "Let's get going. Do you mind driving?"

They switched places, and Ditte started the car and turned on her seat warmer. Anette sat with her phone in her hands, trying to breathe calmly. It didn't help. A text message arrived from Svend that Gudrun was healthy again. They had been to the playground, where she jumped on the trampoline until she collapsed. As Anette was partway through an emoji response to him, her phone rang. It was from Copenhagen.

"Hi, Falck. What's up?"

Pause.

"Are you there, Falck?"

"Ah, did it go through? I couldn't hear you." Falck sounded like he was rubbing a piece of sandpaper over the microphone. "Is the connection bad on your end?"

"I'm on Bornholm, not on the moon," Anette laughed wryly. "Is there any news?"

"We found something on the surveillance video from the camera in front of the grocery store at Esplanaden . . ."

"Wait a second, Falck. I'm going to put you on speakerphone so our colleague from over here can listen in." Anette put the call on speaker. "Okay, Falck, go ahead!"

Pause.

"Falck? We're ready."

"Are you there? Bo Tjørnelund has reappeared. He turned himself in at Station City yesterday for theft, had been hiding in São Paulo. His parents even went there on vacation to see him."

"Seriously?!" Anette sputtered. "So Saidani was right after all."

Falck joined in, laughing from the phone's speaker.

"Hey, Werner, tell me: What's worse than a shark with a tooth-ache?"

"Falck, remember, you're on speakerphone!" Anette smiled apologetically to Ditte.

"A turtle with claustrophobia!" His laughter echoed through the car. "And what's worse than a turtle with claustrophobia?"

He waited but got no response.

"A millipede with athlete's foot!" Falck laughed again but only briefly. Then he ran sandpaper over the microphone again and cleared his throat.

"Well, okay. We've been through the footage. The camera caught a delivery van that stopped and parked next to the Citadel right by the old Resistance museum at two forty-seven a.m. on August thirty-first. A figure takes a suitcase out of the van and carries it over to the moat. It could well be our suitcase. At three twenty-one a.m., the person returns empty-handed and drives away."

Anette gave Ditte a thumbs-up.

"Okay, Falck, that sounds promising. Can you determine the person's identity from the footage?"

"Unfortunately not. But we have a very clear picture of the van. It's one of those with a company name on the side."

Anette hit the dashboard. Finally, a concrete lead!

"Where's it from?"

"From Bornholm, wouldn't you know it? A place called Hedegaarden. It's a slaughterhouse."

Bølshavn, Tuesday, July 19, 1988
Dear Argy,

Do you remember how you normally poke fun at me, saying that it's tough being a new you because the old you always stands in the way? Trips you up every time you try to take a step?

That's how it is for Nikolaj. And before you say anything, yes: that's how it is for all of us, but no one more so than my son. Every time he tries to wipe the slate clean, reality catches up to him and everything turns to shit. Yes, shit!

Is it a male thing? A disastrous testosterone-laden trajectory through life?

Heaven knows, Ida's never been like that. Not that she's easy and sensible, God forbid, but her barometer in life has always been steady. No matter how much we argue and how unreasonable she can be, I'm never nervous about her landing on her feet. But with Nikolaj that's all I am. It's his self-preservation instinct that's missing, his ability to take responsibility. It's always someone else's fault.

This last year has been so good! Having a girlfriend has made all the difference, Nikolaj has made an effort and grown along with his love. He's become a man. He's attended his classes at school and worked for Anton, done his homework, and hasn't been late a single time. He's happy to be earning his own money, proud when he can take his girlfriend out to eat.

We've had fun planning his eighteenth birthday, which will be held the Friday after his actual birthday. We drew up the seating chart together, booked a musician, and agreed on the party games.

The couple who run the Stammershalle Seaside Resort (Mik and Jonna—you met them when we had lunch up there last summer) gave us a great price to hold the party there even though it's right in their high season. I'm still going to have to borrow some to afford it, but Nikolaj himself has offered to chip in.

I've been thinking that he was finally developing some responsibility and maturing. I've been hopeful.

Until yesterday.

He came home last night, earlier than usual, pushing his moped the last part of the way. He doesn't usually worry about waking up the whole neighborhood. I could tell from his hunched shoulders that something was wrong the second he walked into the kitchen. Ironically enough I had time to pray that it wasn't about money because after I sent Ida off to Boston with a little spending money, we had only the small savings for his birthday party left. But it wasn't about money.

Nikolaj stood there for a long time without saying anything, couldn't look me in the eye. My heart sank.

"Mom, I screwed up," he began. His eyes welled up and his voice trembled. "She's pregnant."

At first I couldn't respond. I walked right past him out into the yard and stood in the grass until my slippers were soaked and his words finally sank in. The manifestation of my failed motherhood—my son, an uneducated teenage father and future societal loser. I should have hugged him, reassured him, comforted him, but I was too shocked—I raised my children to travel, see the world, and educate themselves, not to be teenage parents—it seemed like an admission of failure.

I've calmed down a little now, and we've discussed it. I would prefer that she have an abortion, and I think Nikolaj would, too.

But she doesn't want to.

Or to be more precise: she can't. My son with his usual care
selected a Christian girl, who's neither allowed to date boys nor
depart from God's will. Naturally her family is furious about the
pregnancy and the teenagers' promiscuity. I tried to get them to
talk about it, but in vain. They clearly consider us pariahs, not
to say heathens, and aren't even willing to enter into a dialogue
about the young people's future. There's only one path, and that's
marriage.

Nikolaj says that of course he'll marry her, that he loves her, and
that the whole thing will probably all work out. I look into my
son's blue eyes and am divided between the urge to comfort and
help him and to slap him silly until he wakes up. All the things
he doesn't know. The sleepless nights, the schooling, everything
that needs to be sacrificed so you can support the family, a difficult
future. I so wish I could hug him and make it all go away.

Bornholm has been a sanctuary for us for fifteen years, a home
filled with sunlight and the sea and room to breathe. But now
our lives are under a looming threat from a medieval view of
humanity. We are going to have to expand our family to include
people who despise us. Not just for our (lack of) faith and for
Nikolaj's lack of self-control, but for our whole lifestyle. Me as a
single mother, an academic, and independent woman.

I have no idea what the future will bring, but right now I
want to cancel the whole thing. The eighteenth birthday, summer
vacation, life.

Dark thoughts, heavy clouds.

M

THE CARS DROVE in a line like a funeral procession down the pot-
holed dirt road past fields and little tracts of woodland, past pastures
of sheep and cows, until Hedegaarden came into view. Anette sat

behind the wheel in the first car with Ditte at her side and a jittery feeling in her chest. They hadn't spoken for the last twenty minutes.

The cars behind them contained a total of four crime scene investigators from the local Investigations Unit. Anton Hedegaard had grudgingly granted them permission to collect some samples on his property, assuming they were gone again by lunchtime.

His acquiescence had caught Anette by surprise. She had figured they would be forced to obtain a warrant first. Now she was afraid he might have had time to change his mind.

As they approached the farm, she saw Anton standing under the big European ash, the tree that towered in front of the entrance to the farm. Even though its branches were bare, they still bore a shadow of summer's leaves and flowers as an invisible reminder of the life that came and went. Besides the old butcher, the courtyard was empty and unusually quiet. No crows cawing, not a single *baa* from the sheep running free in the fold. Anton looked relaxed, waiting for them with his shirtsleeves rolled up to his elbows.

Anette shivered at the sight. It couldn't be more than about forty degrees out. Standing outside without a coat seemed to send a message, almost a bizarre sort of power display.

The phone vibrated in her pocket. It was Jeppe calling.

He would have to wait.

She turned off the car and glanced over at Ditte, who nodded resolutely, ready and excited.

They got out and let the crime scene investigators catch up before continuing over to Anton under the tree. Six people assembled in a small group. If that made an impression, he didn't show it, just stood there calmly watching them.

"Hi, Anton," Anette began. "Thank you for letting us come by on such short notice. We're here to—"

"To take some tests, yes, I'm aware," he interrupted. "Although I am curious to hear what the reason is."

Anette and Ditte had intentionally avoided telling him the reason for the visit so as not to risk his doing anything to the van before they arrived.

"Your slaughterhouse van was captured on surveillance footage in Copenhagen the early-morning hours of August thirty-first near the location where a body was found. Our technicians would like to examine the van for evidence. And the slaughterhouse. While they do that, perhaps we could sit down somewhere and have a chat?"

He smiled, as if she had said something funny. Then he pointed over to the slaughterhouse.

"The van's around back, behind the building. It's unlocked. The door to the slaughterhouse is open as well. We just cleaned in there, and I would appreciate your leaving the place in the same condition. Food safety hygiene inspections are no joke."

He started walking toward the farmhouse. Anette and Ditte exchanged a glance and followed him.

They walked right into a country kitchen, where the light was on and a radio played soft pop music. As in most of the old farms, the ceilings were low and the windows small, but the kitchen was warm and smelled faintly of freshly baked bread. A place where you would cozy up with a wool blanket and a good book.

Anton pulled a chair out by the worn wooden dining table and indicated that they should have a seat.

"What is it that makes you think our van has anything to do with a murder?"

"The location where the body was found," Anette replied, and then asked him a question. "Do you deliver meat to any restaurants in Copenhagen?"

"A few, yes."

"Where are they located?"

"Let me see . . ." Anton sat down and placed his big palms down flat on the tabletop. Like a parody of a man who has nothing to hide.

"We deliver to Pakhuset in Christianshavn, Brasserie Bon Ami on Esplanaden, and to Gorm's Garage on Øster Farimagsgade. Fresh meat and smoked products. Most of our sales are to the restaurants here on the island, we don't have the capacity for more, even if the demand is there." He held his chin up with pride.

Anette's pulse was racing. Øster Farimagsgade was right behind Østre Anlæg Park, where the first suitcase was found. The whole thing fit together.

"As I mentioned, the van was spotted on Esplanaden in the early hours of August thirty-first. Does that match with a timing of a delivery?"

"If one of the days was a Friday, then yes. We regularly deliver to Copenhagen every Friday."

"Who drove the van?" The adrenaline made Anette's voice high-pitched. A name—they just needed a name.

Anton ran his tongue over his teeth.

"I thought I had explained how many people work here in the summertime. The deliveries are made by whoever has time that day. It could have been Nikolaj, Mads the intern butcher, or André, who's the oldest son from the farm next door. I can't remember off the top of my head."

"But there's a record of that somewhere?"

"Well, we do have payroll records and that sort of thing, but as for who does what when, we don't keep records of that. Every summer the island is swarmed with tourists, and we just run around trying to keep up."

"We'd like to see your payroll records," Ditte interjected. "Everything you have in writing about your employees."

Anton turned his head and looked at her with a small, surprised smile.

"You'll need to get ahold of my bookkeeper, then. I've never been good at that kind of paperwork, so she's got all of that."

"Could you write her name here for us?" Ditte took out her pad and pen and pushed them both across the table.

Anton took the pen and bent down over the paper. He wrote slowly and carefully, like someone who's not comfortable writing.

"These are hard times," Anette said.

"What's that supposed to mean?" he asked, looking up from the notepad.

"The accounts are public," she said with a shrug.

Anton narrowed his eyes slightly and was about to say something, but cleared his throat instead and bent back down over the paper.

They heard a knock on the door, and one of the crime scene investigators peeked in. He had removed his mask but was otherwise covered in a disposable white outfit, gloves, and a hood.

"Could we just borrow you for a second?"

Anette nodded to Anton and got up. Ditte accepted the notepad back from him and followed.

They walked across the courtyard over to the slaughterhouse. The crime scene investigator explained on the way.

"We have two men working on the van. It hasn't been cleaned that well, so there's a lot to be learned, lots of fingerprints and traces of blood. The challenge will be separating the various clues and getting them analyzed. The slaughterhouse is another matter. It gets hosed down every day and cleaned with professional-grade cleaners. We're taking samples anyway, but I wouldn't count on our finding anything. Put the shoe covers on before you go in!"

He opened the door and led them into the cool, tiled interior of the slaughterhouse and over to an open lift, where another crime scene technician stood seven feet up in the air.

"I thought you should see this."

The crime scene technician in the lift tilted a top-mounted saw down into a horizontal position and turned it on. He yelled over the noise: "It's used to cut up the larger animals. You hang them up by their hind legs and divide them with a saw." He turned off the saw. "We'll take pictures and make a molding of the saw blade and send it to Copenhagen so they can see if it's a match. It seems like a possibility, don't you think?"

Anette looked up at the blade, at all the stainless steel around them and the practical floor drains. Yeah, this did seem like a possibility.

CHAPTER 21

Orla opened the door and squinted in the stripe of daylight that fell on him. He looked older and a little frail in a flannel bathrobe that hung open around his skinny neck and made him look like he had shrunk.

"Hello, Jeppe. It's a surprise to see you in the middle of the day." A concerned look crossed his face. "Why aren't you at work? Is something wrong?"

"Not at all. I just wanted to have a cup of coffee and a chat with you about the pastor's daughter."

He waited, but Orla looked blank.

"The pastor's daughter, who fell in the bear cave up by Stammershalle."

"Oh, right, right, of course. I'm sorry, just let me clear away my lunch. Come in and I'll put the coffee on. The kids need feeding as well."

Orla disappeared into his little kitchen. Jeppe took off his jacket and walked over to the cages. Rats lay in piles, sleeping. A few were climbing, running, or doing something, which to his untrained eye resembled play. Girls in one cage, boys in another, Jeppe thought, they've got it all worked out.

"Come and get it!" Orla opened the lids to the rats' cages with some dry-looking feed pellets in his hands. The rats immediately crowded together by the bars.

"They're very fond of food. They'd probably prefer nuts, but this whole-grain diet is healthier for them."

Jeppe watched him feed his pets, petting and greeting each rat individually. He might be old and a bit confused now and then, but as long as he could tell his rats apart and remember their names, things couldn't be that bad.

Orla took his time doling out the pellets, going to great pains to be attentive to the feeding. Jeppe heard the coffee machine beep and brought cups and a pitcher of milk into the living room while Orla washed his hands.

"You'll have to live with my not having gotten dressed today. Luckily I look dashing in a bathrobe." Orla laughed and accepted a cup of coffee from Jeppe. "Plus I got out the scrapbook last night when I woke up and couldn't fall asleep again." He sat down in his chair, which seemed to close in around him so they looked like one combined organism.

"What scrapbook?"

"Ketty liked to keep up with things. When I would sit with my nose buried in a book, she would read the paper or listen to the radio. I've always said that my wife should have been a journalist, she was so interested in the news. Ketty subscribed to a multitude of different newspapers and magazines, and she would cut out articles and paste them into scrapbooks."

"Your wife was like a forerunner of the internet?"

"Ketty was ..." Orla took on a faraway smile. "You were never bored when you were with her." He bent down and picked up a worn three-ring binder off the floor. On the cover a white label read *1988*.

"Well, like I said, I couldn't sleep last night, and while I was lying there, tossing and turning, it occurred to me where I had seen Nikolaj Dybris as a young man. Voilà." Orla pronounced the French word so it rhymed with boiler. He flipped through the scrapbook until he found what he was looking for and showed the entry to Jeppe.

The headline read: "LOCAL GIRL DIES AT PARTY AT STAMMERSHALLE RESORT."

Jeppe skimmed the short article and read that an ambulance and the police had been summoned to a birthday party at the seaside hotel on Friday, August 12, just before midnight, where they found a seventeen-year-old girl had succumbed to death following a tragic fall. There were no other details, and the article didn't include any names.

"What does this have to do with Nikolaj?" Jeppe asked, and shrugged his shoulders at Orla in confusion.

"That's what hit me last night!" Orla tapped the tip of his pointer finger against his temple. "Look at the next page!"

Jeppe turned the page in the scrapbook and found himself looking right into the eyes of the same young man he had seen in the picture in the trailer, Nikolaj Dybris, smiling and with a silver ring in one ear and hair that was long in back. It looked like a school photo that had been printed in the newspaper.

"That party was Nikolaj's eighteenth birthday party," Orla explained. "He and the other guests were questioned afterward."

"Nikolaj Dybris, Margrethe's son?" Jeppe felt like two cables had just connected in his brain, sending sparks flying. The blond girl in the picture of the teenagers was Father Samuel's daughter.

"It was his party, you see. Some of Margrethe's Copenhagen friends had come over on the ferry, but otherwise the guests were mostly local. The family from the sawmill was there, and Nikolaj's friends, of course. And his girlfriend. She was the one who died."

Orla blew on his coffee and drank cautiously before setting his cup down again.

"It was a hot summer that year, some of the kids went down to the water to bathe, others went into the woods behind the hotel. That was where she was found, in the bear enclosure. She had hit her head on the rocks and bled to death."

"Who found her?" A chill ran down Jeppe's spine.

"Nikolaj did. It says so in the article. He went down to the water to sneak a smoke, and when he came back to the party, she was gone. First he chatted with his friends over a beer, waiting for her to come back, but after about fifteen minutes, he started looking for her."

"But," Jeppe protested, "what made him go into the woods and look down into the bear enclosure?"

Orla's eyes opened wide.

"A lot of other people wondered that, too. He said he couldn't explain it, that he was trying to find her and he ended up at the bear cave."

"That sounds weird . . . had he been drinking?"

"They probably all had. Young people back then were allowed to drink alcohol along with the grown-ups."

"Wasn't she the pastor's daughter? Was she allowed to go to parties and get drunk?"

"People figured she lied to her parents. Those religious girls are always the worst." Orla blinked sadly, closed the scrapbook, and set it back down on the floor.

"Be that as it may, the police questioned the guests, investigated the case, and concluded that it was an accident. But there were rumors. Her parents were convinced a crime had been committed."

"A crime?"

Orla nodded and said, "Her father was beside himself with rage."

Jeppe pictured Father Samuel, the affable, smiling man.

"What did they think had happened, then?"

"Rumor was that Nikolaj pushed her to her death. I've never believed that. Why would he do that?"

Jeppe looked down into his coffee with milk. Orla was right. It was hard to believe that a teenage boy would decide to push his girlfriend to her death. But if the girl's father believed it, he obviously had a reason for hating Nikolaj, maybe even murdering him.

He had to get in touch with Anette.

"I remember that she had an unusual name." Orla got up and walked over to his bookshelf, scanning the shelves with his nose only an inch from the spines of the books. "There it is! *The Con Man*. It's been years since I last read it. Are you familiar with Ed McBain?"

"No, but I know someone who is." Jeppe pictured Father Samuel standing in the doorway to the church. "Why?"

"The books are set in a fictional city that's supposed to be New York. The pastor's daughter had the same name as the city, a weird name. Isola."

ESTHER SET DOWN the letter and stretched in the uncomfortable office chair. She felt the beast of grief move as it always did when reading about an unwanted pregnancy. The wound never healed. Annoyed at her own fragility, she got up and walked away from the table, in need of some distraction.

Ida had taken the car to Svaneke to buy groceries for dinner, and Esther was on her own. Esther stretched again and let her back relax gratefully, then yawned and felt the oxygen bringing her brain renewed energy.

If Nikolaj had gotten his girlfriend pregnant, then where was she now? Where was the baby? Ida hadn't mentioned anything about being an aunt.

Esther's eyes landed on the poster from the Bornholm sawmill, which hung next to the bay window. It showed a red building surrounded by trees and tall grass. It was quite faded, its corners warped from many years of damp. There was a word on the facade of the building, written in white capital letters. She walked closer and smoothed the poster so she could read what it said. *ALMINDINGEN*.

Esther took a step back. She recognized that place. Maybe from childhood vacations to the island or something she had seen in a newspaper.

She decided to open a bottle of red wine. After all, it was time to quit work for the day. She went to the kitchen and glanced at the bag of empty bottles on the floor behind the door.

Maybe it was okay to drink wine every day after your best friend just died? Maybe not. There was always some occasion, something to celebrate or a reason to seek comfort. When I get back to Copenhagen, she promised herself, *I'll lay off the wine!*

As she unscrewed the top of a bottle of Shiraz, she remembered where she had seen the red house on the poster before. It had been in the picture she had studied on her phone over breakfast. It was the backdrop for the three young people she now knew were Nikolaj, Marco, and maybe Nikolaj's girlfriend.

Maybe the Almindingen sawmill had been a regular hangout spot for the teenagers? Could that be important?

Esther found her phone, took a picture of the poster in the scant afternoon light and wrote a quick text to Jeppe. *And the girlfriend was pregnant*, she added, just before she hit Send.

"COULD THE SLAUGHTERHOUSE be our murder location?" Anette asked, and then immediately rephrased her question. "I mean, of course it could, in theory. And the tests will hopefully show whether the van has any connection to the murder. What I'm really asking is this: If the slaughterhouse is our murder location, who is our murderer?"

She looked around at the local Bornholm detectives in the open-office landscape. The crime scene technicians had kept their coats on, still cold from working in the refrigerated slaughterhouse. Two detectives who had not been out to the farm had also joined them. Ditte sat next to a male coworker who looked like he was twice her size. Almost like they were father and daughter. Despite that, Ditte radiated a focused authority. When she spoke, no one tried to interrupt.

"We know," she said, "that Nikolaj had a large amount of money lying around in his house. Presumably Louis tried to retrieve that money a few days after Anton was acting threateningly outside his apartment."

"We also know," Anette interjected, "that Hedegaarden is having major financial difficulties and they've exhausted their loan options."

Ditte nodded.

"Without knowing the exact details," Ditte said, "I think Anton involved Nikolaj and possibly also Louis in some sort of shady attempt to raise money, but something went wrong. Maybe one of them got greedy, and then Nikolaj ended up in two parts in the suitcases."

"If so, it was Louis who put him there, because Anton Hedegaard is almost eighty and wouldn't have been able to overpower him."

"Did anything turn up on the surveillance footage from the ferry or the airport?" Anette asked, looking around at the team.

One of the local detectives snapped his fingers and got up off the desk he was sitting on so everyone could see him.

"We've been through everything from the last few days with no result. But when Detective Vollmer"—the local detective nodded over at Ditte—"asked us to check the ferry for the slaughterhouse's van on one of the last days in August, then we got a hit."

Anette nodded to Ditte and mouthed the words *good thinking*. Ditte smiled at the floor.

The detective held up a laptop and showed them the screen. A picture showed the vehicle deck on a ferry, where the cars were parked close together. Hedegaarden's white van sat squeezed between two passenger cars.

"The van was on the eight thirty a.m. sailing on Friday, August thirtieth, from Rønne, and returned the next day on the first ferry from Ystad, at eight thirty a.m."

"That matches the delivery Anton Hedegaard claims took place. We need to check with the restaurants in question . . ."

Ditte gave Anette a slight nod.

"That's been set in motion."

"Okay, good." Anette turned back to the detective with the laptop. "Can you see the driver in any of the surveillance footage?"

"Yes."

"Yes?!" Anette got up and walked over to him. "Well, let's see it then!"

"The image is very grainy, and the person is wearing a cap," the detective hurried to say as he pulled up another image with the driver standing behind the van, his back to the camera.

The body looked like a man's, broad shoulders and narrow hips, and he was wearing cargo shorts and a long-sleeved T-shirt with a little rainbow at the back of the neck. Beyond that, the picture didn't make them any wiser.

"What we'll do now is look through the footage from the rest of the ferry for those two sailings. Maybe we'll spot him in the café line or on deck somewhere."

"You're saying we could have an identification by the end of the day?!" Anette could almost have kissed him.

"If we're lucky. We'll do our best."

"And your best is a damn sight better than anything we could pull off in Copenhagen. Nice work!" Anette slapped him on the shoulder, and he nearly dropped the laptop before he sat back down, blushing.

"Then we just need to confirm that the body's teeth match Nikolaj Dybris's. The forensic odontologist promised results no later than tomorrow." Anette nodded contentedly.

"Um," one of the crime scene investigators, who was still wearing his jacket, said with a sniffle. "I don't know if it's relevant, but we were just talking about something in the car ... something about Louis Kofoed."

"What was that?" Anette sat back down. The restlessness had returned to her body, but this time it was the good kind, tension.

"Well, one of the guys I play soccer with, he's an electrician, and he did some work at a house in Hasle a couple of years ago, for Connie Kofoed."

"Sausage Connie?" Anette's voice struck a blow.

"Uh, yeah," the crime scene investigator confirmed hesitantly. "My friend pulled some cables for her. The job took a little over a week, and she was home and really chatty while he worked." He raised two fingers to his mouth and drank from an invisible bottle. "She said that when she was young, she worked at the Østerlars Sawmill and had an affair with the boss. I don't know if it's relevant, but according to her, Finn Sonne was Louis Kofoed's father."

Anette's brain short-circuited. What the hell was up with these little island communities, where everyone knew everyone, and they were all interconnected this way and that? She got up.

"I need to make a phone call. Get a cup of coffee, people, smoke, do whatever you need to do, and we'll reconvene back here in ten minutes."

Anette walked over to one of the office's dirty windows and looked out at the parking lot. If Finn was Louis's father, then what, if anything, did that mean for the case?

She pulled out her phone. Svend had sent a picture of Gudrun, and Anette was struck by a longing so powerful it was like a horse kicking her right in the liver, the kind of blow that left her unconscious on the ground.

She took a deep breath.

Ditte popped up beside her and put a hand on her shoulder.

"Everything okay?" Ditte asked.

"Yeah, thanks." Anette laughed at herself. "Having children makes you a complete mess, just so you know. One big quivering blob of Jell-O."

She smiled at Ditte, who stayed close to her without moving her hand.

"Do you have someone at home? A partner?"

Ditte looked over her shoulder before answering.

"There was someone, but it's over now. She stayed behind in Rødovre when I moved out here, so now I'm alone." She held the eye contact and smiled shyly.

Anette felt the heat rising in her cheeks. Just as she was figuring out how to respond, she was interrupted by a ringtone. She took the call, answering with relief.

"Is that you, Jepsen?"

"It's Clausen."

He exhaled through his nose so it made a whispering sound in her ear.

"Latest news," Clausen announced. "We found traces of rust on the cutting surface on the body. Actually so much that we can definitively say that the saw blade that sliced our body in half was darn near rusted through."

"But . . ." Anette protested, "there aren't any rusty saw blades at the slaughterhouse. The food hygiene inspection folks would close the place down in an instant."

"I have no idea what slaughterhouse you're talking about, and for good reason. But if there's no rust on their saw blades, then the murder can't have happened there."

CHAPTER 22

After Jeppe had called Anette four times without success, he got in his car and drove to the police station in Rønne instead. The pastor's daughter's death didn't necessarily mean anything for the case, but Anette had to be made aware of all the factors. Besides, he didn't have anything better to do.

The drive to town felt unexpectedly good, even if the car was cold and the road dark. Having a goal again, an urgent necessity.

Just after he passed through Hasle, Anette finally called back. Jeppe pulled over and took the call.

"Hi, Kørner. Sorry I couldn't get back to you until now. We were busy at a crime scene that turned out not to be a crime scene after all."

"Damn it."

"Yeah, pretty much. I thought the murder had been committed at the slaughterhouse, but according to Clausen, the saw blade used was rusty, not clean. What's on your mind?"

Jeppe heard a car pass by, its taillights glowed in the dark before it turned a corner. His pickup was parked along the shoulder; through the window he could see the first stars over the western coast.

"Okay, the short version is that thirty-one years ago Nikolaj's girlfriend was found dead in the woods at his eighteenth-birthday party."

"Dead how?"

"She fell down in an old ruin. The police closed the case as an accident, but rumors flourished afterward. The girl was Father Samuel's daughter, Isola, and apparently he was convinced that Nikolaj had pushed her to her death."

"But," she sighed, "that was a lifetime ago."

"It might still be worth talking to Father Samuel about Nikolaj."

Anette sighed again.

"Surveillance video from Copenhagen places the slaughterhouse's van at the location where the body was found, so we're focusing on Anton Hedegaard and Louis Kofoed right now. But you're right," she conceded, "that is a good motive for murder. Especially such a brutal killing. I can ask the local unit to look up the case. What year did you say . . . ?"

The connection was lost, and the call turned to static.

"Anette?"

The call had been dropped. Jeppe called her back but couldn't get through. He looked at the clock on the dashboard. It was only four thirty in the afternoon, and he had a whole evening ahead of him to play with the building blocks of loneliness. Dinner for one. TV for one. Single toothbrush by the sink. The escalating abuse of painkillers. How had he once again managed to paint himself into a corner, where no one needed him? If he dropped dead, would he melt into the carpet before he was found?

He gave up on calling Anette and saw that Esther had sent him a text with an image. He opened the car window and lit a cigarette while he read it.

And the girlfriend was pregnant.

Jeppe's stomach churned. Had Nikolaj wanted Isola dead to get out of his predicament? And didn't that only strengthen Father Samuel's motive of revenge, if he had lost both his daughter and his unborn grandchild?

Jeppe flipped back and forth between the picture of Margrethe Dybris's poster from the Almindingen sawmill and the old photo of Nikolaj and his friends. Esther was right. He opened the browser on his phone, cursed the island's sketchy cell coverage, and searched for *sawmill in Almindingen*.

Sure enough, it turned out there was an Almindingen sawmill. A family business for three generations and one of the most productive, most prominent sawmills of the island right up until 2006, when it closed. Pictures showed that its ruins were still standing, waiting to be sold off and broken up into building lots for summer homes right by Bornholm's famous Echo Valley. Jeppe had never heard of the place before.

If one wanted to find a rusty saw blade, what better place to look than a defunct sawmill? Not to mention, it was a place where Nikolaj and his friends had gone when they were young.

Jeppe wrote back to Esther and said he would investigate the place right away, then turned his car around and switched on the radio. The melancholy he had felt before was temporarily on hold, he realized, shaking his head at the bearded face in the rearview mirror. Equal parts melancholic and complete idiot.

South of Hasle he turned off onto a road that ran inland, heading for the woods in the middle of the island. He was having a hard time getting his bearings in the dark, took a wrong turn, and had to go back. He got out of the car and walked all the way up to a road sign before he was sure which way he wanted to go. Finally, after a good half hour, he turned onto a small road that led from Almindingsvej to Ekkodalen and rumbled along over its granite roadway.

When Jeppe saw lights off to his right, he slowed down. That must be the forester's house, and as far as he could tell from the map, the sawmill should be right across from that. As he looked out to the left, he saw black shadows against the dark blue sky. That could certainly be a derelict sawmill.

He pulled over and got out, letting his car door slam. The sound spread through the darkness, like a bird taking flight. He took his high-powered flashlight from the pickup bed and stepped over the barrier telling unauthorized people to stay away.

The grounds were completely overgrown, the grass already knee-high a few yards from the roadway, and the bushes thick and wild. He shone his light on a thicket that turned out to contain what was left of an old building. One whole wall had collapsed inward and the ceiling fallen in and was lying on top of the floor in piles of broken roofing tiles and rubble.

He walked on, got caught on a blackberry bush, and continued around a large hole in the ground, which was only partially covered by rotting planks. A chimney rose in the distance behind the trees. The grounds seemed enormous.

Jeppe passed more empty buildings with broken windowpanes and moss-covered steps. They looked like old office buildings, and none of them seemed like they would contain a saw.

The thicket opened up into a large clearing, which could be the area where the sawmill had stored and processed logs. On the far side of the clearing there was a building much bigger than the others. An old door underneath two windows gaped open in the facade, making it look like the building was yelling, *Stay away!*

Jeppe walked closer.

Inside the cavernous old building was a jumble of old machinery. There were tracks and ties and large metal constructions that he couldn't name. In some places there were holes in the machinery, as if someone had removed the most valuable parts and left the rest. Tool hooks were mounted on the walls with little tags over the empty spots and the few items that were still hanging there were rusted beyond recognition.

He proceeded into the building. The ridge of the roof rose thirty feet over his head. He tilted his head back and looked up at the rafters, which were struggling against decay and gravity. The space had atmosphere, like a cathedral.

His toe hit a set of tracks on the floor. The saw must be right nearby. As he walked on, he heard a noise behind him. A crunch in the gravel, two quick footsteps. Then everything went black.

Bølshavn, Saturday, October 8, 1988
Dear Argy,

I wake up every morning thinking I've had a nightmare. I lie in my bed and feel the relief wash through my bones, giddy with happiness. Then reality hits me like a bucket of ice water.

Isola is dead.

Not even the faithful disciples of Jesus with their well-intended prayers can bring the dead back to life. No matter how we try to focus our energies or think positively, it won't change the situation. That's how it is with death. It was like that when Dad died, too, but then there was a naturalness to it. Ceremonies we could lean on when we were feeling blue.

This time it's not like that.

The funeral went well, as far as I was informed. I wasn't allowed to go. None of us were, and that rejection hurt to an extent that I don't have the words to describe. The accusations are unspoken, but I feel them anyway, can sense how our little family is being ostracized. The never-ending police interrogations don't help. They arrive unannounced and sit in the living room or pick us up in the patrol car. They ask the same questions over and over again.

We can't talk about it at home. It's too difficult, and besides, I'm afraid of what answer Nikolaj would give if I asked him straight-out.

So I keep my mouth shut, pretend like I don't listen to the gossip spreading like a wildfire, and isolate myself in the house. I duck when Mrs. Agger looks my way over the hedge, and I ignore the For Sale sign at Finn's place across the street. He is standing shoulder to shoulder with Father Samuel and hasn't spoken a word to me since the birthday. But people won't get the satisfaction of seeing me hanging my head. It's bound to improve at some point, time is on my side. I hope.

For now a feeling of apathy is spreading. Fatigue has settled in my spine, I have to drag myself out of bed, and the letters swim on the pages of the books, so I can't read. I take a morning dip, as I usually do, and try to eat, sleep, and live. I thank the god I don't believe in that Ida is studying in Boston and won't be home until New Year's. If she ever comes home to the island again.

My only hope is to get her back to Denmark so she doesn't fall in love with an American and start a family over there. She dates, of course, as she calls it, as a young woman of twenty-two should. In her latest letter, she sent pictures of her host family and classmates. They all look so clean and have such white teeth. Ida has gained some weight and smiles with rounded, happy cheeks. She's enjoying herself, and I'm glad, even though it bothers me a little when she writes about "my family" and means the American one.

And Nikolaj? My hand grows weary at the thought, lets go of the pen, and doesn't want to write anymore. He is talking about applying for an apprenticeship position with the carpenter in Svaneke, and I don't know if I should play along with his fantasy or not. Is a mother's job to build her child up so he thinks that the world will accept him—no matter what he does—with open arms and love him?

*Reality isn't like that. The carpenter won't accept him, and
there probably isn't anyone else who will now, either.*

*And the question is whether Nikolaj would even be able to
complete an internship in the first place. He's holding his head
up high, but I suspect that's for my sake. I can hear him crying
through the wall when he thinks I'm asleep.*

*My love wasn't enough to prevent this disaster, and it's also
not enough to heal the wounds in its aftermath. Bornholm is
turning against us. Our home has become an enemy. As you can
hear, from where we stand right now, it's not far to the bottom.*

We're decimated.

Yours,
Margy

ANETTE HAD TO go back to the shared office and inform her
Bornholm colleagues that the slaughterhouse wasn't their murder
location. It was Friday afternoon, and the results from the crime
scene investigators' blood tests from the van wouldn't come back
until Monday. No reason to put off the weekend unnecessarily. The
workday was over.

The only detective who stayed in the office was Jakobsen, who
had taken upon himself the task of watching the ferry's numerous
surveillance recordings from the morning trips on August thirtieth and thirty-first in the hopes of being able to identify the van's
driver.

Jakobsen sat in one of the private offices playing back the tapes
frame by frame as he studied every single person who was on the
ferry on the two sailings they were interested in. Man, cap, long-
sleeved white T-shirt: that was all he had to go by.

As long as Jakobsen was working, Anette saw no reason to go
anywhere. Ditte picked up burgers for them and stayed, too. Even

though the van's connection to the murder hadn't been proven yet, the potential identification of its driver seemed like their best shot at a breakthrough in the case.

Anette crumpled up the food wrappings around mayonnaise and salad remnants and tossed the ball in a neat arc into the trash. Svend wrote that they would stay in Kerteminde until Sunday night, and she replied that she missed them and meant it with every fiber of being.

There was something about being on an island out in the sea that made her feel fundamentally alone, both in terms of this case and life in general. It was neither rational nor reasonable, but she couldn't stop the feeling from popping up again and again.

"Here's some reading material for you!" Ditte tossed a thick folder onto Anette's desk.

"I found the Isola Ratsche Jensen case in the archives. So we'll be ready if we need to question Father Samuel."

Ditte pulled her desk chair over, removed the thick rubber band from the file, and opened the folder. On top there were photos of the bear exhibit and the surrounding woods. Eight of them showed the body of Isola lying on the floor of the enclosure, brightly lit by the photographer's flash. She was wearing a blue, knee-length sundress, her blond hair in a ponytail. The blood spread over the rocks like a dark halo around her head. The rest of the pictures showed the cave, the concrete wall, and the surrounding woods and must have been taken at dawn because the light had returned.

"Who the heck decides to build a zoo on Bornholm?" Anette pointed to one of the pictures. "She can't have tripped over that wall, it's too high for that, and the edge is rounded, so it's not exactly the sort of thing you'd balance on."

"Maybe she was sitting on the edge?"

Anette shrugged.

"The report doesn't offer any comments on how it happened but still dismisses the case as an accident, although not until nine months later. See here: closed May 2, 1989. There must have been some doubt."

Ditte browsed through the typed report.

"Here's the autopsy report. Method of death: accident. Cause of death: cranial trauma with subsequent hemorrhage. No bodily trauma other than the fall. She did not have any alcohol or drugs in her blood."

"Wow," Ditte said, turning the report over. "She was sixteen weeks pregnant!"

"As if her death wasn't tragic enough on its own."

"Hmm ... according to her father, Isola always wore a necklace with a cross on it, but it wasn't on the body when they found her."

Ditte browsed further through the interview notes. The vast majority of interviews had taken place the same night and in the days immediately following the death on August 12, 1988, but one person was questioned again and again, up until April 1989, just before the case was closed.

Nikolaj Dybris.

"They think he did it," Anette exclaimed. "They weren't able to prove it, but they hoped he would confess if they pressured him enough."

"Look at this: questioned Margrethe Dybris. That's his mother, isn't it?" Ditte flipped further through the notes. "She was questioned at the station on August 14, 1988, and again September 5, December 5, and one last time on February 10, 1989."

"It makes good sense. Cases like these *need* to be solved, especially when they take place in a small community where everyone knows everyone else." Anette gasped, suddenly short of air. "You can imagine how awful it was for the Dybris family."

"Yes, why didn't they move off the island after that?"

Anette smiled at her young colleague.

"Not everyone can just run away from their problems."

She flipped through to the last page in the report.

"Concluding note from May second: 'The case is being closed and considered resolved. *The survivors have expressed a desire for continued discretion.*' What does that mean?"

"That Father Samuel didn't want people to know Isola was pregnant," Ditte replied dryly. "For a fundamentalist religious family probably the only thing worse than losing a child is losing her virtue."

"Isn't that a bit hyperbolic?"

"Is it?"

Anette's phone rang, and she checked the display.

"It's Forensics in Copenhagen." She hurriedly answered. "This is Werner."

"Hi, it's Nyboe. I got the dental results back. The forensic odontologist compared the body's teeth, to the extent they were preserved, to the X-rays taken by Nikolaj Dybris's dentist."

"And?" Anette's pulse throbbed so strongly in her neck that she put two fingers up to it.

"Teeth, as you know, are remarkably durable. Fillings, crowns, cracks, and bridges, those sort of things paint a wonderfully accurate picture of a victim, making it possible for us to say with a hundred percent certainty."

"The hell, Nyboe, is it him?"

Nyboe hesitated for a second.

"No, the teeth don't match. We can definitively state that the body in the suitcases is not Nikolaj Dybris."

CHAPTER 23

It was the noise that roused him. A rhythmic throb, the sound of riding a night train through Europe. Jeppe tried to ride along with the dream. On his way to Rome, waking up in the sleeper car, and eating breakfast with a view of Brenner Pass. But the back of his head hurt, and the pain kept him from sleeping.

His eyes were stuck shut, and when he tried to wipe them, he discovered that he couldn't move his arms. He was tied up.

The pain from the back of his head radiated to a point behind his forehead and down his spine, making it hard to think. But it also made it clear that he was awake and that the noise he was hearing was real. Where was he? What had happened?

Jeppe tried to focus. He had been driving and had parked his car in the tall grass. The sawmill! Those dilapidated buildings by Ekkodalen, it slowly came back to him. He braved the pain and raised his head so he could look down toward his feet. He forced his eyes to open by blinking them again and again and finally spotted the source of that infernal noise.

Band saw. Turned on.

The blade vibrated in the air only a yard away. He was tied to an enormous tree trunk that was moving steadily toward the saw, as if someone were cutting boards lengthwise off the trunk. But the blade was fixed eight inches above the top of the log, set to hit a different target.

Jeppe yanked at his hands and felt that whatever was holding him wouldn't let go. Panic played tricks, but his only chance was to keep a cool head. He was lying on his side like a sacrificial lamb. His wrists were tied together with a zip tie and secured with a rope to some point on the log that he couldn't see. One ankle was bound the same way.

"Help!"

No response.

"You don't have to do this! Turn off the saw and let's talk about it."

Jeppe raised his free foot and let his safety boot drop down onto the plastic zip tie around the bound ankle. Maybe if he kicked hard enough he could break it. He jammed his heel down onto his bound ankle again and again and heard something break, but a stabbing pain told him it wasn't the zip tie.

White light behind his eyes, the saw pulsing, he yelled for help again, louder than before, yelled until his voice disappeared.

The saw was nearing his feet, and he pictured the blade hitting his body, the blood and the irreversible damage to his flesh. The lonely death.

My mother will be unhappy, he thought. *And Sara.* As the blade neared the sole of his shoe with a whine, he decided that she would be his last thought. Sara.

ANETTE WAS ANGRY. Unjustifiably, childishly angry and disappointed. They had built up their case around the wrong victim, and they still didn't have the correct identification for the body.

She walked out on to the back steps of the police station and punched her fist into the wall, the way she had as a teenager when her body couldn't contain her feelings. In a minute she would go back inside into the office, look Ditte in the eye, and come up with an action plan. They would build the house of cards again, sort through the evidence and figure out which way was up and which was down.

Where was Nikolaj Dybris?

Anette punched the wall again and had to double over to cope with the pain. "Come on," she mumbled, straightening up. "Come on!" She punched again with the same hand. The knuckle of her middle finger hit the crumbling plaster, her skin tore, and blood trickled out.

"Damn it!" Anette stuck her knuckle in her mouth and tasted her own blood, slumped down to sit on the step, and tried to calm down. She was in charge, and she couldn't let herself lose control. The responsibility weighed on her in a way she hadn't anticipated. It reminded her of becoming a parent and discovering that she was now the grown-up in earnest.

Okay. She took a deep breath, exhaled, and repeated until she felt light-headed. Even though the body wasn't Nikolaj, he had been missing for three months. The suitcases, the van, the money, he must be involved in some way. What did they actually know about him?

That he worked for the slaughterhouse and was friends with Louis Kofoed. That he had a reputation for drinking, stealing, and disappearing, sometimes for extended periods. That as a teenager he had gotten a girl pregnant and then was subsequently accused of killing her.

She pulled her phone out and called Jeppe. A gentle voice informed her that his phone could not be reached. Anette swore at the crummy phone network and dialed him again. Same message. She sent a text and asked him to call right away. Today of all days she could definitely use his intuition.

What now? She couldn't go back into the office and look her young coworker in the eye without a plan, some straw to clutch at.

Anette searched through her call log. One thing she could do at least was tell Ida Dybris that her brother was not lying in the medical examiner's office in two halves.

She scrolled down to Wednesday night, when she had called Ida to arrange a meeting, found the number, called, and heard it ring. No one answered.

MAYBE IT WAS the saw approaching his shoe soles, maybe the thought of Sara, but the second the blade squealed, Jeppe decided that he was going to live. He lifted his free leg and hammered the steel-reinforced safety shoe down onto his bound ankle again and again. If he could hit the zip tie enough times to break it, then he could free his leg and get down from the log and safely away from the saw.

Jeppe raised his foot and smashed it at his left ankle until his bones broke and blood was pouring out. The pain was unbearable.

I have nothing to lose, he thought, and roared as loudly as he could. He felt the blade make contact with his boot the very second the zip tie gave way.

Jeppe yanked his knees up, away from the saw. His hands were still bound, and he could barely see. The blade advanced closer; he could feel it vibrating. He had no choice but to jump down onto the floor on the side where his hands were tied and hope for the best.

He jumped.

His leg collapsed beneath him; he tipped over and was left hanging by his wrists. The mother of all pain burned in his ankle, the back of his head, and his wrists. But he was safe from the saw.

He carefully got up onto his knee and leaned all the way in, right up close to his hands, so he could vaguely make out the rope that held the zip tie to a hook in the log. A simple half hitch as far as he could see.

He held the knot with his fingertips and grabbed hold with his teeth. The log kept moving and pulled him along, but he tried to breathe calmly and just focus on untying the knot. Push, bite, push again. The knot loosened and came undone. He was free.

Jeppe rested his forehead on the floor inhaling sawdust and blood.

He was alive.

His breathing grew calmer. He sat up and rubbed his eyes until they were free of the dried blood, and he could see again. With great difficulty, he got up onto one knee and held his wrists to the saw until it cut the zip tie around them with a snap. He looked around and recognized the derelict sawmill that he now knew must be the scene of the murder. It had almost become his own.

He patted his pockets: No phone. Tried to get up into a standing position but collapsed again. How was he going to get away from here with a broken ankle?

Jeppe glanced at the saw that was still rumbling along. Now that he could see it, it was very seriously clear how horrible it would be to die here.

There were boards and wood scraps on the floor next to him. He found two short pieces of wood, which he placed on either side of his broken ankle, and tied them with the rope that had previously held his bound wrists to the log. Then he gritted his teeth tightly, leaned against the log for support, and got up.

The pain was monumental, but so was the relief. He was going to make it. He just had to limp back out to the street now and ring the bell at the forest ranger's house. He could summon help. A trip of three hundred yards, he could do it. He had to do it!

Jeppe took the first step and buckled over. He threw up on the floor, wiped his mouth, and clenched his fists. When he had stood on the leg enough, the break would start to numb itself. Wasn't there something about that?

He took another step and put his feet together, stood for a moment and then moved his injured leg forward and leaned on the machinery. It hurt the least that way. *I think this will work; I can handle this*, he muttered to himself and took yet another step.

"Where do you think you're going?"

The voice behind him sounded surprised and angry. Jeppe turned around and wanted to slap himself. To think that he hadn't realized it sooner! He glanced at the cleaver, which hung heavily pointing down toward the floor, and heard his own hoarse voice.

"You?!"

"SHOULD WE CALL it a day?"

Ditte sounded just as beat as Anette felt. It was six o'clock, and the last two hours had brought them nothing but defeat. Detective Jakobsen was still sitting in his little office reviewing the surveillance footage from the ferry but had warned them that his eyes had about had it.

Anette looked at her phone for the tenth time in as many minutes. No calls, no texts. She called Jeppe again. The number still could not be reached.

She dialed Ida's number instead and let it ring. Just as she was about to hang up, she heard a voice.

"Hello?"

"Ida?!" She practically yelled.

"Who am I talking to?"

"Sorry, this is Anette Werner from the Copenhagen Police. I stopped by your place yesterday with my colleagues ..." Anette could hear her restrained breathing and hurriedly kept going.

"We just received the results back from our forensic odontologist. The body in the suitcases is not your brother."

A long pause followed. Anette let it grow in her ear and resisted the urge to proceed with her own agenda. *You're the grown-up*, she reminded herself.

"But naturally we're continuing the investigation. And the search for Nikolaj."

"Okay . . ." Ida sounded far away.

"It must be hard to take this in," Anette acknowledged. "I'm so sorry to bother you, but Jeppe Kørner doesn't happen to be there by any chance, does he? I need to get in touch with him."

"No, I'm afraid not."

Anette heard the call be disconnected. She searched in her contacts, found Esther's number, and called.

"Hello?"

"Hi, Esther. It's Anette Werner. I'm sorry to bother you, but do you know where Jeppe is? I can't reach him."

"He's probably on his way to the sawmill."

Anette straightened up.

"Østerlars Sawmill, you mean?"

"No, not that one. We found an old picture of Nikolaj in front of a place called Almindingen, which it turns out is a sawmill. Jeppe texted that he was going to drive down there and take a look at it right away."

"The Almindingen sawmill, you say?" Anette looked over at Ditte, who started typing on her keyboard. "So maybe that's why I can't get through to him. If you hear from him, ask him to call me!"

"I certainly will. There's nothing wrong, is there?"

Anette pretended as if she hadn't heard that, said goodbye, and hung up. Then she looked into Ditte's eyes.

"Could that be something?"

"It definitely could!" Ditte grabbed the car keys and got up from the desk.

"It appears to be a disused sawmill in Ekkodalen. It's a perfect fit for the profile of our crime scene."

Anette got up. What the hell was Jeppe up to? If he was trying to solve this case behind her back, the next thing she smashed her fist into wasn't going to be the wall.

She ran after Ditte down the stairs and to the parking lot.

The old police Mercedes's suspension left something to be desired, and Ditte was not stingy with her lead foot. Anette grabbed the panic handle and allowed herself to be swung around the turns and over the hills.

"What happened to your hand?" Ditte asked, glancing at her.

"Just some eczema. Are we almost there?"

The distance between the houses grew, and it was even farther between glimpses of light before Ditte turned down a side street that led toward the forest. The darkness was intense, like the taste of strong coffee, and left Anette's stomach feeling the same way. Damn it, having kids turned her into a real softie!

"Isn't that Jeppe's car? There!"

Anette didn't see the pickup until they were right next to it.

"He must be in there in the bushes."

They parked and got out. Ditte switched on a powerful flashlight, and Anette checked her service revolver in the hopelessly outdated shoulder holster that she insisted on carrying.

"This place is wild," Anette whispered. "It looks like something right out of a horror movie."

Ditte ran her light over the dilapidated buildings and shivered.

"And right here in Ekkodalen, which is crawling with tourists all summer. I've never been here before, never even heard of the place."

A bird flapped over their heads, and they paused to listen to the silence that followed. Something about the overgrown rubble brought back Anette's childhood memories from Karlslunde, all the abandoned farms around town that she and the other children could go play in. Her earliest experience of being a detective and exploring the world on her own.

"Look, there's a light!" Ditte turned off her flashlight and pointed at a large, barn-shaped building a hundred yards ahead of them. Sure enough, a faint light shone from its open doorway.

"Is this our crime scene?" Anette asked, stooping under a thorny branch without waiting for a response.

They crept closer, stepping carefully. At the door they positioned themselves against the clapboard wall, so the light from inside wouldn't give them away. They heard voices, soft but snarling. Anette looked over at Ditte. None of the voices belonged to Jeppe.

Slowly, as slowly as she possibly could, she leaned forward toward the open doorway and peered in.

A large space full of disused machinery, dusty and in disrepair. The voices spoke again, but Anette couldn't see them. They must be standing somewhere amid all the machines, hidden by the tracks and metal boxes.

She pulled out her gun, nodded for Ditte to follow, and quietly slipped inside.

As they approached, the noise level grew. It sounded as if an argument was brewing.

"That was *not* what we agreed! For fuck's sake!"

"What the hell are we supposed to do? He just suddenly waltzed in here. What else are we going to do with him?"

Anette got down on her knees and crawled on all fours toward the light and the voices, hidden from view by the battered sawmill machinery.

Behind her, Ditte did the same.

Her gun clicked against the floor, Anette changed her hold and kept crawling. Her hand hit sand and screws, pebbles and puddles of sticky fluid. Through an opening between two metal boxes, the source of the voices came into view.

Anette lay down on her stomach and wormed her way into the gap so she could see better. Two men, one tall with a cap and a blond, gray-tinged full beard and a shorter one with dark hair and bad teeth.

The tall one stood holding a cleaver in his hands. Jeppe was kneeling in front of him with his eyes closed.

Anette swore to herself.

Jeppe's face was bloody. He looked like he had been beaten half to death. Were they too late?

"There's nothing else to do!" the one in the hat yelled, raising the cleaver over his head. "I'm not fucking going back to jail. Are you?"

Jeppe opened his eyes and raised his face toward his executioner. Even through all the blood, filth, and the ungroomed beard, Anette recognized her partner. Her inflexible, sensitive, fucking irritating partner under a raised cleaver. He was still there. His eyes flashed.

The shot sounded before she had time to think.

Jeppe collapsed and landed on his side, the cleaver dropped to the ground, and the dark-haired man set off at a run.

"What's going on?" Ditte yelled from behind her, but there was no time to explain.

Anette wriggled forward through the hole and into the circle of light. The man with the cap swore and grabbed his shoulder, blood pouring down the filthy T-shirt that must once have been white.

"Police! Put your hands where I can see them!" Anette got to her feet and raised the gun in one, almost fluid gesture, but when she was standing, sighting along the barrel, the man was gone.

"Help me up, damn it," she heard from the floor. "They ran that way."

Jeppe was crawling around himself, trying to stand up.

Anette grabbed his armpit and pulled.

"Are you okay, Kørner?" She could see that he was far from okay. But she knew him well enough to know that it wouldn't stop him.

"Nikolaj tried to saw me in half down the middle, otherwise I'm fine. Come on, we must catch them before they disappear again!" Jeppe tried to support himself on his injured leg.

"Who's the other one?"

"Louis Kofoed." He spat on the floor and gritted his teeth in pain.

Ditte reached them and cast a shocked look at Jeppe's bloody face before she switched on her radio and summoned help.

Anette hesitated. Did she dare leave Jeppe here alone while she and Ditte pursued the men?

Or should she run out into the wilderness on her own?

She had only two seconds to decide.

Right then they heard the roar of an engine, and the light from a pair of headlights swept across the building's hole-ridden clapboard wall.

Anette ran to the door and looked after the car, which was bumping along the rough path to the road. The taillights wobbled red in the darkness. Between them on the silver-colored finish, Anette recognized the characteristic italic logo of a Porsche Boxster.

CHAPTER 24

"Get the car and drive it down here!" Jeppe tossed his car keys to Anette. "Your colleague stays here and waits for reinforcements, the two of us go after them."

Anette gaped at him open-mouthed.

"My pickup is an off-roader, and I have an idea where they're going."

"But . . . your leg," she protested.

"You're driving. Come on, Werner, they're getting away!"

Anette hesitated a second, then set off at a run. A minute later she pulled up in front of the door.

"Hop in!"

He hobbled into the passenger's seat with considerable difficulty.

"I swear, Kørner, if you fuck this up, I'll saw you down the middle myself."

Jeppe braced himself on the car door. His pain was drowned out by the surge of adrenaline rushing through his veins, amplified by a seething fury. He had survived!

These little aches were nothing a good bandage and a shot of morphine couldn't handle. But he wasn't going to allow those assholes to get away! He was going to catch them if it was the last thing he did.

Anette floored it. The car bumped through the rough terrain and threatened to get stuck several times, but she maintained her speed and got them onto the side road in one piece, turned toward the main road and headed north.

"Where are we going, Sherlock?" She changed gear and accelerated.

"Allinge."

"How do you know that's where they're going?" Anette turned left in third gear, so the wheels came up off the road.

"I don't *know*, but we're on an island. They can't leave without flying or sailing. And you can't fly without a license. They must have a boat ready and waiting. Hurry up now, otherwise they'll lose us!"

Anette broke into a laugh.

"After all these years of being sensible and rational, you turn out to have a fiery temperament after all. Who saw that coming?"

The woods became open plains, the moon appeared from behind the cloud cover and lit up the fields. It looked almost divine.

"It's a hunch," he admitted. "But Allinge is in the north, so it's close to the Swedish coast. Plus Louis lives in Allinge, and he must have been the one who arranged their escape."

Anette handed her police radio to Jeppe.

"Tell Ditte Vollmer so she knows where we're going. I really hope you're right!"

"Yes, otherwise it would be . . . unfortunate."

Anette laughed again.

"Exactly," Anette said, laughing again. "*Unfortunate* is the word."

While Jeppe half shouted their destination into the radio, she let go of the wheel for a second and fished her gun out of the holster.

"If Nikolaj just tried to kill you, then whose body is in the suitcases?"

"My guess is the owner of the Porsche we're following, Marco Sonne."

"But he's alive, isn't he?! I don't know how many people have talked to him lately. His own family!" Anette slowed down a little through the dark village of Klemensker and then sped up again on the other side.

"Have they?"

Anette gave him a look.

"Maybe people have only been texting him . . ."

"If Nikolaj has Marco's car, I suppose he could have his phone, too, and be sending texts as Marco."

Anette opened and closed her mouth again without finding the words she was looking for.

"But . . . he has coworkers and friends in London. Wouldn't they notice if the man suddenly went missing for several months?"

"Not if they got a text or an email from Marco that he had to extend his stay on the island," Jeppe suggested. "Nikolaj knows him well and surely also his contacts in London. It wouldn't be hard to come up with a plausible excuse. That his dad was sick, for example. No one would question that."

"My head is spinning." She brought her hand to her head. "I have so many questions; I don't even know where to begin."

"Well, let's catch them, so we can get some answers!"

Anette sped up even more. The narrow country road flew under the car and disappeared behind them. The countryside gradually opened up, becoming barer—heath and sand instead of trees, and rocks instead of grass. When the road reached the shore, small painted houses began to appear as a warning that they were coming up on the little harbor town of Tejn.

"Slow down. I'll keep an eye out! There are three harbors along this stretch: Tejn, Allinge, and Sandvig. If I'm right, they'll be in one of them. They probably haven't turned on any lights, so they'll be hard to spot. On the other hand, they'll be in a hurry, and when people are in a hurry, they make mistakes. Maybe they haven't had a chance to hide the car yet."

"Yes, boss!" Anette quipped and rolled down Jeppe's window for him with a sarcastic little bow.

The harbor was dark and deserted. A couple of fishing boats, a sailboat covered in tarps, and an empty bench under a streetlight.

Jeppe squinted and scanned the marina.

"Everything looks quiet here. I think it's empty. Let's go to Allinge!"

Anette sped up again, and they covered the three miles north in under five minutes.

"Do you see anything?"

"Slow down. We're going too fast!" Jeppe's knee fidgeted nervously under the glove compartment. "Hmm, there's hardly any boats in the water, and they all look completely deserted."

"Are you sure?"

"No, for crying out loud. Are you?" He waved for her to keep going.

Anette pulled out of Allinge and on toward Jeppe's own little marina in Sandvig.

He stared at the coastline with a sinking feeling in his body. If he was wrong, if Louis and Nikolaj had driven to one of Bornholm's other numerous marinas, then they would soon be out on the water and on their way into nothingness.

They passed the coast's fashionable Hotel Nordlandet and came to the minigolf place, where Anette turned down onto Jeppe's small street that led to the Sandvig Marina. He automatically noted that the light was on at Orla's place and was taken aback at how the world could still function normally while he and Anette were in the middle of complete collapse. Just before they reached the bottom of the hill, he spotted the car.

The silver-gray Porsche was the only car in the little parking lot, left between two spots.

Anette pulled up the parking brake and turned off the engine, raised her Heckler & Koch in a silent greeting, and got out.

Jeppe watched her disappear down the hill and realized too late what a precarious situation he had put them in. She was on her way down to face two desperate men by herself, while he remained passively behind in the car with a broken ankle.

Not on his watch! If a ballet dancer could perform a three-act show with a broken toe, he could help his partner with an arrest.

He opened the glove compartment and found the utility knife he used in the woods. The small knife blade was completely inadequate, but he had nothing else to defend himself with.

The door to the pickup opened quietly and he supported himself on it as he got out. He listened but couldn't hear anything from the marina 150 feet ahead. Just waves lapping and seagulls crying.

He glanced at the bed of the pickup and saw his chain saw along with rope, wedges, and all his other forestry equipment. Without a thought, he took the chain guard off, lifted the saw out of the truck bed, and held the business end out in front of him.

He knew what the men down there were capable of. If he and Anette were going to stand a chance, they needed to show them what they were capable of.

What was *he* capable of?

Jeppe walked down the hill. He forced himself to leave all his doubts behind in the car along with his pain and walked the short stretch with only one thought in his head. That Nikolaj and Louis could not be allowed to escape. As he reached the wharf, he heard yelling from somewhere on the jetty to the right and spotted them.

Jeppe sped up.

A lone streetlight dimly lit the small marina and revealed two men standing in a black dory on the water. Louis was struggling to start the outboard motor at the back of the boat, while Nikolaj was trying to push off from the stone jetty. On a ladder leading down from the wharf to the surface of the water, Anette was hanging on with one arm, aiming her service revolver at them with the other.

"Damn it, don't force me to shoot!"

The motion was lightning-fast, and because it came from an unexpected direction, she didn't manage to fend it off. Louis swung something that looked like a mooring fender and knocked the gun out of Anette's hand. It flew in an arc out over the black water and vanished with a splash.

Louis turned back to the motor and got it going with one angry motion. Nikolaj pushed off from the jetty, and the boat pulled away.

Jeppe passed the ladder, where Anette was making her way back up, and proceeded down the uneven surface of the wharf. He turned on the chain saw and pulled out the utility knife. Louis was right, it wasn't the least bit hard to block the chain break with the blade so the saw kept running on its own.

He broke into a run. He didn't notice his leg, didn't hear his heart pounding, just ran with the saw roaring between his hands. The dory was sailing along the jetty, in a minute it would be out on the open water.

Jeppe forced himself to speed up, proceeding toward the harbor's long breakwater. The saw was swinging in front of him, his leg pumping, he tasted blood. Behind him he heard the sound of sirens approaching.

He caught up to the boat in only five paces. With the last of his strength, he raised the saw and threw it out over the side. It fell, rumbling with mechanical rage, and landed heavily in the bottom of the dory, where its rotating blade kept spinning, forcing the men up onto the boat's railing. When first a chain saw is going, it's hard to stop.

They screamed at each other, each from their own end of the boat. Louis was the first to lose his balance and hit the water. His fall started the boat rocking, and Nikolaj started flailing and flapping his arms. For a second he looked like he was going to make it, then he, too, went overboard and vanished below the surface of the water.

IN LATE NOVEMBER the water temperature in Denmark is about forty-two degrees. The sea isn't so frigid that you risk hypothermia for the first hour or so, but it's enough to make you seriously cold after only a few minutes.

Luckily Ditte Vollmer had taken Jeppe seriously and sent first responders up to the northern coast with the instructions to search the ports. They reached Sandvig Marina half a minute after Nikolaj Dybris fell in and promptly started swimming out toward the open waters. It didn't take more than five minutes before two officers in a boat picked him up.

Louis came ashore voluntarily and let them wrap him in Mylar blankets as he glared at Nikolaj and denied having anything to do with the case.

Jeppe was taken to Bornholms Hospital's emergency room where the wound on the back of his head was treated with six stitches and his broken ankle and fibula put into a boot cast.

Anette drove him home afterward, helped him into bed, and made sure that the painkillers were working and that he was half asleep before she snuck out of the room.

Before she shut the door behind her, he whispered, "Werner! Are you going back home tomorrow?"

She opened the door again and peeked in.

"Yes, I think so."

"Will you give me a lift?"

Jeppe lay there with his eyes closed and his foot elevated on a pillow, looking like he was already far away. Anette couldn't help but smile.

"You'd better believe it. Sleep well!"

By the time Anette reached the police station in Rønne, Nikolaj Dybris and Louis Kofoed were dressed in dry clothes and waiting in the interrogation rooms. The station only had two, so it was lucky that they weren't unraveling a larger crime ring.

Ditte sat at her desk updating the reports, but when she spotted Anette, she got up right away and waved the printout of a picture.

"Jakobsen found this shot of Nikolaj on the ferry. So now we have evidence that he was the one who drove the van to Copenhagen. I thought you and I could question him, and let our colleagues handle Louis. Okay?"

"Okay!"

"I talked to Camille Sonne and asked her to call her brother's contacts. She only had the number for his office, but they were able to help us on from there. So far we've reached his landlord and two employees. They all say the same thing: Marco never came home to London after his summer vacation. He told them his father was sick and he had to stay on Bornholm. No one has spoken to him since the end of August, just email and text messages."

"Have the crime scene investigators found anything at the sawmill yet?"

Ditte nodded.

"Marco's telephone, computer, and wallet with his passport, driver's license, and medical insurance card."

Anette took a deep breath and determined that the anxiety in her diaphragm had been replaced by the sense of satisfaction that she normally associated with her work. The result of holding the guilty accountable so justice was served and the victims could achieve peace. This time the feeling was flanked by pride. They were at the finish line, and she was the one who had brought them there. With a little help, to be sure, but she was at the helm.

"Shall we?" she said, clasping her hands together.

Nikolaj sat alone at the table in the little interrogation room. Earlier he had turned down the offer of a lawyer saying, "That's not going to help," and now he sat with his cap in his hand, looking like a beaten man.

His gray-tinged blond hair and beard probably hadn't seen the shadow of a pair of scissors in months, and the skin on his neck was dull with grown-in dirt. A crumpled paper cup sat next to him from the coffee he had said yes to when they arrived at the station.

"Hi, Nikolaj. I'm Anette Werner. I'm with the Homicide Department in Copenhagen. This is Detective Vollmer. We'd like to ask you a few questions."

"Yeah, yeah, yeah. Just get on with it already," he broke in, his voice tired.

"And you're aware that we're recording this conversation on video and you have also been informed of your rights as the accused?"

"Yes, damn it."

Ditte set the photo from the ferry on the table.

"Can you see who that is?"

"It looks like me."

"It *is* you. Taken on the ferry to Ystad, the eight thirty sailing on August thirtieth. You were driving a van from Hedegaarden. Where were you going?"

"I was probably delivering something." He shrugged. "I deliver meat to the restaurants in Copenhagen."

Ditte set a new picture in front of him. It showed the van on Esplanaden and the driver, who was taking a suitcase out of the back.

"This picture was taken that same night. Is this also you?"

"I can't tell."

"The suitcase wasn't found until more than two months later, in the moat at the Citadel," she continued. "It contained half a human body. Do you know anything about this?"

Nikolaj interlaced his fingers and leaned forward on his elbows.

"I've been out of the country on a work-related trip for the last few months, so I haven't been following the news."

Ditte gave Anette a look and let her take over.

"Our forensic pathologists need to collect all relevant samples before we conclude anything," Anette said. "But everything points to the body in the suitcase being your old friend Marco Sonne. Does that ring any bells?"

He looked down.

"Marco, whose car you drove to Sandvig tonight, and whose possessions are at the same disused sawmill where my colleague Jeppe Kørner was almost sawed in half a few hours ago . . ." Anette leaned forward and tried to catch his eye. "No? Nothing ringing any bells?"

"I have no idea what you're talking about," he muttered.

"Then let's stick to talking about the car. How is it that you're driving around in Marco's Porsche?"

He didn't answer.

The crime scene technicians were already testing the saw for blood and fingerprints. The preponderance of the evidence appeared overwhelming. Not to mention the fact that Nikolaj had been caught red-handed holding the cleaver over Jeppe's head. Strictly speaking, they did not need a confession.

"Who's Isola?"

Nikolaj looked at her. His trembling pupils testified to unspoken emotions, but he didn't say anything.

"Isola Ratsche Jensen," Anette continued. "Your girlfriend, who died at your birthday party thirty-one years ago. Do you remember her?"

Nikolaj made a face. His eyes darted around the room.

"She was pregnant with your child. Not exactly the eighteenth-birthday present people dream about, I'm guessing. What happened? Did you kill her?"

"NO!" His roar came out of the blue. Nikolaj clenched his fists on the table. "I was down on the beach smoking, damn it. It wasn't me. I would never . . ."

He shook his head, raised his hands in front of his face, and slumped forward. His shoulders began to shake. If he was pretending, it was extremely convincing.

"Marco never said anything." Nikolaj's voice was rough with pain. "For all those years he let me take the blame. People pointed their fingers at me and called me a murderer behind my back. How do you think that feels, to be suspected of something like that? He fucking ruined my life! Since then, nothing has ever worked out for me. He moved to London and got rich like some kind of hero. He would pretend to be my friend, when he deigned to come home every summer and swagger around. Without a peep."

"Until this year?" Anette looked into his blue eyes. "What happened this time?"

"We were hanging out at the sawmill, Almindingen. We've been going there for years, you know . . . We'd light a campfire and have a good time up there on our own. It was his last night, and we'd been drinking some. Maybe snorted something, too. He said he had a present for me."

Nikolaj wiped his cheeks with his sleeve.

"He pulled his fist out from behind his back and opened it, the way you do with a child. And there was Isola's necklace. Then I knew . . . It was him. He killed her. He acted like he had been *helping* me, like he did me a fucking favor! Do you get how sick that is?! I . . ." He stopped and composed himself.

"I don't remember any more."

"You don't remember tying Marco up and sawing him down the middle?"

He shook his head.

"No, I don't remember anything about that."

"You don't *remember*?"

"You can ask me as many times as you want. I'm not going to give you any other answer. I want that lawyer after all."

He looked up at Anette. The next instant his face crumpled, and he broke into tears.

"And if you found the necklace, I want it back."

Nikolaj put his head down on the table and sobbed.

SATURDAY,
NOVEMBER 23

CHAPTER 25

The morphine stupor lifted gradually as dawn light penetrated the cloud cover over Allinge-Sandvig. Jeppe woke up to a foot throbbing like it was about to explode and had to hobble to the bathroom for painkillers before he could even consider peeing or splashing some water on his face.

His reflection in the mirror gave him a shock. Not the scratches and bruises, not even the bits of blood remaining in his unkempt beard, but the vacant look in his eyes. He had looked death in the eye yesterday. That should lead to some form of realization, shouldn't it? A choice?

Jeppe shook a handful of pills onto his palm and looked at them, knowing that they would not only deaden the acute pain but everything: the anxiety, the loneliness, the heartache.

He turned on the water. When you're the kind of person whose faucet is either all the way on or all the way off, numbing yourself can be a necessity. Either that or once and for all you learn to find a setting in between, he thought, and threw the pills into the trash can under the sink.

He took a pair of nail scissors out of the cabinet and went to war with his beard. It ended up looking not great but at least shorter. His hair couldn't be helped right now. Using a pair of borrowed crutches, he maneuvered his way into the shower, stuck his cast-covered foot outside the curtain, and took a long shower. In reality, he knew very well what he wanted. The question was whether he had the courage to go after it.

Jeppe tossed a change of clothes into a suitcase and put coffee on. Every motion was a reminder of the ruinous state of his body but also the recovery of his mind. The pain was welcome.

While the coffee brewed, he hobbled over to his neighbor's house and knocked.

Orla opened the door and looked at him in horror.

"What happened to you?"

"It's a long story. We found Nikolaj."

"Well, that's a relief." Orla let Jeppe in and tried to help him to the sofa, though he could barely walk himself.

"Is he all right?"

Jeppe thought it over. He couldn't start on the story, which he knew would be the talk of the island all winter. It was still too close and too heavy. Plus there was still a lot he didn't know. Orla would have to wait to have his curiosity slaked.

"He's alive, at any rate."

"That's good news." Orla looked slightly mystified but didn't ask about it further. "What happened to you?"

"An accident in the woods. It's worse than it looks."

"Would you like some coffee?"

"No, thanks." Jeppe moved his cast and made a face. "I just came over to tell you that I'm going to Copenhagen."

"For the weekend?"

Jeppe bit his lip.

"Maybe longer, there's something I need to take care of." He left it at that. "But will you promise to call me if anything comes up? Or just if you want to talk?"

Orla smiled wanly.

"I've never been fond of talking on the phone. You just go take care of what you need to, and we'll see each other when you come back."

Jeppe stood up, accidentally put weight on his broken ankle, and had to double over forward.

"Sorry, I just need to get used to my bum foot." He straightened up and noticed *Selkirk's Island* lying on the coffee table.

"Did you finish it?"

"Yes, I managed to get through it with my old eyes. Exciting story."

"Does he get rescued?" Jeppe asked with a smile.

"Oh, yes." Orla returned his smile. "He comes back to Scotland, gets married, and starts a family. His time on the island stays with him forever, but he doesn't let it destroy him."

Orla picked up the book and browsed through it to a page with a dog-ear.

"Listen to this. This is as the ship is sailing by the island and Selkirk decides to let himself be rescued. I think it is so touching:

> *He knew he must not let this ship elude him. Here was a task at which he must not fail. He threw wood on the beach fire until it blazed. He made The Island bright with flames.*

THE CALL FROM the police came early in the morning. Esther woke up when Ida knocked on her door. She got up immediately.

Ida took the news that her brother was alive but charged with murder with exactly the jumble of conflicting emotions one would expect—relief, shock, unhappiness, and a tremendous need not to be alone.

Esther sat Ida on a chair in the kitchen, brewed coffee, and made toast, which neither of them ate. She wrapped a blanket around her shoulders, hugged her, and made sure that she drank enough water. She felt an enormous sense of relief that Nikolaj's mysterious disappearance was now resolved. Even if the reason was unbearable.

The stench in the living room was gone, and so was the doubt. They could breathe freely now. That's how Esther thought about it, like a shared challenge. Without understanding herself what had changed, it now felt normal to be here in the house. Yes, more than that, it felt necessary.

"I know my brother has done something terrible, something completely incomprehensible." Ida pulled the blanket around her more snugly. "I'm not trying to excuse him, not even to understand him, but it helps to know that Marco started it. Is it all right for me to even say that?"

Esther nodded.

"Everything is allowed here."

"He murdered an innocent young woman and ruined my brother's life." Ida's voice broke, and she drank a sip of water. "If only I had known that, then maybe I could have . . . done something."

"Nikolaj obviously didn't know the truth himself until now, many years later. And he and your mother had good reason to want to put the whole episode behind them, to just forget the whole thing."

Ida shook her head.

"But you can't. The sins of the past have a habit of catching up with us. And when they do, they've only grown in size."

Her phone rang, and she looked at the display.

"It's the lawyer. I'm trying to arrange a proper defense for Nikolaj."

Esther got up and walked into the living room to leave Ida in peace for her conversation. She looked at the layer of letters, invitations, and postcards on the wall. Some of them she knew inside and out, whereas others she was seeing for the first time. *It's a blessing*, she thought, *that Margrethe isn't here to experience this. What mother could bear her child murdering in this most bestial way?*

It hit her in that same instant that it was that fear Margrethe had been living with since Isola's death in 1988, the fear that her son had murdered his pregnant girlfriend. And in a split second, that came and went faster than a breath, she understood Nikolaj's anger. The undue suspicion that had destroyed his life before it had really begun.

She continued into the study, reading the walls as she went. Birthday wishes gave way to brief letters from the electrician and then became sea-blue greetings from Capri. One letter caught her attention. It was the colors that made it stand out from the others, shades of gray rather than an inky black or a ballpoint blue. Like carbon paper. Like the drafts.

Esther pulled the thumbtack out and took the letter down from the wall, skimmed the first lines and felt a shiver down her spine. The missing page of Margrethe's very last letter to Elias! The first letter Esther had read when she arrived on Monday. She brought the letter over to the desk and quickly located the first page, dated January 11, 2017.

Dear E,

  I've been planning to write you for a long time.

The last line at the bottom of the page was:

  perhaps you can find some understanding for my choices, yes, even forgiveness?

And the first sentence on the next page:

  I can't do anything but hope.

They fit together! Her fingers trembling with excitement, she set the pages of the letter in front of her and began to read.

"SHALL WE ROLL? The ferry won't wait." Anette patted the passenger's seat impatiently, urging Jeppe to climb into the car. He had to hold on to the roof handle and lower himself in backward. These things took time.

"Are you sure you don't need help?"

"I can do it, but do you think you could grab my crutch? I can't reach it without getting back out."

Anette rolled her eyes and made a big show of trudging around the car and picking up the crutch for Jeppe. But when she closed her door and started the car, it was with a smile.

"So," she teased, "you couldn't keep away from my investigation after all, you old circus dog!"

"What are you talking about?" Jeppe said. "You're the one who asked for help! I'm holding you personally responsible for my injuries, physical and psychological. You'll be hearing from my lawyer one of these days." He exhaled through his nose and turned his back toward her.

"Maybe I could just buy you a hot dog on the ferry?" she offered.

"And a chocolate milk?" he suggested.

"It's a deal!" she laughed. "But then we're even."

They passed Hammershus and proceeded south toward Rønne. Jeppe sat, watching the coast from the window of the passenger's seat. Every now and then he shifted uneasily in his seat and moaned softly.

"Does it hurt?" she asked.

He turned around and smiled.

"A little. How did the interrogations go yesterday?"

Anette described how the evening had gone in a bullet point list. The extensive evidence that the crime scene investigators had managed to collect at the Almindingen sawmill, and Nikolaj's anger when they asked about Isola. By the time they drove onto the ferry, Jeppe was relatively up-to-date.

"But he didn't confess to killing Marco?" Jeppe moved ahead in the cafeteria line with a tray in one hand and a crutch in the other.

"If a person generally perceives of himself as a victim, it's probably just hard to take responsibility, even when there's no other way out. Here, give me the tray, you stubborn mule. I'm buying."

She paid and helped him to an empty table with the tray. The rolling of the ferry did nothing to help Jeppe's balance.

"The wind has really picked up, hasn't it?"

"They say it's going to snow." Jeppe flopped down onto a chair and pulled the tray over in front of him.

"They've been saying that for weeks. I don't believe it anymore." She took a bite of her hot dog and chewed contentedly.

Jeppe watched her with a furrow in his brow.

"Where did the money come from?"

"Nikolaj stole a payment Anton Hedegaard was going to make on an under-the-table loan, a hundred thousand kroner in cash, that was part of it. But the majority came from Marco's company accounts," Anette explained. "They drained them calmly, quietly, and gradually so as not to arouse suspicion. And then transferred the money into their own accounts and exchanged it at Forex in Ystad, where they took it out in euros. The plan was probably to amass a large sum and then disappear, drive south through Europe, sell the Porsche, and then catch a flight to somewhere far away. Of course that was before you showed up and forced them to flee in their own boat."

"And Nikolaj was hiding at the abandoned sawmill that whole time?"

Anette took a bite and answered with her mouth full: "The investigators found a sleeping bag, clothes, water bottles, and a little generator in one of the buildings. But it actually looks like he's been hiding both at the sawmill and at his mom's house. Until his sister arrived a week ago, anyway. After that, of course, it was difficult for him to be in the house."

"Where the money was hidden." Jeppe fished around in his pocket as if he was looking for something. "What was Louis's role?"

"They don't entirely agree on that. Nikolaj claims that Louis forced him to participate in the scam, and that he had no idea that Marco had been killed."

"So Louis is supposed to have sawed Marco in half for the money? That doesn't sound plausible."

Anette smiled wryly.

"There's nothing but holes in Nikolaj's explanation. Considering how brutal the crime is, he's not a particularly hardened criminal." She drank some of her chocolate milk and gazed fondly at its label. "Louis has a very different take on the case, which I'm more inclined to believe. It seems to be Nikolaj who calls the shots in that friendship, and Louis who toes the line. He says that Nikolaj called him late at night on Thursday, August twenty-ninth, and asked him to come to the sawmill right away."

"Does that match the call log for Nikolaj's phone number?"

"Yup. Louis says that he found a panicked Nikolaj, who had murdered Marco and now realized that he needed help disposing of the body and getting away."

"So Marco was killed on August twenty-ninth?"

Anette nodded.

"He chose his last night on the island to confess to killing Isola. It ended up being his last night, period."

"Marco has been carrying around this secret for all those years. I wonder why he chose to open up about it now."

She sighed.

"Nikolaj suggested that Marco seemed proud of the murder, like he felt like he had done his friend a favor by getting rid of his pregnant girlfriend."

"You mean, to show him that he cared?" The furrow was back in Jeppe's forehead.

"As you know, love has many faces. Some of them are really vile." Anette smiled sadly. "After Nikolaj murdered Marco with the band saw, he realized that he wouldn't get very far without help. So he offered Louis money to bring him food, fill the car up with gas, and handle the practical things, while Nikolaj drained Marco's accounts. Louis jumped at the offer."

Anette swallowed her last mouthful of hot dog and considered buying another just as Jeppe was taking his first cautious bite. He might look like a lumberjack, but on the inside her partner was still a shy, sensitive plant.

She patted his hand.

"Are you okay, Jepsen?"

"Yes, why do you ask?" He looked at her in surprise.

"No reason," she replied, laughing, and finished her bottle. "The technicians also found a large money transfer from the Zealot's Children to Marco Sonne's company at the beginning of August. An amount in the millions of kroner, double digits, presumably set aside to build the new church. It appears that he was going to manage the money and the construction project for them."

"Do you think they suspected anything?"

"Definitely. Finn hasn't heard from his son since August other than brief text messages, and then Nikolaj disappeared. He and Father Samuel must have suspected that Marco absconded with the money, possibly with help from Nikolaj and Louis. Unfortunately the scope of the disaster is quite a bit worse than they could have imagined. It's going to be a hard winter on Bornholm."

Jeppe sighed heavily.

"What about the case? Who's in charge of it now?"

"The case is in good hands with the local Investigations Unit. I promised Ditte Vollmer I'd come back next week and assist, but really they'll manage fine on their own."

Anette thought of their parting that morning and smiled. Ditte had come to the hostel early to say goodbye, which she really didn't have to, but had done anyway to be proper. She had stuck out her hand and said a formal thank-you for their productive cooperation. Funny little creature.

The ferry's loudspeaker announced that they would be docking soon, and Anette got up.

"Well, Crutch Daddy, I suppose you're going to have to choose now if you want to leave your hot dog behind or be left behind on the boat."

"Never mind the hot dog, but I want to squeeze in a smoke before we dock."

Jeppe fell asleep in the car shortly after they had driven off the ferry, and Anette turned on the radio and let him sleep. When they reached Copenhagen, she nudged him gently.

"We're here. Are you absolutely sure this is where you want to be dropped off? I'm going home to an empty house. I'm not in any hurry."

Jeppe woke up, looked out the window, and smiled at her.

"This is perfect. Thank you, Werner." He opened his car door and got to work hoisting himself out onto the sidewalk.

Anette got out, took his bag from the trunk, and set it next to him. She wanted to ask him so many things. Was he planning on coming back to the city, to the police, to their shared work life, but she knew this wasn't the right time. Instead she pulled him into one of their rare embraces and gave him a gentle pat on the back.

"Take care, Jepsen!" Then she got back into the car, honked, and drove home to Greve Strand.

It wasn't until she was halfway in her own driveway that she saw it wasn't empty. Their boxy family car was already parked in front of the house.

She pulled in behind it and got out, slammed her car door shut, and realized she was holding her breath. The dogs barking was the first thing she heard, then the front door flew open and they rushed out to her, excitedly jumping up and letting her pet them in turns. Svend followed them with their daughter in his arms.

Gudrun reached out to her with her chubby little hands and whimpered eagerly. Anette was pulled into a group hug. She dwelled for a long time in the scent of her baby's hair and with her husband's arms around her before she pulled away.

"I thought you weren't coming until tomorrow?!" she said, choking up a little.

Svend smiled.

"We couldn't be without you any longer."

Bølshavn, Wednesday, January 11, 2017
Dear E,

I've been planning to write you for a long time. At the risk of sounding sentimental, I'm writing to say goodbye. And to explain. I feel that I'm losing my strength. This is the end of the line, but that's fine.

Winter is upon us. The cold and dark have settled in to stay, and everything is frozen outside. It seems like a fitting time of year to say goodbye. The home-care nurse has a hard time getting through the snowdrifts, and I only heat the kitchen and the bedroom. It will be a relief to let go. I'm ready to die, whatever that entails, but first—as they say—I need to confess my sins.

I hope I manage to get it all down on paper before it's too late and that you'll read it with an open mind.

If I regret anything in this life, it's moving to Bornholm—or not moving away again in time. I firmly believed it was the right thing to do—and I knew that bringing the kids over here would make it possible for me to give them a nice, safe childhood. If I had known then what I know now, we would never have come. But no matter how much I might like to, I can't change the past or do things over. It's possible that I've failed as a human being and as a mother, but perhaps you can find some understanding for my choices, yes, even forgiveness?

I can't do anything but hope.

My days have all started to look the same. A long string of mornings and evenings with microwaved food and words that flow out and disappear. I hate getting old. You run around your whole life between crying children and faculty meetings and long for just five minutes to read the newspaper in peace, and suddenly you have oceans of time and nothing to fill it with anymore. Where did she go, the Amazon, the straight-backed, indignant woman I once was?

I've developed cataracts and can only read for half an hour at a time, so mostly I sit here at my desk looking out at the sea, counting my sins, writing letters.

I think a lot about whether I've done a good-enough job. That depends on who you ask.

Ida would hopefully say yes. Nikolaj would probably be less inclined to praise his mother. He still blames me because we didn't move away from Bornholm when it all fell apart. Why did we stay?

Because I had faith in the community. And because we couldn't afford to move. Not if I was also going to be able to afford my field studies.

*I suppose the truth is that I've always devoted too much
energy to work and not enough to my children. You think
professional recognition gives you energy and a will to live—
and it does, certainly—but only in flashes, which quickly burn
out. Ambition is a bonfire that destroys all the relationships in
your life until you are left alone, completely alone.*

*Why haven't I written to you before? You would be justified
in asking.*

*My answer would unfortunately be nebulous, like all human
decisions ultimately are in the end.*

*Because I didn't dare. Because time passed. Because I didn't
want to treat my children differently. You see, I don't have the
same information about Nikolaj, and giving Ida something
so essential without being able to give him the same thing has
stopped me again and again. I actually tried to get in touch with
you a year ago through a mutual acquaintance at the university
but got cold feet at the last minute.*

*The truth is that I've always known who you were, and that
I have kept that knowledge to myself. Maybe also out of a futile
fear of being less of a mother to Ida if she knew of your existence.
They've both always known they were adopted, but we've lived
well as a composite family on those terms, even without fathers.
I hope that you can forgive my decision when you hear what I've
taken from you.*

*On March 27, 1966, I was contacted by the Copenhagen
Prefect's office and offered a baby girl to adopt. I had married a
friend, so we were listed as a married couple on the application,
otherwise I don't think I would have stood much chance. But it
worked!*

*A few days later, I held Ida in my arms for the first time. I'll
spare you the sentimental emotional descriptions. Let me make*

do with saying that I knew right away I would do anything to give her the best possible childhood.

I can still remember the feeling of walking down the street in the spring sunshine as a newly minted mother with my baby in a carriage. When I got her, I received two cloth diapers, a clean spare sheet, and a copy of her birth certificate. That's how I know her exact birthdate—March 18, 1966 (Nikolaj, who was abandoned, doesn't have the same luxury)—and that's how I know your name.

For reasons I don't know, you weren't able to raise your daughter yourself. I've done it as best I could, and whether it can be ascribed to my influence or not, she has become a wonderful human being. Ida Dybris.

I hope you will get in touch with her and let her get to know you.

Dear Esther de Laurenti, I never found the courage to tell you the truth face-to-face. I can only hope you're braver than I am.

In gratitude,
Margrethe Dybris

Esther dropped the letter and let it fall. She closed her eyes and grabbed the edge of the desk so she wouldn't fall, too. The world came crashing down. Margrethe hadn't contacted her to get her to write her biography but for something far more important, the most important thing in the world.

Everything came to a standstill, perhaps even her heart. She couldn't— It was too much. What should she do now?

The hand on her shoulder was gentle and warm.

Ida's lips moved, concerned, but Esther couldn't hear what she was saying.

She was too busy looking into her daughter's blue eyes.

JEPPE INHALED THE scents of Copenhagen, sea fog and car exhaust, frost-damaged asphalt and fried food. So far removed from Bornholm's salty rock formations and aromatic forests, more complex and tiring, but also somehow rooted and deeply personal, the scents of home. Home wasn't uncomplicated. Home was the place where difficult things got resolved, he thought, and painstakingly swung the bag up onto his shoulder.

His crutch was still difficult for him to use, but luckily he didn't have far to walk, just across the street to the door.

He could see lights in the windows. The weekend traffic in Christianshavn was lazy and sparse, and he took his time crossing the road and the bike lane.

He stopped in front of the door and looked up at the sky. The year's first snowflake drifted down and landed on his forehead, where it melted and was replaced by another.

Jeppe smiled. So it came after all, the snow.

He hesitated with his finger over the intercom button. He hadn't prepared a big speech, but still he was not nervous. Either she would see him and understand right away, or she would never understand. He didn't need to convince her of anything; he just knew that she was the ship he couldn't let sail away.

The buzzer hummed, and the door opened. Jeppe began the arduous ascent up the stair with his crutch clanking against the railing. He didn't get very far before she came down to meet him.

Sara.

Her face changed from surprise to joy and then back again. He looked at her. Her eyes, the curve of her lips, the unruly curls. The woman he loved.

"Jeppe?"

She was going to ask him something—and the gods knew there was plenty to ask about—but then she shook her head and walked down the last few steps so they were standing at the same level.

He held out his hand and she took it.

"Jeppe," she repeated.

This time it wasn't a question.

ACKNOWLEDGMENTS

THANK YOU!

This book was finished during the coronavirus pandemic, when concepts like *loneliness* and *isolation* suddenly became very tangible to most of us. Feeling lonely is the worst feeling in the world. Thanks to those who reach out and build bridges, offer a cup of coffee, and visit the neighbor who lives alone. Small acts make a world of difference.

Thank you to my beloved Bornholm and to all the people on the Sunshine Isle. You are Denmark's friendliest and most loving. I hope you will forgive me for amplifying and distorting the shady side and letting monsters dwell there. Thanks especially to Jørgen Christensen from Hallegaarden and to Lone and Hans-Henrik Kofoed from Østerlars Sawmill, whose life's work I have rewritten in the crudest sense in this book; to Danny Christensen; Sergeant Gorm Poulsen with the Bornholm Police; Olsker Antiques; Susanne and Torben Lov; Signe and Sebastian Frost; and to my dear friend Henrik Stender.

A big thank-you to professor of forensic medicine Hans Petter Hougen, who is an indispensable mentor to us Danish crime writers;

to forest ranger Asger Thyge Pedersen for essential information about forestry work; to Kenneth Søndergaard for chain saw tricks; and to associate professor Zachary Whyte for help with the anthropology details. Any factual errors are due solely to my incompetence and not their advice and guidance.

A warm thank-you to the Dybris family, who have allowed me to use their last name for characters in this book. It's a great honor. For the record, I would like to emphasize that any resemblance between the characters in this book and any real life Dybris is unintentional and accidental.

I am grateful to Diana Souhami—author of the wonderful *Selkirk's Island*—for supporting the inclusion of a few passages from her work, in editorial context, in my novel.

To my mother, Sysse Engberg, who wasn't alone in teaching me to love literature, but who still to this day patiently reads my first drafts and my translations. Thank you to Anne Mette Hancock for always cheering me on, listening, and supporting me.

To my agent, Federico Ambrosini, and the rest of Salomonsson Agency—you're the best! Thank you to my Danish publishing house, Alpha, and to publisher, editor, and dear friend Birgitte Franch. To everyone at Scout Press, who works so tirelessly on introducing the North American readers to my books, especially to my dear friend Jennifer Bergstrom.

And finally thanks to Jakob and Cassius, without whom my world would be infinitely lonely.